Three for
hot-b
purch

the
Greeks'
BOUGHT BRIDES

Three intense, exciting novels by
three popular writers: Julia James,
Lucy Monroe & Margaret Mayo

the Greeks'
BOUGHT BRIDES

JULIA JAMES
LUCY MONROE
MARGARET MAYO

M&B™ and M&B™ with the Rose Device
are trademarks of the publisher.
Harlequin Mills & Boon Limited, Eton House,
18-24 Paradise Road, Richmond, Surrey TW9 1SR

THE GREEKS' BOUGHT BRIDES
© Harlequin Enterprises II B.V./S.à.r.l. 2010

Bought for the Greek's Bed, Bought: the Greek's Bride and *Bought for
Marriage* were first published in Great Britain by Harlequin Mills
& Boon Limited in separate, single volumes.

Bought for the Greek's Bed © Julia James 2007
Bought: the Greek's Bride © Lucy Monroe 2007
Bought for Marriage © Margaret Mayo 2006

ISBN: 978 0 263 87399 3

010-0710

Harlequin Mills & Boon policy is to use papers that are
natural, renewable and recyclable products and made from
wood grown in sustainable forests. The logging and
manufacturing processes conform to the legal environmental
regulations of the country of origin.

Printed and bound in Spain
by Litografia Rosés S.A., Barcelona

Bought for the Greek's Bed

JULIA JAMES

Julia James lives in England with her family. Mills & Boon® novels were the first 'grown-up' books she read as a teenager, alongside Georgette Heyer and Daphne du Maurier, and she's been reading them ever since. Julia adores the English and Celtic countryside, in all its seasons, and is fascinated by all things historical, from castles to cottages. She also has a special love for the Mediterranean – "The most perfect landscape after England!" – and she considers both ideal settings for romance stories. In between writing she enjoys walking, gardening, needlework, baking extremely gooey cakes and trying to stay fit!

Julia James writes regularly for Mills & Boon; her most recent novel, *Penniless and Purchased*, was published in Mills & Boon® Modern™ in May 2010.

CHAPTER ONE

VICKY could hear her heels clacking on the marble floor of the vast atrium as she headed towards the reception desk, which was an island in the middle of an ocean of gleaming white and metallic grey. The whole interior screamed modernity—ironic, really, Vicky found herself thinking, as the man who ran this whole mega-corporate shebang was as antediluvian as a dinosaur. A big, vicious dinosaur that ripped your throat out with its talons, tore you limb from limb, and then went on its way, searching for other prey to dismember.

Walking into this dinosaur's cavern now made it all come rushing back. In her head she could again hear that deep, dangerously accented voice, carving into her with a cold, vicious fury that had stripped the flesh from her bones with savage economy. She could hear the words, too, ugly and foul, not caring how they slayed her, his fathomless eyes pools of loathing and—worse than loathing—contempt. Then, having verbally dismembered her, he had simply walked out of her life

She had not seen him since. And yet today, this morning, right now, she was going to walk up to that reception desk she could see coming closer and closer, walk up to that svelte, immaculate female sitting there watching her approach, and ask to see him.

She felt her throat spasm.

I can't do this! I can't.

Protest sliced in her head. But her nervous feet kept on walking, ringing on the marble. She had to do it. She'd tried everything else, and this was the only avenue left. Letters had been returned, all phone calls blocked, all e-mails deleted unread.

Theo Theakis had absolutely no intention of letting her get close enough to ask him for what she wanted.

Even as she replayed the thought in her mind, she felt a spurt of anger.

I shouldn't damn well have to go and ask him! It's not his to hand out or withhold. It's mine. Mine.

To her grim chagrin, however, the law did not see it that way. What she wanted was not, as her lawyer had sympathetically but regretfully informed her, hers to have, let alone dispose of.

'It requires Mr Theakis's consent,' her lawyer had repeated.

Her face darkened now as she closed in on the reception desk.

He's going to give me his damn consent, or I'm going to—

'May I help you?'

The receptionist's voice was light and impersonal. But her eyes had flicked over Vicky's outfit, and Vicky got the instant feeling that she had been classified precisely according to the cost of it. Well, her clothes at least should pass muster in these palatial corporate surroundings. Her suit might be well over a year out of date fashion-wise, but its designer label status was obvious to anyone with an eye for couture. Not that she herself had such an eye, but the world she'd once moved in—albeit so briefly—had been ruthlessly observant in that respect. And now this rare remnant of that vast wardrobe she had once had at her indifferent disposal was finally coming in useful. It was getting her the attentive focus of someone who was standing in the way of what she wanted.

'Thank you.' She smiled, striving to keep her voice just as

light and impersonal. It was hard, though, given the mixture of apprehension and anger that was biting away inside her. But, whatever the strength of her feelings about her situation, there wasn't the slightest point showing them now.

So she simply stood there, as poised as she could, knowing that the pale ice-blue dress and jacket she was wearing was perfectly cut, and that the thin silver necklace went with it flawlessly, as did her high-heeled shoes and handbag, which were both colour co-ordinated. Her hair, newly washed and styled—albeit by herself, not a top hairdresser—flicked neatly out at the ends, and was drawn off her forehead by a hairband the exact colour as the rest of her outfit. Her make-up was minimal and restrained, and the scent she was wearing was a classic fragrance she'd got as a free sample in a department store a while ago.

She looked, she knew, expensive, classic, English and—oh, dear God, please—sufficiently appropriate to get past this hurdle.

Right, time to do it—now.

In a deliberately poised voice, she spoke.

'I'd like to see Mr Theakis,' she said. She made her tones slightly more cultured than she usually bothered to do. But this was England, and these things counted. She gave the name as though it were something she did every day, as a matter of course. As if, equally as a matter of course, her giving it were not in the slightest exceptional and would always meet with compliance.

Was it going to happen now? She must not let any uncertainty show in her face.

'Whom shall I say?' the receptionist enquired. Vicky could tell that she was staying neutral at this point, but that she had conceded that it was indeed possible that this designer-dressed female might actually be someone allowed that level of access. Might even, unlikely though it was, given the restraint of her appearance, be a female granted the privilege of personal intimacy with Theo Theakis. But Vicky also knew, feeling another bite of her tightly leashed anger at having to be here at all, that she did not look nearly voluptuously delectable enough to be one of his legion of mistresses.

Vicky gave a small, poised smile.

'Mrs Theakis,' she said.

Theo Theakis sat back in his leather executive chair and felt his blood pressure spike. The phone he'd just picked up and discarded lay on the vast expanse of mahogany desk in front of him, as if it were contaminated.

And so it was.

She was here, downstairs, in this very building. *His* building. His London HQ. She had walked into *his* company, *his* territory, *daring* to do so! His eyes narrowed. Was she mad? Daring to come near him again after he'd thrown her from him like a diseased rag? She must be mad to be so stupid as to come within a hundred miles of him!

Or just shameless?

His face darkened. Shame was not a word she knew. Nor disgrace. Nor guilt.

No, she neither knew or felt any of those things. She'd done what she had done and had flaunted it, even thrown it in his face, and had felt nothing—nothing at all about it. No hesitation, no compunction, no remorse.

And now she had the effrontery to turn up and ask to see him. As though she had any right to do so. That woman had no rights to anything—let alone what he knew she was here for.

And certainly no right—his eyes flashed with a dangerous, dark anger that went deep to the heart of him—no right at all, to call herself what she still did…

His wife.

* * *

Vicky sat on one of the dark grey leather sofas that were arranged neatly around a smoked glass table. In front of her, laid out with pristine precision, were the day's leading newspapers in half a dozen languages. Including Greek. With a fragment of her brain that was still functioning normally she started to read the headline that was visible. Her Greek was rusty—she'd deliberately not used any of the language she'd acquired—and now her brain balked at forming sounds out of the alien writing. But at least it gave her mind something to do—something other than just going round and round in an ever-tightening loop.

I ought to just stand up and walk out. Not care that he's refused to see me. Not sit here like a lemon with some insane idea of doorstepping him when he leaves! Because he might not leave—he's got a flat here, somewhere up above his damn executive suite. And anyway the lift probably goes down to an underground car park, where he's either got one of his flash cars or a chauffeured limo waiting. There's no reason he should walk past me...

So she should go, she knew. It was pointless just continuing to sit here, with her stomach tying itself in knots and her feet slowly starting to ache in their unaccustomed high-heeled shoes.

But I want what I came for. I won't go back empty-handed until I've done everything I can to get it!

Determination gave strength to her expression. What she wanted was rightfully hers—and she'd been cheated of it. Cheated of what she had been promised—what she needed. Needed now, two years later, with imperative urgency. She could afford to wait no longer. She needed that money!

And it was that thought only that was keeping her glued to the grey leather as the slow minutes passed. Pointless, she half accepted, and yet the deep, deep sense of outrage she felt still kept her there.

She had sat for almost two hours before she finally accepted that she would have to throw in the towel this time around. Sinkingly resigned, Vicky knew that, stupid as she would look, she would just have to get to her feet and leave. People had been coming and going intermittently all the time, and she knew she'd been on the receiving end of some half-puzzled, half-assessing looks—not least by the receptionist. With a sense of bitter resignation she folded up the last of the newspapers and replaced it on the table. Useless—quite useless! She would just have to think of some other way of achieving her end. Quite what, though, she had no idea. She'd already done everything she could think of, including looking at the possibility of taking legal action, which had been promptly shot down by her lawyer. A face-to-face confrontation with her husband had been her last resort. Her eyes flashed darkly. Not surprisingly, considering that Theo Theakis was the last person on earth she ever wanted to see again!

Which was why, as she picked up her handbag from the floor and prepared to stand, bitter with defeat, her stomach suddenly plummeted right down to her heels. Right there in front of her appeared a bevy of suited figures, gracefully exiting one of the lifts and sweeping forwards across the marble floor to the revolving doors of the Theakis Corp's London HQ.

It was him.

She could see him. Her eyes went to him immediately, drawn by that malign awareness that had been like doom over her ever since that first fateful encounter. Half a head taller than the other suits around him, he strode forward, his pace faster than theirs, more impatient, as they hurried to keep up. One of the group was talking to him, his expression concentrated, and Theo had his face half turned towards the man.

Vicky felt herself go cold.

Oh, God, don't do this to me! Don't, please!

Because she could feel it again—feel that tremor in her

veins that Theo Theakis could always set running in her whenever she looked at him. It was as if she was mesmerised, like a rabbit seeing a fast car approaching and not being able to move, not being able to drag her eyes away.

She'd forgotten his impact, his raw physical force. It was not just his height, or the breadth of his shoulders and the leanness of his hips. It was not the fact that he looked like a billion dollars in a charcoal handmade suit that must have cost thousands of pounds, with his dark, sable hair immaculately styled, or that his face seemed as if it was planed from a fine-grained stone that revealed every perfect honed contour. It was more than that—it was his eyes, his dark, fathomless eyes, that could look at her with such coldness, with such savage fury, and with another expression that she would not, *would not*, let herself remember. Even now, when he wasn't even looking at her, when he was half focussed, clearly impatient, on what was being said to him. She saw him give a brief assenting nod, and look ahead again.

And that was when he saw her.

She could see it happening. See the precise moment when he registered her presence. See the initial flash of disbelief—followed by blinding fury.

And then it was gone. Just—gone. As she was gone from his vision. Gone from the slightest claim on the smallest portion of his attention. He had simply blanked her out as if she did not exist. As if she had not been sitting there for nearly two whole hours, waiting. Waiting for him to descend to ground level, where the mortals dwelt in their lowly places, far, far from the exclusively rich, powerful people that made up his world.

He was walking past her, still surrounded by his entourage. Any moment now he would be past the sofas and out of the sheer glass door, which one of the group was already hurrying to hold steady for his august passage. Very soon he would be out of the building he owned, the company he owned, and away from the people he owned.

She surged to her feet towards him.

She saw his head turn, just by a fraction. But not towards her. He gave one of the suits flanking the outer edge of his entourage an almost imperceptible shake of his head. Vicky saw the man peel off from the group, cross behind it with a swiftness that was as soft-footed as it was unanticipated by her, and intercept and block her path exactly where she would have been level with her target.

'Get out of my way!' It was a hiss of fury from her. It was like a spot of rain on a rock. The man didn't move.

'I'm sorry, miss,' he said. His eyes didn't meet hers, his body didn't touch hers—he just stood there, blocking her way. Letting Theo Theakis get away from her and stride off with total and complete unconcern for the fact that he had taken something from her that was not his to take and had kept it.

Her self-control was at breaking point. She could feel it snapping like a dry twig beneath her high heels. She felt her hand arch up, gripping the soft leather clutch bag she was holding like some kind of slingshot, and with every ounce of muscle in her arm she hurled it towards the man who was walking past her, walking out on her. Totally stonewalling her.

'Speak to me, you *bastard*! Damn well *speak* to me!'

The handbag bounced off one of the suits' shoulders, falling to the ground. The bodyguard in front of her caught her arm, too late to stop her impetuous action, but in time to force it down, not roughly, but with the strength his profession required of him.

'None of that, please,' he said, and there was a slight grimness to his mouth—presumably because, she thought, with a glance of vicious satisfaction, he hadn't expected a 'nice young Englishwoman' to behave in such an outrageous fashion.

Not that it had done her the slightest good at all. The entourage just kept going—hastened, even. Though the man at the centre did not change his pace by a centimetre. He simply walked out of the building and disappeared into the sleek black limo that was waiting at the kerb. The car moved off. He had gone.

You swine, thought Vicky, trembling all over. You absolute, total swine.

She had never, ever hated him so much as at that moment.

Theo let his gaze rest silently, impassively, on the newspaper clipping that had been placed in front of him. He was at breakfast in his London apartment, and on the other side of the table his private secretary stood, uneasily waiting for his employer's reaction. It would not be good, Demetrious knew. Theo Theakis hated anything about his private life getting into the press—which was ironic, really, since the life he led made the press very interested in him indeed, even though they could never get much information on him at all.

Theo Theakis managed his privacy ruthlessly. Even when the press could smell a really juicy story bubbling beneath the expensive surface of his tycoon's existence, Theo would remain calm. Eighteen months ago, when rumours had started to circulate like buzzing wasps about just why his apparently unexceptional marriage had proved so exceptionally brief, the press had been hot on his tail. But, as usual, they'd got absolutely nothing beyond the bland statement issued at Theo Theakis's curt instruction. Which was exactly why, Demetrious knew with a sinking heart, the tabloid from which the cutting had been taken had snapped up this latest little morsel.

He stood now, watching and waiting for his employer's reaction. He wouldn't show much, Demetrious knew, but he was aware that the mask of impassivity would be just that—a mask. Demetrious was grateful for it. Without the mask he would probably have been blasted to stone already by now.

For a few seconds there was silence. At least, thought Demetrious gratefully, there was no picture to go with the newspaper article. What had happened yesterday in Theakis HQ would have made a photo opportunity for any paparazzi to die for. As it was, it was nothing more than a coyly worded few paragraphs, laced with speculation, about just what had caused the former Mrs Theo Theakis to hurl her handbag at him and call him an unbecoming name. The journalist in question had teamed the article with an old photograph from the press archives of Theo Theakis, looking svelte in a tux, walking into some top hotel in Athens with a blonde, English, couture-dressed woman on his arm. Her expression was as impassive as his employer's was now.

But she certainly hadn't been impassive yesterday. And nothing could hide the glee with which the brief, gossipy article had been written up.

Theo Theakis's eyes snapped up.

'Find out who talked to these parasites and then sack them,' he said.

Then he went on with his breakfast.

Demetrious stood back. The man was ruthless, all right. There were times, definitely, when he felt sorry for anyone who ever got on the wrong side of Theo Theakis. Like his ex-wife. Demetrious wondered why she'd done what she had. Surely by now she must know it was just a waste of her time? She'd been plaguing his boss for weeks now, and he'd not given an inch. He wasn't going to, either. Demetrious could tell. Whatever it was she so badly wanted, she could forget it! As far as Theo Theakis was concerned she clearly no longer existed.

Demetrious turned to go. He'd been dismissed, he knew, and sent on an errand he would not enjoy, but which had to be done all the same.

'One more thing—'

The deep voice halted him. Demetrious paused expectantly. Dark eyes looked at him with the same chilling impassivity.

'Instruct Mrs Theakis to be here tonight at eight-thirty,' said his employer.

CHAPTER TWO

VICKY was ploughing through paperwork. There was a never-ending stream of it: forms in triplicate, and worse, letters of application, case notes, invoices, accounts and any number of records, listings and statistical analyses. But it all had to be done, however frustrating. It was the only way, Vicky knew, to achieve what this small voluntary group, Freshstart, was dedicated to achieving—making some attempt to catch those children who were slipping through the education net and who needed the kind of dedicated, intensive, out-of-school catch-up tutoring that the organisation sought to provide them with.

Money was, of course, their perpetual challenge. For every pound the group had, it could easily have spent five times that amount, and the number of children who needed its services was not diminishing.

She gave a sharp sigh of frustration, which intensified as she picked up the next folder—the batch of quotes from West Country building firms for doing up Jem's house. Jem had deliberately kept the work to the barest minimum—a new roof, new electrics, new flooring—to secure the property and make it comply with Health and Safety regulations. Everything else they would have to do themselves—painting, decorating, furnishing—even if they had to beg, borrow or steal. But the main

structural and safety work just had to be done professionally—
and it was going to cost a fortune.

Yet the house, Pycott Grange, was a godsend. Jem had inherited it the previous year from his childless maternal great-
uncle, and now that probate had been granted he could take
occupation. Although it was very run down, after years of
neglect, it had two outstanding advantages: it was large,
standing in its own generous grounds, and it was close to the
Devonshire seaside. Both those conditions made it ideal for
what everyone hoped would be Freshstart's latest venture. So
many of the children it helped came from backgrounds that
were grim in the extreme—deprived, dysfunctional families,
trapped in dreary inner-city environments that simply rein-
forced all their educational problems. But if some of those
children could just get a break, right away from their normal
bleak lives, it might provide the catalyst they needed to see
school as a vital ladder they could climb to get out of the conditions they'd been born into rather than the enemy. Two weeks
at the Grange, with a mix of intensive tuition and space to play
sport and surf, might just succeed in turning their heads around,
giving them something to aim for in life other than the deadbeat
fate that inevitably awaited them.

But the Grange was going to cost a lot of money to be made
suitable for housing staff and pupils, and a lot more to run, as
well, before Jem's dream finally came true. Disappointment bit
into Vicky again. If the building work could start, without more
delay, then there was a really good prospect that the Grange
could open its doors in time for the long school summer
holidays coming up in a few months. Already Freshstart had a
list as long as your arm of children they would like to recommend for the experience. But without cash the Grange would
continue to crumble away, unused and unusable.

If we just had the money, she thought. Right now. And they

should have the money. That was the most galling part of it. They *should*—it was there, sitting uselessly in a bank account, ready to be used. Except that—

I want what's mine!

Anger injected itself into the frustration. *It's mine—I was promised it. It was part of that damned devil's agreement I made—the one I knew I shouldn't have made, but I did, all the same. Because I felt...*

She paused mentally, then finished the sentence. Felt obligated.

Wretchedness twisted inside her as painful memories came flooding back.

Vicky could hardly remember her father. She had always known that he had been born to riches, but to Andreas Fournatos his money was no more than a tool. At an early age he had taken his share of his patrimony and gone to work for an international aid agency, where he had met her mother and married her— only to die tragically when Vicky was not yet five. It had been his money, inherited by his widow, which had set up Freshstart, and Vicky's mother had run the organisation until Vicky had taken over her role.

She had had very little contact with her father's side of the family—except for her one uncle. Despite hardly knowing her, Aristides Fournatos had been so good to her, so incredibly kind and welcoming. She had always understood why her mother had withdrawn from her late husband's family all those years ago—because it had simply hurt too much to be reminded of the man she had married and lost so early. So, although there had been Christmas cards and birthday presents arriving regularly for Vicky throughout her childhood from her Greek uncle, her mother had never wanted to return to Greece, and had never wanted Vicky to accept her uncle's invitations.

Aristides had respected her mother's wishes, knowing how much it pained his sister-in-law to remember her first husband after his premature death. And when Vicky's mother had remarried, Aristides had been the first to congratulate her, accepting that she wanted to put all her emotional focus on her second husband—a divorced teacher with a son the same age as Vicky—and raise Vicky to be English, with Geoff as the only father she could remember. They had been a happy, close-knit family, living an ordinary, middle class life.

But when Vicky had been finishing her university course Geoff had been given the opportunity to participate in a teaching exchange in Australia. He and her mother had moved there, finding both the job and the lifestyle so congenial that they had decided to stay. Vicky could not have been more pleased for them, but, adult though she was, she'd still felt miserable and lonely, left behind in England.

That was when her uncle Aristides had suddenly swept back into her life. He had descended on Vicky and carried her off to Greece for a much needed holiday and a change of scene. And also for him to get to know his niece better. His arrival had had her mother's blessing—she had accepted that it was only natural that her daughter should get to know, even if belatedly, her own father's family, and now that she had emigrated to Australia she was beyond the painful associations herself.

Having been brought up in England, in an English family, it had been strange for Vicky to realise that she was, by birth, half-Greek. But far, far more alien than coming to terms with the cultural heritage she had never known had been coming to terms with another aspect of her paternal family. Its wealth.

Because her father's money had been spent on charitable causes, she had never really registered just how very different the lifestyle of her uncle would be. But staying with Aristides in Greece had opened her eyes, and she had been unable to help feeling how unreal his wealthy lifestyle was compared to her own. For all his wealth, however, her uncle was warm, and kind, and had embraced her wholeheartedly as his brother's child. A widower in late middle age, without children, he was, Vicky had seen with fondness, clearly set on lavishing on her all the pampering that he would have bestowed on a daughter of his own. While honouring his brother's altruism, and accepting her mother's desire to put the tragic past behind her, Aristides had nevertheless made no bones about wanting to make up for what he considered his niece's material deprivation.

At first Vicky had tried to stop him lavishing his money on her, but then, seeing him so obviously hurt by her refusal to let him buy her the beautiful clothes that he'd wanted her to have, she'd given gave in. After all, it was only a holiday. Not real life. So she'd stopped refusing and had let herself be pampered. Her uncle had taken so much pleasure in doing so.

'Andreas would be so proud of you! So proud! His so-beautiful daughter!' he would say, time and again, with a tear openly in his eye, his emotion unashamedly apparent and, Vicky had found with a smile, so very Greek.

And so very Greek, too, she'd discovered, in his attitude to young women of her age. They were, she'd had to accept, though loved to pieces, treated like beautiful ornamental dolls who must and should be petted and pampered, but also sheltered from the real world.

It had been the same when she'd made her second visit to Greece. She had visited her mother and stepfather in Australia for Christmas the previous year, and Aristides had invited her to spend the next festive season with him in Athens. But that time as soon as he'd greeted her she'd been able to tell something was wrong. There had been a strain about him that she'd sensed immediately.

Not that Aristides had said anything to her when she'd arrived in Athens. He'd simply reverted to his cosseting of her, telling her she was too thin and working too hard, she needed a holiday, some fun, new clothes. Because she'd known that his concern was genuine, and that he took great pleasure in pampering her, she'd once again given herself to his unreal world, where all the women wore couture clothes which they changed several times a day, according to the social function they were attending next. As before, she had gone along with it—because she'd seen the pleasure it gave her uncle to show off his young half-English niece, whose natural beauty was enhanced by clothes and jewellery.

'My late brother's daughter, Victoria,' he would introduce her, and she'd heard the pride in his voice as he did so, the affection, too. Family, she'd swiftly learnt, was of paramount importance in Greece.

For Vicky it had been fascinating, the glittering world she had dipped her toes into, where breathtaking consumption was the order of the day. Sitting around her uncle's vast dining room table, laden with crystal and silverware, with the female guests glittering like peacocks in their evening gowns and jewels, and the men as smart as magpies in their black-and-white tuxedos, she'd found herself realising with a strange curiosity that, had her father not been so determined to abnegate his wealthy background, this could have been her natural environment. Except, of course, she'd amended, she would not have had her English upbringing but one decidedly Greek. It had been a strange thought.

But she'd known that, fascinating as it was to observe this rarefied social milieu, it was, all the same, profoundly alien. She'd felt as if she was at a zoo, observing exotic mammals that lived lives of display and ostentation that were nothing to do with reality. Their biggest challenge would be which new yacht to buy, which designer to favour, or which Swiss bank to keep their private accounts in.

Not that their wealth made them horrible people—her uncle

was kindness personified, and everyone she'd met so far had been gracious and charming and easy to talk to.

All except one.

Vicky's expression took on a momentary darkening look.

She hadn't caught his name as her uncle had brought him over to be introduced to her before dinner, because as she'd turned to bestow a social smile on him it had suddenly frozen on her mouth. She'd felt her stomach turn slowly over.

Greek men were not tall. She'd got used to that now. But this man was tall. Six foot easily. Tall, and lean, and so devastatingly good-looking that her breath had congealed in her lungs as she'd stared at him, taking in sable hair, a hard-planed face already in its thirties, a blade of a nose, sculpted mouth and eyes—oh, eyes that were black as sloes. But with something hidden in them…

She'd forcibly made herself exhale and widen her smile. But it had been hard. She'd still felt frozen all over. Except for her pulse, which had suddenly surged in her veins. Mechanically she'd held out her hand in response to the introduction, and felt it taken by strong fingers and a wide palm. The contact had been brief, completely formal, and yet it had felt suddenly, out of nowhere, quite different. She'd withdrawn her hand as swiftly as politeness permitted.

'How do you do?' she said, wondering just what his name was. She'd missed her uncle saying it.

'Thespinis Fournatos,' the man acknowledged.

She was getting used to being addressed by her birth father's name. At home she'd taken Geoff's surname, because when her mother had married him he'd adopted her, and it was easier for them all to have the same surname. But understandably, she knew, her uncle thought of her as his brother's son, and to him she was Victoria Fournatos, not Vicky Peters.

But there was something about the way this man pronounced

her Greek name that sent a little shiver down her spine. Or maybe it was just because of the low timbre of his voice. The low, sexy timbre…

Because this man, she realised, with another surge of her pulse, was an incredibly attractive male. Whatever it was about the arrangement of his limbs and features, he had it—in buckets.

And he knew it, too.

She felt the tiny shiver turn from one of awareness to one of resistance. It wasn't that he was looking at her in any kind of suggestive way. It was more, she could tell, that he was perfectly used to women reacting to him the way that she had. So used to that reaction, in fact, that he took it for granted. Instantly she schooled herself against him, making herself ignore the breathless fluttering in her insides. Instead, she glanced at her uncle, who made some remark to the man in Greek, which Vicky did not understand. She knew a few Greek phrases, and a smattering of vocabulary, and was with practice and effort just about able to read Greek script haltingly, but rapid speech was completely beyond her.

'You live in England, I believe, Thespinis Fournatos?' The man turned his attention to her, with the slightest query in his voice. More than a query, thought Vicky—almost disapproval.

'Yes,' she said, leaving it at that. 'My uncle very kindly invited me for Christmas. However, I understand that in Greece Easter is the most important time of the year—a much more significant event than Christmas in the calendar.'

'Indeed,' he returned, and for a few minutes they engaged, with Aristides, in a brief conversation about seasonal celebrations.

It was quite an innocuous conversation, and yet Vicky was glad when it finished—glad when a highly polished, dramatically beautiful woman, a good few years older than herself, came gliding up to them and greeted the tall man with a low and clearly enthusiastic husk in her voice. She spoke Greek fluently, and made no attempt to recognise Vicky's presence.

Although Vicky could sense that Aristides was annoyed by the interruption, she herself took the opportunity to murmur, 'Do please excuse me,' and glided off to talk to some of her uncle's other guests.

She was equally relieved when the seating arrangements at dinner put her at the other end of the table, away from the man with the devastating looks and the disturbing presence. The Greek woman who had accosted him was seated beside him, Vicky saw, and she was glad of it. Yet for all the woman's obvious intention to keep the man's attention turned firmly on herself for the duration, Vicky was sure that every now and then those sloe-dark eyes would turn in her direction.

She didn't like it. There was something that disturbed her at the thought of that tall, dark and leanly compelling man looking at her. She could feel it in the tensing of her body.

Why was she reacting like this? she interrogated herself bracingly. She knew she was physically attractive, had learnt to cope with male attention, so why was this man able to make her feel so self-conscious? As if she were a schoolgirl, not a grown woman of twenty-four.

And why did she get the uncomfortable feeling that he was assessing her, observing her? It wasn't, she knew, that he was eying her up—though if he had been she would not have liked that in the slightest. Maybe, she chivvied herself, she was just imagining things. When his dark eyes intercepted hers it was nothing more than a trick of her line of sight, of her being so irritatingly aware of him. An awareness that only increased during the meal, along with her discomfort.

It was as the guests were finally leaving, late into the night, that the tall man whose name she had not caught came up to her. His dinner jacket, she noted abstractedly, sat across his shoulders to perfection, honing down to lean hips and long legs. Again she felt that irritating flurry of awareness and was annoyed by it. There was something unnerving about the man, and she didn't like it.

'Good night, Thespinis Fournatos,' he said, and looked down at her a moment. There was a look in his eyes that this time she could not mistake. It was definitely an assessing look.

Her back stiffened, even as her pulse gave a sudden little jump.

'Good night,' she replied, her voice as formal as she could make it. As indifferent as she could get away with. She turned to bid good night to another departing guest.

Afterwards, when everyone was gone, her uncle loosened his bow tie and top shirt button, poured himself another brandy from the liqueur tray, and said to her, in a very casual voice, 'What did you think of him?'

'Who?' said Vicky, automatically starting to pile up the coffee cups, even though she knew a bevy of maids would appear to clear away the mess the moment she and her uncle retired.

'Our handsome guest,' answered her uncle.

Vicky did not need to ask who he meant.

'Very handsome indeed,' she said, as neutrally as possible.

Her uncle seemed pleased with her reply.

'He's invited us for lunch at the yacht club tomorrow,' he informed her. 'It's a very popular place—you'll like it. It's at Piraeus.'

I might like it more without Mr Handsome there, she thought. But she did not say it. Still, it was a place she had not seen yet—Piraeus, the port of Athens. But, instead of saying anything more on that, she found herself changing the subject.

'Uncle, is everything all right?'

The enquiry had come out of nowhere, but it had been triggered by a sudden recognition that, despite the smile on her uncle's face, there was tension in it, too—a tension that had been masked during the evening but which was now, given the late hour, definitely visible.

But a hearty smile banished any tension about him.

'All right?' he riposted, rallying. 'Of course! Never better! Now, *pethi mou*, it is time for your bed, or you will have dark circles under your eyes to mar your beauty. And we cannot have that—we cannot have that at all!' He gave a sorrowing sigh. 'That Andreas were still alive to see how beautiful his daughter is! But I shall take care of you for him. That I promise you. And now to bed with you!'

He shooed her out, and she went, though she was still uneasy. Had she just been got rid of to stop her asking another question in that line of enquiry?

Yet the following day there was no sign of the tension she thought she'd seen in him, and when they arrived at the prestigious yacht club, clearly the preserve of the extremely well-heeled of Athens, her uncle's spirits were high. Hers were less so, and she found her reserve growing as the tall figure at the table they were being conducted to unfolded his lean frame and stood up.

Lunch was not a comfortable meal. Though the majority of the conversation was in English, Vicky got the feeling that another conversation was taking place—one that she was not a party to. But that was not the source of her discomfort. It was very much the man they were lunching with, and the way his dark, assessing eyes would flick to her every now and then, with a look in them that did not do her ease any good at all.

As the meal progressed she realised she was becoming increasingly aware of him—of his sheer physical presence, the way his hands moved, the strength of his fingers as they lifted a wineglass, or curved around the handle of his knife. The way his sable hair feathered very slightly over his forehead, the way the strong column of his throat moved as he talked. And the way he talked, whether in English or Greek, that low, resonant timbre doing strange things to her—things she would prefer not to happen. Such as raising her heart rate slightly, and making her stomach nip every now and then as her eyes, as they must during conversation, went to his face.

She watched covertly as he lifted his hand in the briefest gesture, to summon the *maître d'*. He came at once, instantly, and was immediately all attention. And Vicky realised, with a disturbing little frisson down her spine, that there was another reason other than his dark, planed looks that made him attractive.

It was the air of power that radiated from him. Not obvious, not ostentatious, not deliberate, but just—there.

This was a man who got what he wanted, and there would never, in his mind, be the slightest reason to think otherwise.

She gave an inward shiver. It wasn't right, her rational mind told her, to find that idea of uncompromising power adding to his masculinity. It was wrong for a host of reasons, ethical and moral.

But it was so, all the same.

And she resented it. Resented the man who made her think that way. Respond to him that way.

No! This was ridiculous. She was getting all worked up over someone who was, in the great scheme of things, completely irrelevant to her. He had invited her uncle for lunch, presumably for that singular mix of business and sociality that those in these wealthy circles practised as a matter of course, and she had been included in the invitation for no other reason than common courtesy.

She forced herself to relax. Her uncle was turning to her, saying something, and she made herself pay attention with a smile.

'You are fond of Mozart, are you not, *pethi mou*?'

She blinked. Where had that question come from? Nevertheless, she answered with a smile, 'Yes—why do you ask?'

But it was their host who answered.

'The Philharmonia are in Athens at the moment, and

tomorrow night they are giving a Mozart concert. Perhaps you would like to attend?'

Vicky's eyes went to her uncle. He was smiling at her benignly. She was confused. Did he want to go? If he did, she would be happy—more than happy—to go with him. Aristides liked showing her off, she knew, and as she did indeed like Mozart's music, she'd be happy to go to a concert.

'That sounds lovely,' she answered politely.

Her uncle's smile widened. 'Good, good.' He nodded. He glanced across at their host and said something in Greek that Vicky did not understand, and was answered briefly in the same language. He turned back to his niece.

'You can be ready by seven, can you not?' he asked.

'Yes, of course,' she answered. She frowned slightly. Why had her uncle spoken to their host about it?

She discovered, with a little stab of dismay, just why on her way back to Athens with Aristides.

'*He* wants to take me to the concert? But I thought we were going?'

'No, no,' said Aristides airily. 'Alas, I don't have time to go to concerts.'

But *he* does, thought Vicky. A strange sensation had settled over her and she didn't like it. She also didn't like the feeling that she had been stitched up—set up...

With no room to manoeuvre.

Well, she thought grimly now, that was how it had started— and how it had gone on. And even now, after everything that had happened, all the storm and stress, the rage and frustration, she still did not know how it had ended up the way it had. How she had gone from being escorted to a Mozart concert by a man whose company disturbed her so profoundly, to becoming—her mouth pressed together in a thin, self-condemning line—his wife.

Mrs Theo Theakis.

CHAPTER THREE

How could I have done it?

The question still burned in her head, just as it always had. How could she have gone and married Theo Theakis? She'd done it, in the end, for the best of reasons—and it had been the worst mistake of her life.

She could still remember the moment when her uncle had dropped the thunderbolt at her feet. Informing her that Theo Theakis was requesting her hand in marriage, as if they were living in the middle of a Victorian novel.

Aristides had beamed at her. 'Every woman in Athens wants to marry him!'

Well, every woman in Athens is welcome to him! thought Vicky, as she sat there, staring blankly at her uncle, disbelief taking over completely as he extolled the virtues of a man she barely knew—but knew enough to be very, very wary of. Since the Mozart concert she had seen Theo Theakis only a handful of times—and she could hardly have said he'd singled her out in any particular way. Apart from knowing that he was rich, disturbingly attractive, and, from the few conversations she'd had with him about any non-trivial subject, dauntingly and incisively intelligent, he was a complete stranger. Nothing more than an acquaintance of her uncle, and no one she wanted to get any closer to.

In fact, he was someone, for all the reasons she was so disturbingly aware of, her preferred option would have been to avoid. It would have been much, much safer...

And now, out of nowhere, her uncle was saying he wanted to *marry* her?

It was unbelievable—quite, quite unbelievable.

She wanted to laugh out loud at the absurdity of it, but as she stared at her uncle blindly she started to become aware of something behind the enthusiastic words. Something that dismayed her.

He was serious—he was really, really serious. And more than serious.

Vicky's heart chilled.

In her uncle's face was the same tension she'd seen when she'd arrived in Athens. The tension that she'd been moved to ask about the evening she'd met Theo Theakis for the first time. And something more than tension—fear.

It was shadowing his eyes, behind the eager smiles and the enthusiastic extolling of just why it would be so wonderful for her to be Mrs Theo Theakis. Behind her uncle's glowing verbiage of how every woman would envy her for having Theo Theakis as a husband, she could hear a much more prosaic message.

A dynastic marriage. Something quite unexceptional in the circles her uncle and aspiring bridegroom moved in. A marriage to link two wealthy families, two prominent Greek corporations.

Oh, Aristides did not say it like that—he used terms like 'so very suitable'—but Vicky could hear it all the same. And more. Vicky realised, with a sinking of her heart, that she could hear something much more anxious. Her uncle didn't just *want* her to marry Theo Theakis—he *needed* her to...

The chill around her heart intensified.

She waited, feeling her nerves biting, until he had finally finished his peroration, and was looking at her with an anticipation that was not just hopeful but fearful, too. She picked her words with extreme care.

'Uncle, would such a marriage be advantageous to you from a...a business point of view?'

There was a flicker in Aristides's eyes, and for a moment he looked hunted. Then he rallied, using the same tone of voice as he had when she had impulsively asked him whether everything was all right.

'Well, as you know, sadly my wife was not blessed with children, and so it has always been a question—what will happen to Fournatos when I am gone? Knowing that you, my niece, are married to Theo Theakis—whose business interests do not run contrary to those of Fournatos—would answer that question.'

Vicky frowned slightly. 'Does that mean the two companies would merge?'

A shuttered, almost evasive look came into Aristides' face.

'Perhaps, perhaps. Eventually. But—' His tone changed, becoming bright, eager, and, Vicky could tell from familiarity, deliberately pitched to address a female of her age, who should not be concerning herself with such mundane things as corporate mergers. 'This is not what a young woman thinks about when a man wants to marry her! And certainly not when the man is as handsome as Theo Theakis!'

It was the signal that he would not be drawn any more from the fairy tale he was spinning for her in such glowing colours. Vicky could get no more out of her uncle regarding the real reason behind this unbelievable idea of Theo Theakis saying he wanted to marry her. It was only the anxiety she felt about what she had seen so briefly in her uncle's face and respect for his kindness and generosity that stopped her telling him that she had never heard anything so absurd and walking straight out.

With rigid self-control she managed to hear him out, and

then, with all the verbal dexterity she could muster, she said, 'I'm…I'm overwhelmed.'

'Of course, of course!' Aristides said hurriedly. 'Such a wonderful thing is most momentous!'

Vicky hung on to her self-control by a thread. Groping about for some excuse to go, she muttered something about a dress fitting she had to get to in the city and slipped out of the room. Her mind was in turmoil.

What on *earth* was going on?

Her mouth set. Her uncle might not give her any answers, but she knew someone who could.

Even though he was the very last person she wanted to go and see.

She made herself do it, though. She went and confronted her suitor.

He did not seem surprised to see her. He received her in his executive suite in a gleaming new office block, getting up from a huge leather chair behind an even bigger desk. As he got to his feet, his business suit looking like a million euros all on its own, Vicky again felt that frisson go through her. Here, in his own corporate eyrie, the impression of power that emanated from him was more marked than ever.

She braced her shoulders. Well, that was all to the good. Obviously sentiment—despite her uncle's fairy-tale ramblings about how wonderful it would be for her to be married to so handsome and eligible a man as Theo Theakis—had nothing to do with why the man standing in front of her had informed Aristides Fournatos that he would be interested in marrying her.

Even as she formed the thought in her head, she had to cut it out straight away. 'Marriage' and 'Theo Theakis' in one sentence was an oxymoron of the highest order.

'Won't you sit down?'

The dark-timbred voice sent its usual uneasy frisson down her spine. She wished it wouldn't do that. She also wished she wasn't so ludicrously responsive to the damn man the whole time. It had been the same all the way through that Mozart concert he'd taken her to, when she'd sat in constrained silence during the music and made even more constrained small talk during the interval. She'd been dreading he'd suggest going for supper afterwards, and had been thankful that he had simply returned her back to her uncle's house, bidding her a formal good night. Since then she'd seen him a handful of times more, each encounter increasing her annoying awareness of his masculinity. His company disturbed her, and she kept out of any conversation that included him as much as possible. She also did her best to ignore the speculative looks and murmurs that she realised were directed towards them whenever they were together.

Now, of course, she knew just what they had been speculating about.

Well, it was time to put a stop to this nonsense right away.

She sat herself down in the chair Theo Theakis was indicating, just in front of his desk, and crossed her legs, suddenly wishing the skirt she had on was longer and looser.

'I take it your uncle has spoken to you?'

Her eyes went to him. His face was impassive as he took his seat again, but his eyes seemed watchful.

Vicky nodded. She took a breath.

'I don't mean to be rude,' she began, and saw the slightest gleam start in the dark eyes. 'But what on earth is going on?' She eyed him frankly; it seemed the best thing to do. It took more energy than she liked.

He studied her a moment, as if assessing her, and she found it took even more effort to hold his gaze. Then, after what seemed like an age, he spoke.

'If you were completely Greek, or had been brought up here, you would not be asking that question.' He quirked one eyebrow with a sardonic gesture. 'You would not, of course, even be here, at this moment, alone with me in my office. But I appreciate I must make allowances for your circumstances.'

Automatically Vicky could feel her hackles start to bristle, but he went smoothly on, leaning back in his imposing leather chair.

'Very well, let me explain to you just what, as you say, is going on. Tell me,' he said, and the glint was visible in his eyes again, 'how *au fait* are you with the Greek financial press?'

The bristles down Vicky's spine stiffened, and deliberately she did not answer.

'As I assumed,' Theo Theakis returned smoothly. 'You will, therefore, be unaware that there is currently a hostile bid in the market for your uncle's company. Without boring you with the ways of stock market manoeuvrings, one way to defend against such an attack is for another company to take a non-hostile financial interest in the target company. This is currently the subject of discussion between your uncle and myself.'

'Are you going to do it?' Vicky asked bluntly.

She could see his eyes veil. 'As I said, it is a subject of current discussion,' he replied.

She looked him straight in the eyes. 'I don't see what on earth this has to do with the insane conversation I've just had with him!' she launched robustly.

Did his face tighten? She didn't know and didn't care.

'Your uncle is a traditionalist,' observed Theo Theakis. 'As such, he considers it appropriate for close financial relationships to be underpinned by close familial ones. A Fournatos-Theakis marriage would be the obvious conclusion.'

Vicky took a deep breath.

'Mr Theakis,' she said, 'this is the most *idiotic* thing I've heard in all my life. Two complete strangers don't just marry because one of them is doing financial deals with the other's uncle! Either there's something more going on than I can spot, or else you're as...unreal...as my uncle! Why on earth don't you just do whatever you intend financially, and get on with it? I've got nothing to do with any of this!'

His expression changed. She could see a plain reaction in it now.

'Unfortunately that is not so.' His voice was crisper, almost abrupt, and the light in his eye had steeled. 'Answer me this question, if you please. How attached are you to your uncle?'

'He's been very kind to me, and apart from my mother he is my only living blood relative,' Vicky replied stiffly. She felt under attack and didn't know why—but she knew she didn't like it.

'Then you have a perfect way to acknowledge that,' came the blunt reply. He leant forward in his seat, and automatically Vicky found herself backing into her chair. 'Aristides Fournatos is a traditionalist, as I said. He is also a proud man. His company is under severe and imminent threat of a hostile acquisition, and his room to manoeuvre against it is highly limited. To put it bluntly, I can save his company for him with a show of confidence and financial strength which will reassure his wavering major institutional shareholders because he is backed by the Theakis Corp. Now, personally, I am more than happy to do that, for a variety of reasons. Hostile bids are seldom healthy for the company acquired, and the would-be acquirer in this instance is known as an asset-stripper, which will dismember the Fournatos group to maximise revenues and award their own directors massive pay rises and stock options. In short, it will pick it apart like a vulture, and I would not want that to happen to any company, let alone Fournatos. However, my reasons for helping to stave off this attack are also personal. My father was close friends with Aristides, and for that reason alone I would not stand by and watch him lose the company to such marauders.'

'But why does that have to involve anything other than a financial deal between you and my uncle?' persisted Vicky.

Cool, dark and quite unreadable eyes rested on her.

'How do you feel about accepting charity, may I ask?' Vicky could feel her hackles rising again, but the deep-timbred voice continued. 'Aristides Fournatos does not wish to accept my financial support for his company without offering something in return.'

'How about offering you some Fournatos shares?' said Vicky.

Theo Theakis's expression remained unreadable.

'Your uncle wishes to offer more.' There was a pause—a distinct one, Vicky felt. Then Theo Theakis spoke again, as if choosing his next words with care. 'As you know, your uncle has no heir. You are his closest relative. This is why he wishes to cement my offer of support to him at this time with marriage to yourself.'

'You're willing to marry me so you can get his company when he dies?' Vicky demanded. If there was scorn in her voice she didn't bother to hide it.

The dark eyes flashed, and the sculpted mouth tightened visibly.

'I'm willing to enter into a marriage with you to make it easier for Aristides to accept my offer to save his company from ruin.' The sardonic look was back in his eyes now. 'Believe me when I say that I would prefer your uncle to accept it unconditionally. However—' he held up an abrupt hand '—your uncle's pride and his self-respect have already taken a battering by allowing his company to be exposed to such danger in the first place. I would not wish to look ungracious at what he is proposing. For him, this is a perfect solution all round. His pride is salved, his self-respect intact, his company is defended, its future is secured. And as for yourself—' the dark eyes glinted again, and Vicky could feel a very strange sensation starting up in her insides '—your future will also be settled in a fashion that your uncle, standing as he feels himself to do in the place of your late father, considers ideal—marriage to a man to whom he can safely entrust you.'

Vicky got to her feet. 'Mr Theakis,' she started heavily, 'you seriously must be living on another planet if you think for a moment that I—'

'Sit down, if you please.'

The instruction was tersely issued. Abruptly, Vicky sat, and then was annoyed with herself that she had.

'Thespinis Fournatos—somewhere between your intemperate reaction, your uncle's very understandable desires and my own unwillingness to stand by helplessly while your uncle's company is taken over we must reach an agreement acceptable to all. Therefore what I propose is this.' His gaze levelled with hers, and he placed his hands flat on the arms of his chair. 'We enter into a formal marriage in the private but mutual understanding that it will be of very limited duration—sufficient merely to see your uncle through this current crisis and satisfy public and social decencies. I believe that when your uncle has his company safe again he will accept the dissolution of our brief marriage and will come to other arrangements for the long-term future of the Fournatos group. If you have the regard for your uncle which you say you have, then you will agree to this proposal.'

Emotions roiled heavily in Vicky's breast. One was resentment at being spoken to as if she were a mix between a simpleton and an ingrate. The other was more complex—and at the same time a lot more simple.

She didn't want to marry Theo Theakis. Not for any reason, period. The very idea was absurd and ludicrous and insane. It was also—

She veered her thoughts away. Pulled her eyes away from him. She didn't like sitting here, this close to him, alone in his huge office. Theo Theakis disturbed her, and she didn't like it. She didn't like it at all.

She forced herself to look at him again. He was still levelling that impassive, unreadable gaze on her, but she could see, deep at the back of his eyes, the glint in it. There was antagonism there, and something else, too, and she liked that least of all.

She jumped to her feet again. This time Theo Theakis did not order her to sit down. She clutched her handbag to her chest and spoke.

'I don't believe there isn't a different way to deal with this,' she said. 'There just has to be!'

And then she walked out.

The problem was, it was one thing to march out of Theo Theakis's executive office in umbrage, but quite another to face her uncle again. It was evident, she realised with a sinking heart, that as far as he was concerned of *course* she would be marrying the man she now knew would be saving his company. That Aristides had kept this information from her only fuelled her sorrow. The awful thing was that, had it not been for her visit to Theo and his brutal explanation of the cruel facts, she would have had no hesitation in telling Aristides, as gently as she could, that she could not possibly entertain the idea of marrying a man who was virtually a stranger. Let alone one who caused such a frisson of hyper-awareness in her every time she set eyes on him.

But because she now knew just how vital it was for her uncle to be able to wrap up Theo Theakis's financial help in a dynastic marriage, she simply could not do it.

Yet how could she *possibly* agree to such a marriage? It was out of the question! Even if it *was* limited to the superficial temporary marriage of convenience that Theo Theakis was advocating.

I can't possibly marry him! It's absurd, ludicrous, ridiculous…

But even though those were the words she deliberately used to describe such a marriage, she could feel her resistance being eroded. The more closely she studied her uncle's face, the more she could see the web of anxiety in it, the fear haunting the back of his eyes. For him, it seemed, everything depended on her accepting this marriage proposal. And as far as her uncle was concerned, Vicky could see, no young woman in her right mind would dream of turning it down! It offered everything—a husband who was not just extremely wealthy but magnetically attractive, who was lusted after by all other females, and held in respect and esteem by all men. What on earth was there to turn down? To her uncle, he was an ideal husband...

It was a clash of worlds, she knew. Her modern world, where you married for love and romance, and his, where you married for family, financial security and social suitability. A clash that could not be resolved—or explained. Every instinct told her that she could not—should not—do what her uncle wanted. And yet her heart squeezed. If she turned down this marriage proposal— even on the terms that Theo Theakis was offering her—the consequences for her uncle would be catastrophic.

I can't do it to him! I can't let him go under! But I can't possibly marry a man I don't know, for any reason whatsoever! But if I don't, then my uncle will be ruined...

Round and round the dilemma went in her head, making dinner that evening a gruelling ordeal. Vicky was horribly aware of the expectant-yet-anxious expression that was constantly in her uncle's eyes, both day and night, and she herself endured a fitful, sleepless night. And so it was with a sense of escape the following morning that she took a telephone call from London.

But her pleasure in hearing Jem's voice swiftly turned to dismay. She had left the running of Freshstart to him while she was in Greece, but before the phone call was over she realised it had been a mistake. Jem was great with kids—he could make emotional contact with the most troubled teenager—but as an organiser and administrator he was, she had to admit, poor.

'I'm really sorry, Vicky, but it seems I didn't get that grant application in on time and the deadline has passed. Now we can't apply again till next year.' Jem's voice was apologetic. 'They were shorthanded with the kids, so I went to help out, and then I was out of time to get the form into the post.'

Vicky suppressed a sigh of irritation. Even with the money her father had left, the charity needed every penny it could raise, and the grant she'd been counting on getting would have gone a long way. Now she had even more on her plate to worry about, despite the unbelievable situation she found herself in here in Greece.

However, soon her attention had to return to that, when, shortly after she'd finished speaking to Jem, there was another phone call for her.

It was Theo Theakis.

'I would like you to join me for lunch,' he informed her with minimal preamble, and told her the name of the restaurant and the time he wanted her to be there. Then he hung up. Vicky stared at the phone resentfully, wishing the man to perdition.

All the same, she presented herself at the designated location at the appointed hour, and slid into her seat as Theo Theakis got to his feet at her approach. Instinctively, she avoided anything but the briefest eye contact with him, and self-consciously ignored the various speculative glances that were obviously coming their way.

Her lunch partner wasted little time in getting to the point.

'I do not wish to harass you, but a decision from you on the matter under consideration is needed without delay,' he began, as soon as the waiter had taken their orders. 'The marauding company has just acquired another tranche of shares. Other shareholders are clearly wavering. Unless a very clear signal is sent to them imminently to say that I am aligning myself with Aristides they will start to sell out in critical numbers. So…' His dark eyes rested on her without expression. 'Once again I must ask you whether you are prepared to accept the recommendation I made to you yesterday.'

She could feel her hands tensing in her lap.

'There *has* to be another way of—' she began tightly.

'There isn't.' Theo Theakis's voice was brusque. 'If there were, I would take it. However, if you are still of the same mind as you were yesterday afternoon—' again Vicky could hear the note of critical condemnation in his voice, and it raised her hackles automatically '—then allow me to mention something that was omitted from our exchange then.'

He paused a moment, and Vicky made herself meet his eyes. They were quite opaque, but there was something in them that was even more disturbing than usual. She wanted to look away, but grimly she held on.

He started to speak again.

'Because of your upbringing in England I appreciate that the concept of a dynastic marriage such as your uncle hopes for is very alien to you. However…' He paused again minutely, as if deciding whether to say what he went on to say. 'There is another aspect of such arrangements which your lack of familiarity with them might require me to make plain to you. It is the matter of the marriage settlement. Although the issue is complicated by the matter of the threat to your uncle's company, nevertheless in simplistic terms the outcome for yourself would be a sum of money set aside—in the form, if you like, of a dowry. No, do not interrupt me, if you please— I appreciate you find the term archaic, but that is irrelevant.'

He broke off while the sommelier approached with the wine he had chosen for lunch, and went through the ritual of tasting it, approving it with a curt assent. Then he continued. There was a slightly different tone to his voice as he spoke now. A smooth note had entered it, and Vicky felt it like a rich, dark emollient over her nerve-endings.

'It must be hard for you,' Theo Theakis said, as he contemplatively took a mouthful of the wine, setting back the glass on the table but never taking his eyes from her. 'Staying with your uncle and appreciating, perhaps for the first time, just how very different your life would have been had your father not been of the philanthropic disposition that he so abundantly was. In the light of that, therefore, and in respect of the sum of money I alluded to, which in the event of a normal marriage would remain with me, I am prepared, since I am proposing a highly limited marriage, to release this sum to you on the dissolution of the marriage.' His veiled gaze rested on her. 'Additionally, I am willing to make you an advance on this sum at the outset of our temporary marriage. The figure I have in mind is this.'

He named a sum of money that made Vicky swallow. It was about three times the amount of the grant that Jem had just failed to apply for.

Her mind raced. With that money they could…

She dragged her thoughts away from all the things that Freshstart could spend that kind of money on, and back to the man sitting opposite her, in his superbly tailored business suit, with his dark, sable hair and his opaque, unreadable eyes that nevertheless seemed to send a frisson through her that went right down to her bones.

'Well?'

She opened her mouth, then closed it again.

'The final sum released to you when our marriage ends would be twice as much again,' he said, into the silence.

Twice as much?

What we could do with such a sum!

She stared, unseeing for a moment, ahead of her, oblivious even of the disturbing figure opposite her. What would her father have done? She could not remember him, but her mother had told her so much about him.

'He gave away his inheritance to those who needed it. He didn't think twice about it.'

Her mother's well-recalled words echoed in her head. She felt her throat tighten. What should she do? If she went ahead with this insane idea she could not only save her uncle's company, but inject into her father's charity a sum of money that would help so many children blighted by poverty and wrecked families...

But I'd have to marry Theo Theakis...

Slowly her eyes refocussed on the man sitting at the far side of the table. The familiar frisson went through her.

If he were just an ordinary person I could do it...

But he wasn't—that was the problem. He was a man like no other she had ever encountered, and to whom she reacted as she had never done in her life before.

It's too dangerous...

The words formed in her mind and etched into her brain cells.

No—it didn't have to be dangerous! In fact—she pressed her lips together determinedly—it was absurd to even think of that word. Absurd because it didn't *matter* that she reacted so strongly to Theo Theakis. The point was that *he* was not reacting to her at all! It was all on her part, and if she just succeeded in keeping a totally tight lid on the way he affected her then she could just go ahead and...

She inhaled sharply. Good God, was she really thinking what she was thinking? Was she really, seriously thinking that she could go ahead with this insane scheme? Surely to God she couldn't be?

Yet she could feel her mouth shaping words, hear them sounding low across the table, coming from somewhere she didn't want to think about.

'How long would we have to stay married?'

* * *

The phone on her desk was ringing, and Vicky heard it from a long, long way away. Sucked down into the past. Painfully, she dragged her mind back to the present—the present in which frustration and bitter anger warred in equal proportions.

'How long would we have to stay married?'

The fateful question she had posed that day over lunch reverberated in her head. It had been the moment that she had mentally acceded to the idea of entering into the kind of marriage that Theo Theakis had outlined to her. She'd known that even at the time.

And he'd started to cheat her from that very moment! Because the kind of marriage he'd outlined had been nothing, *nothing* like it had turned out to be!

He cheated me right from the start—and he went on cheating me right to the end! The brutal, merciless end...

Anger buckled through her again. Oh, Theo Theakis might have paid out upfront all right—the money he'd said was an advance on what he would make over to her when they were finally free to end their marriage—but as for the rest of it...

It's mine! He promised it to me—it's not his to keep!

He's got no business hanging on to it! Just because I...

The insistent ringing of the phone finally broke through her angry reverie. She snatched it up.

'Yes?' she said tersely.

The voice that answered was accented, formal, and studied.

'This is Demetrious Xanthou. I am aide to Theo Theakis. He has instructed me to inform you that he will receive you this evening. If you will be so good as to give me your address, I will arrange a car for 8:00 p.m.'

For ten seconds Vicky went totally still. But the emotions that warred in her were not tranquil. Turmoil seethed in her. Haltingly, hardly able to concentrate, she gave her address. Then, hand shaking only very slightly, she set the phone down.

She stared ahead blindly for a moment. Then her face set again, and a grim, ruthless expression entered her eyes.

She was finally going to get her face-to-face with the man who had rent her limb from limb with his savage words. Well, she wouldn't care about that now—she had one thing only in her sights.

I want that money. It's mine. I want it—and I need it.

And I'm going to make him give it to me—whatever it takes!

It was the only thought she was going to allow herself.

Anything else was much, much too disturbing. Much too dangerous.

Theo Theakis stood by the window of his London apartment, looking out over one of its most historic parks. His face was expressionless, but beneath the impassive exterior one emotion was uppermost.

He rested his eyes on the woman in front of him.

Unlike during her attempt to accost him the day before, she was dressed without the slightest effort to look the part today. It was deliberate; that much was obvious. Yesterday she had been playing the role of Mrs Theo Theakis—even though she no longer had the least right to that name, he thought, with a savage spurt of anger. Tonight she had chosen a different image. Jeans and a chainstore sweat top. Her hair was caught up in a ponytail, and she wore not a scrap of make up.

His lips pressed together. She would not be wearing that outfit for him again—

'Well?'

The voice was curt, demanding. The line of his lips tightened. How dared she stand there, shameless and insolent, and speak to him in such a tone? His eyes darkened.

'You wanted to talk to me. In fact, you were very expres-

sive on the subject.' His voice was clipped, and he didn't bother
to hide the note of sarcasm in it. 'So,' he invited, 'talk.'

He watched her eyes narrow. After all she'd done to him she
still thought she had the right to call the shots. Take umbrage.
Make demands.

Well, she could make them all right—and she could pay the
price, as well.

'I want my money.'

The bald, bare, shameless words fell from her. Theo felt his
tightly controlled anger stab again.

'Your money?' He echoed her words, eyes spearing hers.
'*Your* money? The law takes a different view—as you very well
know. The settlement that Aristides drew up with me is very
clear—the money is mine.'

He could see fury leap in her face, and it gave him grim
amusement. She spat back at him venomously.

'You promised it to me! You told me it would be mine when
the marriage ended! And now you're cheating me of it!'

Anger leapt into his face uncontrolled.

'You *dare* accuse me of cheating?'

Her expression contorted.

'It's my money! And you're keeping it! What the hell else
is it but cheating?' she demanded furiously.

Cold fire poured from him.

'*Christou*, are you really so terminally stupid that you
imagine I would have the *slightest* inclination to let you have
that money? After what you did? You deserved nothing—and
nothing is what you got!' His voice changed, become harsh and
deadly. 'What else does an adulterous wife deserve?'

CHAPTER FOUR

VICKY could feel her face whiten. She was back in the past again, and Theo Theakis was laying into her with his vicious talons, ripping her to shreds with his vituperation. She had tried to defend herself but it had been impossible. He had allowed her no chance—no quarter.

Well, this time she would not even make the attempt. She would not stoop that low.

But it was hard—much, much harder than she had allowed for—to stand here, face to face, with that overpowering presence in front of her, the full force of his self-righteous anger bearing down on her. It was like an intense, overwhelming pressure coming at her, trying to make her buckle and crack. Trying to destroy her.

Her spine steeled. She didn't destroy that easily! She'd survived that first hideous onslaught of his, which had ended their unspeakable farce of a marriage, even though she'd been shaking like a leaf before he'd done with her, desperate only to run, run from his presence as fast as her trembling limbs would carry her.

It might have served its purpose, but that did not mean she could ever forgive or forget that brutal scene, his vicious, self-righteous judgement of her.

So now, gathering a nerve she had to dig deep to find, she slid her hands into her back pockets, shifted the weight of her leg, and looked across at him, her face a mask. Her voice, as she spoke, was cool.

'I'm not here to discuss ancient history, Theo. I'm here to get the money you've been keeping from me. I don't give a toss how our marriage ended, only that it did—and that you owe me.'

As she finished she had the strangest feeling she'd just lit the blue touch paper—but the rocket didn't go up. Instead, something slid across his face, almost as if he were wiping it clear of any expression or emotion. She'd seen him look like that often, usually when he was talking to people but revealing nothing of what was going on inside his head. It had been a common expression when he'd been talking to her, as well.

His tone was smooth suddenly, but with the smoothness of steel. 'We've already established that you have no entitlement to it whatsoever. However...' His eyes rested on her, and there was that same concealed characteristic about them as in his face. 'I may, perhaps, be willing to change my mind. Tell me—' the question came out of the blue '—what do you want the money for?'

Vicky started. Automatically she veiled her expression. No way was she going to tell him that Jem was anything to do with why she wanted the money—the memory of Theo's verbal gouging of her two years ago was too deep for that, and Jem's name would be like a red rag to a bull.

'What business is that of yours?' she countered, still keeping that cool, deliberate voice going.

She could see the anger lick through him at her reply. Theo Theakis was a man who liked getting his own way—she knew that, to her cost. Whatever he wanted, Theo liked to get it.

Even when it was personal.

Especially when it was personal.

And he wasn't fussy about what he was prepared to do to get his own way…

Her mind sheered away. Memory was dangerous, very dangerous. Much safer was Theo being angry with her. His anger might be a vicious onslaught of savage fury, or it might be the cold, contained, implacable power of a very rich man, but both of those were easier to endure than—

No. She cut her mind off again.

Focus! Focus on what you want here—your money. That's all you're here for. Nothing else! Nothing else at all.

But if that were true, why—dear God—did her eyes keep wanting to smooth over that tall, lean body standing so short a distance away from her? To rest on that planed, ludicrously compelling face and just gaze and gaze, like a hungry animal long deprived of food…?

He was replying to her, and she forced herself to listen.

'It's a substantial amount of money. You are not used to being in possession of such sums. Therefore you may be the target of unscrupulous operators who wish to part you from it.' His voice was smooth, the lick of anger gone completely now from the visible surface.

But Vicky remained wary—she knew she had every reason to be.

'I'm putting it in the bank, that's all. I want to spend some of it on a house, the rest stays in the bank.'

It was an evasive answer, and she knew it. True in some sense, but implying, falsely, that she wanted to buy a house, not do one up, and that there would be a lot left over—when there would probably be none at all. But she didn't owe Theo Theakis the truth. She didn't owe him anything.

She held his gaze, resolutely keeping hers steady.

'Very prudent,' he murmured, and again Vicky got the feeling that there were currents running deep beneath that smooth surface.

But what did she care about those, either? She just cared about getting her money. That was all.

'Very well—I'll release the money.'

The words fell into the space between them—and that was much, much more than the few metres that separated them. For a second she stood still, not believing she could have heard right. Then her eyes lit—she could not stop them.

'But there will, of course, need to be conditions.'

His voice was smooth still. So smooth.

The light in her eyes flashed into anger.

'You have absolutely *no* right to—'

His hand came up abruptly. 'What I have,' he enunciated, 'is something you want, and if you want it then you accept my conditions.'

She was the insubordinate minion again. Her chin came up in defiance.

'And they are?' she demanded, eyebrows rising with the same cool deliberation she'd used before.

His eyes rested on her a moment. She could not read them—could not read the smooth surface of his expression. But suddenly, quite suddenly, out of nowhere, the barest fraction before he spoke, acid pooled in her stomach.

'They're very simple,' he said. 'You'll return to Greece with me, and to my bed.'

The acid leached from Vicky's stomach and into her veins, draining down into every limb.

'You *cannot* mean that,' she breathed. It seemed to take all the breath she had left in her lungs to do so. Her eyes had widened like a rabbit's, seeing a predator step in front of it.

Something flickered in the back of his eyes, and she felt her lungs crush yet more.

'It's exactly what I mean. If you want the money, you'll comply.' His voice was unperturbed.

'It's *outrageous*!'

'So is adultery.' His voice was cold, as cold as steel.

'I won't do it.' Her teeth were gritted, so tight it hurt.

He shrugged, the material of his jacket moving over broad shoulders.

'Then there's nothing more to be said, is there? So you'd better go, hadn't you? But if you do—' his voice hardened '—don't trouble to get in touch again. You decide now—right now—what you intend to do.'

She stood transfixed, staring at him horror. And from behind the horror came memories, marching forward, one after another, like the frames of a movie, surging forward in vivid, punishing colour...memories she never, ever allowed herself...

I can't do it! Dear God, I can't!

'Well?'

She could feel her stomach churning with acid.

'No! God Almighty, of *course* I won't do it! You must be insane to think I would!'

'Very well. If that's your decision.' He started to move towards the door.

She spun round. 'I want my money!' Her voice was all but a shriek of anger and frustration—and horror.

'Then comply with my conditions.' His voice was cool, impersonal. He didn't even look round, simply walked out into the hall and made to open the door of his apartment.

She strode after him, the acid still churning in her stomach.

'*Why*? Why the hell do you even want to...to...?'

She couldn't say it—it was impossible. As impossible as believing he'd actually said that to her!

He turned. For a moment he was still, very still. She stood, her insides churning. Then suddenly, before she had a chance to realise his intent, he reached out a hand to her.

Long fingers slid around her jaw, grazing into her hair. His eyes looked down at her. Their expression jellied her stomach.

With leisurely insolence his thumb grazed along her lower lip. The touch shot weakness through her body.

'I like to finish what I start,' he said.

His thumb smoothed again. She couldn't move. She was transfixed, her heart slugging in her chest. Then he smiled. The smile of a predator. He dropped his hand away.

'I'm flying to Athens tomorrow at noon in my private place. You have till then to make up your mind what you're going to do.'

He pulled the door open and waited, expectantly, for her to go.

On shaking legs she left.

London flowed around her like an unseen river as she walked blindly along its darkened streets. At some point she must have walked down into the Underground system and taken a train, changed to a different line, kept going, emerged, and walked back to her tiny studio flat. When she got indoors she went into the kitchen, and with the same disconnected brain started to make herself a cup of tea. Then, on sudden desperate impulse, she poured herself a glass of white wine, took a large gulp as she headed to the living area, and collapsed on the sofa.

She stared blankly ahead. She could feel her heart thumping in her chest.

I've got to think about this. I can't not think about it. I don't want to think about it. I don't want to do anything other than pretend that whole encounter tonight just didn't happen. Deny it completely. Wash it from my brain, my memory, my consciousness.

But I can't. I can't do that because I know, though I desperately don't want to. I know I've got to make a decision.

She took a second gulp of the alcohol. Another voice seemed to shoot through her brain.

What the hell do you mean, you've got to make a decision? There isn't any decision to be made! You can't possibly, possibly think otherwise! What he said is unthinkable—it's disgusting and outrageous, and he can damn well go to hell for even saying it to you!

She stared ahead still. Her heart seemed to be thumping more heavily, and there was a sick feeling inside her, like nerve-ends pinching in her guts.

But he said it was the only way I can get my money...

The other voice slammed back. *Well, you'll just have to do without it, then!*

She swallowed heavily. Do without it. But they couldn't. That was the problem. Without the money that she'd promised Jem there was no way the house could be ready for the summer—which meant they'd have to wait another season before being able to take in any kids, if ever. The whole scheme depended on her getting the money.

We need that money! We've just got to have it!

Anger spurted through her again. Theo had no *right* to that money! It didn't matter what the damn law said, the money was for *her*, at the end of their stupid, insane marriage, and him keeping it was sheer bloody vindictiveness! Petty revenge, that was all!

She took another vicious gulp of wine. It was coursing through her system, making her feel angry and aggressive.

It was a marriage of convenience. That was the whole point! Something just to keep Aristides happy, to make him able to accept Theo Theakis's help without losing face. That's all I went along with it for! And that's what Theo said, too! A temporary marriage of convenience, for my uncle's sake.

Indignation burned along her veins.

It had been a deliberate, business-based marriage of convenience, and therefore obviously, *obviously*, the issue of fidelity was irrelevant! How could anyone think otherwise?

Her face darkened. But Theo Theakis had. The all-time original dinosaur—with vicious talons and an even more vicious tongue, that had verbally ripped her to bloodied shreds before he'd done with her!

Angrily she answered him in her head—the way she had that terrible day when he'd confronted her.

It was a marriage of convenience, Theo! Not a real one! An empty façade, meaning nothing—nothing at all! And you damn well should have treated it as such, instead of...instead of—

Her mind cut out. No. No, no and *no*. She wasn't to think of that—never. Ever. Forbidden. Locked door. Never to be opened.

Except that tonight, to her face, Theo had opened that door and made her look inside.

Her face drained of expression. She knew what Theo wanted. His taunting, insolent words formed in her brain— *'I like to finish what I started.'* But that wasn't why he'd made that outrageous condition tonight. It had nothing to do with it. He wanted something quite different.

Revenge.

And he knew exactly, *exactly*, how to get it.

A shudder went through her.

Adultery—that had been the crime that Theo had thrown so viciously in her face. So unjustly.

She could have defended herself in terms that even he would have had to accept—but if she had...

No, that had been impossible! It had been impossible then, and it was impossible now.

And for the same reason.

Her fingers clenched around the wineglass, threatening to break the stem. She must not, *must not*, let her mind go in that direction. It wasn't just dangerous—it was suicidal...

Desperately she pulled her mind away from the precipice it tottered on. Adultery was not the only crime she had committed in Theo's eyes. There was another, far, far worse, and he wanted revenge for that, too.

And he would get it, she knew, with a terrible chilling in her guts. The revenge that he would exact from her would be an exercise in humiliation.

Her humiliation.

And Theo would extract every last gram from her until he was satisfied—satisfied that her crime against him had been paid for.

I can't go through with it! I can't! It's impossible! Impossible!

Anguish filled her, and she could feel herself start to shake.

I can't face the humiliation—I can't face Theo taking that revenge on me! I can't!

Abruptly she got to her feet, and went and refilled her wineglass. She took another large slug from it, and stared blindly around her small studio flat. It was a world away, a universe away, from the life she'd led in Athens as Mrs Theo Theakis.

I can't possibly go back there!

How could she ever go back there? She could never do it to her uncle, for a start. Since leaving Greece so precipitately she had not seen Aristides. She had written him a stiff, painful letter, simply saying that, regrettably, her marriage to Theo Theakis had 'broken down irretrievably' and left it at that. She had not received a reply or any communication from her uncle since. She knew why. Theo had told him why he had taken an axe to their marriage.

Her face darkened. Why the hell had Theo gone and done that? There had been no need—no need whatsoever! What he had accused her of had never been made public, and however much speculation there might have been in the gossiping circles of Athenian society it had remained merely that—gossip.

Theo could just have told her uncle that their marriage had broken down, without having to spell out why. After all, that was

precisely what they had been going to do anyway, by prearrange-
ment. She had merely precipitated their divorce, nothing more...

Merely...

The word mocked her. There had been nothing 'merely'
about it.

Not for her and not, she knew—dear God, she knew!—for
Theo, either.

And now he wanted his revenge for it.

Why had he waited this long?

The answer followed hard on the question. *Because you've
handed him the possibility on a plate by demanding your
money! He's got you over a barrel, and if you want the money
you'll have to do what he wants...*

But she couldn't. It was as simple as that.

She would never, ever subject herself to the humiliation he
had planned for her. Because that was what it would be, she
knew—oh, how she knew! A calculated, assiduous, deliberate
humiliation of her...

Her eyes narrowed suddenly. Her body stilled.

*Why? Why does it have to be? That was what Theo would
want—but why did she have to comply?*

Why didn't she simply...simply refuse to play along?

Or rather...

Her narrowed eyes hardened, and she took another belligerent slug of wine.

Theo wanted revenge—and his revenge would be in her humiliation at his hands.

A tight, grim smile twisted her lips. Revenge? Well, revenge
was a two-way street. A double-edged sword. Theo intended
to sweep one edge of the sword down on her—but she could
use the other side of the blade for her own ends.

Not revenge. Something far, far more important to her.

She drained her wineglass. The alcohol was swimming in

her veins, but she welcomed it. Dutch courage? Possibly—but it was steeling her, giving her the resolve she needed. Needed to get through what lay ahead of her. But if she did it, if she went through with the outrage that Theo was plotting to perpetrate on her, then when it was over she would emerge with something she had never possessed before.

And it had nothing, absolutely nothing, to do with the money she wanted.

Her chin lifted.

I can do this. I can do it. And when I've done it I'm going to walk off with the money that's mine, and Theo Theakis can go to hell!

She set her empty glass down in the sink.

I can do it, she said again to herself. *I can.*

I must.

Because if she did—if she succeeded… Emotion ran through her like a river of lightning in her veins. If she succeeded, then at last…at *last*…she could finally be free of the man she had married. Free in every sense of the word.

I can do it…she repeated. *I can…*

It was a mantra she had to keep repeating to herself over the following hours. Otherwise she knew she would never have been able to travel the distance to the aerodrome where Theo Theakis's chartered jet would be waiting to whisk him home at luxurious speed and convenience. She'd deliberately underdressed, wearing jeans and a cheap sweater, with a backpack hoisted on her shoulders. Her hair was in a loose plait and she wore no make-up. Despite the chilly, cloudy weather she wore a pair of sunglasses—but it wasn't the sun they were protecting her from. She had no intention of risking eye contact with Theo.

But even just setting eyes on him again, shielded as she was by her dark glasses, was an ordeal. For one awful moment, as she saw his tall figure swing round towards her, it was all she could do to stop herself turning tail and running as far and as fast as she could.

There was nothing in his eyes as they flicked over her. Neither satisfaction that she'd given in to his despicable terms nor disdain at her scruffy appearance. He simply said something briefly in Greek to the young man standing rather upright and nervously attentive at his side, who promptly came up to her.

'I am Demetrious Xanthou—Mr Theakis's aide. Please let me know if there is anything you would like for the flight.'

He was new to Vicky. She didn't remember him from before. His manner was impeccably polite, but the expression on his face was studiedly incurious. The word 'discretion' all but shrieked from him.

'I'm fine, thanks,' she answered. She tried to make her voice offhand, as if it were nothing that Theo Theakis's ex-wife was flying off to Greece with him two days after throwing her handbag at him in a fit of temper.

It certainly seemed nothing to Demetrious Xanthou, and her face tightened, little more to his employer.

Well, she thought grimly, if Theo wanted to treat her like the invisible woman she should be glad of it! She was only too happy to treat *him* as the invisible man.

Except that it was very difficult to do that. As they boarded the plane, Theo letting her board first with a gesture that was light years away from true consideration but merely social habit, she was horribly conscious of him following her, too close behind. The interior of the jet, with its huge leather seats and mahogany tables—light years away from flying economy class—caught at her suddenly. Memory jabbed into her, sharp and intrusive.

Private jets, squillion-pound yachts, supercars and designer wardrobes—a lifestyle that was the stuff of dreams for so many.

But not for her. For her it had turned into a nightmare.

Abruptly she dropped herself down in the seat she hoped would be furthest away from Theo, and dumped her backpack at her feet. She refused both offers of help to take it from her or to stow it, and busied herself pulling out a paperback from a side pocket, clipping her seat belt across her in a businesslike fashion, and settling down to read. Determinedly, she kept her nose in the book, pausing only to look out of the porthole window for takeoff, which never failed to bring a rush of adrenaline to her, until the jet had reached its cruising altitude. Across the wide aisle she could see that Theo had settled himself down and was talking incisively in Greek to Demetrious, who had a sheaf of papers laid out on the table between them.

The mellifluous tones of the language of her father tugged at her. Since her marriage had ended she'd avoided anything Greek like the plague. Even though she had never managed to learn the language beyond anything other than hesitant reading and simple conversation, hearing Theo give instructions to his aide brought the words teasing back into her mind. And words that were more than business terms…

She felt her stomach plunge, her skin contract over her flesh. All her Dutch courage of the night before had vanished completely. All her vain resolve to turn this outrageous situation to her own advantage was gone—completely gone! All that remained was panic—blind, blind, panic. She was sitting on Theo's plane, being flown back to Greece.

He's going to have sex with me, and I've consented! My very presence on this plane is my consent!

She must have been mad! She would have to run—run the moment the plane landed. Use her credit card to buy a return flight and get out the moment she could!

But if she did she would never get her money.

Jem would never get her money. Pycott Grange wouldn't be able to open that summer. Children who needed it desperately would have to do without. And she—she would not achieve what last night had seemed finally within her grasp…

Her ultimate freedom from the power that Theo Theakis wielded over her. The power she dreaded more than anything else in the world…

You've got to do it. You've got to—it's the only way.

Just don't think about it—don't think about it till you have to.

Hurriedly, she scrabbled about in the rucksack for her music and stuck headphones in her ears, flicking on the soothing counterpointed intricacies of Bach, instantly silencing the rest of the world around her. Doggedly she forced herself to keep reading. When, a little later, the smiling stewardess came to ask her what she would like by way of refreshments, she asked for coffee, refusing the champagne that was proffered. The very thought of alcohol now was stomach churning. So was food. Acid was running in her stomach, and she felt sick.

But she mustn't, *mustn't* let it show! To let Theo see her nerves would be to pander to his vicious need for revenge, and she would not, *would not* give him that satisfaction.

At least he was not in her line of sight, and nor could she hear his deep, dark voice any more, and for that she could be grateful. When her coffee arrived she lifted the cup, taking little sips, staring out of the window over the fleecy cloudscape, willing herself to be calm as the *Brandenburg Concertos* wove their compelling rhythm through her head. The morning had been such a rush she'd had no time to do anything other than surface, groggily, after a restless, tormented night of unpeaceful intermittent sleep and tearing emotion, then throw the essentials into her backpack.

As for Jem—she'd changed her mind half a dozen times about whether to phone him and tell him she was on the trail of the money. Half of her wanted to reassure him, but half was terrified he'd start asking her questions about how she'd finally managed to change Theo's mind...

Jem must never know. Never. He would be outraged, and rightly so. No, she mustn't think about Jem. She must keep him ignorant for his own sake, to protect him. Just as she'd kept him ignorant about how brutal Theo had been when he had ended their marriage so precipitately. She'd done so partly to protect Jem, but also because he'd have been bound to storm off and confront Theo on her behalf, and then Theo would know...

No—she cut off her thoughts abruptly. Jem now, like then, had to be kept out of this. This was between her and Theo. That was all. She and Jem went back a long, long way, and he was vitally important to her—but she didn't want him dragged back into the ungodly mess that had been the ending of her farcical marriage.

I'll do what I have to do—achieve what I aim to achieve. Then I'll come home again, to Jem, hand him the money, and never say a word of what I had to do to get it.

What I'm going to have to do...

As she sat, tense as a board, sipping hot coffee, the full enormity of what she was doing hit her like slugs to her chin. Disbelief drenched through her, and a sense of dissociation from reality that she had been clinging to for dear life.

I can do this—I can.

I must.

The mantra went round her head, carried by Bach, stopping her thinking of anything else. Anything at all.

And especially, above all, what 'this' would actually mean...

She could feel her eyes flickering and managed to replace the coffee cup on the table in front of her, her head starting to loll. Her restless, tormented night was catching up with her.

The dream she slipped into was vivid. Instant.

She was on the island. That magical, maquis-clad island,

where the azure bowl of the sky cupped land lapped by a cobalt sea, enclosing it in a private, secret world, a world where the outside world ceased to exist, where everything—everyone—was reduced to the elements of which they were made. Sky and stone, sand and sea, air and water, light and dark. Flesh and blood.

And heat. Heat beating up through the rocks, burning down from the blazing sun, heat running in her veins like a fire. A fire she could not quench, a heat she could not cool, heat in her skin, her veins, her nerves, her flesh…flushing through her, pulse, after pulse, after pulse…

She woke—eyes wide, staring. Heart pounding. Terrified.

Words screamed through her.

I can't do this! I can't! I can't! I can't!

Her hands clenched over the arms of her seat.

The plane flew on.

Theo listened as Demetrious brought him up to date on a dozen different items on his always crowded agenda. But his mind was elsewhere.

So she had come. He had half wondered if she would. It could have gone either way, he knew—her self-righteous fury was quite capable of cutting off her own nose to spite her face. His face tightened. It was that, above all, that enraged him— her self-righteousness! Her self-righteous fury at being denied what she dared, *dared* to consider her entitlement to her uncle's money! The uncle she had insulted and shamed, who even now still felt the burden of what she had done.

As for himself—the lines around his mouth incised more deeply—did she really think she could do what she had done and then expect him to meekly hand over the money? His eyes flickered to where he could just see the edge of her body, almost invisible to him. He felt again that stab of raw black anger go through him. Then another emotion countered it.

Should he have made her this offer, given her the chance to get the money she craved? Shouldn't he just have continued to stonewall her, ignore her very existence, as he had done since he had thrown her out, raining down on her the censure she so richly deserved?

With his head he knew that that was indeed what he should have done—every gram of sense in him told him so.

But sense was not uppermost in his mind now. He knew that, deplored it, and yet even so knew he was going to pursue this— knew he was going to carry out what he had every intention of doing. What he had promised her last night when he'd felt again the touch of her flesh against his.

He had unfinished business with her.

And only when he had finished it—finished with her— would he finally throw her from his life permanently.

CHAPTER FIVE

As THE plane made its final descent, Vicky felt her stomach acid go into overdrive again. Not just because she was that much closer in time to the ordeal ahead of her. Nor just because of the nightmare memories that were ready to spring like banshees into her brain, with every familiar sight of Greece around her. But because something else had dawned on her—something that would make the ordeal ahead even worse. Where, exactly, was Theo planning on taking her—and did he intend her to be seen with him in public? On show at his side...?

Dear God, surely he can't be planning to do that?

She swallowed. That had turned out to be the worst aspect of her brief, ill-fated marriage. It was ironic, really. It had been, after all, purely for show that she had gone along with the insane idea of marrying him in the first place! To show the world that Aristide Fournatos was not going cap in hand to Theo Theakis to save his company, but was merely doing something that every Greek family could approve of: forging a link for the mutual benefit of both commercial dynasties, between his niece and a suitable—oh, so highly suitable—husband. Saving his company was almost incidental.

And so being on show had been an essential part and purpose of their marriage. Vicky had thought she could cope with it—

after all, a marriage for external show only was all she had signed up for.

But it had proved far, far more difficult than she had ever imagined.

And then—impossible…

Quite, quite impossible…

She tensed in recollection as the memories started to march across her brain.

As Aristides Fournatos's niece she had been of interest to her uncle's circle of friends and acquaintances, accepted by them despite her Englishness, because of Aristides. But as the wife of Theo Theakis she'd become an object not of interest, but of almost virulent curiosity.

Especially from women, and in particular—the gleeful words of her uncle that every woman in Athens would envy her had not been an exaggeration—women to whom her husband was an object of their sexual interest.

There were so many of them. Women like the one who had commandeered him the evening she had first been introduced to him at her uncle's dinner party, women who had quite obviously either had an affair with him or wanted one. Or wanted another one. Athens, it seemed, was awash with women who found the man she had married magnetically attractive, and who all shared something in common—envy of her, or resentment, or both. Vicky had soon realised that she had committed a social solecism of the highest order—she had walked off with the prize matrimonial catch in Greek society.

Without deserving it.

Crime enough—except for something even worse.

Without appreciating it…

Her gaze hardened.

Vicky knew, as the jet made its descent, that she had spectacularly failed to appreciate the enviable good fortune of having Theo Theakis for a husband. The needling and barbed comments she had received from other women had been proof enough of that. Comments openly directed at her by women congratulating her on her great good fortune in capturing such a prize, as well as more malicious observations from women who had, with sweetly smiling insincerity, expressed the hope that Theo Theakis would manage to be as interested in her as a bride as he evidently was in her uncle's company. Her studiedly blank reaction in the face of all this antagonism had seemed to irritate them even more. The provocation had got worse, making her dread those social occasions when she'd had to be on show with Theo, until finally, to her relief, she had been castigated as a cold-blooded Englishwoman, dull and passionless, and dismissed from their further attention.

But it hadn't just been the scores of women for whom Theo Theakis was an object of desire who had regarded her marriage to Theo as a big mistake

Her eyes darkened balefully and her hands clamped in her lap involuntarily.

She knew to the exact moment when she had realised, with a terrifying hollowing of her stomach, just how big a mistake she had made when she had finally agreed to marry Theo.

Talk about being lulled into a false sense of security…

She had always, right from the start, been a reluctant bride. Quite apart from anything else, the terms of her marriage had meant deceiving her mother and stepfather. It had appalled her when she'd realised that Aristides had been planning to invite them to Athens for the wedding, and she'd had to urgently cite her parents' inability to take leave in the middle of the school term to stop him doing so. She had also lied to him, saying that she had told them about her marriage. Of course she had not! If her mother had got the slightest whiff that her daughter was marrying a man she scarcely knew, for the reasons she was doing so, she would have been on the first flight to Athens to stop her!

Telling Jem had been imperative, of course—if for no other reason than he'd wanted to know when she was going to take over at Freshstart again. It had been incredibly awkward telling him, and even though she had assured him fervently that it was of *course* a marriage in name only, she knew he'd been dismayed by her decision to go ahead with it. Even the knowledge that as soon as it was decent she would end the marriage and return to the UK with a handsome donation to her father's charity had not made him warm to it. Nor had he relished having to run Freshstart in her absence, even though she'd promised him she would only be, after all, at the end of a phone if he needed her. But it had been yet another complication, and the more she'd got sucked into the whole business of marrying Theo Theakis, for however short a duration, the more reluctant she'd become—and the more inextricable her commitment had become, as well.

Only the visible relief in her uncle's eyes had kept her going. That, and one other thing. Since making the fateful decision she had spent minimal time with Theo, during which he had treated her with an impersonal formality that had managed to get her through the ordeal not just of the brief betrothal period but the wedding, as well. Despite the wedding being nothing more than a business arrangement it had been conducted with jaw-dropping extravagance. A lavish civil ceremony—to her uncle's disappointment—had been followed by a huge reception, during which she'd stood at Theo's side, stiff and disbelieving at what she had just done.

It hadn't been until they'd arrived at their honeymoon destination that the reality had hit her with the force of a sledgehammer. There had been something about being ushered into the honeymoon suite of a five-star hotel with the doors closing on her and Theo that had brought home to her the fact that in the eyes of the world he was her husband.

There was, she had realised, staring in horror, only one bedroom—and only one bed.

She had turned in the doorway. Theo had been behind her.

'What is it?' he asked, seeing her aghast expression. His enquiry was brisk.

'There's only one bed,' she said.

His eyes glanced past her shoulder. Then they went to her face. For one brief moment something flickered in his eyes. Then it was gone. He gave a shrug.

'It's the honeymoon suite. What did you expect?'

She took a step backwards. Already the bellhop had deposited their suitcases in the bedroom. One by each of the vast wardrobes. At the touch of a bell, the maid service would arrive to unpack them, lay out their nightclothes on the bed...

Did he wear any?

The thought formed in Vicky's mind, and the moment it was there she could not undo it. Worse, an instant image accompanied it—Theo's tall, lean frame, stripped of its five-thousand-euro suit...stripped right down to the hard, muscled flesh beneath...

She gulped. No! Dear God, that was no way to begin this totally fake marriage! There was only one way to get through this to the other side—the way Theo had been behaving. As if they were nothing more than passing strangers, temporarily sharing accommodation.

But that's just what we are. Passing strangers...

For the briefest moment emotion shafted through her. For an even briefer moment she recognised it for what it was—and was horror-struck. No—she could not *possibly* be feeling regret that they were nothing more than passing strangers.

She steeled herself mercilessly. Oh, sure, Theo Theakis was compellingly masculine—but what the hell had that to do with the current situation? The whole point of this set-up was not to take any notice of her awareness of him, to completely and resolutely ignore it. Because what would be the point of doing otherwise? Theo Theakis had entered into a temporary, unreal marriage to save her uncle's company. And nothing… *nothing*…else came into the question!

And it wasn't just her who thought so. Even as Theo made his remark he glanced behind him, his gaze picking out the long three-seater sofa in the sitting room behind them.

'I'll sleep on that,' he told her.

That idiotic emotion fleeted through her again as she registered what he intended, and again Vicky tossed it aside and stamped on it. Hard. Very hard.

'Thank you,' she said stiffly.

'Not at all,' said Theo. His voice was formal. There was an inflexion in it she did not pick up.

Their sleeping arrangements set the tone for the rest of the honeymoon—which Theo passed in meetings with various government trade officials and other businessmen, and Vicky in sightseeing tours—and continued thereafter when they returned to Athens, to take up residence in the huge Theakis mansion in an exclusive district of the city. There, they hardly ever saw each other, and Vicky was grateful. The house was so large it was easy to keep out of his way, though she was always relieved when he went off on business to other parts of Europe or, better still, farther afield to America.

It was quite difficult enough coping with the bizarre situation she was in without him being around to add to the strain. Being Mrs Theo Theakis was just that much easier when he wasn't around.

Not that it solved her other problem—boredom. The main occupation of the social circle she found herself in seemed to be spending money and socialising with each other, neither of which Vicky took pleasure in. Shopping seemed mindlessly extravagant, and because of the prurient envy and resentment that she so often received from other women, socialising was out of the question. She would have happily spent more time with her uncle, had it not been clear that right now, as was understandable, his prime concern was his business—seeing off the corporate raider now that he had accepted the financial support of Theakis Corp. Besides which, she was also worried she might let slip just how much of a contrived sham her marriage was.

To pass the time she explored Athens, and all the cornucopia of ancient sites in this region of Greece. She also, inspired by discovering the heritage of her father, started to learn Greek, struggling with the difficulty of the alien script to get to the language it embodied, as well as assiduously studying Greek history, art and philosophy. Then there were concerts, opera and the ballet to divert her, and she became a regular at the theatre. Back at the Theakis mansion she also spent a good two hours a day in the pool, swimming lengths, as well as making the most of the fully equipped gym.

But that, as it turned out, was the easy bit of her marriage. Much, much worse was the time—far too much of it!—when Theo was back in Athens and they had to take part in what seemed to her a never-ending round of social activities. She didn't want to, but it was, she conceded, all part of the show that was the purpose of their marriage in the first place.

But being part of a 'couple' with Theo was a highly uncomfortable process. She felt eyes on her, curious and critical, only adding to her feelings of acute self-consciousness in the role she was being required to play. It was the reason, she knew, that she was so particularly stiff in her manners, and the reason why, too, though she was forced to buy ridiculously expensive clothes for such occasions, she always chose styles that were above all discreetly understated—outfits that did not emphasise or overly reveal her figure, or make her conspicuous. They might draw disdainful looks from the chicly sophisticated women from whom Theo Theakis selected his sexual partners, but what did she care?

Her concern was simply to get through the ordeal of being Mrs Theo Theakis. Constantly at her husband's side, conscious all the time—punishingly so—of his tall, commanding presence beside her, was making it impossible, quite impossible, for her ever to relax.

The hardest occasions, she came to realise, were those when she had to play the role of Mrs Theo Theakis in his house, entertaining others. It seemed to exacerbate her pointless, enervating awareness of him, to put her in an oh-so-visible position where she was indelibly linked to him. Bride of a man that other women wanted and resented her for having.

Help yourselves! she wanted to shout at them.

And especially one of them.

She'd glided up to Theo at one of the social events Vicky had attended with him on their return from their fake honeymoon, and Vicky had recognised her instantly. She was the spectacularly svelte woman who had had been at her uncle's dinner party the evening she had been introduced to Theo, who had been all over him, ignoring Vicky completely.

She ignored her now, too.

'Theo!' Her voice was a rich purr, and she spoke Greek, effectively cutting out Vicky while she used a low, intimate voice to the man at her side. She stood too close to him, in his body space, and the contrast between her closeness and the stiff distance that Vicky habitually kept from Theo was marked. So, too, Vicky registered, with a sudden tension in her muscles, was the difference in the smile that Theo bestowed on the woman.

It was a smile of familiarity—sensuality.

He's never smiled at me like that...

The words formed in her head before she could stop them. Immediately she dismissed them. Of course Theo had never smiled at her like that—it was a smile for a lover to give a woman whose pleasures he had enjoyed.

Not for a woman he'd married in a token arrangement for the sole purpose of saving her uncle's beleaguered company. A woman who meant absolutely nothing else to him...

Forcibly, she stiffened her spine. What on earth was she thinking of? Let him have as many lovers as he wanted. It was nothing to do with her.

And this woman now wasn't anything to do with her, either. To prove it, she held out her hand.

'Hello—we haven't met yet, have we? I'm sure I would have remembered you,' she said sweetly.

The woman's sloe-like eyes flickered to her. Vicky's voice had been bland, deliberately sticking to English, but she could see the other woman register the subtle insult. Theo's lover—past or present—was not a woman that other women forgot having seen before.

'Christina Poussos,' she returned dismissively. 'An old friend of your...husband.' She hesitated pointedly before giving the descriptor of the man she was too close to.

Vicky's smile was even sweeter.

'Oh, no,' she murmured in a saccharine voice. 'Not that old, surely?'

Her gaze upon the other woman's immaculately made up, thirty-something face was limpid.

At her side, she could hear Theo clear his throat suddenly. She almost frowned. That couldn't possibly have been a smothered laugh, could it?

Then he was intervening, his voice smooth and emollient.

'Christina—Victoria, as I'm sure you know, is Aristides Fournatos's niece.'

The other woman smiled. It was her turn for a shot now, and she took aim pointedly.

'Of course—and I'm sure you will both allow me to congratulate you on an excellent match. Fournatos and Theakis—a formidable commercial combination. And now, my dear Theo,' she went on, having relegated her lover's marriage to nothing more than a corporate merger, 'you must tell me when you will be free for lunch. I need your business acumen in selecting the best investment of my divorce settlement.' She reverted to Greek, once more cutting out Vicky.

Vicky could feel her muscles tense again. If the woman was talking investments in that slinky voice she'd eat her non-existent hat! She stood there, a fixed, doggedly polite smile on her face, sipping at her glass of wine, until with a final throaty laugh Christina Poussos reached up, brushed her mouth against Theo's, and glided off again.

'Until Friday, then, Theo darling,' she murmured, in a Parthian shot that found its mark dead on Vicky, whose fingers suddenly tightened around the stem of her wineglass.

Forcibly she made herself relax them. She didn't care *squat* what Theo got up to with Christina Poussos. Or anyone else.

Deliberately she raised her wineglass and took a larger mouthful than usual.

I don't care. I don't care squat.

Not even microsquat...

And why should she? She hadn't even *wanted* to marry Theo Theakis, so of course she didn't give squat about him carrying on with any women. She just didn't particularly want to know about it, that was all.

Brightly, she turned to Theo, fuelled by the wine inside her.

'Sorry about making that bitchy remark about her age. A bit of a low shot. I do hope I didn't hurt her feelings.'

Theo's dark gaze swept over her before answering. She pinned the bright look to her face with sustained effort.

'I'd say she got her own back quite easily, wouldn't you?' One eyebrow quirked sardonically.

Vicky widened her eyes. 'What, talking about the commercial advantages of a Fournatos-Theakis marriage? What's bitchy about that? It's only the truth.' Her tone was dismissive. 'So long as she doesn't blab to my uncle that it's a totally fake, totally temporary marriage. Speaking of my uncle—isn't that him over there?' She craned her neck slightly, seeing past the people around her. 'Yes, it's definitely him. I'll go over and say hello. I can't stick here by your side like I'm on a string all evening.'

She made to move, but a light touch on her arm stayed her. Theo's long fingers loosely circled her wrist. She felt a current of electricity go through her that dismayed her, and she froze.

'Why not?' Theo's voice was easy, but she could discern something underneath it—some note that made her muscles tense yet again. 'We are newlyweds, after all.'

She gave a pointed shrug. 'Oh, if you think the show must go on, so be it. Shall we go arm in arm?' she said, with deliberately heavy, terse jocularity.

'Why not?' said Theo again, with smooth assent this time, and now there was a blandness in his voice that somehow managed to grate at her. He tucked her arm into his and drew her forwards towards her uncle. Stiff as a board, Vicky went with him.

The moment she could, she disengaged.

She knew it was only for show, but it didn't make it any easier. Keeping her distance from Theo Theakis was the only way to get through this ordeal.

Her mood was bleak. What the hell had she gone and let herself in for? She wanted to go home—to London, to Jem, to Freshstart, and her safe, familiar world.

A long, long way from Theo Theakis and her ridiculous fake marriage that meant nothing, nothing at all to either of them.

And let's keep it that way! she thought vehemently.

It was far, far too disturbing to think of anything else.

But at least, to her relief, she only had to play the part of Mrs Theo Theakis in public. In private, audience gone, she could finally go off duty and let the tension racking her slacken off. And Theo could, too. He could drop all the pretence he had to put on of being the attentive husband and do nothing more than treat her with indifferent civility, his expression completely neutral. When he spoke to her she might have been anyone—anyone at all—fifteen or fifty, male or female. She was glad of it, and told herself so. It was totally abundantly obvious that Theo Theakis was as indifferent to her as she could possibly want. Off duty, she could revert to the truth of what she and Theo were to each other. Passing strangers who'd united to help her uncle in the only way he would accept help.

Nothing more at all.

Until that fatal evening. That fatal moment.

When she realised that she was facing a danger she had never, ever dreamt she would have to face.

It came right at the end of a large, gruelling dinner party. It had not been an easy evening—such evenings never were—but she had done her best, wearing a carefully selected designer gown and appropriate jewellery, her hair styled, her face perfect, every inch the immaculate hostess, smiling and conversing and being very grateful that the expert Theakis staff kept everything running like clockwork. It had gone on and on, and her face muscles were aching as much as her feet in their elegant narrow shoes. But finally it was over, and the last of the guests took their leave. She stood at the foot of the stairs that swept grandly to the upper floors as Theo, in a dinner jacket that sat superbly across his broad shoulders, turned from saying good night to the very last guest.

As he turned, his eyes rested on her for just a moment. And in that single moment she realised, with seismic shock, that she had been totally, completely wrong about him.

She could still feel the echo of that shock wave. Felt it resonate now, as she sat in the padded leather seat, gazing blindly out of the aeroplane window, heading back to Athens.

From that moment on, as that seismic shock had jarred through her, her marriage had changed for ever.

At first she had not believed it. She had assumed that in that moment when his eyes had rested on her with that expression in them she had been mistaken. She must have been mistaken. There was no other explanation. It had been late, she'd been tired, she had drunk wine—and so had he. That expression in them, therefore, had been nothing to do with her. Had been a recollection—or an anticipation. But not of her. Never of her. How could it have been?

Their marriage was a sham, a façade, a hollow charade. They had entered into it for no other purpose than to be exactly that. And until that moment he had treated her with complete and studied indifference. So how, *how* could that look possibly have been directed at her...?

But it had been—

And it had been unmistakable. Completely and absolutely unmistakable. A look as old as time. As clear as day.

Directly unambiguously, transparently—devastatingly— right at her.

A single look. Nothing more.

Nothing less.

And by it she had known, with a churning in her stomach, with a weakening of her limbs, a debilitating flush of betraying blood in her veins, that her fake, sham charade of a marriage had become something completely, absolutely different.

It had become a hunt.

She closed her eyes in worn, mental exhaustion, drawn back down into that inescapable past.

A hunt. That was what Theo Theakis had conducted. From that moment on, from that one single glance that had stripped away from her all the puerile illusions she'd had, she had become a hunted creature. Prey to a skilled, ruthless and unrelenting predator. A predator who had made her his target and kept her ruthlessly, remorselessly, in his sights.

His campaign had been so skilful. Slow, assiduous, bringing to bear all the expertise he had so abundantly at his disposal, honed to perfection on so many, many women. And she had been the focus of it.

As the days, weeks had followed, and Theo had slowly moved in for the kill, she'd realised that there was only one place that he was guiding her to, only one destination he had in mind for her—his bed.

CHAPTER SIX

LIKE a recording set to endless replay, Vicky again felt the hollowing of her insides that she had experienced when it had finally dawned on her just what Theo had in mind for her. And just as she had that time, she felt the same reaction—absolute blind panic.

Followed by absolute blind fury.

What the hell did he think he was doing?

That was what had screamed through her mind then. It still did now. But now, dear God, now she knew what she had not known then. That Theo Theakis was a man who would balk at nothing—nothing at all—to get what he wanted.

She felt her palms grow cold. God, she knew that all right! Her presence here, now, was terrifying, outrageous testament proof of that!

She heard his cold, chilling words echo in her mind.

'I want to finish what I started...'

She opened her eyes, staring ahead of her, blind and unseeing. In her ears Bach's convoluted intricate harmonies wove a universe of order and serenity. It mocked the raw, ragged torment in her mind.

I have to do this. And I can—I can do this.

Because I must...

And when she had—when she had done it—she would finally be done with Theo Theakis. For ever.

I'll have finished what he started—what I never, ever wanted him to start.

And then Theo Theakis could go to the hell he deserved.

Grim, dogged determination filled her, and a loathing of the man who was doing this to her crammed every cell of her body.

She felt the plane tilt, circle down, come into land, touch down, the jet engines screaming into reverse thrust to brake the plane, decelerate to a standstill.

Limply, she let her hand lie in her lap, then jerkily she unfastened her seat belt and looked around. Theo was already on his feet, and so was his aide. Theo did not look at her, simply headed for the exit, pausing to murmur brief thanks to the steward and stewardess, and acknowledge the pilot and co-pilot. Demetrious followed him, carrying his briefcase. He half hesitated, Vicky saw, as if to turn and speak to her, then simply hurried off after his employer.

It was the stewardess who came down to her to escort her from the jet. Theo was long gone, and Vicky knew why and was glad of it—even though she knew perfectly well that Theo had only been concerned about himself, not her. But at least it meant that she was spared what she had been dreading—being spotted by the paparazzi that hung around waiting for VIP passengers to come through.

If they knew I was back in Greece with Theo they would have a field-day!

She shivered involuntarily. Hadn't it been bad enough being an object of virulent curiosity to every woman who had had, or wanted to have, an affair with Theo? But on top of that she had also, thanks to her marriage, been an object of voyeuristic fascination to the Greek paparazzi, and to her consternation she had become used to the flash of photographs being taken whenever she went anywhere public with Theo, and often when she was on her own, as well.

A grim light glowered in her eyes. It had been the paparazzi, trailing her to that hotel, who had precipitated the vicious ending of her marriage...

She pulled her mind away. She would not let herself recall that hideous scene again, in which Theo had poured down on her all the savage fury he was capable of. Just as she would not, *would not*, let herself think about what she was doing now, returning to Greece.

A car was waiting for her, large, sleek and expensive, with tinted windows and a chauffeur. The moment she realised that that was to be her form of transport Vicky felt relief flush through her. The car indicated that she was staying on the mainland. God alone knew just how many beds Theo owned across his myriad properties, but there was one above all others that she dreaded.

No—no thinking of that. No memories allowed. Total shutdown of brain function—that was all that was allowed when it came to that subject.

Don't think—don't think about the island...

The island where she had endured her greatest ordeal.

Far more unbearable than the vicious savaging with which he had disposed of her as his wife.

Far more unbearable than that...

Cold snaked down her spine at the thought of Theo maximising his revenge by taking her back to that place...

But if she had been spared the island, where was he then intending to keep her? Pincers nipped at her insides. Was he planning on having her stay in the Theakis mansion? Please, no! It would be far too easy for her uncle to discover her presence there—

As ever, when she thought of Aristides, anger flushed

through Vicky. Theo had not spared her uncle either in his vicious savagery. He had destroyed her relationship with Aristides, her only living paternal relative, and she would not forgive him for that any more than she would forgive him anything else.

As the car started to leave the airport complex she saw it was not heading towards Athens, and the pincers in her stomach stilled. Nor were they heading for Piraeus, the port of Athens, so it was not to be his yacht, either.

So where, then?

It was as the car headed for the coast, and she made herself look at the road signs, that she finally realized. And when she did she felt a spurt of uncontrollable, furious anger.

She knew *exactly* where she was being taken!

Bastard! The absolute bastard!

Fury bit in her.

He was doing it on purpose—that was obvious. Making his point. Rubbing it in. Showing her, very visibly, what he intended to make of her! She felt her temper seethe. Then, out of her bile, another emotion emerged. The same one she had summoned last night, as she'd steeled herself to do what she had to do. This was a game two people could play. He thought he was calling the shots—well, he could think again!

He could damn well think again!

She had her own agenda for this hellish interlude, and she'd stick to it through thick and thin.

She sat back in the soft leather seat as the chauffeured car whisked her luxuriously to her destination. It did not take very long to get there, and she was not surprised. After all, it had to be a convenient distance from Athens. A quick enough run to fit in with the crowded agenda of a busy chief executive whose time was scarce and valuable.

'*Kyria?*'

The voice of the driver was impersonal, but his glance, as Vicky got out of the car at her destination, was less so. As she caught the discreet appraisal in his eyes, his expression of brief puzzlement only confirmed that she had been delivered to the correct place. Why else would Theo's chauffeur think it odd that he had just delivered a woman dressed in jeans and a cheap top to a place like this? The women who were brought here were light years away from her—they would never have worn chain-store clothes, or have been seen without a full face of make-up and hair done up to match. They would be svelte and chic and sophisticated, and above all always stunningly beautiful—the way Christina Poussos was.

And they would be preeningly gratified to be the object of his attentions. Even more gratified, Vicky knew, with another caustic glint in her eye as she surveyed her destination, to have been brought here.

Her eyes ran over the house in front of her. It had been built well off the main coast road, tucked discreetly away, far from prying eyes, deep in lushly watered gardens, surrounded by a high wall and the usual electronic security the wealthy found normal. It was small by the standards of the rich, not a mansion, but it was opulent and luxurious and Vicky knew exactly what sort of place it was.

She'd been told about it—but not by her husband. By a woman who had been at one time a guest here—'*Many* times, my dear'—so she had informed Vicky, with one of those sweetly insincere smiles she had become accustomed to. Vicky hadn't reacted—why should she have? It had meant nothing to her—and her blankness had clearly annoyed the woman.

She reacted with the same blankness now as she walked into the house, the door opened for her by a member of staff she had no reason to recognise from her marriage. The staff here would be quite different from those at any of the other Theakis properties in Greece—the vast mansion in Kifissia, the apartment in the city centre, the ski lodge in the mountains and the *faux*-primitive beach villa on the island.

Even if they did recognise her, it would not matter. The staff here, Vicky knew, would have been selected not just for their ability to be invisible, but primarily for their absolute and total discretion, blind and deaf to the identities of their employer's 'guests'. There would be no leaks to gossip columnists or paparazzi from these servants.

It was cool indoors, compared to the brief heat of the exterior between the air-conditioned car and the air-conditioned interior, and Vicky gave an unconscious shiver. It was the sudden chill that had made her shiver, she told herself. Nothing else.

With studied blankness she strolled forward, across the marble floored entrance hall and then into the shaded reception room beyond. It had been, she surmised, professionally designed for style and luxury, lacking any kind of personal touch. Through the slatted blinds she could make out a veranda, and the sea beyond.

Hefting her backpack to her other shoulder, she walked back out into the hall and headed upstairs. There was no sign of any more staff anywhere, but Vicky knew that if she dumped her backpack on the hall floor it would invisibly be taken upstairs at some point, and its meagre contents unpacked for her.

On the upper landing were several doors, and she opened one at random. It was a guest bedroom. The next was a bathroom as large as a bedroom. A small, scornful smile nicked her mouth, devoid of humour—with a sunken bath easily able to accommodate two people, plus a Jacuzzi and a walk-in shower. The next door opened to what must be the master bedroom, with a bed the size of her own bathroom.

She shut the door abruptly and returned to the first bedroom. That, at least, though still opulently decorated in the same pro-

fessionally anonymous style of the downstairs décor, lacked a
football pitch of a bed in which sleeping was obviously not the
designated activity.

Like an automaton she crossed to the window, drawing up
the blinds and staring out. She could see down over the gardens
and the swimming pool to a small, private shingle beach, with
a jetty to one side and the sea glinting with a blue that the colder
shores of the UK never saw.

Emotion moved within her, and she slammed down on it.
Her face set, she dumped her backpack on the bed and started
to empty the contents over the counterpane. Unpacking would
help to pass the time.

Stop her thinking.

That was essential. Quite essential.

But her unpacking took almost no time at all, and within
minutes it was done. She glanced out of the window again. The
shadows were lengthening; the two-hour time difference, plus
the flight time, had eaten up the day. On a sudden impulse she
lifted the house phone. It was answered immediately, and she
issued a request for coffee to be served on the terrace. Then,
armed with her book, she went downstairs.

The temperature on the terrace, despite the time of day, was
still warm enough to make her wish she'd changed into more
lightweight clothes. But if she'd done that she would have had
to have a shower first, and she was in no mood to do that. It
would have meant stripping off, seeing her naked body.

Her stomach plunged. Suddenly the reality of why she was
here hit her all over again like a sledgehammer. She felt panic
explode in her chest.

Oh, God, I can't do this! I can't! I can't!

Panic beat like a wild animal, and she could feel her heart rate
leaping. Then, clenching her hands, she forced herself to calm.

Stop it—stop it right now. Ruthlessly she clamped down on

her burst of emotion. *You can do it—but the only way is to not think. Just don't think about what you're doing. That's all you have to do.*

That's all...

Grimly, she forced herself back into that state of deliberate blankness she'd managed before, sitting herself down on one of the padded chairs set out in the shade from which she could see the swimming pool, one end curved around into a whirlpool, with a set of waterproof switches inset into a stone slab at one end. She looked away and flicked open her book, making herself start to read. A few minutes later the coffee arrived. It was filter coffee, not Greek, and there was a plate of little Greek pastries and biscuits to go with it. She eyed them a moment. She ought to make herself eat something, she knew, because she'd been unable to eat on the plane, and breakfast had been an impossibility, too. But she contented herself just with sipping coffee instead.

Sip and read. Sip and read.

Don't think. Sip and read. Sip and read.

But thoughts came all the same. Threading into her brain between the words of her book, pooling like acid into her stomach.

She was here, in Greece. She had not been here for two years. All around she could hear the chitter of cicadas, feel the warmth of the southern clime, see the Mediterranean vegetation and the sparkle of the sun on blue, blue water. This time yesterday she'd had no idea at all that she would be here.

No idea of the ordeal ahead of her.

Am I mad to do this? Even to think I can do this?

Doubt assailed her, eroding what little dogged determination she was retaining. Disbelief swept over her, and then panic again, and she had to fight them both down.

I can do this—I can get through it, and I can come out the other side. And I will. That's exactly what I'm going to do. I'm

*going to come out the other side, and I'm going to get my
money, and then I'm going home—home to my real life. Home
far, far away from here—and farther away from Theo Theakis
than he can ever reach again.*

She felt anger and loathing for him pool deep within her.
She let it gather, taking strength from it. Let his image form
in her mind.

Tall, dark, deadly.

Abruptly she jumped to her feet, dumping her coffee cup on
the tray and letting her book tumble to the floor. She strode off
the terrace, past the pool, with its purpose-built whirlpool, and
plunged down the set of steps that led on to the shingle beach.
It was only a tiny beach, hardly enough to stride along. The
vegetation at either end was too thick for her to negotiate, and
she was reduced to crossing and recrossing the patch of shingle
as all around her the warm Mediterranean dusk gathered like
a thickening blanket, pierced only by the noise of the cicadas
in the foliage.

Agitation poured through her, a sick anxiety, as she strode
up and down, backwards and forwards, the soles of her trainers
crunching the gravel. Then, without knowing why, she halted.
Her skin seemed to prickle. She had heard nothing, but she was
spiked with awareness.

Slowly, very slowly, she turned to look back at the villa.

Theo was standing on the veranda.

Watching her.

Theo let his eyes continue to rest on her, even though she was
now aware of his presence.

She was agitated. That was good. It meant that the air of
blankness she'd pulled over herself during the flight had been
nothing but a pose. She was good at poses, he knew—all too
well. Posing at being his wife—until she'd been caught *in fla-*

grante by the gutter press who had, for once in their sordid, voyeuristic lives, come in useful.

A familiar fury gripped him—fury on so many, many counts. Fury at her sheer gall, at her daring to do what she had and then, when confronted with it, being without shame or repentance. Fury at her continued shamelessness, thinking she was entitled to the money Aristides had set aside for her, for which she had repaid him with dishonour and disgrace. But she hadn't cared about that, either. Or about anyone else…

Deliberately he let the fury drain out of him. It had had two years to drain out now, and there was no point letting it return. Emotion was out of place now. All emotion. He did not need to be Greek to know that the first rule of revenge held true whatever the nationality of the injured party. Revenge was a dish to be eaten cold.

It was a dish he would start to dine on tonight.

Abruptly he raised a hand, and summoned her to him.

Vicky went back up to the villa. She didn't want to. She wanted to find a power boat—a fast one—climb into it, let out the throttle and carve a way through the sea until the land behind was gone. Until Theo Theakis was gone.

But she couldn't. So instead, with steady tread, she walked up the steps and on to the veranda. She stood, saying nothing. Not meeting his eyes.

But punishingly aware of his physical presence.

For a moment he stayed silent. Then he spoke.

'Get changed. Clothes have been delivered for you. I'll meet you for drinks in an hour.'

She didn't deign to answer, just walked past him into the villa and out into the hall to go up the stairs. In the room she'd selected there were two people. One was a member of the house staff, and the other, she assumed, was some kind of personal shopper. They were placing clothes in the closet, on rails and in drawers.

'I'm going to take a shower,' Vicky announced, and went through to the bathroom, shutting the door firmly. Inside, she felt the bitterness starting to pool again. She took a sharp breath, stared dead ahead of her into the mirror above the vanity unit. But she did not meet her own gaze. She did not even look at herself. She looked at the reflection of the far wall in the glass. Then, counting to three, she steeled herself and started to pull her clothes off.

By the time she emerged a few minutes later she was clean, her hair towelled dry, swathed in a bathrobe. It was too skimpy on her, and she felt too much of her legs exposed. Both the other women were still in her room, clearly awaiting her. She forced a polite smile to her face, thanked them and dismissed them. She did not want anyone around while she dressed.

With a calmness she had to impose rigidly on herself she set to, sliding open drawers and sifting through the plastic-swathed clothes now hanging in the closet. It didn't take more than a few seconds to see exactly what instructions the personal shopper had been given. For a brief moment anger surged in Vicky. Then, with a grim tightening of her mouth, she reminded herself that that choice of attire suited her purposes entirely, as it happened. Whatever Theo's agenda was, she had one of her own. One that she must not waver from.

With iron discipline, stony-faced, she made her selection and started to get ready.

She hadn't brought a stick of make-up with her. But the personal shopper had seen to that, as well. A vanity case bearing the logo of a famous parfumier had been set out for her.

It took nearly all of the hour Theo had allocated her to do what she had to, and she did it with all the blankness she could summon to her aid. Then, with nothing more than a last, expressionless glance at her own reflection, she made her way downstairs.

He was in the reception room, and he was on his mobile. She walked in, crossed to the cocktail cabinet which had been opened to show a lavish display, and poured herself a vermouth. A large one.

Then she turned, glass in hand.

Her ex-husband had stopped talking.

Slowly, very slowly, he slid the phone back into his jacket pocket. Then he just stood and looked.

CHAPTER SEVEN

THEO could feel his body react. It would have been impossible for it not to have done. Emotions surged through him along with his body's animalistic response.

One emotion was obvious, but the other—

The other was completely out of place. He thrust it aside.

Then, like the connoisseur of fine women he was, he allowed his overriding sensation free rein—along with his eyes.

She was wearing eau-de-nil silk, clinging to her body more closely than her own pale skin, the material cupping her breasts and revealing their deep, exposed cleavage. Her fair hair was swept loose around one shoulder, falling seductively over one side of her face. Her eyes were huge in her face, lashes sooted with mascara, deepened by shadow, and her mouth was a lush curve of shimmering colour.

She stood, weight on one leg, one hand loose, the other raising a glass to her mouth. She took a slow, deliberate sip, then lowered the glass again. It was a calculated, provocative gesture.

So, he thought, that was how she was going to play this, was it? The mix of emotions clashed in him again, and, as before, he thrust aside the irrelevant one.

He knew what the woman in front of him was. He'd known it for a long time now, and it was not knowledge that drew from him anything other than the desire to do exactly what he was going to start tonight. The dish he was going to consume cold, and so very, very enjoyably.

He started to walk towards her.

Vicky stood, completely frozen, glass in her hand, like a rabbit that was being approached by a lean, intent predator. But beneath the frozen stillness of her pose something was running. Running in her veins, her nerves, her skin, like a fire through tinder-dry grass.

And it was tinder-dry all right.

Two years—two *years*—since that fire had last run in her veins.

Memory crashed through her, fusing present with past in a searing moment.

Theo, walking towards her, with one intention, one intention only, in his eyes, eyes that held hers, not letting her go, not letting her move.

Not letting her escape…

She'd wanted to—desperately—but she hadn't been able to. Hadn't been able to run, hadn't been able to move. Had only stood there while he walked towards her, reached for her…

He was reaching for her now, his hand fingering down the long fall of her hair beside her face. Hair was supposed to be unfeeling, and yet, if so, how was it that a million nerve-endings had started to fire within her?

For a long, endless moment he said nothing, just held her eyes, his eyelids lowering infinitesimally as he contemplated her. She stood immobile, quivering with awareness of him. Of his closeness.

Of his intent.

Then, in a gesture that was almost leisurely, he let his hand fall.

'Dinner first, I think,' he murmured.

He strolled through into the dining room that opened off the drawing room. Vicky followed behind. Her heart had started to thump. She tried to make it stop, but it wouldn't. So she took another mouthful of her vermouth. Its spiced headiness made her feel better.

Stronger.

And she needed to be strong. She needed to be absolutely strong.

One of the house staff was holding her chair, and she took it with a murmured thank you. It came out automatically in Greek, and the realisation made her uneasy. She didn't want to feel she was in Greece. Didn't want to do anything.

Except get this over and done with.

She cast a belligerent eye at Theo as he took his own place.

Why the farce of dining with me? Why not just lug me straight up to that ludicrous bed and do what you brought me here to do?

But she mustn't think about that—that was a bad idea, very bad. She took another mouthful of vermouth. Then, seeing that a glass of white wine was being poured for her, she seized that and drank from that instead. It didn't mix well with the vermouth, but she didn't care. She wanted the alcohol.

Needed it.

'If you're thinking of passing out cold on me, think again.'

Her eyes flashed to the far end of the table. Words rose in her mouth, words that would tell him that being out cold would be the best way of facing what he had in mind for her. But the presence of the staff, however impassive their expressions, stilled her. Instead, she made a show of pushing her wineglass aside in favour of the tumbler of sparkling mineral water that had also just been poured for her.

They ate in silence. It was difficult to do anything else while the staff hovered. Vicky wasn't sure whether she was glad they were there or not. Their presence kept a veneer of normality over the proceedings, but to her that only made it even more hypocritical.

How she got through the meal she did not know. Theo said nothing more to her, seemed preoccupied. And she did her best not to look at him. Nor to let herself think. Or feel. Feel anything at all. She must not, she knew. She must just sit there, lifting food to her mouth and lowering her fork again. Taking sips, repeatedly, of the wine poured for her by the silent, soft-footed staff who waited on them. Did they find it odd that their employer and his latest mistress sat and ate in complete silence? If they did, she didn't care—wouldn't care. God knew what they'd seen here in their time! She didn't want to think about it. Let alone imagine it...

Theo, with all his willing, willing women...

Well, not me! Not me!

Anger spurted through her. Then, like a house of cards, it collapsed.

A voice sliced into her head. Low, insidious, and so, so deadly.

Liar...

She stilled. Every muscle in her body freezing.

Liar, came the voice again, the one inside her head.

You were willing once...

In the end...

Of their own volition, drawn by a power she could not resist, her eyes went to him. She felt her breath catch in her lungs.

Why—why did it happen every time she looked at him? Because ever since she had first laid eyes on him she had felt it—felt his power. Power to disturb her. Dismay her.

And power to do much, much more to her. To make her do what she so did not want to do.

Her mind slid away to the past, the wine in her veins making it all too easy to do so, and memory suffused through her.

From the moment, so vivid still in her mind, when he had let his eyes rest on her as she stood at the foot of the stairs, and she had seen and felt his intent, he had hunted her down.

Relentless, purposeful, knowing what he wanted and set on getting it. Until, at the last, he had breached her resistance.

The island. How had she been insane enough to go there? She had thought it a refuge, a haven. A place where she could hide—escape. She should have known it was not that at all. That it was a trap, a lure, and once there she would have no place to run. No retreat.

She had fled there, to the private island Theo had mentioned in passing, never realising, in her stupidity, that she had done exactly what he had wanted her to do. Played right into his skilled hands. That the deliberate pressure he had exerted on her in the immediately preceding days, when he had racked up the tension so that she was incapable of rational thought, had all been part of his campaign.

The campaign had not been hurried or precipitate. No, it had started slowly, oh, so slowly, from that fateful initiation. A slow, deliberate process of letting her know, little by little, what his intentions were. Even when she had realised, disbelievingly, that she really was not misunderstanding the signs, that for some insane reason Theo Theakis thought he could enjoy her in his bed, he had continued.

I should have challenged him right there and then! Told him where to get off!

But she hadn't—little by little, week by week, he had worked on her. A look, an assessing regard, a flicker of awareness of her, the way he spoke to her, set his eyes on her. Until, finally vulnerable, trapped within the demands of her fake marriage with all the terrifying opportunities for an intimacy that had never, never been in the contract, he had turned on her the full force of the potency of his power and magnetism.

He had succeeded in making her weak and vulnerable—and gullible.

So gullible.

It had come to a head when, returning to Athens after nearly a week in Zurich on business, he had informed her that there was a gala ball to which they had been invited. It had been bad enough just realising that her heart rate had quickened discernibly when she had returned to the mansion and heard Theo's deep tones issuing instructions to one of the house staff. Worse when, hearing her arrival, he had emerged from his study, still wearing his business suit, and her lungs had squeezed out the air in them at the sight of him after a week. Had he seen her betraying reaction? With hindsight she knew he must have. He was far too experienced not to know. He had strolled forward, enquired after her health in a formal fashion, then reminded her of the hour at which they would have to leave that night.

The ball had been her worst ordeal yet. She had had to dance with Theo.

Of all things, a waltz.

She had been wearing a ballgown of red satin, strapless, with a high bodice that wrapped her torso tightly, gliding in to her waist then falling in a long, straight skirt to her ankles. A diamond and ruby necklace, one of the dozen items of similar jewellery that Theo had bestowed on her to wear for the duration of their marriage, had glittered at her throat, diamond and ruby drops at her earlobes. Her hair had been up, in a severe French pleat, and her make-up had been subtle and subdued.

Theo's eyes had narrowed very slightly, she recalled, as she had descended the staircase in the Theakis mansion, to where he waited, tuxedo-clad, in the hall below. As she'd come up to him, her expression impassive, she'd seen and been sure of it, a glint in his dark veiled eyes.

'Very English,' he observed, and the glint came again, making nerves flutter in her chest.

'Shall we go?' was all she said, and started towards the door.

Only the sudden pressure of her fingers on her satin evening bag betrayed her agitation.

All through their arrival and the early part of the proceedings Vicky managed to maintain her composure. Aristides was there, and she was glad of it, making a beeline for him when the sultry divorcee, Christina Poussos, who was clearly determined to resume her affair with him, commandeered him, shamelessly taking his arm and pressing her black-sheathed body against his as she led him away because he 'must meet' a most influential Argentinean financier.

But she was less glad of her uncle's presence when, after letting her chat to him for fifteen minutes, he said to her, with a mixture of indulgence and reproof, 'Go and rescue your husband from Christina Poussos before she thinks she can steal him from you, *pethi mou*!'

Vicky stifled an urge to say that Christina Poussos and her entire sisterhood could whisk him away any time they fancied, knowing she must say no such thing to Aristides. So she made her way to the cluster of people where Theo stood, his arm still held by the woman who, Vicky idly assessed, probably fell into the category of females whom Theo had once enjoyed, and had since replaced, but who had ambitions to return to his bed. Certainly the Greek woman's eyes glittered malevolently at Vicky as she arrived to join the group. But her reception by the middle-aged Argentinean was quite different. He broke off in mid-sentence to pay her a fulsome compliment, his eyes working hotly over her. Christina introduced her, and Vicky could almost hear her teeth gritting. Then, as the orchestra started to play, the other woman's eyes lit.

'Dancing at last! Theo, you know I love to dance!' She smiled flirtatiously at him before switching her gaze to the Argentinean. 'Enrique, take care of Victoria, won't you? Theo—' The flirtatious smile was back on her red-painted lips.

How it happened, Vicky did not know. Presumably with the same cool, ruthless skill and will that he brought to bear on everything. But the next moment Christina Poussos was disengaged from Theo, and her own hand taken. Then he was saying, in deceptively casual tones, 'The first dance must be with my wife, I think,' and she was being led out on to the huge dance floor as the orchestra swept into a waltz.

It had happened so fluidly she had no chance to realise his intention—and now it was too late.

She had been taken in his arms. His hand slid around her waist, resting lightly, firmly—immovably—in the small of her back, and his fingers laced through hers.

'Your left hand goes on my shoulder,' he murmured, glancing down at her.

Numbly, she did as she was bid, her feet starting to move as he impelled her forward. Her heart seemed to have gone from being frozen solid in her chest to lodging breathlessly in her throat.

They started to dance. And as they did Vicky understood for the first time in her life just why waltzing had once been considered scandalous.

She was so *close* to him! Closer than she had ever been! Held almost against him, her body posed and positioned by the subtle pressure of his hand splayed at her waist, his long, strong fingers laced through hers, and worst, worst of all, his lean, muscled thighs brushing against her skirts as he moved her backwards into the dance, turning her as he did so.

She gazed up at him—quite helpless. His face was so close to her, too—far, far too close. She could see the blade of his nose, the lines around his mouth, the firm outline of his lips, the smooth, freshly shaven jawline and more devastating yet, the dark glint of his eyes half veiled by thick black lashes.

And there was something more powerful still. Primitive, potent. The scent of his masculinity, the faint spice of aftershave, teasing at her. Her left hand rested as lightly as she dared on the smooth, expensive surface of his jacket, and through the fine material she could feel the sinewy muscles of his broad shoulders.

The music was haunting and rhythmic, old-fashioned but reaching deep, deep into her psyche, and they moved around and around, turning and turning on the dance floor, so that she could see nothing else, nothing at all except his lean, tanned face looking down at her, and her eyes locked to his—the only still point in a turning world. She was breathless, floating, caught and held, moving along the path that he set for her, guiding her, taking her where he wanted her to go…

Into a realm where only he existed for her.

And she gave herself to it as the music flowed in her limbs and her body. Helpless to do otherwise.

When, after an eternity, the music died, he stilled her, but her mind was whirling still, and all she could do was stand and gaze up at him, into his fathomless eyes.

And she recognised, deep, deep within her blood, what had happened to her. For one long endless moment she went on standing there, as all around couples were moving away, re-forming, talking and laughing. She just stood there, trembling in every limb, and gazed at him, lips parted.

He looked down at her. Looked at her from his dark, dangerous eyes.

And smiled. The smile of a predator who had captured his prey at last…

She did not know how she got through the rest of the evening—had no recollection of it, no awareness. All her consciousness was focussed on one thing only.

She must escape.

Where—how—with what excuse? What reason?

It was during one of the distracted conversations she had during the course of that endless evening, when she made some remark about how hot and breathless Athens was at the end of September, that Aristides suggested the island Theo owned.

'It will be cooler there. Fresher than here. You should have a holiday, both of you.' He beamed at them. 'You could go there tomorrow!'

Vicky stiffened automatically, and Theo said, 'Impossible, unfortunately. I can't get away until the weekend.' He glanced at Vicky. 'You could go, however, and then I could join you on Friday evening.' There was a bland look in his eyes, but Vicky had seen the glint in them.

But all she murmured was, 'Very well.'

'Splendid!' Aristides exclaimed. He beamed at both of them again.

Vicky forced a smile to her face. Oh, she would go to this island, all right. But she would not be there, waiting like a tethered goat, when Theo arrived at the weekend to finish off his kill. She would be gone by then. Where, she didn't know or care—but agreeing to go to this private island of Theo's would buy her the precious time she needed. From there she could make her own arrangements.

So she had gone. Like a fool, an idiot. Thinking she had found a haven, a refuge from what she fled.

But Theo outmanoeuvred her effortlessly. She set off after lunch, Theo safe in his offices in Athens. When she landed on the island he was already there.

The island. Fragrant with the scent of thyme, cooled by the breeze off an azure sea, a place of magic and enchantment. An enchantment that sapped her will and lulled her senses even as it awakened them.

When had the moment of yielding come? She did not know, but it came all the same—a moment so silent, so imperceptible, that she was not even conscious of it. As she walked up to the tiny white-walled villa, framed by olive trees, splashed crimson with bougainvillea, in all its bewitching simplicity, she felt her heart lift, her spirit lighten. Beyond the whiteness of the building she could see the cerulean blue of the sea, merging into the infinite sky above.

She felt a strange tranquillity steal over her, a sense of journey's end and resolution. Her pace slowed and she looked about her more deeply, drinking it in.

Then the sound of a door opening made her turn back towards the villa.

Theo stood in the doorway.

For one brief moment she stood, transfixed.

Waiting for the fury. The dismay.

But they did not come.

He held his hand out to her. He was not wearing his perpetual business suit. His short-sleeved shirt was open, the bronze of his chest darkened, his trousers nothing more than long swimming trunks, his feet bare, his hair feathered by the breeze. She felt desire shimmer in her. More than desire. Finally, more than desire.

There was nothing more she could do. She had fought, and run, and resisted.

But it had still come to this. She walked towards him and he looked down at her, took her hand, and led her in.

It was, in the end, all she could do.

Yield to him.

Why had she given in to him? Gone to his bed? Let him do to her what she had fought so hard against? She knew the truth of it—because she had not had the strength to go on resisting him. That was all.

He had sensed his victory from the moment she had walked up to him, and from that moment on she'd been lost. It had been as if all the fight had gone out of her—and he had known it. He'd said nothing of that, however, simply greeting her as if it had all been prearranged by both of them.

Maybe it had been the remote beauty of the island, their iso-
lation, with no one else there once the helicopter that had
brought her from the mainland had whirred off into the sky,
letting the peace crowd back again into the silence.

'Come down to the beach,' Theo had said, taking her small
suitcase and carrying it into the single bedroom. A simple
room—whitewashed walls, stone floor, an old-fashioned bed,
wooden furniture and slatted blinds.

Not a room for Theo Theakis—head of a mighty corpora-
tion, corporate captain *par excellence* and one of Greece's
richest men.

And yet, as Vicky watched him curiously, he seemed at
home here.

As did she. That was the strangest thing of all—the way she
simply accepted what had happened, abandoned her fight. Let
herself be taken over by him at last, to spend a lazy, easy day
together on the beach, in the water, in the sun and the shade,
letting the island work its strange, alluring magic on her, and
then, as night fell, eating simple food, cooked by themselves in
the low-tech kitchen, sitting at a rustic wooden table set out
under the olive trees, drinking wine while the stars burned
golden holes in the patches of the sky between the silvered
olive leaves.

What they talked of she did not know, for another conversation was taking place, running silently between them,
weaving their eyes together, until at last Theo rose to his feet,
took her hand, and took her to his bed.

In the early morning, as he lay asleep beside her, she got up
and dressed, and phoned from her mobile for the helicopter.

And fled.

CHAPTER EIGHT

MEMORY twisted inside her like a garrotte around her throat. She gazed now, down the length of the table, at the man who was going to wreak his revenge on her for what she had allegedly done to him.

Gone from his bed into another man's arms.

She'd had no idea—none—that she had been photographed with Jem at the airport where she'd met him, or that she had been trailed leaving with him as she fled. No idea at all until, three days later, knowing she could put it off no longer, she had returned to the Theakis mansion.

To be eviscerated by Theo's savage fury and thrown from her marriage in bloodied rags.

Never to be spoken to again, never to have her existence acknowledged—until now. When he had decided it was time for a little exercise in revenge…

Her eyes darkened. Revenge for her having committed the greatest crime of all, in his eyes—preferring another man to him.

That was all it was…

All it could possibly be. Their marriage had not been real, had been a sham, simply for show, so how could there even be a question of adultery?

No one even saw those photos! Only him!

So how could he have grounds for anger? Her mouth twisted. Was it just about the money it had cost him to buy them from the photographer who had, so Theo had hurled at her in that nightmare exchange, thought he could make more money by selling them to him rather than the newspapers? Well, so what? Theo Theakis had more money than he knew what to do with, and she wasn't responsible for the ludicrous interest the press took in him and his affairs!

He shouldn't have so damn many himself if he doesn't want the press all over him!

Well, she thought balefully, no one was going to find out about the 'affair' he was having right now, that was for certain.

With his own ex-wife.

She gazed down the table again, reaching automatically for her glass of wine. She wished she could pass out cold. Wished she could simply shut her mind, completely and totally, to what was going to happen. But she couldn't. She felt her stomach tighten. She had to do his. For Theo, it might be about revenge for his injured conceit about himself, but for her, oh, for her it was for a quite different reason.

Her eyes rested on him with tight deliberation, and she set down the glass again. She felt the wine wind into her bloodstream like a slow coil of satin, gliding over her nerve-ends subtly, so subtly, easing into the cells of her body. With the fringes of her mind she knew it was taking effect.

She looked about her, eyes drifting around the dining room. It was opulent, like the rest of the house, decorated in that same rich, uniform style—a setting, nothing more, for the true purpose of the house: to provide a discreet, luxurious place where sexual congress could take place with absolute privacy.

It was a house that had seen a great deal of such activity...

A pinched look haunted her eyes for a moment. Then she dispelled it. Her gaze went on drifting around, looking anywhere, everywhere, but at the man sitting at the head of the table.

Yet she could sense his presence as if it were solid. It was impossible not to. She was quiveringly, pulsingly aware of him with every beat of her blood. Finally, she lifted her eyes to do what she had refused to do all through the endless meal. Look down the long table to the man who wanted to take his revenge on her. A vengeance she had no choice but to let him take. No choice at all.

Starting right now.

In slow motion her gaze slid through the space between them and locked to his.

It was instant. Tangible. Physical. His eyes held hers as surely as if his hands had caught her. It was like being speared, caught and held, like a fish on a line. For a fraction of a second she wanted to pull away, but he would not relinquish her, and even as she tensed she felt the dissolution in her veins as she gave herself up to the leash on which she was being held. He had felt her moment of yielding. She could see it in the minutest relaxation of his face. He knew that she would not break the gaze between them, knew that he could go on holding her eyes with his, making her the recipient of the slow, probing exploration of his look. She saw the lines around his mouth begin to deepen into a smile—a smile of satisfaction.

Anticipation.

She got to her feet. Still without unlocking her gaze, she picked up her wineglass and took one last mouthful. Slowly she lowered the glass, but kept it between her fingers. Then, with the same slow movement, she turned away and walked towards the door.

Her hips were swaying, she could feel it through the line of her legs, her feet in their high heels. She could feel the fall of her hair rustle over her bare shoulder.

Feel his eyes follow her every step.

At the door she did not pause or turn. One of the staff was there before her, opening the door for her, but she did not acknowledge it. This was not the moment for other people. This was the moment only for her—and the man who would any moment now push back his chair and follow her.

She crossed the hall, her footsteps loud on the marble, and began to ascend the stairs. The wineglass was still in her hand and she paused halfway. She didn't need this now. She could feel its power already creaming in her veins like a silken veil.

As she moved she felt the sleek material of her dress move against her body, like a whispered caress over her skin. She could feel her body, feel its contours, feel the heat flushing slowly through her flesh as she made her swaying ascent. She paused at the landing, and then made her languorous way to the bedroom. The master bedroom.

The mistress bedroom.

Well, that was, after all, exactly what she was about to become. One of Theo Theakis's mistresses. One of so many. Enjoying with him an affair that was sensual, sophisticated and entirely pleasurable.

Just right for a mistress.

And therefore, with immaculate logic, entirely appropriate for her now...

So, now that she was to become Theo Theakis's mistress, she must do only what a mistress would do in these circumstances. Be only what a mistress would be.

Feel only what a mistress would feel.

Pleasure. Nothing but pleasure. Sensual and sophisticated and above all untainted by emotion. Quite, quite untainted by anything so completely unnecessary...

As she walked in, still with the same slow, undulating walk, she left the bedroom door open behind her. Moving towards the vast bed, she drew back the pristine counterpane and pressed the light switch to illuminate the room with a soft, flattering light. Then she slipped off her sandals and lowered herself down on to the bed. She posed herself carefully, languidly, one arm stretched out over her head, which lifted her breasts, the other hand splayed on her thigh, her legs slightly crooked. She could feel the hem of her dress, taut and high across her upper legs, feel the mounds of her breasts strain against the silky material covering them so skimpily.

She felt ripe and wanton.

And quite, quite alien.

But that was good. It was fine.

More than fine.

Necessary.

I can do this—I must...

The last echo of her mantra sounded in her head, then faded away, quite away.

She did not need the mantra any more. The ripe, wine-laden wantonness of her body was all she needed.

Right now, at this moment, as she lay arranged in her deliberate, knowing pose, her breasts full, her skin warmed and lustrous, deep within the slow heat building, it was all she wanted...

There was a shadow by the door—a dark presence electrifying her senses.

He was there. Coming towards her. His gait steady, purposeful. His features taut. His eyes—

Dark, so dark. Intense.

Intent, so very, very clear, on one purpose only...

She felt her breath catch, felt the shiver of what she knew—welcomed and rejoiced—was raw sexual excitement. The wine that filled her veins was had been replaced by this new feeling, and she could feel it absorbing into her consciousness. Nothing mattered except this moment, this sensuous, voluptuous *now*. The *now* that filled her, possessed her—changed her.

He came up to her. He was still formally dressed, and the sight of him in his business suit, with his broad shoulders moulded by the superb tailoring, the glimpse of the grey silk lining of his jacket, the pristine whiteness of his shirt stretched across his chest, slashed by the expensive discreet silk of his tie, made her feel, with a shiver of that same raw, sexual excitement, the full frisson of his power.

For a long moment he looked down on her, and she was what he saw—a woman displayed for him—beautiful, willing, and waiting for him. A mistress…

Some last, frail shadow of herself haunted the recesses of her mind, but it died away. She simply lay there, her sensuous pose displaying her, as his eyes worked leisurely along the languorous length of her supine body.

He sat down beside her, and she felt the mattress dip beneath his weight. He contemplated her one moment longer, without touching her. He said nothing, and nor did she. There were no words to say. This was not about words. This was about the fire in her blood, making her someone quite, quite different.

A mistress. The woman he wanted her to be.

The woman she now was for him.

And she would be that woman, willingly, wantonly, letting him, as he did now, reach a hand towards her face, letting his thumb graze sensuously along the lushness of her lip. His touch dissolved into her, and with a movement she could not stop she bit slowly, softly, into the hard pad of his grazing thumb, letting her tongue ease along it.

She saw the deep flare in his eyes, fathomless eyes, framed with long, impenetrable lashes. She bit softly again.

His thumb left her mouth, travelled slowly down the curve of her jaw, the line of her throat, pausing in the hollow at its base to feel the pulse with its slow, insistent beat. His hand moved on, palming over her bare flesh, fingers dipping into her cleavage, and then, with a considered, leisurely movement, he drew down the bodice of her dress to display her breasts to him.

Heat pooled between her legs. Her breath caught in her throat. She lay, breasts bared, while he drifted the tips of his fingers across them. He did not look at her, only at her breasts, and she felt them engorge and fill, their peaks flowering like exquisitely sensitive buds. The touch of his nails on them, so light, so devastating, dissolved her spine.

For a little while he continued to caress her breasts, almost in an exploratory way, seeing what his touch would do to them. She felt her fingers clench as sensation after sensation shot through her.

She could not think; she could only feel. She was only this— an exquisite net of sensation, playing through her body. Tiny shoots of fire laced from her nipples through the taut swell of her breasts, racing down, down the length of her abdomen, to feed the heat pooling between the vee of her legs.

Her lips parted and she gave a low, soft moan.

As if it were a signal, he moved with sudden swiftness, sliding one hand beneath her shoulder and turning her over with effortless strength, before she even realised what he was doing. The room swirled and settled, and then, with another, deeper shiver of excitement, she felt his hands smooth along the silk of her short skirt, riding up over her thighs. He smoothed the material upwards, ruching it towards the small of her back.

Exposing the bare mounds of her bottom.

She wore no panties. What would have been the point? They would only have had to be removed.

She felt him still. He had not expected that, for her to be so naked. She knew it deep inside her, where the heat was pooling, and the knowledge made her feel even more wanton. Her cheek was pressed against a pillow, her hands reaching up above her, fingers pressing into the edge, while the taut silk of her dress cut across the bared flesh of her bottom, displayed for his view.

Sensation surged through her. She felt arousal—full-on, incredibly erotic—flood her. Instinctively she stretched her spine, indenting her body into the mattress, her thighs falling very slightly apart.

'Don't move.'

The instruction was a low rasp, and she felt the mattress tilt again as he stood up. He was stripping his clothes off, she could tell, hearing the sound of rapidly discarded garments. Then there was the sound of a drawer in the bedside unit being pulled roughly open. There was a pause. She did not look. She knew what he was doing.

What he was preparing for.

She felt her heart rate increase, flushing through her veins, heating her yet more. Then, abruptly, the bed dipped again, but now the balance was different. Now she felt strong, muscled thighs either side of hers.

He was caging her, kneeling over her legs as she lay, displayed and semi-naked for him. She pressed her groin into the bedding again, feeling that incredible surge of erotic sensation, knowing what he was seeing. Her hands kneaded at the pillow.

Hunger filled her. Hunger and need. Displaying herself was not enough. She wanted more...much, much more. She stretched her spine again, minutely lifting her half-bared bottom to him. Inviting him.

He took the invitation. Hands curved hard over her, and pleasure flooded her. The tips of his fingers were beneath the silk hem of her dress, and his thumbs—his thumbs were dipping into the cleavage between the mounds of her bottom. Dipping and dragging, down, down, into the hidden valley between her thighs.

It was unbearable, incredible, so fantastically arousing that she lifted her head and shoulders, straining the curve of her spine.

A moan broke from her, and from him a soft, satisfied laugh.

For countless blissful moments he toyed with her, and then, in another sudden movement, his hands were at the zip of her dress. He unzipped it, hoisted her off the bed with a single sweep of one strong forearm around her waist, and peeled the dress off her completely, shucking it away down her legs and discarding it on the floor.

She was completely naked.

He flipped her over.

Her eyes went to his instantly, her hair tumbled around her face, lips parted. Her nipples were swollen aching peaks, her hands helpless and limp beside her head.

He caged his body over hers, his fingers sliding between hers, holding her, holding her exactly where he wanted her to be. Which, right now, was the only place in the entire universe where she wanted to be.

For a moment, a brief, slicing moment, disbelief consumed her. Then it was gone, gone completely, like a drop of cool water on a sizzling hotplate. Heat flared in her, excitement and arousal. There was only this—now, here. Lying aroused and pleasured, caged and waiting—waiting for what she wanted now, right now, right now...

Her eyes locked to his, challenging him, inviting him.

His body was so powerful, the bare muscled chest honed and sleek, every plane and muscle taut—and she wanted it. She wanted to feel its hard weight pressing her down, feel its strength, its rampant, urgent desire for hers. Wanted to feel that long, strong shaft fill her, thrust up into her, again and again and again, and she didn't want to wait—she didn't want to wait one moment more.

Her spine arched, and she strained her hands against his grip.

His thighs were pressing against hers, and she strained against them, lifting her hips to him.

'What are you waiting for, Theo?' she said, and her voice was a challenge, a husk, her eyes twining with his, writhing like twisting ropes. 'This is what you want, isn't it? It's what I'm here for, isn't it? To finish what you started—'

She lifted her hips again, her breasts rising, thrusting forward as she moved. Raw, urgent excitement, erotic and sensual, overrode everything, blotting out everything else.

It was just her body and his. And she wanted only one thing. She wanted it so, so badly...

He gave it to her.

With slow, taunting control he lowered himself down, sliding into her in one single, fluid movement.

She gasped, and threw her head back, sensation exploding in her. Oh, God, it was good! It was so, so good! She lifted to meet him, lifted against his thrust, wanting him to thrust again, right up to the very neck of her womb, as her muscles tightened around him. She was on fire, urgent, hungry, as hungry as a vampire scenting blood.

He thrust again, hard and hot, and she cried out, a sharp, high sound. Her fingers wound in his, every muscle clenched tightly in her body as she arched up to meet his scything downstrokes. Her spine sweated, her body was jerking, as the hard, relentless thrusts came again and again. Her body was melting, melting all around him, as if it was turning into something else, something that was hot, liquid metal, searing with heat, glistening with absolute, total arousal.

She could see his face and it was taut, intense. He was caught up in his own consuming pleasure as he scythed into her, hard, insistent, over and over again. And with every thrust the hot, metallic liquid that was her body came closer and closer and closer still to the moment she was gasping for with every urgent rasp in her straining throat. The moment that was almost, *almost* there, with every hard stroke against the inflamed, distended flesh inside her, that incredible spot she had heard about but never, never...

Sensation sheeted through her, a pleasure so powerful she could not believe it, crying out with a high, unearthly sound as every cell in her body fused into molten silver. And as they fused she seemed to feel his arms tighten convulsively around her, holding her so close against him that she could feel the hectic beating of his heart against hers. Something seemed to take her over, flooding through her, something that was nothing to do with the intensity of physical pleasure consuming her. Something that seemed to take her out of her own pulsing body, soaring upwards, higher and higher. An emotion so powerful that she could feel her arms wrap around the body in her arms as if it were the most precious thing in the universe...

No! The cry was silent, anguished. Theo wasn't precious to her—he was just a highly skilled sexual partner exerting his formidable expertise to ensure she got the maximum pleasure from his body.

That was all he was.

All this was.

Desperately her body arched and bucked, and she jerked her hips upwards, again and again, to keep that incredible pleasure going. Because she never, never wanted to lose it. She wanted to keep it, ride it, hot and greedy, wanting more and more and more of it. Because it was essential—essential she did not lose it, that she clung to it, fused with it, became one with it. Because if it started to fade, if it started to ebb, it would be, it would be...

It was fading. Ebbing.

Panic took her. She thrust up her hips, again and again, but there was nothing there, nothing to thrust herself against, no hardness, no fullness. And as the dawning recognition of that, and the reason for it, came to her, so, welling up in her like cold, icy water, came something else—something she could not, must not, *must* not, let into her mind.

But it came all the same. Seeped in on the cold, icy water that was filling her veins now, replacing the hot, greedy pleasure she had sated herself on, which had faded now, ebbed away. Leaving her on the bleak, bare shore, bereft of all sensation.

Bereft of everything.

Except one thing.

The knowledge of what she had just done.

She shut her eyes. It was instinctive, imperative. As if by refusing to see there would be nothing to see. Nothing to know. Nothing to feel.

But feel she must. She could not escape.

Her body ached. Ached from being distended, strained. Ached from the overloading of her sensory capacity.

He drew out of her. She could feel it—feel him unclasping her hands, which went on lying there limply, her whole body flaccid, collapsed. She kept her eyes tight, tight shut. They burned beneath the lids.

Her body felt cold, so cold.

What have I done?

The question coiled in her brain.

What have I done?

But she knew. She knew the answer. She had done what she knew she would have to do. Unfinished business, Theo had called it. He was right.

'Open your eyes.'

His words cut through her coldness.

She forced her eyes open. He was looking down at her, and his eyes were colder than she had ever seen them before in her life.

'Don't play your tricks with me again—not if you want your money. Understand?'

Then he was gone, walking into the en suite bathroom, shutting the door. She heard the shower start to run. Slowly, very slowly, she pulled the bedclothes over her.

A stone, hard and painful, blocked her lungs.

Theo's hands curved tightly around the steering wheel of his car, and he pressed his foot down on the accelerator. The low, lean vehicle sprang forward with a throaty roar. Gravel crunched under its tyres as he headed down the drive, opening the gates with a flick of an electronic switch and turning out on to the road beyond, dimly lit by a tired, waning moon.

He drove fast. But not fast enough to outrun his memory. Hot, pulsing memories of the sex he had just had.

Black emotion filled him. A dish eaten cold? No, it had been scalding, molten hot! His mouth thinned. She'd tried to turn the tables on him, manipulate him. Call the shots.

He'd let her do it—this time.

This time—deliberately, knowingly—he'd gone along with her. Let her play the vamp, lure him upstairs, set the pace. He'd chosen to let her do so, wanting to see just what she would do.

And now he knew. *Theos*, now he knew!

It had taken all his strength—all of it—to get out of there the way he had.

Leave her the way he had.

When every burning instinct had wanted to keep him there...

Cold snaked down his back. What had happened in his moment of white-out had been nothing, *nothing* of what he'd intended.

It was just a reflex—nothing more. Nothing more than that.

Or an illusion. He hadn't really felt her heart beat against his. Her arms tighten around him like that.

Deliberately he forced a hard, contemptuous smile to his lips. It had been just another trick of hers, that was all. One of the repertoire of tricks she'd tried out on him all evening, showing him her true colours, as he had known them to be since the moment he had seen those damning, condemning photos and discovered the truth about her

His hands clenched on the driving wheel as he pressed down yet harder on the accelerator, cutting through the night, back towards Athens.

He knew what she was. He didn't need to know anything else about her.

And what he knew about her damned her. Damned her completely.

The way she'd been tonight only confirmed it—as if he'd needed any such confirmation about just what kind of woman he'd married. Victoria Fournatos was as shameless as she was adulterous, and she deserved no quarter. None.

And that was exactly what she'd get from him.

It was all she deserved.

He drove on, into the blackness of the night.

But he would be back. Oh, he would be back, all right. He hadn't finished with her yet.

Not by a long way.

And next time he would stay absolutely, totally in control

It was essential he do so. Quite, quite essential.

He came again to her the following night. She was wearing a different dress this time. Red, with a halter neck and a short, swirling skirt. This time he did not dine with her. He'd eaten at a business dinner in Athens. She was sitting in the lounge, with the air-con on too high, watching an English language news channel.

As he walked in her eyes veiled immediately. She stood up.

Tonight she was different. She stood passive, not displaying her body, just standing there, not meeting his eyes, not posing as she had been last night.

Her passivity lasted the entire encounter. He took her

upstairs, turning her around in the bedroom to unzip and remove her dress. She was wearing panties this time, little wispy things that made him instantly hard. He stripped off his own clothes rapidly, and took her over to the bed.

She lay quite still while he reacquainted himself with her breasts. Only their physical response to his caresses told him that she was becoming aroused. That and the parted lips through which her breath was coming in soft, quick breaths, and the blind, glazed look in her eyes.

His hands made a leisurely progress, stroking and teasing until her nipples were hard and coral-red, his eyes always watching her body's reaction to him. Then, when he judged her sufficiently aroused, he let his hands slide downwards.

She was wet already, the delicate tissues plumped and swollen. He let his fingers glide in their satin folds, watched her bite her lip, the blind, glazed look becoming more unseeing. Her fingers, lying inert on either side of her, bit into the softness of the bed. A low, helpless moan escaped her constricted throat.

He moved over her.

This time he controlled the pace. Controlled it absolutely. He parted her thighs and paused at the entrance to her body. Then he began to inch himself into her, his control total. He saw her eyes flare, and when he had filled her completely knew that her pupils were at maximum dilation.

Then he began to move in her, slowly, skilfully, building a rhythm, his body under his complete control. Her body, too.

With the same absolute control he gave her her first orgasm, and then, as it subsided, he gave her a second. Each time he watched her skin flush, her breath freeze, felt her heart rate burst, felt her internal muscles flux wildly, drawing him in yet more deeply. Each time he let her subside, let the sweat dew on her body, the pulse at her throat slow down again.

Only then, finally, did he take her one last time, with himself, to that same point of sensation.

Only then, in his own pleasure, did he stop watching her.

When he had climaxed he left her immediately.

He could not bear to be in the same house as her.

Let alone the same bed...

Vicky lay, staring upwards. The ceiling seemed to be revolving. It was an illusion, she knew, caused by the fire in her bloodstream.

She lay unseeing as the room moved around her. She was still in the same position he had left her in. She had not moved a muscle. He had gone some time ago, walking out of the room fully dressed, not looking at her. She had been spared that, at least.

But nothing else.

Nothing else at all.

Revenge—that was what he wanted, and that was what he was taking. But for her it was something different.

It was exactly what he had planned for her.

Humiliation.

Cold ran through her, and a despair so deep within that she did not know where it came from.

It wasn't supposed to be like this!

How—how had it gone so wrong? She had been so sure that she could do it—could be exactly what she had to be in order to take from this what she needed to take.

I was going to turn the tables on him—not let him do what he wanted to me—humiliate me and take his revenge on me. I was going to be exactly the kind of woman he likes—sexually sophisticated, dedicated to sensual pleasure, wanting nothing more from him than physical sensation. I was going to stay in control and call every shot.

Instead he had turned the tables back on her. Seen through her pathetic attempt to resist him. To retaliate against him.

And now resistance and retaliation were impossible.

Now... Her eyes bleached with despair. Now there was only survival.

Getting through to the end.

Fear bit into her, like a stab in the belly. When would the end come? She had never bothered to ask just how long Theo intended her to stay here, because what would have been the point? He might not have told her, and it would simply have shown him how much she longed for the ordeal to be over. And that in itself would have given him a satisfaction she would never, ever willingly grant him.

But how long would he keep her here? How many nights had she still to endure?

Her fingers clutched into the sheets. There was nothing, nothing she could do. She would endure as long as she had to endure. Until Theo had finally finished with her.

Because only then would she, too, be finally finished with him...

Whatever the price she had to pay to do so.

Night after night he came to her. In the daytime, when the bright sun beat down, she was like an automaton. She got up, ate breakfast on the veranda, sat and read, swam in the sea from the shingle beach, up and down, back and forth, over and over and over again. She ate lunch and read. Drank coffee. Watched the sea, its tireless constancy marking the sameness of her days.

Then, by night, she went upstairs to her bedroom and adorned herself for Theo Theakis.

Every night he came and took her to his bed, gave to her body a physical pleasure that she could not bear to remember, either in the light or the dark, and then, when it was over, he left.

Leaving her slowly bleeding from wounds she could not stanch.

On the seventh night he emerged from the bathroom, fully clad in his business suit once more, and placed a piece of paper on the bedside unit.

'Your money,' he said. Then he walked out.

CHAPTER NINE

VICKY sat in the bed, looking at the piece of paper in her hand. The money she needed. The money she had come to Greece to get.

Well, she had it now

She went on staring at the piece of paper, with the curtly written signature on it, the zeroes of the figure in the box.

She could hear the sound of him walking down the stairs, out of the door, his monstrous car revving loudly, then swirling away down the drive—away, away, away.

When she could hear him no more she slowly placed the cheque back on the side table, then lay down, drawing the bed-clothes over her. She should sleep, she knew. Tomorrow she would be taken back to the airport, put on a plane, despatched to London. To get on with her life. And she could, now. She had her money, after all.

Think of the future. Think of when you start helping Jem restore Pycott. Think of the work ahead and the things to achieve. Think of the first schoolchildren arriving, the new hope they will have. Think of that. Think only of that.

Don't think about anything else.

You've got the money—be glad of that at least.

Closure.

That was the word, the word psychologists used to describe how essential it was for people not to have things hanging over their head emotionally. Closure to seal one part of life from another. The past from the present. The present from the future that was yet to come.

She had come for closure, but for her there could be no closure—not yet.

What Theo had done to her in his bed ensured that.

Instead of closure, something else was swelling inside her— something powerful, unstoppable. Something that was seeping through her, blotting through all her body.

And she knew exactly what it was.

And exactly what she was going to do about it.

She was packed and ready to go by eight in the morning. She had slept eventually, a heavy, dreamless sleep, and now she was calm, very calm, and that was good. As she painted on her face her hand did not tremble. When she was done she eyed herself objectively. Her full face of make-up did not go with the casual clothes she was wearing, but that didn't matter. She wouldn't be wearing them for long. They would not be suitable for her purpose.

Before she set off downstairs she checked her wallet one last time. Yes, the cheque was still there. She gazed at the dark, incisive handwriting, the strong scrawl of his signature. For just a moment she felt the emotion that had started to build up in her last night lash out, but she leashed it back in.

Not yet.

Soon.

She stood up, lifted her backpack, and headed out of the room. Along the corridor the shut door of the master bedroom looked back at her blankly. As blank as her own expression. Downstairs she took her leave of the staff, not looking any of them in the eye. She didn't like to behave like that, but for her own sanity she knew she had to. Then she walked out to the waiting car. The warmth after the perpetual air-conditioned cool of the interior made her shiver—or something else did. She looked back at the house.

A love-nest. That was the coy expression that used to be in vogue. Well, nothing to do with love had happened in there this week.

She shivered again, and got into the car. But as it started to move off she leant forward.

'I'm going into Athens,' she said to the driver.

He nodded, incurious, and she leant back.

It was strange, very strange, to see Athens again, to sit in one endless traffic jam after another and catch glimpses of the familiar outline of the Acropolis crowned by the Parthenon. Even though she did not want to, she felt herself react. Felt emotion start to run in her veins. She stopped it because she could not allow herself to do otherwise.

And because it was the wrong emotion.

There was only one emotion she was allowing herself now. Only one that was right and proper for the occasion.

Her first port of call was the bank. She'd opened her own account before they'd married, arranging to have funds placed there from her own British bank account in London. It was irrelevant that her uncle would happily have bankrolled her, and that as Mrs Theakis Theo had opened a separate account for her at his bank. She trusted only her own bank, her own name.

It did not take long to pay in the cheque Theo had left for her. But paying it in did not achieve the closure she needed. She had known it would not. Not now. Something much more was needed.

For that, she would need an outfit. One that suited the face she wore and the sleek styling of her hair. She ordered the driver to deposit her at the premises of one of the designers she had most favoured when she was Mrs Theo Theakis. The vendeuse was new, and she was grateful, but she kept her dark glasses on all the same. Nor did she linger over her decision, emerging less than fifteen minutes later wearing a classic shift dress in mint-green, with an off-white handbag and sandals to match. As she left the shop she took one last glance at herself in a full-length mirror.

She gave a small, tight smile to her reflection. Oh, yes, Mrs Theo Theakis was back in town all right!

And she wanted more than the money she was owed. Much more.

Now it was her turn for vengeance. And she would make sure it really, really hit Theo where it hurt. In his giant-sized masculine sexual ego.

Back in the car, she phoned his office. The voice that answered was familiar—it was Theo's aide, Demetrious. Vicky spoke crisply in English.

'This is Mrs Theakis here. Put Theo on the line, please.'

There was an imperceptible pause. Then, 'One moment, please, Mrs Theakis.' The aide's voice was as neutrally incurious as it had been on the flight over. He came back on the line a moment later.

'Mrs Theakis, I'm so sorry. Mr Theakis is in conference.'

The voice was smooth—apologetic, even—but Vicky knew that it was pointless to repeat her request. This time around was not going to be an action replay of her vigil in Theo's London offices. This time *she* was calling the shots. Starting right now.

'Oh, dear,' she answered. 'That's a pity. Would you let him know I'm going to be lunching at Santiano's, if he'd like to join me there? Thank you so much. I'm in the car at the moment, so he can reach me on that number.'

She hung up and sat back as the car continued to wind its way round Athens' infamously traffic-laden streets. Santiano's was the biggest hotbed of gossip in Athens. Everyone who wanted to be seen went there, and it was a favourite haunt both of gossip columnists and the paparazzi, waiting to see who was lunching with whom. And, of course, a lot more than lunching…

If the former Mrs Theakis was seen there, back in Athens, tongues would start to wag straight away. Even without the slightest shred of evidence the columnists would be speculating on whether she was going to be getting back with Theo Theakis again. A momentary pang went through her—if Theo called her bluff, then it was inevitable that Aristides would find out that she was back in Athens. She didn't want him hurt— not any more than he had been already.

But that was thanks to Theo anyway, she reminded herself mercilessly. There had been no need for Theo to tell Aristides why he was going for a divorce. No need to upset him the way he had, by telling him about those incriminating photos! He could just as easily have trotted out the story they had agreed they would tell her uncle all along—that the marriage had simply not worked out, and they were parting amicably.

Amicably…

Vicky felt her stomach hollow.

No, amicable their parting had *not* been.

Fierceness filled her again.

It's Theo's fault—it's all Theo's fault! I never asked for any of this—none of it! And I didn't deserve it! I absolutely did not deserve it. Even if I had—

The phone in the car went.

For a moment she let it ring, feeling her stomach hollow out. Then she picked it up.

'Hello?'

It was Demetrious again.

'Mrs Theakis? Mr Theakis has suggested you lunch with him in his apartment here. Would that be convenient for you?'

Mentally, Vicky punched the air.

'What a lovely idea,' she trilled. 'I'll be there as soon as I can. We're at—'

She cast her eyes around and told Demetrious what street they were on.

It took a little while still to reach the headquarters of Theakis Corp. As the car drew up, Vicky felt the lick of memory. She hadn't been here very often during her marriage, and she only recalled being in Theo's private apartment at the top of the building a couple of times. But it was still strange—unnerving, even—to walk into the building.

Just being in Athens again was strange. Unnerving.

She pressed her lips together. Their marriage of convenience had been working out fine—why, *why* had Theo had to go and ruin everything? Why?

His ego. That was all. His overweening sexual ego that had decided that he might as well have her panting for him, as well...

Memory drenched through her. Not of the time of her brief, wretched marriage, but of last night. And the night before, and the night before that.

She could feel her body react in hot, humid recollection of what it had done a few hours ago, in the darkened tumult of her inflamed desire...

Her nipples were hardening, the pulse at the vee of her legs quickening.

No! God, no! Stop it—just stop it!

With monumental effort she slammed down on her reaction. That wasn't what she must feel! That was fatal—fatal. Even with her cold, light-of-day reasoning about exactly why she had gone along with Theo's outrageous demand that she come to his bed, it was fatal to let her mind go back to what she had done.

Never again. That was what she had to remember. Never again would Theo touch her. Never again would his body move over hers. Never again.

I'm safe now—safe from him. That's all I have to remember. There is nothing more he can do to me. Because I have every-thing I want from him. Everything.

Except one thing.

She took a breath—a deep one,

What she wanted now from Theo was not something she had to fear. Only be grimly, blackly satisfied by.

I want my own back. I want my own back for what he did to me. And I know exactly how I'm going to get that.

She lifted her chin, picked up her new handbag, and got out of the car.

If it was disturbing to be back in Athens again it was even more disturbing walking into Theo's HQ. This time around, unlike in London, she was shown up to his office straight away, and as she entered Theo's executive suite Demetrious came forward to greet her. If he wondered what she was doing there, why she was suddenly dressed not in chainstore clothes but indeed as 'the former Mrs Theo Theakis', nothing showed in his professionally blank face as he ushered her into Theo's inner sanctum.

Only then, just as she walked in and heard the double doors click shut behind her, did a sense of *déjà-vu* suddenly hit her. This was exactly what she'd done the day that her uncle had announced his bolt-from-the-blue idea—that a man she scarcely knew, but who'd had such a disturbing effect on her right from the very first time she'd laid eyes on him, had asked for her hand in marriage.

She had marched in here, demanding an explanation for so ludicrous a proposition.

Her eyes went to the man now unfolding his tall, lean frame, the same way he had that fatal day.

How on earth had he persuaded her to marry him?

Why the hell did I agree? There must have been another way for Aristides to accept Theo's investment! It was just ludi-crous—ludicrous to go along with what I did!

But she had, and that was all there was to it.

You made your bed...

The echo of the familiar proverb stung in her head, and with an awful hollowing of her stomach she heard not the metaphorical meaning but the literal one.

Bed. Sex. Theo.

That had been what had gone so hideously wrong in their brief, disastrous marriage. And it had been entirely and totally Theo's fault.

If he'd just bloody left me alone...

But he hadn't. And so, without the shadow of doubt, without the slightest sliver of any other possibility, this whole ugly, vile business was *his* fault.

The emotion she had felt building up in her since he had dropped the cheque for *her* money beside her naked body slashed through her again. Powerful, unstoppable—and now roiling in her like a black tide.

Her chin went up. Theo was on his feet.

His face was tight and taut. His eyes dark with cold, icy anger.

'What the hell do you think you're playing at?'

His voice cut at her like a knife.

For a moment, just a moment, Vicky felt a new emotion go through her. She buckled under it, reeling from the vicious hostility in his voice. Memory came at her again, with sickening vividness. This was how Theo had spoken to her on that hideous, hideous day when she had arrived back at his mansion from Jem's and he'd tossed the paparazzo's revealing, condemning photos of her and Jem down on the table in front of her shocked, appalled face.

She felt her throat spasm. *Why does he have to be so angry with me? Why?*

Her throat tightened. There was almost pain in it.

But what was the point of pain? Pain just made her weak, defenceless. She had stood there while Theo carved her into shreds that awful day. Her stammering attempts to justify her actions had been scathingly demolished even before she could get them out. Theo had not listened—had only attacked. Savagely, ruthlessly, totally.

Then thrown her out.

Thrown her out and taken his petty revenge by refusing to hand her over the money she had been promised.

And then—her stomach hollowed—then he had taken a revenge that had not been petty at all...

She felt her spine stiffen. When Theo had thrown his outrageous demand at her in London, her only thought had been how she could protect herself from his vengeance.

But he had not let her do so. He had imposed on her exactly what he had planned all along—her humiliation, at his skilled and expert hands. Allowing her no quarter—no hiding place.

Her eyes hardened.

Well, now it's my turn. My turn for a little revenge. And I will really, really enjoy sticking the knife in you this time around...to give you back what you paid out to me, night after night...

This is just a fraction of what you did to me!

She walked forward. Strolled forward. Her high-heeled sandals moved her hips, the fine material of her dress eased over her body. Her freshly washed and styled hair lifted from her shoulders. Her outfit might have taken an uncomfortably large bite out of her credit card, but she didn't care right now, she just didn't care—she felt and looked exactly the way she wanted.

Elegant. Classy.

A knock-out.

And as she saw the pinpricks of his pupils flare suddenly at her approach she felt confidence flood back into her.

Something else came with the confidence. But that wasn't important. Not now.

She raised an eyebrow quizzically.

'What am I playing at? Why, Theo, I'm here at your invitation. You've invited me for lunch, remember? Upstairs in your penthouse.'

His eyes were masked. Out of nowhere, all the emotion in his face vanished. It was like a smooth, unreadable surface. She knew that face, was very familiar with it. It was a face to be extremely wary of. Well, she was wary, all right. But that wasn't going to stop her. Wasn't going to intimidate her. Not this time. She was, after all, in possession of information that Theo would find it bitter to swallow. But he was going to swallow it all the same. And there was nothing he was going to be able to do about it.

So she just went on standing there, her expression as bland and as smooth as his.

He walked around the edge of his desk. Her eyes stayed fixed on him. For a tall man he was very graceful as he walked. The grace of a tiger approaching its prey.

Instinctively she tensed, then forced herself to let her muscles relax. She wasn't Theo's prey. Not any more.

Never, ever again.

She stood her ground. She would do this. She would do this and win. For once, in their final encounter, she would win.

'Well, in which case, let's head upstairs. I'm sure Demetrious has sorted out lunch for us. Shall we?'

He ushered her from the office, past his PA, and across the lobby to his private lift. As the doors sliced shut on them Vicky felt a burst of claustrophobia. She was not fearful of lifts—but the enclosed space made Theo seem closer to her than she ever wanted him to be again.

When the doors opened directly into his penthouse apartment she stepped out hurriedly. Too hurriedly? Was she betraying her reluctance at being so close to Theo? Well, tough—and too late. She walked forward with the same deliberate, confident air with which she had walked into his office one floor below, and made a beeline for the windows on the far side of the room. She could see the outline of the Parthenon on its rocky hill, the Acropolis, guardian of Athens for time immemorial. She ought to take another visit before she left for London. It was a good time of year to be in Athens—so much cooler than it had been that long, hot summer of her marriage. She could stay a few days in a hotel and see the sights again. No one would know who she was, and she would not come here again, she knew.

Sadness plucked at her. Then a harder emotion. That was yet another crime to be laid at Theo's door. Not just what he had done to her, and to her relationship with her last paternal blood relative, but the fact that he had parted her from her own Greek heritage.

She turned back, so that she could no longer see the outline of the city she loved.

'Would you like a drink?'

Theo was crossing to the drinks cabinet against the wall. Through the double doors that gave on to the dining room Vicky could see a team of staff, busily setting the table, despatched to do so from the executive kitchen on the floor below. It was not the first time she had lunched here. There had been several times when he had had business acquaintances for lunch who had brought their wives, necessitating her presence, as well, to make polite small talk while the men talked business.

Did he bring his women here? The thought stung in her mind before she could stop it. It would be convenient, after all, and the lift descended straight to the car park, so 'guests' could arrive and leave without having to go through the office levels.

Her eyes flickered around. The décor couldn't have been more different from that 'love-nest' on the coast! It was stark and masculine, functional and minimalist. Any women he brought here would have to accept that this was the space of someone who was not prepared to make concessions to their feminine sensibilities.

Well, right now, 'feminine sensibilities' were something she was going to be decidedly short on. This was hardball time. Plain and simple. She wanted to hit at Theo. Hit him in the only spot that was vulnerable.

His ego.

Not that he looked in the slightest bit vulnerable right now. As ever, that aura of power sat on him as seamlessly as his superb hand-tailored suit. As her eyes rested on him, a sense of protest stabbed at Vicky. It wasn't fair—it just wasn't fair! He looked *so* damn compelling that even now, steeled as she was, she could feel the familiar deadly weakness start up inside her just by looking at him.

Let alone remembering…

'Mineral water, thank you,' she said crisply, cutting like a necessary blade through her own treacherous thoughts.

'Still or sparkling?'

The smooth dark tones mocked her, she knew. But she would mirror his cool if it killed her.

'Still will be fine.'

Anything would be fine—anything without alcohol. She needed control—perfect control.

He poured out her drink, adding ice, and handed it to her without expression. Yet there was something moving behind his mask, she knew. Well, she didn't care. He could think what he liked. It was nothing to do with her—not any more.

She lifted her glass.

'*Yassoo*,' she intoned.

He did not respond, merely lifting his own highball to his mouth and taking a slow, considering sip. His eyes did not leave hers.

Something ran between them. Unspoken. Like a line of wildfire in tinder dry grass.

The world stopped around her. Just stopped.

She heard a silent cry in her head. Fear. Absolute fear.

More than fear…

Worse than fear…

'Lunch is served.' The sonorous tones from the doorway to the dining room made the world start again. As her fingers closed more tightly around the chilled column of her glass, she walked into the room beyond. Going through the required rituals of taking her place at the table gave her the chance to regain control of herself.

'I only ever have a light lunch,' Theo said, indicating the array of salads on the table. 'But of course if you would like something more substantial, you have only to say.'

She gave a curt nod of her head. One of the staff was setting out a coffee tray, with a jug of coffee keeping warm on a hotplate. A quick word in Greek to their employer, asking if anything else was required, a brief negative from Theo, and they took their leave. She was left alone with Theo.

She started to reach for the salad bowls, making a selection. She was not hungry. Her stomach was a tight knot. She watched covertly as Theo did likewise, his movements as smooth and economical as always. It came to her that this would be the last time she would set eyes on him…

The world seemed to still again, and then stop completely.

She forced it to keep going again.

Focus—that's all. Just focus.

Theo lifted his fork to his mouth. 'What's this farce all about, Vicky?' he asked.

His voice was off-hand, indifferent. She felt her back go up. Deliberately she delayed in answering him, making a play of taking a mouthful of salad and eating it.

'Well?' There was more curtness in his voice as he prompted her. He did not like to be kept waiting for answers when he wanted them.

Even more deliberately she took a drink from her water glass, forked up some more food.

'I wanted to thank you for the money, Theo,' she answered, her voice bland.

His eyes narrowed infinitesimally. Then, gliding in with a knife thrust she did not see coming, he said, 'It was my pleasure. My very considerable pleasure. Yours, too, of course.'

His eyes unveiled as he spoke, touching her like a caress. A slow, sensual caress. She felt colour flare in her cheeks.

Bastard! He was doing it deliberately. *Don't react—do not react to him!*

She blanked him. It was hard, excruciatingly hard, but she did it.

'I've paid the cheque into my bank already. I stopped off on the way here. I've kept my personal account going—the one I opened before we married—which of course makes it easier for paying in a euro cheque. I dare say I'll suffer from the exchange rate when it's transferred to my London bank, but, given the size of the sum, that won't be too much of a loss.'

She took some more food and continued, her voice with the same light, bland tone. 'Mind you, it will need to stretch quite a long way. The house that Jem's inherited needs a lot of work doing to it to make it habitable again. But it's a wonderful opportunity, of course, and we're both so very excited. A complete new start for us both! We'll be moving there in the summer, which will be lovely. Did I mention the house is in Devonshire? Very near the coast? It's an old house—Victorian, I believe. Rather appropriate, given my name, don't you think?'

She gave a little tinkle of laughter and drank some more water. Her throat was dry with tension. 'We're going to have to do huge amounts to the house, of course. Roof, new electrics—all that boring sort of stuff. That's before we get on to the fun bits like decorating. Still, it will keep us busy! And together, which is even nicer. I always miss Jem when he's not around—we go back *such* a long way, and we stick together through everything. Thick and thin.'

Her eyes were like diamonds. Sparkling and hard. But her gaze as she looked along the table at Theo was limpid, like clear, transparent water. She was hiding nothing from him— every word was the truth. Nothing but the truth.

Theo had stilled. Not a muscle moved in his body. His face was a mask. Then, lifting his highball to his mouth and lowering it again, the movement completely controlled, he spoke. His voice was casual, so very casual.

'You're a fortunate woman. Not every woman can boast a lover who's happy to whore her out for cash.'

His eyes were blank. Expressionless.

'Or aren't you going to tell him how you got the money— by having sex with me?'

She pushed back from the table. Her chair scraped on the tiled floor. As she stood up, she had to cling on to the table to keep upright.

'Will it just be our little secret? Is that it?' he continued, his eyes still with that same strange, expressionless look in them. 'So many secrets to keep, though. The way you like me to stroke your breasts, the way your body ripens for me, the way you give that cry in your throat when you orgasm, the way—'

'You *bastard*!'

Her voice was shrill, ripped from her lungs.

His eyes still looked at her, but now there was a dark, black glitter to them. 'The way you cry out my name as you climax. Will you tell him that, I wonder? Or will that just be another little secret from him?'

'*Shut up!* Shut *up*! You unspeakable *bastard*!

He didn't even register her outburst. His voice was as smooth, as unperturbed as ever.

'No? Not planning on going into that much detail? Not even planning on saying how you whored yourself to me for it?'

Her hand crashed down on to the surface of the table, shaking the crockery violently. Pain shot up her arm, but it was nothing, *nothing*, to the tempest inside her.

'It was *my* money! Mine! You had no right to keep it! No right to it! No right to make me do what you did! I don't have to feel bad about it! It's you, *you* who should feel guilty. You who—'

He was on his feet. His face was a snarl.

'You shameless little bitch! You committed adultery— without the slightest ounce of shame or remorse or guilt!'

She stepped back. Her heart was pounding, pounding with fury and outrage.

'Oh, that's rich—that's rich.' Her voice was hollow. She had started to tremble, the way she had when he had eviscerated her that first, hideous time. '*I* committed adultery? God Almighty, every damn day I was here I had women falling over themselves to tell me they'd had affairs with you—'

'Past tense! I never touched another woman while you were here!'

Her mouth opened, then closed. Then, simply staring at him, she spoke.

'Why the hell not?'

For a timeless moment there was silence. A silence you could cut with a knife. The snarl left his face.

'Why not?' he echoed. 'Because—' he bit out each word '—I was married.'

Her brows drew together. She stared at him uncomprehendingly.

'It wasn't a real marriage. It was fake from beginning to end. A total sham.' She took a deep, shuddering breath. 'Are you telling me you never…you never carried on with *any* of your women? But you *must* have! It's ludicrous to think otherwise!'

He was staring at her. 'You really thought that?'

'Of course I did! We weren't *really* married! It was for show, that was all! Of *course* someone like you would have gone on having sex!'

His mouth tightened. 'Unlike you, I am not in the market for adultery.' His voice was as cold as ice.

Something snapped inside her. 'It wasn't a question of adultery! Adultery doesn't come into it!'

'Spare me your moral take on things,' he shot back contemptuously. 'And don't think to worm your way out by using the basis of our marriage to exonerate your behaviour!' His voice chilled even more. 'Let alone by trying to make out you were no worse than me! You committed adultery. I did not.'

Shock was ricocheting round her. Theo had not continued with his affairs while they were married. It was impossible to believe, and yet—

No wonder he seduced me! He had no intention of remaining celibate…

He had used her. Deliberately and callously. Used her for sexual relief…

She felt an anger that surpassed anything that she had felt for him till now. Even when he had thrown at her what he had.

'You absolute bastard,' she said slowly.

Something flashed in his eyes. 'For calling you what you

are? Shameless, conscienceless, without remorse or regret! Bringing shame down on your uncle for—'

Anger leapt in her again.

'*You* were responsible for that! There was no need—no need at all—to tell him why our marriage had ended!'

His face darkened. 'I did my best to avoid telling him. Unlike you.' His voice was scathing. 'I wanted to spare his feelings. But he persisted, insisted on knowing why you had returned to England, why our marriage was being dissolved, and in the end I had to tell him the truth. That there had been someone else, another man.' His eyes lasered into her. 'Perhaps in London, in sophisticated, liberated circles, adultery means little. Here, there is a different attitude. Your behaviour hurt your uncle very much—something that still completely fails to prick your conscience.'

'My conscience is clear!' Her retort was instant, vehement.

'How convenient. How very convenient. You go from my bed to his in the space of mere hours! *Hours!* From sex with me to sex with him before the sun has set!' His voice whipped her, lifting the flesh from her bones. Remorselessly he ploughed on, each word another crack of his cruel whip. 'Then, when you get greedy for the money which you think—you *really* think!— you're entitled to, you come crawling back to me! You sell your body back to me for cash. And you come here to tell me you are giving it to your oh-so-accommodating lover, seeing no need to tell him how you managed to get it. What a very convenient conscience you have, to be sure. But just how convenient, I wonder?'

He had started to walk towards her, down the length of the table. His voice as he spoke was smooth, but it caught at her like fine barbs. In all the hideous maelstrom of emotions inside her she could feel, quite suddenly, her heart rate start to quicken, adrenaline start to run. Fear licked through her. He was still ap-

proaching her. She started to back away. It was essential, quite
essential, to back away—

His eyes were holding hers, dark and glittering. She felt her
stomach hollow.

'How, I wonder, how far will that wonderfully flexible,
elastic conscience of yours stretch?'

He was getting closer. She backed away, backed against the
wall. He went on coming towards her.

'Stay away from me!' Her voice was high-pitched, adrenaline streaming in her blood, fear—it must be fear!—jumping
in her veins.

He did not stop. His eyes still held hers, immobilising her.
His voice was smooth, as smooth as the devil's.

'Stay away from you? But that isn't what you want, is it,
Vicky? You don't want that at all. *This* is what you want. You
wanted it every night this last week—over and over and over
again. You couldn't get enough of it…'

He reached his hand out to her. Smoothed down the silken
fall of her hair. A shiver went through her, trembling in her
body. His hand cupped her face, his thumb stroking along her
cheekbone. She felt it in every part of her body.

No! No—don't let him! Don't let him!

She wanted to move—run, hide. But she could not. She could
only stand, paralysed, immobilised, the hard, unyielding surface
of the wall behind her. The hard, unyielding figure in front of her.

'This is what you want,' he said again, and his other hand slid
around the nape of her neck, his fingers slowly moving, sensuously, seductively, on the sensitive skin. She felt weak, boneless.

His eyes caressed her.

'You want this, and you know can have it—don't you? You
don't even need to tell yourself it's to get the money you want.
And you won't have to tell your lover because of that convenient conscience of yours—the one that allows you to do this…'

His mouth lowered to hers. It moved on hers slowly, languorously, devastatingly. She felt her legs give, and in the same moment his fingers at her nape strengthened, holding her head as he took her mouth, opening it to his.

It was bliss. It was heaven. She could not stop, could not resist, could not do anything except give herself to the sensation firing through her.

He lifted his mouth from hers. The dark glitter in his eyes shot through her like sparks of fire. Igniting her.

'Still more? Allow me to oblige you—'

He scooped her up. Her body was boneless, clinging. She didn't care. Could not care. Could not do anything except lift her mouth to his as he lowered it again, striding through the room into the lounge. He didn't bother with the bedroom, or a bed. Even as he lowered her to the sofa he was stripping off his jacket, tie, shirt. Swiftly, ruthlessly discarding what was unnecessary for the moment. Then he turned his attentions to her. Her zip was gone in an instant, her dress discarded. Blood pounded in her veins, hunger in her eyes, her mouth. Oh, dear God, she wanted him. Wanted the hard, lean length of him on her, in her. Arousal consumed her like a fire in the undergrowth.

This was no slow coupling. Urgency burned through her, as if she knew, somewhere dim and dangerous to her, that what she was doing was madness, folly, a crime so stupid that it would never be forgiven.. But she could not stop. As his mouth suckled her, pulling strongly on the rigid, sensitised peaks of her breasts, she held his head to her, her thighs straining against his. He was hard against her, so hard, and she felt a leap of raw, primitive excitement lunge through her. She writhed against him, hungry and urgent. Wanting him. Wanting him now, right now. His possession, his body in hers, now, right now. She lifted her hips to him, her free hand straining down over his naked back. He was still half clothed, but she didn't care. Wanted only what he was withholding from her...

Her hand slid beneath his waistband, and then her other hand was there, too, unfastening him, freeing him…strong in her hands, powerful and potent, so potent. She gave a rasp in her throat, lifting her hips to him as his tongue laced around her nipples, shooting peaks of pleasure through her that she thought she must die from. But it was not enough, not enough. She had to have more…she had to have all…

'Theo—now, *now*!'

Her voice was urgent, desperate. His head lifted from her, eyes still burning like lasers into hers.

'Theo!' she gasped again, and parted for him.

He drove into her, and she gave a great gasp of pleasure as he filled her. Sensation exploded through her, driving on and on, fire was raging in her. Her hands slid around his back, gripping him to her.

His mouth swooped on hers, devouring her, and she gave him like for like, as urgent as he, more urgent still. He drove into her again, and then again, and each time the sensation that exploded in her was like a hammer of pleasure. With every thrust the ultra-sensitive zone within her sent more and yet more excitement through her. More and more, over and over, and over again, thrust after thrust…

'*Theo!*'

Her voice was a cry, a gasp of incredulity, as a pleasure so intense that she felt it like a white burning heat flashed out from where it had ignited and sheeted through her body, burning down every fibre of her being.

'Oh, God, *Theo*!'

She gasped for air, for oxygen, but it only fed the flame, sending yet another wave of even deeper intensity and pleasure through her. Every muscle in her body had tautened, and the extreme tension seemed to amplify what was happening to her. She cried out yet again.

Then he was surging in her. She could feel him, filling her, engorging her, convulsing into her. His hands were pressing down on her shoulders, his torso rearing over her, his head lowered from his powerful, straining shoulders.

She clung to him. Clung like a swimmer in a drowning sea, clung to the hard strength of the body over her, clung to him while his body convulsed into hers, and while hers, every nerve inflamed, strained against him.

The moment went on and on and on.

And then, at the limits of exhaustion, it died away.

Leaving her on the shore of the realisation of what she had done.

His weight came down on her, muscles slackening. His head was at her shoulder, and she could feel the heat of his racing breath on her dampened skin. Her exhaustion was total, as if she'd run a mile. Her heart beat in hard, heavy slugs, her pulse, too.

She could feel his face against her. Feel his skin cooling, feel the sleek sweat of desire spent draw the heat from her body. Leaving her cold, so very cold…

His head lifted from her. His eyes looked down into hers. For one moment there was something in them, then it was gone. Quite gone. Now there was only that dark glitter in them again. With long fingers he smoothed the hair back from her sweated brow, a touch that made her shudder deep, deep within, and gazed into her distended eyes.

'Will you tell him about this, your hapless lover? Tell him how you cried out for me as I took you? Tell him how this time—' his voice changed, cutting like a knife into her '—you did not even do it for the money…'

He levered up from her. Standing there, adjusting his clothing. Picking up his shirt from where it hung half off the arm of the sofa, where it had caught, and shrugging himself into it.

Then he walked towards the phone on the sideboard and lifted it.

His Greek was too quick for her, but when he hung up and turned back to her she did not need to understand.

'The car will be waiting for you in the basement. Your flight will be rearranged for when you reach the airport.' His eyes flickered at him. 'I suggest you use the bathroom in the guest room to repair your appearance. You'll forgive me if I make my farewell now.' He walked towards her, lifting her supine, naked body upright. She sagged, unable to support herself, and his arms held her, his fingers around her flanks, indenting into her ribcage. He looked down into her face a moment. Her hair was tousled wantonly over her bare shoulders, her eyes were wide, distended, her mouth bee-stung from his arousal of her.

His eyes had that strange blankness in them; his face was a mask.

'So beautiful on the outside,' he said. 'So deceptive.'

He let her go and walked away, heading, she dimly remembered, for the master bedroom, and presumably its bathroom.

Like a zombie she picked up her clothes. Like a zombie she found the guest bedroom and its en suite bathroom. Some time later, when she was sure the apartment was empty again, she took the lift down to the basement and got into the waiting car. She was driven to the airport where a first-class ticket back to London had been arranged for her.

She wanted to die.

Two days later, when she phoned her British bank to ensure the money had been transferred from her Greek account, she was informed that the cheque had been stopped by its issuer.

Theo had taken his revenge on her yet again.

CHAPTER TEN

THINGS were not going well for Theo. His business affairs were thriving, as ever. His investment in Aristides Fournatos's company was returning handsome profits, and he and the old man had formed a consortium to turn the tables on the company that had tried to buy him out. They were very close to acquisition, but Theo was adamant that the directors of the company should not personally profit financially from any takeover bid. He did not like to see the undeserving reap rewards from their misdeeds—whether they were unscrupulous corporate asset-strippers or an adulterous wife.

But he must not think of that. Must not think beyond the fact that he was now finished with her. Absolutely. Permanently. Stopping the cheque had been the last action he had taken to dispose of her once and for all.

It had been, he now knew, a mistake to do what he had. He had thrown her from him two years ago, and he should have left it at that. He had known this, but for some insane reason he had been unable to stop himself when she had accosted him in London.

Bad mistake. A very bad mistake.

But then his whole disastrous marriage had been a mistake. No, that was not to be thought of. Not to be referred to. It was to be put aside, ignored. It was bad enough that he had to live in the same city as Aristides Fournatos, bad enough that he had to look the man in the eye every day and know that he knew the shocking truth about his niece. And that had been another mistake—telling Aristides why their marriage had ended. He should have stonewalled him, refused to explain. But Aristides had been set on trying to patch things up between them, on visiting Vicky, getting her to come back to Athens. Then Theo would have had to see her again…

And yet he *had* seen her again, and of his own volition He had succumbed to that unforgivable lapse of judgement after seeing her in his office, outraged at being ignored, fire and ice flashing in her eyes.

Mistake. Bad mistake.

And worse to follow.

Offering her that devil's deal, so that he could take his revenge for what she'd done to him two years ago. It had been easy to lure her with the promise of the money she was so greedy for. So self-righteously convinced she was entitled to. Adulteress though she was…

Her words of self-exoneration bleated in his memory—*'It wasn't a real marriage…'*

He slammed his mind shut. But not before one final memory had blazed inside his head.

The last, shaming time he had taken her—the ultimate indulgence.

Ohi! No!

His fingers curved around the pencil in his hand and snapped it like a toothpick. He tossed it aside and reached for another, continuing with his rapid scanning of a printout of latest sales figures. Sales were up, profits were up. His business affairs were thriving.

But he, Theo, was not doing well.

* * *

'More coffee?'

'No, thanks, I'm fine. I'd better make a move anyway.'

Jem got to his feet. His lanky frame made Vicky's studio flat seem even smaller than it was. She could have fitted the entire place into the dining room of Theo's Athens penthouse...

But then, that was what being rich did for you. Bought you penthouses and private islands, ski lodges in the mountains—and 'love-nests' on the coast to take your mistresses to.

Mistresses galore for Theo Theakis—except when he was married.

Because then, of course, he'd had a wife to satisfy his sexual needs.

Like a program running in her brain, thoughts formed in her head as they always did, over and over and over again, without pity, without cessation. So what if Theo had not continued with his affairs during their marriage? That only made it worse—much worse.

He used me. Used me for the sex he hypocritically refrained from getting from his usual sources!

Hadn't it been bad enough thinking he'd seduced her simply as an exercise in his own sexual egoism? Now she had to face something even worse.

I could have been anyone! Anyone at all! Any woman would have done—any woman who was his wife. There for the purpose. The purpose of being a vessel for his sexual relief...that's all I was—all my body was.

Just as her body had been nothing more than a means of exacting his revenge on her. Ruthlessly, deliberately using her pathetic weakness, her criminally stupid vulnerability to him, turning it against her, using it as a deadly annihilating weapon against her.

Right to the very, very last.

Cold flushed through her, sickening and shaming.

Even when she'd been yelling her fury and defiance at him he'd still had to do nothing more than walk up to her, touch her, kiss her...

And take her.

She shut her eyes, shame burning through her.

'Vicky—are you all right?'

Her eyes flew open. The concern in Jem's voice making her instantly tense.

'Yes—fine.' She got to her feet. 'Just a bit depressed—which isn't surprising really, is it?'

She tried to keep the edge from her voice, and failed. Like a pressure cooker with the lid tightly screwed down, she could feel the fury and rage boil within her.

'You know,' Jem was saying, 'I still think the best thing to do would simply be to tell him what Pycott Grange is going to be used for. Surely the man can't refuse to release the money then?'

Vicky's face tightened instantly.

'It wouldn't do any good. He'll never hand the money over. Never.'

Her mouth snapped shut like a clam.

Jem gave a heavy, exasperated sigh, and ran his hand through his hair.

'Well, what about my other suggestion, then? Give the story to the press. OK, the guy's in Greece, but even so, surely the tabloids there would snap up a story about some rich tycoon who won't fund a holiday home for deprived kids?'

'No!' A shudder went through her. 'I could never do that. And anyway, it won't work. Look, Jem, *nothing* will work! The man is a total and absolute *bastard*!'

'Well, what about your uncle, then? The money came from him originally. Maybe he'd give you what he agreed, and then get the original amount back from your ex?'

'No!' Her negation came again, more high-pitched this time. 'Jem, stop it—there isn't any way. There just isn't!'

'Maybe your uncle would simply make a charitable donation, then, irrespective of any deal or whatever that was set up when you married—'

'Jem! No! It's impossible. I can't go to my uncle—I can't!'

Jem's face set. 'Vicky, it's your family, I know, and I don't want to interfere. But think about it—your uncle is rich. It's insane to ignore that. We need the money so urgently—we really do. We can do what we can—get some local help, try and raise money here—but it's just so frustrating knowing that you're owed that money and your ex is too bloody tight-fisted to hand it over.'

Vicky's hands clutched together. 'I'm sorry, Jem. I'm really, really sorry. But I can't get in touch again—I just can't. Please don't ask me to.'

She kept her voice calm, as calm as she could. But Jem's searching eyes looked at her.

'OK, I'll back off.' His arms came around her in a warm, comforting bear hug. 'You're very important to me, Vic, and I don't want you upset by anything or anyone.' He released his hug, but slid big hands either side of her face. Then he dropped a kiss on her forehead. 'You take care now, OK? Promise me?'

He smiled reassuringly at her. 'We'll work something out. Don't you worry. We haven't got this far just to give in now. Look, I tell you what—I'll drive down to Devon tomorrow, see what the latest state of play is down there. Maybe there are areas the builders can suggest we do a temporary, cheaper job on, just for the moment, so we can still open this summer. There are ways and means—there always are.'

He dropped a last kiss on her forehead and let go of her. But even as he released her her arms wrapped around his waist, and she pressed her cheek against his chest.

'Oh, Jem, I'm so sorry—I really am.'

He patted her back. 'That's OK, Vic—truly. I know that whole marriage scene was a bad time. But you've got me—you know that. We go back a long way, you and I. Thick and thin.'

She pulled away from him, smiling up at him.

'Right back to when you thumped Peter Richards from the year above, for lobbing that conker at me!'

'Yeah, and then he thumped me back. I can still remember the nosebleed.' He gave a rueful laugh. 'Well, I always was fool-hardy. Weighing in to fight the big, bad guys.' He glanced at his watch. 'I'd better go. The tube will be shutting down soon.'

'You can stay the night if you want.'

He shook his head. 'No, I'll make a dawn getaway tomorrow morning. Be in Devon by mid-morning.'

She saw him to the door. Her smile was strained by then, but she kept it pinned to her face.

Only when he had gone did it crumple into little pieces.

Theo eased his dinner jacket over his shoulders. He was due at the opera within the hour, and he still had some phone calls to put in to the States. Not that he was eager to get to the opera, either. Or, indeed, to escort Christina Poussos there. But it was a gala of some kind, and she wanted to show off—and show him off, too, at her side.

His face tightened as he checked his dress tie and slid his wallet into his tuxedo. He'd take her back to her own apartment afterwards. He had no intention of bringing her back here, either, to the Theakis mansion, or to his office penthouse.

Above all, not there.

He hadn't used it much recently. It was a damn nuisance that it was part of the Theakis HQ or he'd have sold it straight away. He must buy another city apartment. It might not be as conven-ient as the one at his HQ, but it would have fewer....associations.

It was irritating that he could not dispose of this mansion, either. But it had been the Theakis family residence for too long for him to sell. Even so, he was spending less and less time there.

He'd already sold another property he possessed. One with a sea view.

And far, far too many memories...

He picked up his mobile and headed downstairs. Christina wanted him to arrive early, to collect her from her apartment, but he did not intend to do so. She would want sex, and he was not intending to oblige her. He was not in the mood for sex.

These days he was seldom in the mood for sex.

And when he was it was definitely not Christina that he wanted.

Or any other suitable woman.

He stalked across the wide hallway and into his study, shutting the door with unnecessary force. Then he started to make his calls.

He needed something to divert him. His mood was not good.

Damn her—damn her to hell...

Anger stabbed through him. She was nothing but a shameless, adulterous—

He cut the thought out of his head. He knew what she was—so what was the point of repeating it? She was out of his life now, and no power on earth could let her intrude again. She had been a mistake—a bad mistake. But that was hardly a reason for making a bad situation worse.

Deliberately, he conjured an image of Christina Poussos to his mind. She was chic, beautiful, desirable. Better still, she quite obviously wanted to restart their former affair—the one that had been interrupted when she'd decided to marry. But now she was back in circulation, her marriage over, and she was eager to show the world that she was still capable of picking the lovers she wanted. Well, maybe he would change his mind and oblige her after all. She had meant little to him the first time

around, and she would mean less this time, but her advantage
was that she was a known commodity. With Christina Poussos
he knew exactly what he was getting.

Unlike—

He cut out again. Like a circuit breaker. A safety trip.

The ring tones on his phone ceased, and the voice of the
person he was calling answered. He leant back in his chair and
started to talk business.

Another safety trip. He needed a lot of them these days.

It was some twenty minutes later that the house phone went.
It would be his chauffeur, reminding him they must set off or
miss the start of the opera. That wouldn't bother him, but it
would put Christina in a sulk—she liked making a grand
entrance. And since he wanted sex from her tonight he didn't
want to have to dispose of female sulks beforehand. Not that
Christina would deny him her bed. She would be too triumphant
to risk taking that tack. She knew all too well that there were
any number of women who would follow her. There always had
been. He'd always taken it for granted that since he was Theo
Theakis he would never be short of willing females to interest
him sexually. He was not conceited—merely realistic. It was
not a big issue.

Nor was it a major concern in his life. His major concern
was Theakis Corp, and ensuring that those in his employ kept
their jobs. It was all too easy to see how danger could
threaten—Aristides Fournatos was demonstration of that.
Theo's expression changed. Despite the disaster that his ill-
judged marriage had proved, he did not regret it. He had done
the right thing, he knew. Business was a close-knit affair, and
mutual co-operation was mutually profitable. He had made
substantial money from his investment in Fournatos, and
honoured his father's memory, as well, standing by one of his
close friends.

His eyes hardened. Honour. A strange word. Meaning nothing—and everything.

She should have told me. Told me right from the start that she could not marry me because she was still involved with another man. Aristides might not have approved—might have wanted to know why she was not marrying this man if he meant so much to her as to have an affair with him—but he would not have persisted in his hopes and plans for a dynastic marriage to underpin and justify my investing in Fournatos.

But she had said nothing. Why? She had been vociferous enough on the whole subject of the kind of marriage that was commonplace in his and Aristides' circles. Vociferous and scathing. Yet not a word on the one subject that would have put an instant stop to the whole notion.

About that she had kept completely silent.

Keeping it her little secret...

Her dirty, dishonourable secret.

Not worth disclosing.

Again in his head he heard her indignantly self-justifying outburst. *'It wasn't a real marriage...'*

Did she really think that gave either of them *carte blanche* to ignore its existence? Did she really think that was what he had done? Had she actually thought that he would continue with other women for the duration of their marriage?

I gave her no cause to think that. None! And she knows it!

No, she had just trotted out that convenient disclaimer of all responsibility for her own act of adultery! Trying to make out he was as culpable as she! Just to exonerate her own despicable behaviour.

He felt anger knife through him, as emotion so strong it seemed to white out in his head.

She went to him from me...

From my bed to his...

The violence of his emotion shook him.

The house phone rang again. Insistent. Intrusive. But he needed its interruption. With visible force he wiped his mind. Took back control of himself.

He lifted the phone.

It was not his chauffeur, but the on-duty security guard. A visitor was at the entrance, asking for him.

'He refuses to give his name or state his business, *kyrios*. Should I phone the police? I have him on camera, if you wish to view him.'

The monitor in Theo's office flickered, cutting to the exterior view of the electronically controlled gates to the driveway. A taxi was pulled up, and standing by the intercom, in full view of the security camera trained on him, was the man who was asking for him.

For a second Theo just looked at the image in front of him. Then, slowly, his face drained of expression.

'Show him in,' he instructed.

'Vicky, these figures don't add up to that total.'

Vicky looked up from her work. One of her colleagues was holding a printout of some financial calculations she'd just produced.

'Oh, Lord, sorry. I'll sort it—' She held out her hand for the papers.

Her colleague handed them over. 'So long as the master file is accurate. I've marked where the sums went wonky,' she said with a smile, and headed back to her own desk.

Vicky stared bleakly at the figures in front of her. They were blurring even as she looked. She just couldn't get her head around numbers these days. Or around anything else. She seemed to be moving in a perpetual fog. Everything seemed so very hard to do—even the simplest things, like making a cup of coffee, or getting up in the mornings. Let alone anything that required the slightest brain power.

Depression—that might be the clinical name for it.

She had another name. But it was not one she must ever, ever give voice to.

It was her secret. Her terrible, unspeakable secret. And she could tell no one. No one at all.

Certainly not Jem. He would be so angry—so appalled and horrified.

Thank God he was away at the moment. Last night she'd nearly cracked in front of him, and it had taken more strength than she could bear to use to hold it together until he had gone. But now at least she had a couple of days without him. Not that the knowledge of where he was did anything to cheer her. She glanced at the clock on the wall. Even now he was probably walking around Pycott with the builder, realising just how daunting the task of making it even partially habitable would be without the money they had been expecting.

Despair crushed her. If only she could go to Aristides! He would give her the money, she knew he would—he was kind and generous, and his heart would be moved by what she and Jem were attempting to do. But she could never go to him. Not now Theo had told him just why their marriage had come to its abrupt premature end.

She was trapped—trapped on all sides. There was nowhere she could go, no one she could turn to.

If only she could go to her mother and Geoff! They couldn't help financially, she knew that, but just to see them again—just to get out of here, flee somewhere as far away as Australia! She was good at fleeing…

But sometimes… Her stomach hollowed with cruel self-knowledge. Sometimes when she fled from the unbearable, what happened thereafter was even worse.

Like when she had fled the island…

She pressed her lips together. No, leaving the island had been essential. And Jem had been there for her—a wonderful, life-saving surprise she had clung to. But she still could not tell him what she had done. She could not. Shame flushed through her.

And if she did run away again this time it would be even worse! Her mother would ask questions, want answers. Would want to know how it was that she had done what she had…

No, she was trapped. Trapped here, in the prison of her enforced silence.

I can't tell anyone—I can't tell anyone what I've gone and done…

Numbly, rubbing a hand across her weary forehead, she called up the master file of the report she'd compiled, and slowly and laboriously started to retype the corrections.

They took a long, long time to do.

Around her heart a cold, tight shell of despair was forming.

Theo crossed to the drinks cabinet in the corner of his study. He normally never went near it unless he had a visitor. But the visitor on his way into the house now would not be offered a drink.

With controlled, economic movements he opened a single malt, poured a shot into a glass, and knocked it back. It was doing grave disservice to a fine malt, but he didn't care. Right now he cared about nothing—except the visitor who was about to walk into his house.

Was he mad to let him in? No man would let such a visitor into his domain.

And yet he had.

But then, he had his reasons.

He wanted to look into the man's eyes. See him face to face.

Tell him just what he thought of him. He might… He felt his left hand fist. He might just do more than that…

But not in anger. He would remain, as it was imperative to do, in total and absolute control. That was essential.

With total, absolute control, he set back the empty glass and closed the cabinet. Crossed back to his desk. Pulling back his chair, he sat down, and with total, absolute control he waited for the study door to open.

He could hear the visitor arrive. Hear the front door open and two voices speak, but both were inaudible. Then his door opened. The man walked in.

Theo looked at him. Looked at the man whose face he had last seen looking out at him from the photographs that scum of a paparazzo had placed in front of him in this very room, on this very desk, standing back, waiting—waiting for Theo to take his fill of what they meant, to reach for his chequebook. To pay him the money he required to ensure the photos never saw the light of day.

His eyes rested on him. Expressionless and implacable, dark and impenetrable. The other man's eyes were blue, and they were filled, like the rest of his face, with one expression only.

Anger.

Theo leant back. The movement was again controlled. Then he opened his mouth to speak. To enunciate his views on the man who stood on the other side of his desk.

But the other man spoke first, anger sparking electrically from his eyes, his voice vehement.

'You can tell me one thing, Mr Theakis—and one thing only. You can tell me right now, to my face, just what the *hell* you think you're playing at! And what the *hell* makes you think you have the *slightest* business in keeping my sister's money from her?'

With total, absolute control, Theo froze.

CHAPTER ELEVEN

VICKY was washing out a jumper. It was two in the morning, but she didn't care. She couldn't sleep. Not these days. If she went to bed she simply lay awake, staring up the ceiling, listening to the dying sound of traffic outside in the street.

Thinking.

In the dark it was impossible not to think.

Not to feel.

She would lie there, hour after hour, staring upwards, her emotions stripped naked.

As naked as her body had once been.

Thinking about that. Remembering.

So that was why she was standing here at the kitchen sink, in her thin cotton bathrobe, her hands in suds, rhythmically squeezing warm, soapy water through the woollen jumper. On the draining board a soggy pile of washed clothes was accumulating, waiting to be rinsed. On the other side of the sink was a heap of more clothes to wash. She'd set the radio to a classical music station, and it was playing softly from the top of the cooker. It wasn't a very good choice of music right now, however. Strauss's *Four Last Songs*.

The terrible, ravishing, dying elegies wound in and out of her, the voice of the soprano tearing at her with emotion.

But she must not feel emotion. It was forbidden to her. Forbidden absolutely.

So she went on rhythmically squeezing and dipping, squeezing and dipping.

The sound of the key in the lock made her freeze.

Then she jerked around. The kitchen area of the studio flat was separated from the living/sleeping area by a half-wall that was designed as a breakfast bar, with cupboards underneath for compact storage. An archway to the right of it shielded the front door via a tiny coat lobby.

'Jem?'

Her voice was sharp. He was the only person to have a key both to the block of flats and her own studio.

There was no answer, so she hurriedly, panicking, seized an unwashed garment and hastily mopped the suds from her hands with it. Then she seized a kitchen knife from the knife-block by the toaster. She turned around, heart pounding with fear.

Shock and disbelief blasted through her. The knife dropped from her hand, her fingers suddenly nerveless.

Theo stood in the archway.

He tossed the keys onto the breakfast bar.

'Jem lent them to me,' he said.

Faintness washed over her.

'Jem?' Her voice was weak. Uncomprehending.

'He came to see me,' Theo said conversationally. His voice sounded normal, its familiar deep, faintly accented tones no different from what they had always been in the days when he had spoken to her in such a conversational manner.

But his eyes held the dark glitter that had been in them the last time she had seen him.

Her heart started to pound. Not with the panicked fear of a burglar that she had first felt. With a familiar, heavy pounding that she was very, very used to.

Which was impossible. Because what Theo had just said to her was impossible.

'Jem's in Devon,' she said.

'Wrong,' said Theo. 'He's in Athens. He arrived this evening. We had a very interesting conversation. A very...enlightening...one.'

His eyes were holding hers, holding them with the power of that dark glitter. He stood still, very still, paused in the archway. Vicky's eyes went over him. He was wearing evening dress. It seemed an odd thing for him to be wearing in the circumstances.

But then the circumstances were...unbelievable.

She tried to get her head around them, fixing on the thing that was least unbelievable.

'You were in Athens this evening?' She frowned. But he was here, now, in London.

'Then I flew here,' said Theo. 'You see,' he went on, and something altered in his voice, something that slid along her nerves like acid, 'enlightening as my conversation was, earlier on this evening, it failed to answer all the questions arising therefrom. There are so many questions, but they all have one expression.'

He paused. His eyes glittered with that strange, terrifying darkness.

'Why?' he said softly. 'Why?'

He moved suddenly, and Vicky jumped. But he did not approach her. Instead he walked across to the armchair by the window and sat down. He crossed his long legs, resting his hands on the arms of the chair.

'Start talking,' he said. 'And don't,' he instructed, in the same voice that raised hairs on the back of her neck, 'leave anything out.'

The world was splintering around her. Breaking up into tiny shards, each one so sharp it was cutting her to ribbons. Slowly she reached for a tea towel, dried her hands properly. Then she bent to pick up the knife from where it lay on the floor, wiping it with the tea towel and replacing it in the knife-block. Finally she reached to switch off the radio.

'*Can this be death?*' asked the soprano with tearing beauty.

But death came in many guises. This was one of them.

She walked to the breakfast bar. She needed its support. Her legs had jellied. Shock—that was what it was. Shock was having a physical effect on her that was too great to bear.

'Talk, Vicky.'

She opened her mouth, but no words came. Then, with a rasping breath, she said, 'I don't understand. Why did Jem go to Athens?'

There was a flicker in the dark, glittering eyes.

'He wanted what you wanted, Vicky. He wanted your money.' His voice changed. 'He seemed to think that I was withholding it unreasonably.' The eyes glittered again. 'He was quite aggressive about it. Which was curious, really, because, you see—' the glitter intensified '—I only let him into my house on the grounds that I was going to personally beat him to a pulp...'

He paused. 'It was as well, was it not, therefore, that he spoke first? After all—' his voice was a blade, sliding between her ribs '—what possible cause could I have to beat your *brother* to a pulp?'

'He's my stepbrother.' Her voice was blank. As blank as the inside of her skull. 'My stepfather Geoff's son from his first marriage. We were at primary school together. That's how Geoff met my mother after his divorce—through my friendship with his son.'

Something flashed in Theo's face. A fury so deep that it should have slain her.

'Why? *Why* did you let me think he was your lover?'

She looked at him.

'Because it ended our marriage and I wanted out.'

Her voice was calm, so very calm. What else could she be? The inside of her head was blank—quite, quite blank.

At her answer she saw his hands bite over the arms of the chair. 'A simple "I want a divorce" would have sufficed.' The scorn in his voice gutted her.

She couldn't answer. It was impossible. Impossible to say it. To anyone.

It was her own terrible, shameful secret.

No one could know. No one in the world. Not Jem, or her uncle, or her mother. No one.

She watched Theo's mouth thin into a tight, whipped line. His eyes were like spears touching her skin, ready to indent into the flesh beneath.

'Your brother is unhappy. He feels—besmirched. Slandered.'

'He was never supposed to know. He shouldn't have gone to Athens. He should have gone to Devon, like he said. I told him you wouldn't give me the money. I told him.' Her voice was still calm.

He mirrored it back. 'But you omitted the little detail of why.'

Her eyes flickered. 'It wasn't relevant.'

The tightening of his hands over the arms of the chair came again.

'Nor relevant to your uncle, either, I presume?

'No.'

'Nor, of course—' his voice was very calm now, his eyes resting on her, the glitter gone, quite expressionless '—to me.'

She gave a little shake of her head.

'No,' she said.

There was silence. Only the sound of traffic in the street below. And the thudding of her heart, beat by beat by beat.

'Yet you wanted, that money very badly,' he said. 'So badly, you made a whore out of yourself.'

She met his eyes. 'No. Whores get paid. The money was not for me. I expect Jem has told you that.'

'Yes. He was quite discursive on the subject. You may be glad to know, if you consider it in the slightest *relevant*, that I have handed him a cheque that will cover the entire restoration and refurbishment costs, plus running costs for five years.'

'That's very good of you.' Her voice was hollow.

'If you had told me what you wanted the money for I would have given it to your stepbrother. And if you had told me he was your stepbrother, not your lover, I would not have thought you an adulterous slut.'

His voice was still conversational. It sliced through her like a surgeon's blade.

'So why did you?' he asked. 'Let me think you an adulterous slut? Because you did so quite deliberately. You had so many opportunities to put me straight...'

The glitter was in his eyes again.

'You didn't take one of them. Why?' The softness of his voice eviscerated her, as once his fury had done.

She had thought his fury unbearable. She had been wrong.

His dark, glittering eyes rested on her across the small space of her studio.

'Vicky, I have flown fifteen hundred miles. It's four in the morning for me. I scrambled my pilot when he was having dinner with his wife. So you *will* give me answers. Believe me, you will give me answers.'

His eyes were slicing through her. Inch by inch.

'Why did you let me think you were a faithless bitch?'

Her fingers were pressing onto the tiled surface of the breakfast bar. Pressing so hard that at any moment, any moment now, they must surely snap.

'I told you—I wanted out of our marriage. And it worked, didn't it?'

'You slandered yourself and your stepbrother, you shamed your uncle. Or wasn't that *relevant*?'

'No.' None of that had been relevant.

'So what *was*, Vicky?'

She couldn't answer. She could never answer. Silence bound her for ever. Bound her to her terrible, shameful secret.

'I've had a long time to think about this, Vicky. If you won't give answers, I will.' He stood up. The movement made her jerk.

He was starting to come towards her. Tall and lean and dark. And terrifying. Her eyes distended. Flaring with terror.

The unfastened jacket of his tuxedo swung, revealing the muscled narrowness of his waist, the whipped leanness of his hips.

She could feel his power. She had always felt it.

And it had always, always terrified her. Time dissolved away and she saw him again, turning to be introduced to her, those dark eyes looking down at her so impassively. She had felt his power then.

She felt it now.

Desperately she clawed her hands over the surface of the breakfast bar.

'Stay back, Theo—'

The words broke from her.

'Answers, Vicky.'

He stood there, on the far side of the bar, a foot away from her. So close. Terrifyingly, terrifyingly close.

'Tell me why you let me think you had a lover. Tell me—'

His voice impelled her. His gaze compelled her.

Terror consumed her. Terror and desperation.

She threw back her head.

'Why do you *think*, Theo? You'd just had sex with me!'

There was scorn in her voice, forcibly injected under an intensity of pressure. Her fingertips were still pressing into the tiles, the veins on the backs of her hands standing out like ropes.

'Sex with the only woman you were going to allow yourself so you didn't have to be celibate while married to Aristides Fournatos's niece! So don't damn well stand there and look for answers—because *that's* the reason! I met Jem at the airport because I picked up a text message on my mobile from him, saying he was Athens. I was so upset over…what had happened on the island…I just had to get away. We went sightseeing and talked about the house he was sent to inherit, how it would be brilliant for a youth centre, only we would need a lot of money to do it up. He asked me if I could line up the funds out of what you'd promised to release to me when our marriage ended. The time away from you had me realise that I had to get away from you—permanently. So when you threw those vile photos in my face I grabbed at the chance to make it the reason for ending our marriage immediately. And it worked, didn't it? *Didn't it?* You couldn't wait to lay into me—to slash me to pieces! And then throw me out like garbage!'

She fell silent, finishing on a harsh, indrawn breath, her eyes spitting at him.

He was standing very still. A nerve was ticking in his cheek.

His voice was controlled. Very controlled. 'When you came to the penthouse you accused me of adultery myself. All through our marriage you assumed I was sleeping with other women. Was that why you let me think you had a lover, too? To get even with me?'

'It was to get *away* from you! What the hell does it matter whether you were carrying on with other women or using me as some kind of bloody sexual relief?'

His eyes were resting on her. 'You're right, it doesn't matter. Because neither is true. But what does matter…' his voice was conversational again, but the nerve was still ticking at his cheek in his stark, expressionless face '...is why you thought either was true—and why that upset you.'

'I wasn't *upset*—I was *angry*! Angry at being used like that!'

'But I didn't use you in that repellent way. Nor did I commit adultery with any other women during our marriage. So now you don't need to be angry any more, do you?'

Her face contorted. 'How the hell can you say that?' she demanded viciously. 'After the way you treated me—forcing me to have sex with you for the money, saying what you said to me!'

He gave a shrug, his eyes never leaving her. 'I behaved like that to you because I thought you had taken a lover, that you still had a lover, and yet were prepared to have sex just to get the money you thought you were entitled to. All you had to do to stop me behaving like that was tell me the truth. But you didn't, did you? You let me go on thinking that about you even when it was no longer necessary. So why, Vicky? Why did you do that?'

He had cut the ground from her feet. She felt herself falling—falling down into the bottomless pit that waited to consume her.

But she mustn't fall. She must fight. Fight with all the weapons she could.

There was only one problem—she had no weapons left. No words. Only a terrible, gaping hollow of horror opening up inside her. She stared at him, wordless, defenceless.

His eyes were moving over her face. The nerve at his cheek had stopped. His voice, when he spoke, had changed.

'Tell me something, Vicky. If I do this now, will you be angry?'

His hand reached to her. Thumb moving across her lips.

'Does that make you angry, Vicky? What about this? Does this make you angry?'

The backs of his fingers drifted over her cheek, then turned to stroke with soft, searching movements over the delicate flesh of her ear, spearing gently, so gently, into her hair.

'What about this, then? Do you feel angry when I do this to you?'

His fingers closed around her nape. Drew, with ineluctable pressure, her face towards him, as with slow, aching descent his mouth moved down to hers.

His kiss was velvet, his lips as soft as silk, his touch as smooth as satin.

He lifted his head away from her.

'Angry, Vicky?' he asked softly, so very, very softly.

Her body was boneless. Her palms collapsed against the cool surface of the tiles. She looked into his eyes. Deep, fathomless. Eyes to drown in.

His face swam before her. On the surface of the breakfast bar a single tear splashed like a diamond.

'Theo, please—don't do this to me. Please.' Her voice was a whisper. 'Please.'

Another tear splashed.

He was looking at her. She could not see him. He was out of focus. Tears were spilling from her eyes.

'Please don't do this to me. Please.'

Greek broke from him. She did not know what it meant, but she heard the shock in his voice. The disbelief.

She knew why. She wanted to die. Fall through the earth into that bottomless pit beneath her, the one that swallowed up all those like her. The fools of the world.

She stared at him through the tears blurring her vision.

'Please go, Theo. Please. Just go. *Just go.*'

She felt her body slacken, felt herself grope for the high stool and heave herself onto it before she collapsed. Her head bowed. Tears were streaming down her cheeks.

'Vicky! *Cristos!* Vicky!'

He had come around the edge of the bar, his arms enfolded her. For one brief, anguished moment she let herself cling to him. Then she drew away. Dragged herself from him.

'Is this answer enough for you, Theo? Is it? *Is it?* Are you happy now? Have you got what you wanted? Just like you got what you wanted from me when you hunted me down? Got me into your bed! And you're right—so bloody, bloody right! What does it matter whether you used me or not? It was all the same to you in the end! Sexual relief or sexual ego! What did it *matter*? What did it matter? It was all the same to you and—oh, God—it didn't make any difference to me! How could it? How *could* it? You made a fool of me either way! A stupid, idiotic fool!'

A laugh broke from her. High and humourless.

'Did you read me wrong, Theo? Did you think I was like all those other women, falling over themselves to tell me they'd had affairs with you, or wanted one, or wanted another one? That I'd just be like them? Enjoy the physical pleasures you had to offer, be chic and sophisticated and blasé about the whole thing like them? Well, I couldn't! And I *knew* I couldn't! I went into that marriage never thinking for a single instant that you'd take that line! I never for a moment dreamt you'd think anything else! Our marriage was a sham, just for show—of *course* you would go on having your normal sex life! When you turned on me I didn't know what to do! I tried to stonewall you—tried so damn, damn hard. But you wouldn't lay off! You kept right on coming. And I tried to stop you—I tried and I tried. And it was the same when you pulled that devil's deal on me! Making me go back to you if I wanted my money for Jem's project! Do you know why I went along with that—do you?'

She glared at him, her face contorted through the tears still running down her cheeks.

'Do you think I did it for the damn money? Well, I didn't!

I wanted the money for Jem, but that wasn't the reason I did what you wanted me to do! I did it to show myself—to show *you*!—that I *could* be just like all those bloody other women! I *could* have totally meaningless sex with you—the only kind you like! The only kind you want! I did it so I could make myself immune to you. To make myself hate you, big-time! And, my God, it should have worked! After everything you did to me, said to me, and that very last nightmare time of all—my *God*, I should have hated you! You were so vile to me, and horrible, and…and…'

She couldn't go on. Couldn't do anything. She had told her terrible, shaming secret, the one she shouldn't tell anyone— anyone at all. And she had told it to the very worst person in the world to tell.

'I should have been immune to you,' she whispered.

But she wasn't. She wasn't immune to him. She would never be. That was the power he had over her, the power that terrified her.

She took a deep, shuddering breath.

Looked at him. Looked right at him.

'Just go, Theo,' she said. Her voice was cracking. She was cracking. Cracking into fragments. 'Just go.'

But he didn't go. He stepped forward to her again, to where she had shrunk from him. He said something to her in Greek. It might have been Greek for idiot—she wasn't sure. Her Greek wasn't very good any more. If so, she wasn't surprised. The word suited her. It was what she was. An idiot. A fool. A moron. One after another the words tolled through her brain, each one breaking her into smaller and smaller fragments. Her tears had stopped now. All run out. She was just a sodden, dripping mess.

Like her life.

She heard him say the word again—the one that probably meant idiot. *Elithios*. That was what it sounded like. Did he have to keep repeating it? She knew she was that—an idiot. Who else but an idiot would have done what she had?

She started to cry again. It seemed to be the only rational response in the circumstances.

Then Theo's arms were coming around her. She was being crushed against him, his arms like steel bands around her. It made her cry more. The tears soaked into his shirt, because there wasn't anywhere else for them to go. He hugged her more tightly, saying more things to her she couldn't understand. Then he slid his arms from her and she nearly toppled off the high stool, but he caught her, held her face between his hands.

'Idiot,' he said, in English this time. His eyes looked into hers. 'I thought myself a clever man—and all the time I was an idiot. Blind to what was right in front of me. Blind to everything—except one thing. One thing.' His gaze searched hers. 'This,' he said.

He kissed her. Warm and close and for such a long, long time. Then his lips left her mouth and kissed her eyes.

'*Matia mou,*' he told her. 'My eyes. My lips. My heart. My wife.'

He kissed her mouth again. This time it was warm, and close, but more—more than that. She felt the flame light in her body

Then she was being lifted off the stool and carried, still being kissed.

Fear sprang in her.

'Theo! No—please! I can't do this! I can't. *I can't!*'

He crossed the short distance to the bed, its duvet crumpled from where she had thrown it back, sleepless and tormented, an hour ago.

'You can,' he said to her, and lowered her down. 'You must. And so must I.'

He took off his jacket and tossed it aside, and then his dress tie and shirt. Then the rest of his clothes.

Then he came down beside her. 'It's imperative,' he said to her, 'that we do this. Or the idiocy in our blood will take us over for ever. And we must not allow that, either of us. Not any more. Never again.'

He parted her bathrobe, spreading wide the material.

'My most beautiful one,' he said. Then he lowered his head and kissed each breast.

She shut her eyes. There was nothing she could do. Nothing at all. All will was gone. There was nothing left except sensation. Slow and sensuous and sweet. As sweet as honey…the honey that was easing through her veins.

His body was warm to her touch. Warm and strong. He murmured Greek to her, words she did not know, had never known, never heard. But they were honey in her ears, as his touch of her body was honey in her veins.

Slowly he kissed her, slowly he aroused her, slowly he entered her, holding her and cradling her, taking her with him on the journey he was making, to a land he had never visited before. Nor she.

They went to the land together, and found that distant shore, which was so close, so very close, after all. As close as their bodies to each other.

She cried again as the climax consumed itself in her, tears that came from a place deep within her.

'Don't cry,' he said, and held her close. 'Don't cry.'

He soothed her till her tears had ebbed away, easing from her but never letting go of her, folding her to him so that her cheek rested on the strong wall of his chest. Her heart was full within her, but a great grief ran through her still.

She lifted her head to look at him.

Her eyes were troubled. So very troubled.

'Theo—thank you. Thank you for giving me this time now. It's taken away so much of the stain of what happened in

Greece. And I'm grateful, very grateful to you for that. But go now—please. Please go.' She swallowed painfully.

She sat up more, so that she was farther away from him and could half wrap the duvet around her. Then, with another swallow, she began to talk.

'I should never have married you. I knew right from the start that I should not. Not just because I didn't approve of our reasons for doing so—I gave in to the pressure anyway, for my uncle's sake—for another reason. One I refused to face up to until it was far, far too late.' Her eyes gazed down at him, still troubled. 'A marriage like the one we went through could only possibly work if both parties felt the same about it, and about each other. To me it really was a sham, a show, nothing more— a charade meaning absolutely nothing beyond the mere surface. It was nothing more than play-acting, with me cast very temporarily in the role of Mrs Theo Theakis. The play would have finite run and then we'd both go off stage and get on with our real lives again, the purpose of the play achieved. That's why...'

She swallowed yet again, and though she did not want to speak, she did, 'that's why I was so horrified when it actually finally dawned on me that you were...were making a move on me. I kept thinking I must be mistaken—I *had* to be mistaken! I mean, of *course* you couldn't be doing what I thought you were! This wasn't a real marriage—it wasn't anything! The very idea that you would look at me...think of me...in that way was just absurd! And when I finally accepted that in fact you *did* think of me in those terms—it made me angry. It made me so, so angry. How *dared* you do so! Because to me there could only be one possible reason why you were doing it. It was an exercise in power. That was all. Flexing your sexual ego while you continued merrily with the women who'd made it so clear to me that that was your usual practice.'

A painful breath shook through her.

'But I couldn't cope with that—I knew I couldn't. I knew I couldn't treat sex with you the way those other women did. And I knew—oh, God, I knew—that for you I wouldn't be anything more than any other woman was.'

She shut her eyes again, then opened them determinedly. 'Even when you threw at me that you had never slept with any other woman during our marriage, it just made it *worse*! It threw a whole new hideous light on what you'd done to me. You'd played the arch hypocrite—observing the letter of our marriage, refraining from your usual practice—but then, of course, realising you were facing months of celibacy, you'd decided that you might as well recourse to the one woman with whom you could, by your terms, have sex. Me.'

She shook her head slowly. 'Oh, God, that made me even angrier! To be *used* like that! *Used!* Because it meant it didn't matter who the hell I was—anyone you'd married for the reasons you and my uncle thought necessary—anyone would have done!'

'So it didn't matter. Because the outcome would be the same either way. When our marriage came to its allotted end, that would be the end of what you wanted from me. I would go home, as arranged, and that would be that.'

She pulled the duvet more tightly around her, as if it were to stanch a wound.

'That would be that,' she said again, and her voice was bleak. As bleak as winter wind. Then she forced a smile to her mouth. It was a little twisted, a little wry—and very rueful.

'I didn't handle things very well—did I, Theo? I should have been up-front with you. After all, you'd been up-front with me, that time I came to see you after Aristides had done his Victorian novel stuff on me. You were very up-front about why, in fact, a marriage on the terms we made did make sense—was necessary. So, when I finally realised you were making a move on me, I should have been up-front with you, shouldn't I? Simply told you that, unlike your other women, I couldn't handle an affair—as it would have been, in essence—like the one you wanted. And if you really thought our marriage meant you couldn't or shouldn't continue with other women, then I should have told you that you either had a choice of celibacy or dissolving our marriage earlier than we had intended to. Because I just couldn't handle anything else.'

Her smile twisted painfully. 'So in a way it's all been my fault, hasn't it? My fault for not being up-front with you. My fault for being stupid and weak enough to go along with what you wanted of me, and then, worst of all, to panic the way I did and let you totally misinterpret my relationship with Jem so that I could escape from you and know you wouldn't come after me again.'

Her fingers started to pleat the edge of the duvet.

'I just should have been honest with you all along.' Her eyes rested on his face, as impassive as his eyes, which were just looking at her steadily. He had one arm crooked behind his head. Absently, with a slice of pain that seemed to scrape along every raw nerve in her body, she took in the roughened line of his jaw, the feathered sable of his hair, the complex musculature of his shoulder and lifted arm, the strong column of his throat. She would not be seeing them again. She would not be seeing him again. Everything was sorted now—all the truth told. Now it was time for Theo to go. Anger spent, poison lanced, all the secrets and lies disclosed. They could both now get on with their lives.

She would move to Devon with Jem to help run Pycott, visit her mother and Geoff in the autumn, hopefully even make peace with her uncle. But she would not go to Greece again.

That would be too painful, even now. Especially now.

Now there was only one more secret left—one more lie of omission.

That could never be told. Must never be told.

Because there was no point in telling. It would serve no purpose. None at all. So she would keep silent still, the secret deep within her to the end of her days.

'So why did you sleep with me?'

His voice startled her.

He was looking at her, his expression still impassive. 'You say you didn't want an affair with me, as you termed it, and yet you *did* sleep with me when I met you on the island. I'm curious why.'

There wasn't any feeling in his voice, but it was not emotionless in the way that could chill her like freezing water seeping into her shoes. His voice was simply—curious. Enquiring.

She gave a half-shrug. 'I just gave in, that's all. I mean, Theo, after all, it would hardly have come as surprise to you. I'm sure better women than me have given in. You're pretty hard to resist.'

'You managed pretty well.' His riposte was dry.

His eyes rested on her. They were still impassive. But they were veiled—veiled in a way she had not seen before.

'I'll be honest with you—your reaction surprised me. I'd realised how alien the whole concept of a dynastic marriage was to you, and when I realised that was what Aristides wanted as part of our financial arrangement I was very sceptical that it could ever work with someone who had not been brought up to accept such things as normal. Yet I decided in the end that your phlegmatic English temperament would actually make it possible after all. You were capable of being composed and formal, I had noticed that the few times we were together before our marriage, and so I decided to go along with it. However, even within the temporary terms we'd agreed, it was still clearly something you found it hard to get your brain around. Then there was the whole business of adapting to life in Greece, having not been brought up there. You didn't speak the language well, you were feeling your way into being Mrs Theo Theakis, with a life and lifestyle you weren't used to. So I gave you time—it would have been stupid to do otherwise. Besides, I was so busy at work with Aristides's company, as well as keeping my own affairs in order. Time is always the scarcest resource for me, Vicky. I knew from what had happened to your uncle's business that the danger comes when you take your eye off the ball, and that wasn't going to happen to me. So I know I didn't have a great deal of time for you. But I argued that that was all to the good—it gave you the space you needed to make the adjustments you had to make.'

He shifted his weight slightly, his fingers beneath his head flexing at his neck.

'Besides, though you were half-Greek, your nature was English. That was obvious. Obvious not just in your appearance, but in your taste and behaviour. All those understated clothes you wore! Very elegant, very restrained. Just like the way you conducted yourself. You didn't get emotional, you weren't demonstrative, you never picked up on any of the darts thrown at you by the likes of Christina Poussos. And you never picked up on something else, either.'

For a second so brief she thought she must have imagined it, the veil from his eyes lifted. Then, with a sweep of long lashes, it had come down again.

'I have to tell you, appalled as you may be, that it was always my assumption that our marriage would not be a sham in one respect. You said just now that I would have married anyone who was Aristides Fournatos's niece for the reasons I married you, but that isn't actually true. I would never have married a woman I did not find sexually attractive. It would not have been…kind…to her to do so. But you, obviously, were sexually attractive. It would therefore be perfectly possible to have a non-celibate marriage. However, as I've just said, I knew I needed to allow you time to make the adjustments necessary to being my wife for the duration we'd agreed on. By then, you will appreciate, I had been celibate for longer than was usual for me. So I was…keen…to remedy that situation.'

It wasn't icy water that was seeping into Vicky as she listened. She had seen Theo arctic with fury, had felt his freezing anger strip the skin from her bones.

But this—this was worse. This was Theo being a man of his class, his wealth, his circle, his normality. Deciding it was time to have sex with a woman he'd always intended to have sex with, whom he would not have entered into such a show marriage with on any other basis other than that she was sufficiently sexually attractive to him to warrant it.

He went on speaking. That same light, discursive tone.

'So that is what I set about doing. It was very simple—I merely had to signal to you that the time had come to do what we would both enjoy. I had realised in those initial weeks that I would actually enjoy it more than I had originally assumed. That was because of you, you see. I was finding that your Englishness—all that understated, under-emotional cool—was proving surprisingly alluring. Intriguing. And as I proceeded with "making a move" on you, as you phrase it, it became yet more so. I realised that I was starting to want you really very much. Even if we had not been married, by then I would most definitely have sought an affair with you. Being married to you, in fact, merely added yet another layer of…allure…to you. It presented me with a façade of intimacy, and yet I had not laid a single finger on you. And then, I'm sorry to say, you made the most significant contribution to my condition.'

He looked at her, and somewhere very deep at the back of his eyes she could see something. Something that started, very slowly, to turn her inside out.

'You resisted me. Avoided me. Blanked me. Stonewalled me. Fatal—completely fatal. Were you doing it on purpose? A feminine manoeuvre? I didn't know, and I didn't care. It wasn't relevant anyway. Because there was only one place you were heading for. Only one place I wanted you to be. And I got you there. Of course I did. There was no possibility of anything else. You wanted me as much as I wanted you. So I got you to the island, was there waiting for you, and I took you to my bed.'

There was something strange in his eyes.

'If you had simply stayed there none of this would have happened, you know. We would have done what I had assumed all along we would do. We would have had a mutually enjoyable affair, for the duration of our marriage, and then, when it was no longer necessary for us to be married, we would have parted very amicably and gone our separate ways. That was my intention.'

He stilled. Vicky felt her heart slow. Her fingers clung to the duvet cover as she gazed down at him, half-fearful, half-numb.

'But you didn't stay, did you? You ran. You ran to another man. And in the moments when I looked at those photos of you with him I felt something I had never in my life felt before. Do you know, Vicky, what it was?'

She swallowed. 'Your ego denting.' Her voice was hollow.

He gave a laugh. Harsh and humourless.

'Jealousy. Raw and primitive and leaping in me like a monster. The green-eyed monster, devouring me. I'd never felt it in my life before—why should I have?—and I didn't even realise what it was. I just…possessed it…and it possessed me. Raged through me. It ate me alive from the inside out.'

She could see the cords of his neck standing out, the muscles of his arms tensed like steel.

'Why? *Why* did it do that? What the hell was it, this

jealousy? When Christina was my lover and announced to me that she was marrying I gave her sapphire earrings and my best wishes. When any other lover terminated a relationship before I did, my reaction was the same. The most I felt was irritation if the timing was inconvenient, or if it had been done deliberately to try and get a reaction from me. So where the *hell* did that monster come from when I saw you in those photos?'

She fingered her duvet.

'You're Greek, Theo. It's probably some kind of atavistic response, seeing how I was legally your wife at the time. So it wasn't really jealousy, just a bit more than a dented ego. It was that Greek macho male pride, self-regard, whatever…'

He said a word in Greek. She had a bad feeling she knew what it was, and it was something to do with the male reproductive system of cattle. Or possibly the far end of the bovine digestive system.

Then he spoke again. His voice was different now.

'But there was something else besides the monster eating me alive. Something else that, although it didn't devour me in tearing strips, drained me—quietly, silently, almost unnoticeably—drained me of my lifeblood.'

His right hand, which had been lying inert at his side, lifted. It touched along her knuckles as her fingers clutched the duvet to her. Then he twined his fingers into hers.

'I hurt, Vicky. I hurt so much.'

His voice was quiet.

'I hurt. But it was mortal pain, so I could hardly feel it. Not beneath the monster tearing me to shreds. But it was there all the same, all the time. Invisible, unnoticed, ignored. Until tonight. Until now.'

His fingers tightened on hers. Everything had gone very, very still all around her. Nothing moved. No breath in her lungs. No blood in her veins. All quite, quite still.

He looked up at her. With eyes that were not veiled.

'Why did you run from me that morning on the island? You said you panicked—but why? Why didn't you just turn on me and berate me for what I'd done? Why did you let me tear you to shreds about your adultery? Why did you let me do what I did to you when I made you come back to Greece? You've given me answers, Vicky—but there's one more truth to tell, isn't there? *Isn't there?*'

His grip on her was drawing her down to him. She could not pull back.

'Isn't there, Vicky?' he said again. Insisting—insisting on the truth. *All* the truth. One last secret, one last lie undone.

His hand slid from his neck to hers, holding her with effortless power, so that she could only look down into his face from so, so close.

'I'll answer for you,' he said. His eyes poured into hers. 'You did what I did—and, like me, you never intended to, but it happened all the same. To both of us, Vicky. To *both* of us. And I'm going to say the words to you, so that you can hear them from me and not be afraid—not any more, never again. *S'agape.* I love you. Now say the same, Vicky— say the same. You can do it because I can do it. It's weird and strange and unbelievable—but we must believe it because it is the truth. *S'agape.* Say it, Vicky, *matia mou.* My eyes. My love.'

How hard it was, to say the truth. Even in a whisper.

'*S'agape*, Theo.'

He drew her down to him and kissed her gently. Then he cradled her in his arms and drew the duvet over them both.

'What would you say,' he said, and his breath was warm on her cheek, 'to another wedding?'

She felt love—hers and his—flow between them. A levelling tide that floated them away to the shores of that land they would never leave now, through all that might ever happen, safe in what they had.

She smiled against his mouth.

'I'd say yes,' she said.

EPILOGUE

SUN dazzling on the sea. The scent of thyme, crushed beneath the feet of the wedding guests. The whiteness of the chapel walls against the blue of heaven above.

Vicky stood with Theo, arm in arm in the narrow doorway of the tiny chapel on the hill, on the island, and all around in the clear bright sunlit air was light, pouring down like a blessing on their union.

The guests came forward to embrace them. Her mother and Geoff, hugging her, then her uncle, tears unashamedly in his eyes, and Jem, wrapping her in his bear hug and telling her to avoid the paps in future because he was done with being fool-hardy and rushing off to confront vengeful husbands intent on grievous bodily harm to him.

She laughed, and cried, and laughed and cried again. Her mother was kissing Theo, and Geoff was pumping his hand, and Jem was slapping him on the back, and Aristides was enveloping him in the kind of embrace that no Englishman could ever give another man, then turning to her mother and embracing her even more tightly, telling her thickly that his brother was calling down blessings from heaven on his beautiful daughter. Then he was steering them all down the narrow path to the stonewalled villa, which was nowhere near big enough for the party except on the shady terrace, where the wedding breakfast was spread out for them.

The officiating priest, a personal friend of Aristides, had received his brother's daughter into the Orthodox church for her wedding—her real wedding this time, her real marriage. The bride and groom were seated side by side, while her parents and stepbrother and uncle raised their brimming champagne glasses to toast their happiness and their future.

Then a team of staff emerged from the sleek cruiser moored at the tiny quay, and proceeded to present a meal fit for a Michelin starred restaurant.

It was several hours later, and the sun was westering, before the wedding guests started to make their way along the quay to embark upon Theo's cruiser, which would take them back to the mainland. With many embracings, and yet more tears and laughter, they took their leave, and Vicky and Theo watched them go, their arms wound about each other's waists. A final wave, a final blown kiss, then the engine roared and the cruiser cut its wake through the azure waters, heading away.

They watched till it was out of sight.

Then turned to one another.

'So, Mrs Theo Theakis, what do you propose we do now?' asked Theo.

'We could clear the table,' said Vicky.

'Done already. My staff are well trained.'

'Do the washing up?'

'Also done already.'

'Well, there must be something we should do.'

His eyes glinted.

'There's certainly something *I* should do. This.'

His fingers smoothed the fabric of her wedding gown from one shoulder.

'And this,' he said, and his lips smoothed the skin beneath. 'And similarly…'

He performed the same task to her other shoulder.

'Then, of course, there is this.' His hand went to her back, and with a single fluid movement drew down her zip. 'Why, Mrs Theo Theakis, you do not appear to be wearing underwear…'

'It's the heat,' she murmured.

'Ah, well, that is something we can remedy, I believe.' The glint in his eye, the deliberate not touching of her naked back, was sending tiny delicious sparks through her. 'You may find it, Mrs Theo Theakis, cooler indoors. Shall we?'

He guided her inside the villa, into the single bedroom. With the double bed.

'Much cooler,' she murmured.

'Oh, I think we can do better yet,' he said. The jacket of his wedding suit had long ago been discarded, and still hung around the back of the chair he'd sat in for the breakfast. His cuffs were undone and his shirtsleeves rolled up. His tie hung loose around his neck, the top button of his shirt unfastened. Now he proceeded to unbutton the rest of it.

'Allow me to help,' said his wife. 'Wives should always help their husbands in all those little tasks they like help with.'

One by one her fingers slipped his buttons, drawing the fine material apart, slipping it from his broad shoulders. Then, as he stood stock still, no muscle moving, she unbuckled his belt and started on the fastenings of his trousers.

His hands moved like lightning, imprisoning and lifting.

'Some tasks,' he said, and there was a tightness in his voice she'd have been deaf not to hear, 'may prove a little…precipitate…if helped with. Allow me, instead, to reciprocate.'

He drew her loosened dress from her, exposing first one breast and then the other. They were full, engorged already, their tips like coral. He touched each lightly, felt them flower at his touch. Sensation shot through her.

He let her gown fall to the floor. She left it there. She would tidy it later. But now, right now, it was time for one thing only.

She took his hand and lifted it above her breasts, to her heart.

'Roll back time, Theo. Make the past come back again. But make the present now the past. This the reality. Now. For us both. Now and for ever.'

He turned his hand in hers, and took hers with his, raised it to his lips.

'Now and for ever,' he said.

For one long, timeless moment they gazed into each other's eyes, and all the needless pain and torment were undone.

Then he let go her hand and replaced his own at her breast.

'Now,' he said, 'where were we?'

'You were starting to make sensual, passionate, bliss-inducing love to me on my wedding day,' said Vicky helpfully.

'Ah, yes, so I was. Well, then...' His thumb started to tease her nipple, sending weakness and desire dissolving through her. 'Let's continue, shall we?'

'Yes,' said Vicky faintly, as her body turned boneless, 'let's.'

Bought: the Greek's Bride

LUCY MONROE

Dear Reader,

Have you ever played the 'What if?' game? It's part and parcel of my daily life, but some 'What ifs?' are so intriguing they demand real time at my computer. The story ideas for two books came to me a couple of years ago as I explored the question, *What if there was a set of twins raised apart, who didn't know the other existed?*, but Ellie and Amber did not completely form in my mind until this last year. When they did, I knew the books I was going to pitch to my editor to write. Luckily for me, she found their stories just as compelling as I did.

Ellie is one of my favourite characters yet and her hero, Sandor, is no slouch. Love may not be on his agenda, but losing this amazing woman isn't either. As secrets from the past are revealed and dealt with, you're going to see deeply into hearts that have spent too many years hiding behind a protective shell. I hope you find it as emotional a journey as I did.

Hugs,

Lucy

Look for Amber's story, *Taken: the Spaniard's Virgin*, in *The Spaniard's Pleasure* from Mills & Boon By Request® in August 2007.

Lucy Monroe started reading at age four. After she'd gone through the children's books at home, her mother caught her reading adult novels pilfered from the higher shelves on the book case...alas, it was nine years before she got her hands on a Mills & Boon® romance her older sister had brought home. She loves to create the strong alpha males and independent women that people Mills & Boon® books. When she's not immersed in a romance novel (whether reading or writing it) she enjoys travel with her family, having tea with the neighbours, gardening and visits from her numerous nieces and nephews. Lucy loves to hear from readers: e-mail Lucymonroe@Lucymonroe.com or visit www.Lucy Monroe.com

Lucy Monroe's latest novels, *The Shy Bride* and *The Greek's Pregnant Lover*, were out in May and July from Mills & Boon® Modern™. Look for another new book from Lucy in the autumn.

For my mom and sisters...because there is a love so strong and so unconditional it lights life even during the darkest moments and makes the joyful ones so bright they are incandescent.

That love is the one we share – a sister's and a mother's love is so precious and beautiful and I thank God that He put me in this family to share this deep love with you all.

Always in Christ,

Lucy – daughter and sister.

CHAPTER ONE

HIS BIG, WARM HAND against the small of her back, Ellie allowed Sandor to guide her into the exclusive Boston restaurant. It felt good to walk into the air-conditioning. Boston in the summer was muggy and hot, but the instant cold sent shivers chasing along her arms and made her nipples bead behind the black silk bodice of her dress.

Rather than discomfort, her body reacted with a sensual pleasure that was her constant companion in this man's company.

It had marked their first meeting and had not abated since, leaving her with a need to explore a side to her character that she usually ignored. Her feminine sexuality. She found herself dressing more sexily around him than she ever had in the past and reveling in the small, possessive touches he peppered their dates with.

Tonight, she'd worn a dress by Armani that she loved because it was both elegant and sexy. Its sleeveless design and scooped neck left her arms, a good portion of her chest and her back exposed, but the hem swirled modestly below her knees. The black silk clung to her understated curves and the thin fabric offered no real barrier between his hand

and the sensitive skin of her back. And that single point of contact was enough to send her nerve endings rioting.

She had to concentrate on maintaining a bland façade for him and the other restaurant patrons, but she couldn't help wishing they were someplace private. Someplace she might actually get the nerve up to ask why he'd never pressed for deeper intimacy when his good-night kisses were powered by a wealth of barely leashed passion. Passion she'd decided she wanted to explore.

She recognized several faces as the maître d' led them to their table and wished she didn't. She would like to go out, just once, to a restaurant that was not one of the accepted watering holes for their kind. But Sandor Christofides demanded the best. In everything.

Sometimes, it made her wonder what he was doing with her.

She had been born to the world he had worked so hard to enter, but as far as she could see, that was all she had to offer him. At five foot nine, with small curves, average features, and rather boring dark blond hair, she was not particularly beautiful; she did little to cultivate the contacts others would kill to obtain; she abhorred the standards set by money and frequently refused to uphold them. Her job as an employment counselor for the state was as unglamorous as it got. Her clients wouldn't make it on to the "Who's Who" list of anything, for that matter…neither would she. Not anymore.

Her dad considered her career a complete waste of her Ivy League education, but she didn't care. She considered his overwhelming preoccupation with his business a waste, too. Not that she dismissed his company as unimportant, but she hated the fact that it always had and always would come before her, anyone or anything else.

Interrupting Ellie's thoughts, the maître d' stopped beside the same table they always had when Sandor brought her here. Its placement was an indication of Sandor's importance, something her father would take for granted, but she didn't think Sandor did. His dark brown eyes would glow with satisfaction for a brief moment at small things like this, as if they really mattered to him.

Which was another reason they weren't exactly well suited. Stuff like that just did not impress her. Maybe she was jaded by growing up around it, but she got a lot bigger thrill out of one of her clients getting a job, or a certification necessary to do so, or additional education.

She knew why she said yes to every one of Sandor's invitations. Because she was quite literally enthralled with the man. But she didn't understand why he kept extending them. Especially if he didn't want to sleep with her. He just didn't seem like the celibate type, but that might be her own libido talking.

Sandor seated her though typically the maître d' would have done so. She took it as a mark of his Greekness...or his possessiveness. She wasn't sure which, but for as little as she understood what Sandor saw in her, she knew she would not be the one to end their relationship. Because the little actions like him seating her personally made her feel special.

They also exhibited a side to his nature she found enticing. He didn't bow to the dictates of the world he inhabited, but insisted it take him on his terms. And when she was with him, she felt truly alive for the first time in her twenty-four years.

She couldn't help watching with a hungry intensity she tried to hide as he folded his six-foot-four frame into the chair across from hers. His dark, wavy hair, cut just a little long framed chiseled features she could stare at all night. His superbly muscled frame filled out his dinner jacket in a way few businessmen did.

His hands were well groomed, his nails buffed from a masculine manicure, but they were big and marked with tiny scars from a background very different to hers.

After placing their napkins in their laps, the maître d' left without giving them menus, but Sandor did not remark on it.

He was too busy looking at her, his knowing gaze acknowledging the desire she tried so hard to hide.

His even, white teeth slashed in a smile. "I am not on the menu, *pethi mou*." He paused and his smile turned to a predator's grin. "But I could be."

"Promises, promises…" she boldly teased back even as she felt the blush burning her cheeks.

Her body wasn't feeling any embarrassment, however. It was too busy reacting to his teasing as if to a caress. Unrepentant heat pooled low in her belly while her breasts tingled with the need to be touched. Her already hardened nipples felt like they increased in size, aching for his attention.

She wasn't precisely a virgin, but she'd never responded to anyone the way she responded to him.

He laughed, but didn't deny that he had no real plans to follow through on his taunt. The truth was, though they had been dating for three months, he had never pushed for the ultimate intimacy and he'd ignored her subtle hints in that direction.

She stifled a pang of disappointment and asked, "How did the negotiations go with the department store chain?"

He and her father had combined forces to try to lure one of the biggest worldwide retailers into using their combined shipping companies' resources and Sandor's import/export network.

"It is in the bag."

She loved the way he often talked American slang in his slight Greek accent. Unlike others of different nationalities that she'd met through her father, Sandor did not speak with the flawless accent of an Englishman, trained by exacting teachers. He'd told her he'd learned most of his English after coming to live in the United States when he was a child. His mother still spoke with a heavy accent that required a lot of concentration to understand sometimes. Luckily it was something Ellie was good at.

"I'm glad and I'm sure Dad is pleased."

"Yes, but we are not here tonight to discuss business."

"We aren't?"

"You know we are not."

She laughed softly. "I won't argue. I know more about my father's business since we started dating than I ever knew before and everything I do know, I've learned from you. I'm not exactly the best choice for a partner in that kind of discussion."

"But I think you are the ideal partner for other things."

Was he teasing her again…about the sex thing that she was fairly certain he had no plans to act on? Or did he mean something else? She looked at him in confusion, but though the corner of his mouth tilted enigmatically, he said nothing.

The waiter arrived at their table and poured them each a glass of Sandor's favorite wine. She liked it, too, and had never balked at his standing order for this particular predinner drink. But she was surprised when he confirmed their food order without asking her preference. He had never done that before. But then, both he and the waiter acted as if he'd ordered before even arriving at the restaurant.

That impression was further enforced when the waiter returned to their table seconds later with appetizers.

She sniffed appreciatively at the garlic baked shrimp dripping with melted butter and topped with a grated medley of three cheeses. "My favorite."

"I know." He put a piece of shrimp on a slice of baguette, carefully drizzling the garlicy butter over it and making sure there was just the right amount of melted cheese on top before handing it to her. "I know you very well, Eleanor."

"Do you?"

"After three months, do you doubt it?"

"That depends on what you mean. I think you do know a lot *about* me, but I am not sure you know *me*." Her dad would have known to order this appetizer, too, but that didn't mean he knew what made her tick. As far as she could tell, Ellie's dad had no desire to know her on any level but the surface.

She couldn't stifle the hope that Sandor would be different.

"Is there a distinction between the two?"

"Yes."

"If tonight goes as I plan, I will have a great deal of time to learn what *you* mean."

"And how do you plan for tonight to go?" Was he finally going to make love to her? Was she ready for it?

She almost laughed aloud at her inner voice. Ready? She was desperate for him. She'd already decided she wanted him, but the possibility of actually having him was throwing her into mental chaos. Which was silly. She wanted this man and while she had no intention of telling him that at this very moment, she would not lie to herself and pretend differently. She refused to indulge in those kinds of games.

"Allow me to reveal my plans in sequence."

She should have guessed he had an agenda of some sort. It was so like him. It was one of the more disconcerting ways he reminded her of her father. She didn't dislike it exactly, but it worried her a little. Were his agendas as coldly determined as her father's?

"By all means, I wouldn't think of attempting to divert your schedule."

He took a sip of wine, his dark eyes filled with mock menace. "Are you laughing at me?"

"Maybe, a little. Spontaneity is not your thing."

"You know me well."

"As well as can be expected after dating three months."

"Well enough." There was meaning behind his words, but she wasn't sure what it was.

"Aren't you going to have any of the shrimp?" she asked.

"I suppose, but the real pleasure comes from watching you eat them."

She had just taken a bite and her eyes closed in bliss. *Divine*. "To each their own."

He laughed. "I assure you, I am very happy with my own appetizer."

They were sharing the shrimp and he wasn't eating any, so it took her a second to understand his meaning. When she did, her eyes flew open. He was looking at her with a distinctly predatory light in eyes that had grown dangerously dark.

She took a deep breath, trying to calm the rapid pulse that was making her light-headed. Oh, my. When this man went for it, he held nothing back. She could not wait for later. Tonight, he would not leave her with a good-night kiss that made her toes curl and her body feel hollow with wanting. Not with that look in his eyes.

The appetizer was followed by butternut squash soup. She'd never had it at this particular restaurant before. "The chef must be trying something new."

"At my request."

"You *did* preorder the meal."

"Yes."

"Why?"

"Tonight is special, I want every aspect to be right."

"Special?"

"Yes."

"I like the sound of that." She smiled and took a bite of the soup he'd had one of the most temperamental chefs in Boston make just for her. "It's delicious."

"I would expect no less."

"I'm surprised you talked the chef into trying something new for your benefit alone."

"Money speaks most languages."

"Even that of a temperamental chef?"

"As you see." He indicated their twin bowls of the golden-orange soup. "But he did not make the soup for *my* benefit."

"No?"

"No. He made it for yours."

"At your request."

"Yes."

"Because tonight is special."

"Very."

She didn't know what else she would have said because at that moment, two things happened that derailed any thoughts of talking on her part. The first was that a trio of violinists took up residence in a spot near them that had on the last occasion they'd eaten there held a table of other diners. The musicians began to play a piece she had always found emotionally evocative and soothing at the same time.

The second occurrence was that she was presented with two dozen long-stemmed red roses by the maître d'. She took them and inhaled the scent of the perfect blooms. The heady fragrance bathed her senses.

She looked at Sandor. "They're beautiful."

"You are so certain they are from me?"

She laughed, her voice surprisingly husky. "Of course."

But she picked up the card to read anyway. It was small and white and read, "Sandor." Nothing else. He'd signed it himself, however. She recognized the black slashing writing.

"Thank you," she said, her face still buried in the roses. For some reason, she needed to hide there for a moment.

This was definitely more romance than she'd expected from him for the advent of the physical side of their relationship and it made her wonder if he had feelings for her she had not detected. The prospect sent a swarm of butterflies fluttering through her insides.

"It is my pleasure."

The maître d' took the flowers, returning moments later with them in a gorgeous crystal vase that he set at the side of their table.

She snuck peeks at them throughout the soup course, her mind spinning with what all this meant. Hope swirling through her along with a desire she gave herself permission to feel fully. Tonight, she would not go to sleep wishing for the moon, or Sandor's caresses. She was sure of it.

But when the main course was cleared—again a dish he

knew she enjoyed—a small black ring box appeared on the table and her breath ran out.

She stared at it. That couldn't be what she thought it was. The roses...the violinists... Suddenly her mind snapped with shattering clarity to a conclusion she had not even considered. The romance had been prelude to a proposal?

She couldn't believe it and yet, no other reason for the ring box could penetrate her racing mind. A man did not give a woman a ring simply to embark on an affair.

He reached across the table and took her hand. Feeling strangely numb, she could feel him looking at her and willing her to meet his gaze. She forced herself to do so, her eyes moving up the strong chin with its adorable cleft, past the long straight nose to a gaze as penetrating as a laser beam.

"Eleanor Wentworth, will you do me the great honor of becoming my wife?"

Even expecting the question, her usual aplomb deserted her and she gasped and stared, her mouth opening, but no sound emerging. He'd asked her to marry him, but she had no idea how he felt about her. If he loved her, wouldn't he have said it? Wouldn't she have sensed it?

He cocked his head to one side, one brow rising in an obvious prompt for a response.

"I don't know," she blurted out past a constriction of emotion in her throat.

The words sounded unnaturally loud to her ears. She couldn't believe she'd said it...like that. And from the look on his face, he couldn't, either. He had been expecting a very different response.

"Come, you must have been expecting this."

"Um...no, I wasn't. Honestly." She bit her lip, thinking

maybe she'd been naïve, but it had never occurred to her that a man as dynamic and sensual as he was would ask a woman to marry him that he had never slept with. "This has come as a complete surprise."

And she sounded more gauche than she ever had in her life. She'd been handling difficult social situations with grace since deportment classes when she was a mere six years old, but she'd never been proposed to…by a man she wanted, but was not at all sure wanted her. She hoped, had an inkling he might…but no certainty.

"An *unpleasant* surprise?" He didn't sound in the least vulnerable when asking that question. Not like she would have. Instead he sounded demanding, as if he wanted answers and he wanted them *now*.

"Not unpleasant." She shook her head, trying to clear it. "Just *very* unexpected."

"We have been dating for three months."

"Yes." They had already established that.

"Exclusively?"

"Yes…I mean I assumed…"

"For me, it has been exclusive."

Something inside her that she had not even realized had gone tense, relaxed a little. "For me, too."

"Where did you think this relationship of ours was going, if not marriage?"

"I thought maybe first…to bed," she answered honestly. Did they even have a relationship?

Casual dating yes…but a *relationship?*

He cursed in Greek. She recognized the word from a summer she had spent studying ancient civilizations in his former homeland. It was a very nasty curse. "I don't believe you just said that."

That caught her up short. "Why?" To her, it was a perfectly natural conclusion to make.

"It is unlike you."

"Perhaps you don't know me as well as you think you do." It might not be considered appropriate to discuss such matters in a public place, but she didn't give as much credence to proper behavior as everyone seemed to think she did. Or as her father thought she should.

Honesty was far more important to her.

And the fact was, he clearly did *not* know her all that well if he was shocked she'd had the temerity to mention sex. Marriage to a man who was that ignorant of her inner person was not a wholly appealing proposition. If it had not been *him* doing the proposing, it would hold no appeal at all.

"I do know you," he insisted.

Exasperated, she shook her head. "Not *that* way."

"I know enough to be certain of our compatibility."

"Because we've shared a few kisses?"

"We have shared more than kisses." His now molten gaze reminded her just how much more.

But as far as they'd gone, he always pulled back. Except once. The first time they'd kissed, it had almost gotten out of hand very quickly. Frightened by a wealth of emotion she wasn't used to experiencing, she'd pulled back. Since then, he had done more than kiss her, but he'd never let the passion flare so hot and he'd certainly never made love to her completely.

"Yes, we have, but it's the very fact that we've shared *just so much* that makes me wonder if we are as compatible in that way as you seem to think."

"Why should you wonder this? It is obvious that you want me." His Greek accent got thicker when he was upset.

She'd noticed that during a heated business phone call she'd overheard once, but it had never happened between them before.

She couldn't feel badly that it was happening now. She was glad to know she could make him angry. She needed the assurance that she could impact his emotions because he certainly impacted hers. Though she would much prefer evidence of another sort of emotion and she didn't appreciate his sentiment at all.

"Yes," she said between gritted teeth, "I do want you, but I'm not so sure you want me. And I'm not going to spend my life married to a man who is going to look for his passion outside of our marriage bed."

"Who said I would do this?" he demanded, his voice guttural and so thick with accent she had to concentrate to understand the words.

"Who said you wouldn't?"

"I say."

"I want to believe you, but—"

"There is no but. My honor is not in question here."

"I wasn't talking about your honor. I was talking about making love."

"You brought up the possibility I would violate the bonds of our marriage…that is a matter of personal honor and one I do not take lightly."

She was glad to hear that, but it didn't answer the real problem gnawing at her. He was business associates with her father, how much did that have to do with this marriage proposal? She simply couldn't convince herself that Sandor was suffering from shyness in admitting undying love. The man was far too confident…if he felt something for her, he would have said so. Yet, how did a woman ask if the man proposing was doing so as part of a business arrangement or if he wanted her personally? The blunt approach would probably be best.

Sandor wasn't the type to respond well to subtlety.

"Do you want me…I mean for my own sake, not simply because I'm my father's daughter?"

He frowned. "I would think that is obvious."

Maybe it was. To him. But it wasn't to her. When he kissed her, he made no effort to hide the barely leashed passion coursing through him, but he never acted on it. It confused the heck out of her.

"If it was obvious, I wouldn't be asking."

"I do want you." His voice dropped an octave, to a sexual purr. "Very much."

She licked her lips. "That's…that's good."

"But for me, the commitment comes first…then we make love."

She doubted he was a virgin, but apparently he ascribed to the standard some men still maintained about the women they intended to marry. "You've got some very old-fashioned views."

"Yes. I am not ashamed this is so. I was born in a traditional Greek village. My grandfather's beliefs may not find wholesale acceptance in me, but his influence is there."

"Sandor," she said, latching onto a topic less volatile to her emotions. "You never talk about your past. I don't know if your dad is dead, if your parents are divorced or why it is that you never mention your father, but your grandfather pops up in conversation on occasion. I know he's gone…at least I know that much," she muttered under her breath, "but I don't know why you and your mother live here in America. I don't know so much about you."

"Chief being the way I screw."

"*Sandor*," she hissed while her entire body blushed.

He glared. "I can be crude. Yes. It comes from the background you know so little about. But another thing comes from that past…the belief that a man does not take a virgin to his bed unless he is engaged to, but preferably married to her."

"Is that something your grandfather taught you?"

"He drilled it into me every day of my life while he lived. Only a man totally lacking in honor would do so."

"I see." She had a feeling there was a lot more to this topic she planned to explore, but first she was going to set the record straight on something else. "However, between us…the point is moot because I'm not a virgin."

"Of course you are."

CHAPTER TWO

"AND WHAT HAS made you draw this brilliant conclusion?" she demanded in a tone her dad would have recognized with trepidation.

Ellie didn't get mad easily, but once she was angry…she didn't back down.

"Look at the way you blush when we discuss sex."

"Married women blush. If that's your full supporting argument, you need to hone your deductive reasoning skills."

His eyes narrowed. "Do not play games with me about this. I know what I know."

"What you think you know."

"Stop this foolish claim. I am sorry if my observation has piqued your feminine pride, but I will never allow you to lie to me."

"Have issues with honesty do you?"

"Yes."

"That's surprising. Most businessmen at your level can be very inventive with the truth."

"But I will not tolerate untruth from those in my personal life. Ever."

"And will you give the same level of integrity to a relationship?"

"Count on it."

"In that case, let me repeat…I am not a virgin."

His jaw tautened and white lines appeared at the corners of his mouth. He was getting seriously upset by her adamant claim to sexual experience. "You have never had a serious relationship."

"Is that what my father told you?"

He didn't even look uncomfortable at being accused of talking about her in very private terms with her father. "Yes."

"Well, he obviously doesn't know everything about me, which should hardly come as a surprise." He had to have seen ample evidence during the time they'd been dating how far from close she was with George Wentworth.

"He has reason to know certain things."

"You mean the bodyguards I supposedly no longer have?"

Sandor managed to look slightly chagrined. "You know about the security service?"

"Of course." She rolled her eyes. "Please. Just because I told my dad I didn't want a bodyguard any longer doesn't mean he listened to me, but at least with them as silent and *distant* watchers, I have a little more privacy than I did when my bodyguards remained within touching distance."

"Not *that* much privacy."

He meant not enough for her father not to know if she had a man stay the night or had done so with one. "I don't have to sleep over with a man to have sex with one."

"But you would have to have had a relationship that went beyond a few casual dates because you are not the type of woman to sleep with a man on a whim."

"You're so sure about that?"

"Yes."

She couldn't deny it because he was right. And she did

not lie. Like him, she hated lies. Like the lie when a person told you they loved you but didn't. Not really.

"So…I have had more than one relationship that lasted a few months. I'm twenty-four years old, after all."

"But none of those relationships were deep."

"How do you know? My father said so," she guessed. "You can't trust the judgment of a man who thinks that balance sheets are more comprehensible than people. He doesn't *know* me."

"Like I do not know you?"

"I'm afraid so, yes."

Sandor shook his head with an impatient jerk. "You are wrong."

But she wasn't. Sandor did not know her any better than her father did, which meant he couldn't care for her any more deeply than her dad. While the knowledge hurt, it also really begged the question why Sandor wanted to marry her.

He was looking at her as if he expected another argument, but she didn't have to convince Sandor of her point of view. In this instance, it was her opinion that mattered and his confident insistence wasn't going to change it.

"I am not relying on his word alone," Sandor said. "I had you investigated." His expression showed not even a hint of remorse at the claim.

"What? *Why?*"

"When I first started considering you as a potential wife, I thought it prudent."

"You are kidding."

"No."

"I would have thought you too arrogant to believe you needed anything besides your own reading of a person in a situation like this."

"You have called me arrogant before."

"Have I?"

"Yes, the time I told you who would win the Super Bowl."

"You were so sure you were right and you aren't even a football fan."

He shrugged. "And yet I *was* right."

"Well, you're wrong about me being a virgin." And as much as the memories of the reason for her lack of innocence hurt, she felt a certain grim satisfaction in catching him in the wrong.

Maybe she should be offended he'd had her investigated, but she wasn't. She was, however, bothered. If Sandor wanted a relationship with her, why hadn't he made the effort to get to know her better rather than having her investigated? Maybe it wouldn't be so worrisome if he'd done it in addition to the investigation, but he hadn't.

The similarities to her dad were piling up and not in a good way. She'd been raised by a man who would have done the exact same thing in such a situation, who even now kept her under constant surveillance—ostensibly for her safety's sake. After all, she was the daughter of a very wealthy and influential man. However, he wasn't above using that so-called security to monitor more than her safety. She didn't know what her father thought his knowledge was going to do for him.

If he wanted a better relationship with her, he wasn't going to have it via a silent security detail. Only maybe that was just the way he liked it. He felt like he was doing his fatherly duty without getting emotionally involved.

"My investigator is very thorough," Sandor said, breaking into her derailed thoughts.

"Even the best investigators make mistakes."

"Perhaps." But she could tell he didn't believe her.

Instead of annoying her, it made her laugh. "We could go back to my apartment and I could prove it to you."

He looked far from amused. His dark eyes glinted with a warning she had no intention of heeding. "Are you trying to shock me, *pethi mou*?"

"Challenging you, I think." Recklessness filled her to bursting.

She didn't know if it came from the unexpected proposal that had mentioned not one word of love, from memories she'd prefer to forget, or from the renewed evidence that her father wanted no emotional connection to her, but the strictures of a lifetime were falling like dominos around her.

No, she wasn't the type of woman to view sex casually, but she wasn't a virgin and she was darned if she would marry a man who could turn himself off from her so easily. She didn't want Sandor to be like her father. She couldn't stand for their relationship to be as cold and distant.

"Why do you feel the need to challenge me?" he asked, sounding baffled.

It was almost cute, in an arrogant, macho reaction to what should have been a straightforward topic kind of way.

"Why don't you want me enough to have seduced me?" Or even accepted her sometimes not too subtle invitations?

"I told you."

"You believe I'm a virgin, so that puts me off-limits until the wedding night."

"Essentially…yes. Perhaps not until the wedding night, but definitely until the wedding is a date on the calendar."

"This is not the Dark Ages."

"Integrity has no time limit."

"Is that one of your grandfather's sayings?"

For a second his eyes burned with a pain that could not be mistaken. "As a matter of fact, yes."

"I don't understand why you want to marry me. You don't love me."

"And your friends have all married for the sake of some ephemeral emotion that cannot even be counted on to last past the cooling of the sheets in most cases?"

"No." She wouldn't pretend that all her acquaintances had married because they were in love. "But they aren't me and I happen to believe in that *ephemeral emotion*. I want more from marriage than a businesslike merging of two people's lives." She wanted more from life than that, period…but had no idea how to get it.

Other people found love so easily, but not her. But that didn't mean she had given up hoping to find it.

"And you will have more. We are compatible, in every way. We will have a family. You even enjoy my mother's company."

"She's easy to like, but you say that like it's a major consideration."

"Since I choose to have my mother live near me like a good Greek son, it is."

"I wouldn't mind living with your mother, but I'm not so sure about her son."

"So, you *are* considering my proposal?"

Was she? Her heart beat too fast, the pain of uncertainty squeezing her chest tight. She *was*. No matter what he believed about love, she was afraid she was already irrevocably in love with him—or headed there fast. What a hopelessly terrifying thought. "Yes, but I can't give you an answer right now."

"Surely you were expecting this."

"Funnily enough…I wasn't. I told you that."

He sighed. "Yes, but I would have thought you would have at least considered the possibility."

She just shrugged, not knowing what to say. They'd already been over the whole sex thing and their views were polar opposites. She'd been sure he wasn't ready for a deeper relationship because he hadn't pursued that angle and he'd assumed she'd realize he wouldn't pursue it until she was committed to him.

"And you cannot make the decision now, knowing what you know of me, of yourself?"

"No." Because if she did, it would have to be *no*. And her heart both demanded and rejected that answer.

"Is it my background?"

She stared at him. "I don't know enough of your background for it even to be a consideration and I hope you aren't implying I'm some sort of snob who would only marry someone born to the same world of privilege I was."

"I am not saying that, no. In fact, your refreshing refusal to judge others based on where they come from appeals to me greatly."

"I'm glad, because I don't want to change that part of me."

"But you are willing to change in other ways?"

"People grow…change is inevitable, but that's with me to stay."

"I am glad."

"But you are annoyed I won't accept your proposal right now."

"Not annoyed…disappointed. I would think you could see the advantages to a marriage between us."

He was disappointed, but not hurt. Which meant his emotions were not involved at all. That did not bode well.

She bit her lip, realizing she must have done so before because it felt tender. It was a bad habit, but she had enough to think about without trying to break it at the moment.

"I'm sorry. I'm not like you and my father. I don't make personal decisions based on business logic."

"What do you base them on?"

"Emotion."

His lips twisted with distaste just as she knew they would. He and her father had a lot in common. Maybe too much. She suspected he would be no more impressed with an emotional commitment from her than her father was.

She took a fortifying sip of water. "I know. That's a dirty word to you and men like my father, but it's how I live my life. You'll have to give me some time to think."

Silence pulsed between them until he pushed the ring box across the table. "Put it in your bag. We'll discuss the proposal again later."

She wasn't sure why he wanted her to take possession of the ring. Maybe he thought that since possession was nine-tenth's of the law, if she took the ring, she might have a harder time saying no and giving it back. The man was wily enough to have considered every angle.

"Please keep it until I give you my answer."

"I'd rather you kept it."

"Even if I say no?"

"I had the ring made for you. Whatever your answer, it is meant to be yours."

Unable to hold back from looking after such a statement, she opened the box. It was a square-cut precious stone exactly the color of her eyes. Aquamarine-blue. To either side was a perfectly cut square diamond of crystal clarity, only slightly smaller than the center stone.

Emotion that had no place in their discussion welled inside her and she husked, "It's beautiful."

"Like you."

She shook her head, dislodging the empty words. "I'm hardly that."

"After all we have said about honesty tonight, you think I lie about this?"

"I think you want to flatter me, but I have a mirror. I'm passable, but I am not beautiful. You should see pictures of my mother. She was beautiful." And she'd taken what existed of George Wentworth's heart to the grave with her.

"You know the saying, beauty is in the eye of the beholder."

She barely kept from rolling her eyes. "Yes."

"You are beautiful to me, Eleanor."

"False flattery isn't going to get me to agree to marry you."

"It is not false." His voice was a low rumbling growl. She'd managed to make him mad again.

"If you say so."

"I say so. Your beauty is timeless and very alluring to a man with my background."

"I don't understand." What did his background have to do with it?

"You are kind. Truly compassionate. You seek to make life better for those born without your advantages. Your care for others is ingrained to the depths of your soul. In that, you remind me much of my mother. Physically you are perfect to me. Your features are soft and feminine, your body a delight to my senses, but particularly that of sight. Yet, as much as you spark my desire, you are elegant and refined, even in jeans and a T-shirt. These things are beautiful to me."

She didn't know what to say. She could tell he meant

the words and that did something to her insides, tipping over a heart that had teetered on the precipice of love straight into its warm, sweet depths. Because as much as she'd learned he did not know about her, he had just proven he did know something about the woman she was under the skin and behind the image of a wealthy man's daughter.

"Private schooling and deportment training can do wonders," she said, trying to laugh it off while her heart contracted and expanded with her newly acknowledged feelings until she was dizzy with it.

"You were born with these traits, they are not something a person can learn."

She didn't agree. "You learned."

"I am far from compassionate and kind."

She'd seen the way he treated his mother. "I don't agree, but that's not what I'm talking about."

"What then?"

"How to fit the society we move in." She indicated the rest of the restaurant with a wave of her hand.

"But I do not fit."

"You do."

And yet, in a way he was right. He wore his suit, which was by a top designer and handmade, like he'd been born to it, but there was an aura of power around him that came from hard work and determination, not being born to wealth. His slight Greek accent. His direct way of speaking. They all spoke of a man not born to their world, but made.

But then she didn't fit her world perfectly, either. All her little idiosyncrasies stemmed from the inside and only showed themselves on close inspection. In that they were alike.

"Tell me about your childhood."

His eyes widened. "Why?"

"I want to know."

His jaw hardened. "And if I do not want to tell you?"

"I'll have you investigated." She grinned at his shocked expression.

And then he laughed and she fell just a little harder as she laughed with him.

"I was born in Greece."

"I knew that," she teased.

"We lived there, with my grandfather, until I was ten."

"We?"

"My mother, she was his only child, and I."

"Where was your father?"

"Gone."

A day ago, she would have respected the boundaries she sensed he'd erected, but a day ago, he had not asked her to marry him. "What do you mean, gone?"

"He was an American tourist. On the island for only a couple of days. By the time my mother realized she was pregnant, he was long gone. She did not even know his last name." Sandor did not sound condemning...of his mother at least.

"That must have been very difficult for her."

"Yes. But it could have been worse. My grandfather did not kick her out of the family home despite the shame her condition brought him. He supported her and me in the years that followed."

At what cost though? Definitely Sandor had not come out of that home unscathed.

"What about your grandmother?"

"She had died the year before. Grandfather often said that it was a lucky thing, for the shame would have killed her."

"He sounds like he was a harsh man."

"He was. In some ways. But he loved my mother and he took care of her even though what had happened went against his entire belief system."

"She was young." Hera Christofides had to have been a teenager when she had Sandor because she barely looked forty now. She had to be older than that, but Ellie was guessing it wasn't by much.

"She was sixteen. Grandfather forgave her, but he never forgave the man who made her pregnant."

"The *only a man without honor would take the virginity of a woman he's not married to,* thing?"

"Yes. And that man's blood runs in my veins."

She wondered if that was something else his grandfather had maintained, but she didn't ask. She merely said, "You can't know he wouldn't have stood by her, if he'd known about you, I mean."

"He knew she was a virgin, but he left her. He never returned to check on her. He did not care."

"Maybe. He probably wasn't much older than she was. There might have been reasons for why he didn't come back."

"Yes. Those reasons were that he *was* an irresponsible teenager himself who should have kept his pants zipped if he wasn't prepared to deal with the aftermath."

"Like you said, he was a teenager. It probably never occurred to him that there even was an aftermath."

"Ignorance does not change the outcome."

"No, it doesn't, but I have a hard time believing that any man who fathered you could have been totally without a sense of responsibility."

"I get my sense in that direction from my grandfather and mother."

"You can't know you got nothing from your father... since you didn't know him." She didn't know why she argued, only that is seemed important to make him realize life was not as black and white as his grandfather had obviously taught him it was.

"What is this about? Are you worried bad blood will tell?"

She sighed. "I hate that saying. It's just so wrong. Even if he was an all out jerk without a bit of good in him, that has no bearing on who you are today."

"Not everyone sees things that way."

"I know, but I'm the one who is right."

"And perhaps I am not the only arrogant one at this dinner table."

"Knowing when I am right is not arrogance," she teased.

"I will have to remember that defense."

"You do that, but somehow I don't think it's a new concept for you."

He just smiled.

"For the record, I for one am glad your dad didn't keep his pants zipped and I bet your mom doesn't regret it, either."

The smile disappeared and his expression looked hewn from granite. "Why would you say such a thing?"

"Because, if he had, *you* wouldn't be here."

"And you think that is a good thing?"

"Yes, and I'm sure your mom agrees."

"But you hesitate to marry me."

The man was tenacious. "My reasons have nothing to do with you not being a pretty amazing person I'm glad is alive."

He raised his brows at that. "Then what are your reasons?"

"More to the point, what are yours?"

CHAPTER THREE

"I HAVE EXPLAINED...I find you beautiful inside and out. I am ready to marry and have a family. I want to do that with you." Sandor knew instinctively that if he mentioned the business deal with her father, it would make Eleanor balk.

It was not the overriding reason for him choosing her to be his wife, but it had played a role. That did not bother him, but he suspected she would react very differently to that knowledge. As she had said, she did not make her decisions based on the same considerations that swayed men like him and her father.

She wanted an emotional reason for marrying him. She wanted to be loved. He had gleaned that much, but that was not something he could give her. It was not something he wanted to give her. Love was an overrated emotion he preferred to steer clear of. He had loved his grandfather and he loved his mother, and that love had come with a price. He had paid in vulnerability when nothing else and no one else got to him.

His mother's unhappiness hurt when he let nothing else touch him. His grandfather's disapproval left wounds he swore no one else would ever get the chance to emulate. He would have to convince Eleanor there was enough going for them without the love he wanted no part of.

"My mother said she fell in love with my father at first sight." He didn't know why he'd mentioned that, but it supported the argument he was about to make, so he did not regret it. "The emotion you think such a panacea for pain is in fact one of the biggest instigators of it that I know. Her love led her into his bed. My grandfather's love kept her with him even though he could never overlook her indiscretion completely. His love for me drove him to push me harder, to demand more of me than he would have his own son. He would not allow me to become like the man who had sired me. Irresponsible and without honor. But his lessons were often painful and I knew they were born of love."

"Love does not always lead to pain."

"Yes, it does, and I do not want the pain that is inevitably born of love in my marriage."

She gasped and he grimaced. He had said more than he intended, but if it helped to convince her, he would not begrudge her the truth.

"What *do* you want?" Her sea-blue eyes were filled with a softness that called to something deep in his soul.

It had from the first moment he'd seen her across a crowded charity ball. She'd been with her father and Sandor had been instantly intrigued by this woman who was so clearly of the world he wanted to conquer, but not like it.

"I want children, a legacy—a legitimate legacy, to inherit what I have built, to build onto it. I want to please the woman who sacrificed so much to give me life and keep me with her. Even in Greece thirty years ago, a woman could find ways to end an unwanted pregnancy, but she never even considered it."

"How do you know?"

"I asked."

The compassion he liked so much sparked in Eleanor's eyes. She was exactly the kind of woman he wanted to spend the rest of his life with. A woman who could help to calm the demons that raged in his soul.

"Your mom wants you to marry?"

"You know she does."

Eleanor smiled. "Well, she's not very subtle...but I figured she hinted that way to all your dates."

"Actually, no."

"You mean I'm special?" she asked facetiously.

"Yes. She has hinted at me enough, but never to one of the women I dated. Until you."

"She wants grandchildren. A lot."

"Yes. What about you?"

"I'm too young to be a grandmother."

That was one of the things he really enjoyed about his little Eleanor. She teased him. She made him smile and she was always ready to do so herself.

"I meant do you want children?" He did not doubt her answer, she was too perfectly suited to motherhood not to want to be one, but he wanted to hear her say it.

"Yes. Very much."

"I thought as much."

It was her turn to grimace. "You think you know everything."

"Apparently I do not. I thought you would accept my proposal without a lot of fuss."

"Fuss?" she asked delicately and suddenly he knew he was treading on very shaky ground.

"I did not think it would be a difficult decision for you to make," he amended.

"It would have been easier if you had said you loved me."

He could only respect her courage and her honesty. "Do you want me to say it?"

"A lie of expediency designed to get you the outcome you want? What of your insistence on truth from me? I told you I won't accept any less."

Yet, he had a sneaking suspicion that they defined honesty differently. He dismissed the niggling worry and said, "I will give all the loyalty and dedication to your happiness a man who professes such feelings would do. There would be no lie in my saying the words if you need them to feel more comfortable about our marriage."

"Except that you don't feel the emotion and neither do you want to feel it. They'd still be a lie, Sandor."

"But the intent behind them, my dedication to your well-being, is not a lie."

"I understand that we see things very differently. Not only do you not want love, but I'm not sure you believe in romantic love at all or you could not blithely talk about saying the words as if that's all they were. Mere words."

"Romantic love is not something I have any personal experience with."

Pain flashed in her pretty blue eyes, but was gone so quickly, he could not be sure he had seen it.

"Will it help if I promise I will never say those words to another woman?"

"Can you promise that? What if you fall in love? Just

because you don't love me doesn't mean you are incapable of loving someone else."

"I do not want to love anyone else."

"It doesn't always come with a choice."

He did not agree. "I keep my promises. It is up to you to decide if you trust me to do so."

"I do trust you."

A flare of triumph coursed through him.

She saw it and frowned. "I'm not saying I'm going to agree to marriage, but I think I'm beginning to understand why you asked me at least."

"I would have thought that was obvious."

"There you go being wrong again. This can't be good for your ego, but your reasons for picking me to share the rest of your life with are far from obvious."

"You will tease me one time too many," he warned on a mock growl.

"And you'll do what?"

"Perhaps I will make love to you and slay that dragon of doubt at least."

"Do you think a planned seduction will decimate my concerns about the fact that you find it so easy to control your libido around me?"

"I think, little one, that there are depths to you that I have yet to plumb." It startled him to have her take him to task for such a thing, but it also aroused him. "Trust me, I do not find it easy to control my desire around you, merely necessary."

"Because you don't want to be like your father."

"That is one reason."

"Tell me another."

"If you do not want to marry me, I do not want to spend my life addicted to a body I have no access to."

She burst out laughing as he'd meant her to, but there was a grain of truth to what he said. If he made love to her, he did not think he would ever want to let her go.

On the other hand, making love might be the very solution to their impasse. He would prove his passion to her and regardless of what she wanted him to believe, he knew she would only accept him into her body if she was making a major commitment to him.

He had already made his commitment to her and while he'd rather they were officially engaged with a wedding date set before he took her to bed, he had no doubts about the ultimate outcome. He was not taking advantage of her. They would marry. He was not a man who allowed anyone or anything to thwart him when it came to getting something he wanted.

And he wanted Eleanor Wentworth as his wife.

When they arrived at Ellie's apartment, Sandor requested her key card to park in the visitor's area of the secure garage under her building.

"Are you planning to come up for a while?" she asked as he pulled into a parking slot.

He waited until she looked at him to ask, "Are you planning to invite me?"

She usually did, but tonight she'd hoped to have some time to think.

He reached out and cupped her nape. "Invite me up, *pethi mou*. I am not ready for the evening to be over."

Just as it did every other time, his slightest touch impacted her senses with the power of a Level 10 earthquake.

"Even though it didn't have the outcome you wanted?"

she asked breathlessly, knowing she would not turn him away if he was intent on staying.

"You did not refuse me. It is enough."

"Is it?"

"I learned early to be patient when going after something I wanted. Rushing the outcome can sour it faster than facing opposition."

Why did the unabashed business-speak liquify her insides? She shouldn't be reacting to corporatese as if he'd said something intoxicatingly alluring, but the problem was that he'd said it in that low, sexy voice that had been shaking up her equilibrium since the first time she heard it. And, in effect, his sentiment *was* sensual. He was talking about convincing her to marry him, which *would* land her in his bed. Even if unbridled passion had not.

"I see. So, I'm a corporate merger you'd like to make?" she asked, trying to keep it light…trying to temper her own reaction to what shouldn't be nearly so much temptation.

"You are the woman I would like to marry, not a company I plan to buy—but the similarities exist, yes."

She couldn't help smiling wryly. Of course he would see most of his life in business terms. It was all he knew, that and the lessons on integrity he'd learned at his grandfather's knee. She shivered when she thought what it must have been like to be raised by a man who loved him, but not enough to see past his illegitimate birth. A man intent on making sure that what he considered *bad blood* would not show itself in his grandson.

If the older Christofides were alive today, Ellie would have a few choice words for him. But then if he were alive, Hera probably would never have left Greece and taken her son with her. Ellie and Sandor would never have met.

Coming on the heels of her inner revelation regarding her feelings for him, the thought chilled her.

"Come up," she said on a defeated sigh.

Sandor had not conquered her desire to be alone and think; her own conflicting needs undermined it. She wanted to spend time with him. She craved his presence like a drug and was just glad he wasn't one. She'd always thought she had a strong sense of self-control, but when it came to Sandor, she lost touch with it and her sense of self-preservation as well.

Which was one very good reason for not giving him an answer to his proposal tonight.

He climbed out of the car and came around to open her door. Always the gentleman, even more so than a lot of men born to money, social elevation and manners. He helped her from the car, transferring his hand to the small of her back once she was standing. She realized he did that a lot, this guiding her where he wanted her to go with a possessive-protective hold.

He kept his hand on her even in the elevator. He did that a lot, too…simply touching her for the sake of doing so, not because he needed to. He touched her like she was already his. It was one of the reasons she had been so confused over him not pressing to make love.

She understood better now, but wasn't sure that with understanding came acceptance.

Silence reigned in the elevator on the way to her fifth-floor apartment and no one else joined them to break it. It wasn't an awkward silence, but she was lost in her own thoughts and she sensed that Sandor was content to leave her that way.

He waited patiently for her to open her apartment door

and deactivate her alarm with the code and her thumbprint. The double locks on the solid steel door molded to look like a classic paneled wood door undid with a *snick*. She pushed the door open and led him inside.

"I like the security here."

She laughed. Sometimes, she got the impression that, like her father, Sandor considered the security at the Denver Mint no more than routine. "I picked out the apartment in a secure building to help Dad make the transition to me no longer living at home. That wasn't good enough for him. He gave me a security system installed by Vitale Security for a housewarming gift."

"I have used that firm before myself. They are very good."

"I'll say and the installation expert was to-die-for gorgeous."

"Was he?" Sandor asked in a rough voice.

"Totally delicious." She licked her lips. "But too short for me. He came all the way from the head office in Sicily. Dad demanded the best."

"I must then be grateful I inherited some tall genes somewhere, hmmm?"

She eyed his six-foot-four frame. "I bet that's one good thing you got from your father."

Sandor frowned, but he didn't deny it. Considering the fact that his mother was barely over five feet, maybe he couldn't.

"We all inherit things from our parents, and we hope they are the best things," she said as she led him into the living room. "I got my dad's stubbornness. Just ask him."

Sandor waited until she sat down on the bright yellow leather retro sofa before settling right beside her. "I have no need, having seen ample evidence of it myself."

She laughed again, loving just being there with Sandor at

that moment in time. She kicked off her sandals and curled her feet under her, turning her body slightly so she faced him.

He wasn't smiling in response to her laughter. Instead he was looking at her like he was trying to piece together what made her tick. "You're very understanding of George's need to protect you."

"I love him." She sighed. "And I understand that as the sole heir to a man as wealthy as he is that I'm a good candidate for a kidnapping."

"Yet you insist on living alone."

She barely stifled the urge to snort. "I don't exactly live alone, do I? His security team has the next apartment over. They monitor me as well as my apartment while I am gone."

"Wouldn't it be easier to simply live in your father's home?"

"Maybe, but while it may not be perfect, I have a lot more independence than I would have if I had stayed at home." It was also easier to convince herself that the reason she saw so little of her father was that they lived apart, not because he didn't care enough to make any time for her. "Besides, I really don't want my dad's money dictating every aspect of my lifestyle."

"You would prefer to be able to live without the security detail."

"Yes."

"But you make the concession to George's *feelings*— to his fears for you."

"And to practicality. But don't you do the same, for your mother?"

He smiled, laying one arm along the back of the couch. "Touché."

His scent enveloped her, the subtle fragrance of his spicy

aftershave mixed with his own essence. She'd read that a woman's sense of smell was more refined than a man's but it was the first time *she'd* ever noticed the individual scent of another person. Maybe it was because to her senses, Sandor was infinitely unique. In every way.

His warmth and sexy masculinity called to her and she forced herself to speak instead of closing the distance between their bodies. "I bet you find it as difficult to carve time out of your work schedule to have the family dinners and the excursions Hera insists on as I do to allow my dad to keep a security detail watching over me."

"I think you are right, though I never considered it in that light. I only know that since I was a small boy I was determined to give my mother the life my father *should* have." Something in his expression said his words surprised him as much as her.

He was an intensely private person, that he had shared as much of himself as he had with her was incredibly special.

Allowing herself one tiny touch, she brushed his arm and smiled. "Well, I'd say you surpassed that goal and then some."

"You think?"

She smiled with emotion shining in her eyes because it sounded like he really was asking the question. As if there could be any doubt. "I doubt your dad is a hugely wealthy tycoon and I'm certain he wasn't as a teenager. You've surpassed anything he could have done for her, even if he had stuck around."

"I think you may be right." The wealth of satisfaction in his voice told Ellie something else about this enigmatic man who wanted to marry her.

He had things to prove to himself…to his grandfather…*and* to the father he'd never met.

Remembering her role as hostess, she asked, "Would you like coffee...or an after dinner drink?"

"Neither, thank you."

Now, why did the way he said that make shivers dance along her nerve endings? "It was your idea to come up," she reminded him.

"To settle one of your concerns in regard to marriage, not because I crave more liquid refreshment."

"You plan to settle my fears?" How very noble of him. "In what way?" Though she thought she could guess.

He leaned forward, invading her personal space completely and his body heat called to her while his dark eyes mesmerized. "Guess."

"What about the no sex before marriage integrity thing?" She'd meant to ask the question in a sarcastic tone, but her voice came out breathless and much too inviting. Darn it.

"I plan to marry you. It is up to you to set the date." He might as well have shrugged, he sounded so casual in that pronouncement.

And right then she realized he really did plan to marry her. Not hope. Not want. But the man had a *plan* and was fully confident in his eventual success.

"So, it's okay to seduce a virgin if you intend to marry her?" Again that breathless voice that was really starting to get on her nerves.

She sounded like she wanted his reassurance, but she didn't. Did she? Not this way...not planned. But Sandor was a planner and he worked best with a schedule. She'd known that since the beginning. She just hadn't expected it to dictate this part of their relationship.

"You have said you are not a virgin." He didn't sound like he was bothered either way.

"And you didn't believe me."

"You have no reason to lie."

"No, I don't." But he'd still doubted her. Why was that again? Oh, yes…her father's security reports and his own investigator's report. But still he should have believed her. Shouldn't he?

She tried to catch thoughts that spiraled away as her body's reaction to his nearness began to take precedence. "If I was a virgin, would you be planning to seduce me in cold blood?"

That made him smile, a purely predatory expression that held no comfort for her feminine concerns. "I assure you there will be nothing cold about it."

"Now, you see, I have a hard time understanding how you're going to…" Her brain short-circuited as his hand moved from the back of the couch to her shoulder.

He brushed her collarbone with his thumb. "Yes?"

"Yes?"

His lips hovered above hers. "You were saying?"

"I was saying…" She desperately grasped for reality. "You…I…"

"You…I…what?" he taunted, his voice laced with laughing, masculine triumph.

His amusement sparked her pride and her memory and she pressed her head back into the couch, away from his descending mouth. "I still don't see how you expect to convince me of your passion when you are touching me with the *intent* of convincing me. It's no different than offering a potential client an enhanced guarantee."

The words sounded positively brilliant to her befuddled brain, especially when she considered how many she'd managed to string together.

He looked less than impressed however with her argument. "I can promise you that I do not see you as a client."

She wasn't so sure about that. Now that she'd verbalized the thought, it had taken surprisingly strong root in her mind.

He moved infinitesimally closer. "I want you. Once I have had you, the truth of my desire will be impossible for you to ignore, *pethi mou*."

"You're so darn sure of yourself." She crossed her arm over her small chest and did something totally out of character. She pouted, her lip protruding…the whole bit. And it felt good.

He smiled as if he found her reaction charming and brushed his fingertip down her arm to where it crossed with the other, and then traced the one closest to her body so the back of his fingers made contact with skin bared by her low neckline.

Heat and pleasure rolled over her in a tidal wave of sensation and she gasped.

He stopped with his fingertip in dangerous proximity to her breast. "It is the fact that I am so sure of you that really bothers you, I think."

He was right, darn him. Only she had no time to dwell on that fact because his mouth finished its descent and locked to hers with rock-solid possession. This was no tentative kiss, no prelude to seduction, but the thing itself. In living, glorious color that had starbursts going off inside her and her brain going into a meltdown.

And she went under just as he'd predicted she would. Without a whimper of protest. Without so much as a token attempt to push him away. And she couldn't even claim it was because her hands were trapped between them because he immediately uncrossed her arms for her so that he could get closer with his big, hard body.

She might have been embarrassed if she wasn't enjoying the kiss so much. But nothing had ever felt so right. Well, nothing except his kisses. It had been this way since the very first one. She'd acknowledged then what she knew now. She belonged here, in his arms. Whether he felt a corresponding need, she did not know, but she craved his touch.

Did he sense it? Was that why he was so sure of himself? Of course he did…he was too world savvy not to. But none of that explained why *he* wanted to marry *her*.

CHAPTER FOUR

EVEN THOSE THOUGHTS splintered as his tongue demanded and received entrance into her mouth. His taste intoxicated her and she let him pull her firmly into his body, reveling in the electric charge of contact when her breasts pressed against his chest.

She pulled at his shirt and then scrabbled for buttons, hungry for the feel of his hot skin. They came undone despite the clumsiness of her fumbling fingers and she luxuriated in the silky dark curls that swirled over his chest. He was such a masculine man…everything about him screaming *prime specimen* of the male of their species.

His muscles were granite hard against her exploring fingertips. His sheer size both intimidated and aroused her feminine sensuality.

He made a growling sound in his throat and dragged her into his lap. Planned or not, his desire for her pulsed between them as he had promised it would. She could not deny the harsh reality of his erection pressed against her thigh or the way the hands holding her trembled against her own flesh shimmering with sensation.

But it was so much more than mere physical feeling.

She loved this man and her heart craved this intimate connection as fervently as her body.

His hands slid over the silk of her dress, caressing her curves and inciting feelings that never ceased to shock her. This was what passion was supposed to feel like—not forced, not muted, but so full, so real that every atom in her body shimmered with delight. His hand skimmed up her calf, taking the dress with it and baring her legs to him. He stopped when his fingertips brushed the apex of her thighs through the sheer lace of her panties.

He groaned and pulled his lips from hers. So he could see what he had touched. "Very sexy."

She couldn't form a word to respond. She looked down at herself, sprawled in abandon across his thighs, her legs spread slightly, her thighs quivering with need. She could smell her own musk and rather than embarrass her, it excited her further to think she could respond so totally to this man's kiss.

His bronzed chest gleamed under the muted light cast by the single torchère lamp she'd left on for her return home. His dark body was such a contrast to hers that she was lost in the visual pleasure for long moments.

"I'd like to see you in front of a fireplace, lying naked on a thick rug. Aroused," she said, shocking herself as she admitted one of her favorite nighttime fantasies out loud.

He didn't look taken aback, though; he looked interested. "There is a fireplace in my bedroom. After we are married, I will be very pleased to see that you get your wish."

"I haven't said I'll marry you." Where the wit to say so came from, she didn't know, but she suspected that self-preservation was as instinctual as sexual intimacy.

"You will."

"Maybe."

He chose that moment to slide his finger up and down along the edge of the scrap of fabric that covered her feminine center. She moaned and arched toward his touch, wanting him to move his finger just a fraction of an inch to the left.

He repeated the caress, his expression feral. "I will convince you."

"You can try," she invited, one hand diving to cup the hardness that proved his desire was every bit as real as hers.

She was not a bold lover, but it was imperative for her newly discovered feelings to make him acknowledge, if only tacitly, that this was far from one-sided.

He gasped and then cursed and it was her turn to smile.

Pleasure zinged through her at his response. Perhaps her lack of boldness in the past was because her single sexual liaison had occurred when she was barely nineteen. Her previous lover had been older and a whole lot more experienced than she.

As Sandor's touch ignited raging fires of need inside her, Ellie realized her former lover might have known more, but he had not been particularly good at lovemaking. And that knowledge took away some of the lingering sting the memories had on her emotions. If that man had been as good at evoking a response as Sandor, she would never have escaped the relationship relatively unscathed. She might not have escaped at all, despite what she'd learned back then.

At the time, she'd thought her heart was decimated by his calculation and betrayal, but five years on, she had to admit that it could have been so much worse. That truth served as a chilling reminder for the present, bringing her back to reality with a vicious jerk to her emotions. Because this *was* Sandor. She *did* love him and his potential to hurt her was beyond anything she'd ever known.

Terror coursed through her, cooling blood heated by wanton desire.

She'd learned to expect less from her dad, but would she ever be able to affect the emotional distance necessary to accept that kind of relationship with Sandor? She didn't want to, even if she could. She didn't want a half-life in her marriage. She wanted something fully vibrant between them. But was that a fool's dream?

"What is the matter?" He was looking at her face now, his expression marred by a slight frown.

She blinked and stared at him realizing he'd stopped touching her completely. "Nothing."

But it was a lie. Worries were pounding inside her mind with painful frequency and power. He could hurt her. So much. Was letting him make love to her the smartest thing she could do? Did she want to give him a bigger hold on her heart than he already had?

He wanted to marry her, the side of her brain that housed her libido reminded her with strident urgency. He wasn't going to leave her in the dust. But her first lover had wanted to marry her, too. Only his reasons hadn't been what he'd said they were, or what she needed them to be. Love had not even been a minor variable in the equation.

"You were thinking of something else," Sandor said, not willing to let it drop.

"And that bothers you?"

"Considering what we are doing. Yes."

"Ah, male ego. No need for yours to get dented. I was thinking about you." The words this time were *more* sarcastic than she intended, but she felt powerless to change her tone.

His dark brows drew together, but he did not pull

away. "Right now, I want you being *with* me...thinking only of *this*."

She wasn't expecting another assault to her senses so quickly. Probably because her thoughts and feelings were so divergent, she expected his to be impacted as well. But Sandor knew what he wanted and he went for it.

This was a kiss so carnal, it shattered her fears and her ability to think, leaving her reeling in a maelstrom of need she could not navigate. This was touching and caressing that left her mindless with need and so incoherent she didn't even realize she had been undressed until she was naked and being carried to her bedroom in Sandor's strong arms. She must have done some clothing removal herself because his torso was fully exposed and his bare feet slapped against the hardwood floors of her apartment.

Her body burned with the need to fuse with his and she pressed against him as if she could achieve it in that position.

"Yes, go wild for me, Eleanor. You are everything a man could wish for."

"Ellie," she gasped, needing him to call her by the name she preferred, the one that in her mind fit the true woman she was. This was too intimate for the formal name no one but her father used anymore.

Dark eyes glittered into hers. "Ellie." Then he said a short Greek word that carried a wealth of meaning. *Mine*.

He was claiming her and right that second she could not gainsay him. She needed him more than the air she breathed...she did belong to him. At least for tonight.

Pressing feverish kisses along his collarbone, up his neck and along his jaw, she refused to think. She could only feel. Emotions deep inside, physical pleasure along every nerve ending, joy and purpose radiating off of Sandor. It all mixed together in a combustible package that rocked her to her very soul. She had been born for this moment and she would revel in its splendor.

"Sandor…" She licked under his jaw.

He growled and fell on the bed with her. She landed in a sprawl on top of him, but he quickly flipped her over and took her mouth. She opened her lips, inviting his tongue and deepening the kiss. He rubbed his lower body against hers and she went rigid with shock at the pleasure.

He'd gotten rid of his pants with the rest of his clothes and his erection was touching a place no one else had gotten near in five years. It felt amazing. He was rock-hard and yet the skin was soft and felt totally delicious pressing against her most feminine place.

He yanked his head back. "You are ready for me."

"Yes!" She tried to wriggle to invite him in.

He wouldn't let her move. "Protection?" he gritted.

For a brain totally fuzzed by sexual desire, hers worked quickly to figure out what he needed and the answer to that need. "Drawer by the bed."

She'd bought the condoms when they started dating, assuming he would press for intimacy. There was enough of her brain functioning to appreciate his re-membering to ask.

He wanted her to marry him, but he wasn't going to try to trap her with pregnancy. Warmth unfurled inside her at the knowledge. Her other lover had not been so noble. She thanked God that his ignoble intentions had born no fruit, but she'd never forget the sense of betrayal when she realized what he'd tried to do.

Sandor reared off of her and rushed to the nightstand, ripped open the drawer and then grabbed a condom from the box with flattering speed. He rolled it on and then climbed back on the bed and stalked toward her on his knees. It felt just like a predator was preparing to leap at his prey. A surprisingly pleasurable atavistic shiver shook her frame at the knowledge she was that prey.

He cupped her small breast and kneaded it, sending delirious enjoyment arcing through her. She moaned.

He whispered in her ear, "Your desire for me is real, as is mine for you."

"Yes."

"The passion, it is here between us," he said in a thick Greek accent. "It is real."

"Yes," she repeated.

"Believe," he said and then kissed her again.

She wasn't sure what he meant, but she accepted his mouth and his touch, freely returning both. When he moved on top of her, she spread her thighs in blatant instinctive invitation. He maneuvered his shaft so it pressed against her silky, wet opening.

He stopped. Stopped moving. Stopped kissing her. Even stopped making those sexy male noises of pleasure that had been emitting from his throat.

Her eyes fluttered open and met a dark gaze intent on her.

"Do you accept me into your body?" he asked.

He had to know she wanted him, so this question meant something more, but she wasn't sure what. Only it didn't matter. Her answer was, "Yes."

He nodded as if sealing a pact and then pushed inside her.

Silken tissues stretched and her body absorbed him as if they had been created to fit together perfectly. She felt filled to capacity, yet instead of hurting...it felt good. Really, really good.

Feminine fear that had nothing to do with wanting to stop fluttered through her, but it did not decrease her arousal. It increased it, making her crave movement and total possession. "I want all of you."

"Can you take all of me?"

"I was made to." She wasn't sure what she was saying, but it felt right.

He rocked his pelvis forward, sliding further into her humid depths. Continuing the motion, he took her body slow inch by slow inch until his pelvic bone pressed against hers. Both sensations made her gasp.

He said something in Greek she didn't get.

She luxuriated in the feeling of oneness for a timeless moment. "I told you we would fit."

He husked a laugh. "Usually it is the man comforting the woman with that line."

"Is it?" she asked, not knowing and caring very little what the norm was between other men and women.

She knew only what was right between them and this was right. She tried to arch against him. "I need you to move."

And he did. So perfectly that tears washed into her eyes and leaked down her temples. He seemed to understand because he sipped at them and continued to make love to her as her body built toward a cataclysm of pleasure that was unlike anything she'd ever known.

Then something happened that was surely a miracle because his body went tense above hers at the same moment that she felt the explosion inside. He shouted. She cried out. And their bodies shuddered together in mutual abandon. He continued to move in small, caressing motions that drew the pleasure out for both of them.

Her body jerked with spasms of release while he

groaned and bucked against her a few more times before collapsing on top of her in a heavy, but welcome heap.

His breath bellowed in her ear and her chest labored to draw air in. "That was amazing," she whispered, afraid of ruining the perfect moment with too much sound.

"Yes, it was," he rumbled against her neck, sending shivers along her oversensitive skin.

She turned her head and kissed the side of his face. "Thank you."

"The pleasure was as much or more mine."

"I'm glad you didn't say all yours."

"It would not be true."

She laughed softly at his arrogance, but fell silent quickly. He was so right. It would not be true. She'd never felt anything so wonderful. And she wanted to feel this again. And again. And again.

Which was why he had made love to her, wasn't it? To convince her that they were meant for each other. If not in love, in lust and in like.

"I am going to adore having you as my wife in my bed," he said, confirming his thoughts ran parallel in content if not intent to hers.

"That is not a done deal, yet, Sandor."

He leaned back to fix her with his "get serious" look. She'd seen it a few times before, but it was funny in their current situation and she couldn't help laughing again.

"I do not find this funny. You will marry me, Ellie."

At least he got the name right. She stifled her laughter and cupped his cheek. "Making love with you was incredible, but I still need time to think."

"After what we have just experienced together, how can you need time to think?"

"Because we won't spend our entire life in bed, Sandor."

"It is worth considering."

She shook her head. "You're such a man."

"I am that." He carefully rolled off of her and padded naked to the bathroom. "I would be little use to you in this situation if I wasn't," he called back over his shoulder.

She couldn't argue that logic and did not even try.

He stayed the night and made love to her again in the wee hours of the morning and then again when they awoke to her alarm. Both times left her a boneless, quivering mass of satisfaction. But he did not push again for a definitive answer from her. It was as if he was so sure of her, he was simply biding his time.

She didn't really care why he refrained from pressing her, but was merely glad that he did. He left her house after a brief shower to go home and change for work, while she rushed through her morning routine in order not to be late herself.

There was no time to think or try to decide what the night before had meant.

He called her later that morning, but she was with a client and didn't get a chance to call him back until midway through what should have been her lunch hour.

"I had hoped we could share lunch, *pethi mou*, but I see that idea is a washout."

She looked at the case files dumped on her desk that morning by another counselor before going home ill and sighed. "Unfortunately, yes it is."

"Dinner tonight? Mama hopes to see you."

If he hadn't phrased it like that, she might have said no. She needed some time to get her head together and it wasn't going to happen during work hours filled with the overbooked caseloads of both herself and her absent co-worker. But she liked Hera Christofides. A lot.

And Ellie had no intention of hurting the very sweet older woman's feelings. "I'd love to. What time would you like me to arrive?"

"I will pick you up at six."

"I'd rather drive myself."

"I prefer to see to your comfort."

"You know I'm followed by a security team. I'll be perfectly safe driving myself to your house and home again."

"Nevertheless, I would rather drive you. It is the male prerogative."

"In a former decade maybe."

"Some traditions are best not left behind. Besides, it has not escaped my notice that you do not like to drive."

He was speaking the truth. She didn't. She hated negotiating city traffic and would prefer to ride public transport to work, but with her "secret" security detail following her every move, that wasn't an option. She could accept her dad's offer of a car and chauffer, but something seemed wrong about showing up for a public service job that way. And she wasn't a wimp.

She could drive, she just didn't like to. And Sandor had noticed.

"You're going to be stubborn about this, aren't you?" she asked, but there was no ire in her voice.

She was too busy feeling cherished. She should probably tell him thank you, but she didn't want to feed his already overly certain belief that he always knew what was best.

"Can you doubt it?"

She laughed softly. "Not when stubborn is the thing you do best."

"I would say after last night that you would consider I had at least one or two other attributes."

Despite the fact that no one else could hear his words, she blushed a hot crimson. "Sandor!"

He laughed, the sound low and sexy, affecting her in ways she tried to ignore. The fiend.

She waited for him to stop laughing and then said by way of dismissal, "I'll see you at six."

"I shall look forward to it."

She hung up the phone feeling just slightly outmaneuvered, but she didn't really mind. One of the problems she'd had dating was that after growing up around her father and having to push so hard against him for any sort of independence, most other men seemed a little too easily led in comparison. At first, she'd thought that was what she wanted.

She didn't want to be used again and she didn't want to be dominated, so she very selectively dated men that were from her world and weren't looking for her father's millions to support them, but who were also patently non-aggressive. Men who spouted feminist ideals better than she did and who were sensitive. Men who did not have Sandor's vibrancy or personal power.

She'd grown weary of the dating scene quickly and it wasn't until Sandor bulldozed into her life that she realized what was missing. She wanted a man of integrity, but not one she could lead around by a ring through his nose. She wouldn't tolerate being dominated, and if he didn't already know that, he would learn, but she was glad he was so strong.

She'd learned that a man could be aggressive and powerful and sensitive to her feelings. At least some of them. Which was more than she'd ever had, but not the same as having his love. However, Sandor was always careful to look after her. His recognition of her dislike of driving was not an isolated incident. He watched her. He paid attention.

And that was very different from her father. Which considering how many similarities she saw between the two of them was a very good thing.

Added to that, she didn't live in fear of denting his fragile male ego because he wasn't *overly* sensitive. The fact her father approved was a double-edged sword. His lack of emotional connection to her had resulted in a sense of rebellion toward all that he stood for. But there was a tiny part of her that still wanted his approval. That still hoped deep inside that if she could please him enough, he would love her like a daddy was supposed to love his little girl.

Marrying Sandor would definitely please her father, but his similarity to the man who had lacerated Ellie's heart time and again with twenty-four years of almost complete indifference gave her pause. How could it do anything else?

She couldn't live the rest of her life in that same emotional wasteland with a husband. Even if *she* loved *him.*

Her disturbing thoughts were interrupted by a phone call and she didn't have another second to call her own for the rest of the day. She left work late and had to rush through getting ready for dinner at the Christofides home.

Sandor asked about her day when he picked her up and spent the entire drive to his home listening. It was a heady experience, being the central focus of his attention. With pleasure, she ticked a mental mark on his scorecard…on the side that said, "Not a carbon copy of George Wentworth."

He helped her from the car and she stayed him with a hand, reaching up to kiss him on the corner of his mouth. "Thank you."

His brows drew together. "For what?"

"For listening. I can't imagine that my attempts to help my clients better their lives is all that fascinating, but you never tell me to shut up."

He leaned down and kissed her full on the lips. "You are wrong."

She was clinging to his biceps for support after the short but devastating kiss. "About what?"

"Everything about you interests me, but your desire to help others is both admirable and yes, fascinating to me."

"You're a special man, Sandor." But was it true? If everything about her interested him, why was he so ignorant about some basic elements to her nature? Most important being her need for an emotional connection with him.

"Remember that."

"It's not something I could forget."

He just smiled and led her into the house.

CHAPTER FIVE

HERA CHRISTOFIDES WAS every bit as pleased to see Ellie as Sandor had said she would be and made her welcome with warm effusiveness.

"It is so good you come. Sandor, he is like a caged lion lately, but when you are here...he is better." She squeezed Ellie's hand before taking a seat on the large white sofa and indicating Ellie should join her.

"Mama, I do not mind being likened to a lion, but I am far from caged."

"There are many kinds of cages, my son," Hera said wisely. "Though I agree, you are very like a lion in the cage or out of it...because you see the world as your prey." She sighed, her eyes so like Sandor's filled with concern. "It is always the business with you. You want to win, win, win."

Sandor shrugged. "Better that than I be a lazy layabout, no?" His speech pattern always took on a more decidedly Greek bent when he was around his mother.

Hera pursed her lips and appealed to Ellie with her eyes. "I cannot imagine this one lazy. Can you?"

Ellie shook her head solemnly, though a smile flirted at the edges of her mouth. "No. I really can't."

"There, you see?" Hera said as if making a point.

Though Ellie had to wonder if Sandor knew what it was supposed to be because she wasn't sure she did. She smiled regardless.

"And what am I supposed to see, Mama?" Sandor asked.

"That to work all the time is its own cage," the older woman said, as if it should be obvious.

"Better that cage than many others I could name."

"Perhaps, but it would be better not to be caged at all. Do you not agree, Eleanor?"

"Yes. Freedom is a beautiful thing and something we often have to sacrifice other things to attain."

"Ah, this one, she is smart. You hold on to her, son." Hera patted Ellie's arm.

Sandor smiled. "I intend to, believe me."

Hera nodded. "Good."

Thankfully that was all she and Sandor said on the subject and Ellie had to be grateful that he had not told his mother he had asked Ellie to marry him. She had a feeling Hera wouldn't be above trying to convince Ellie she should say yes.

So, why hadn't Sandor pulled his mother in to argue his case? It seemed like a tactic he would use.

On the other hand, she'd asked for time to think and apparently Sandor intended to respect that. Which was a pretty darn effective argument in his favor, if he but knew it.

Since she wasn't pressuring Ellie to accept her beloved son's proposal, having Hera there as a buffer made the evening more relaxing. But nothing could mitigate the fact that Ellie's mind insisted on playing the events of the night before over and over in her head. Being slammed at work had helped to keep her thoughts under control, but being in his company made it impossible to keep the memories at bay.

She would catch Sandor looking at her like a shark ready

to gobble her up and she would stammer and blush and in general react without her usual aplomb. His mother would take him to task for embarrassing her and Sandor would just grin, pleading innocence if not ignorance.

An important call came in during dessert and Sandor excused himself to take it in his study.

Hera shook her head after he left. "He puts too much importance on business, that one. I thought bringing him to America would give him a better life. It is not so easy to be a child without a father in a small village like the one we came from, but now I wonder if I made the right choice. Had we stayed there, he would not be so driven by business maybe."

"I don't believe Sandor is the kind of man to be defined by his surroundings. He is who he is and would be that man, no matter where he'd spent the last years of his childhood. It wouldn't have mattered if he started in a small town in Greece instead of Boston, your son would have climbed his way to the top no matter what. I think if you'd stayed there, though, that it would have taken longer and been harder for him. He might not be where he is right now, but never doubt he would have achieved what he set out to achieve."

"Thank you, Eleanor. You are a kind and very perceptive young woman."

The praise filled Ellie with a sense of well-being, of belonging. She grinned. "And just think, if he had to work harder to get where he is, he would have taken longer to begin considering matters besides business."

She wasn't about to spill the beans about his proposal, but she figured Hera was savvy enough to realize her son's thoughts had turned to domestic matters.

The older woman's expression turned-horror struck.

"You think he might have made me wait even longer to get grandbabies?"

Ellie laughed. She knew the other woman was intuitive where her son was concerned. "I'm afraid so."

Hera shook her head again. "I still worry about him. He never stops achieving. When is it enough?"

"He seems to have things to prove to himself," Ellie said carefully.

This time Hera's sigh carried a wealth of sadness. "Yes. He wishes to prove he got nothing bad from his father. My papa, he was a good man, but he was hard. He made Sandor to think he was responsible for things that he had no control over. Papa said nothing good about the young boy I loved, but he was good. Too young to be as strong as he needed to be maybe, but he *was* good."

"Do you ever tell Sandor that?"

"I tried, but while Papa lived, it would have been disrespectful to say his words were not all truth. By the time he died, his beliefs were settled so deeply inside Sandor, I could not sway them. And part of me…I blamed Jimmy for never coming back. There were things I did not know at the time. I now regret never speaking against my father's words."

Ellie reached out and touched Hera's arm. "It must have been hard for you."

"It was. I was raised to be a good girl…to hold my innocence for marriage, but the love I had with Sandor's father…it was overwhelming. I have never known anything like it since. You will think me a fool, but he has always been the husband of my heart."

"I don't think it is foolish at all. I've heard of love like that." And for the first time, she wondered if she really wanted feelings that deep with a man.

That kind of love had always been her idyll, but now, seeing Hera's pain, the hurt in those beautiful brown eyes so fresh it could have happened yesterday, Ellie's own heart twinged with both sympathy and fear. Compassion for the other woman filled her along with a terror that Ellie's own feelings were already as at risk as Hera's had been.

She was no naïve sixteen-year-old with her first lover, but she had a suspicion that the kind of love Hera was talking about transcended age and even experience.

Hera's smile wiped the pain from her eyes as they glowed with a remembered feeling so powerful it could still bring her joy as well as hurt. "To feel it is beyond any other riches this world has to offer. To have it returned, a gift of unimaginable pleasure. We both felt it. He loved me as much as I loved him."

"Yet he left." Ellie didn't say it because she doubted Hera, but because she could not understand walking away from something so special. Still, belatedly, she realized, she should not have said the words aloud. "I'm sorry. I should not have said that."

"Why not? It is the truth. But only part of the truth. Papa caught us together and he beat my love until he could not get up." Tears filled Hera's eyes. "I tried to stop him, but Papa slapped me hard and Jimmy told me to leave. He could not stand for me to be hurt. I would not listen to my papa, but I listened to Jimmy. It wounded his pride for me to see him beaten like that also, I could tell. He would not raise his hand to my father, so he had no defense. Papa thought it was his right to do what he did, but he drove Jimmy off the island."

"So, he didn't leave you voluntarily?"

"No. He had no way of knowing I had become pregnant.

He was only a teenager himself. A young boy on holiday with his friends. He tried to see me once after that."

Ellie's insides clenched. Did Sandor know that?

"I did not know he had done so until after Papa's death. I found the letter in his bureau. At first, I did not tell Sandor because he was already grieving the loss of his grandfather, but later...I did not know what purpose it would serve. It had been so long and I had convinced myself Jimmy had married and had more children. Sandor already struggled with so much, to expose him to such a situation would have hurt him even more I thought. And he was bitter toward his father. I thought to wait would be best."

"You were probably right."

Hera's eyes filled with doubt. "I wonder. I never married. I had opportunity, but I had no desire. Was it the same for my Jimmy? I had to choose between using the money I got from selling my family home and possessions for Sandor's schooling or to search out his father. I made my choice, but I often wonder if it was the right one."

"But now that you have the money, you could find him."

"I broached the subject with Sandor once. I learned to regret it. Had I not asked, I could have done so without repercussion, but because I told him what I wanted to do, he asked me not to use money from his hard work to find a man who had abandoned us both. I could not change his mind."

"Did you tell him that his father wrote?"

"It did not matter to him."

"Sandor is very stubborn."

"Yes."

Said stubborn man returned soon thereafter, but Ellie could not get her discussion with Hera out of her mind.

When he took her home, he once again parked in the

visitor parking garage and asked to come up. She knew what was coming, but she wanted to talk to him about what Hera had told her and if she was honest with herself (and she had a policy of being scrupulously so) she wanted what he wanted. Very much.

This time, she went directly to the kitchen and put the kettle on for tea.

"I am not thirsty," he said from behind her.

"I want tea." *And time to talk*, she added silently.

His dark brow rose, but he bowed slightly. "Then we shall have tea."

"You're making fun of me."

"I am humoring you. It is not the same."

"I see. Why are you humoring me?"

"For obvious male reasons. I hope to sweeten your temperament toward me so that I may have my wicked way with you."

She laughed. "I think you know you can seduce me without a pot of tea first."

"But I prefer not to seduce."

"You want me to offer myself?"

"Is that so bad?"

She shrugged. She didn't suppose it was, but she frowned anyway. "You think indulging before bed will make me more inclined to invite you to share mine?"

"I will do my best to convince you."

"I thought you weren't out to seduce me."

"Reminding you of the pleasure we shared last night is hardly a seduction."

Right. "And that's your plan, to remind me?"

"And entice you with thoughts of what tonight could bring."

Luckily for her already heating libido, the teakettle whistled and she jumped into action, making a pot of herbal tea that would not keep either of them awake. Though she had a feeling Sandor would effectively do so anyway.

They were sitting at her small 1950s restored yellow Formica kitchen table when she broached the subject of his dad. "Have you ever considered finding your father?"

Sandor's body tensed. "I suppose it was too much to expect that my time on the phone would not provide the opportunity for Mama to open this particular can of worms tonight. What happened, did she drag out the sorry tale of how my grandfather beat James Foster and chased him away?"

"You're uncannily prescient." She grinned teasingly, wanting to keep it light, but not sure that was going to be a possibility with the look on his face. "I don't suppose you were eavesdropping?"

He sighed and drank his tea. "No, but it's a story she's tried to feed me more than once."

"It's not a story. Your mother wouldn't make something like that up."

"I have no doubt my grandfather did as she said, but what does that change? My father was too weak to return for her. That is the bottom line."

"He tried."

"She told you about the letter, too?" Sandor sounded pained.

"Yes."

"Look, I read that letter and it was hardly the missive of a love pining away for her company. He had finished university, he thought they could see each other again…for old time's sake. He said nothing of the love she insists they both felt so strongly. He said something about thinking she might have married by now because Greek girls married younger than American ones, or some such rot."

"Did you think he should have poured his heart out in a letter to a woman he couldn't even be sure wasn't married?"

"If his love was as great as my mother claimed, he would have." Sandor's tone was hard, brooking no argument.

She gave it anyway. "Would *you* have?"

"I do not believe in that kind of love."

"Yes, I know, but even if you did, I don't believe you would put your heart on the line until you knew the lay of the land."

That seemed to take him back a little. "What is the point of this conversation?"

"I think you should find your father, if not for your sake, then for hers."

Sandor pushed his tea away and leaned back in his chair, the caged lion coming to mind again. "You think I do not take her feelings into account when I refuse to seek him out?"

"Do you?"

"Yes." He rubbed his hand over his face as if tired all of a sudden. "Tell me, what do you think it would do to my tenderhearted mother to discover my father married soon after graduation and has other children and a wife he adores?"

"Does he?" Had Sandor had the man investigated?

"I do not know and that is the point. In this instance, ignorance is bliss. At least as far as my mother is concerned."

"But if he is married, you would not have to tell her about him."

"I would not...could not lie to Mama."

"But is a lie of omission always a lie, if you are just protecting her? Wouldn't it be better for you to know?"

Sandor shrugged. "I love my mother. To withhold that

information from her if I had it would be wrong. It would breach the trust we have between us. I won't risk her being further hurt."

Wow. How could she help loving this man?

"But what if you are wrong?"

"Then he would have come for her in all this time."

It was a telling argument. "What about you? Don't you want to know him?"

"He deserted my mother, he abandoned me though he did not know about me. He is not a man I want in my life."

"Your grandfather kept them apart."

"There was only one letter, Ellie, not ten, not five, not even two. Just one. He struck out on the first swing and never picked up the bat again."

"You can't imagine doing that, can you?"

"No. Not when it pertains to something important to me."

"I'm stubborn, too, you know."

"We have established that, yes."

"I believe you are wrong."

"I believe I would rather discuss the way your nipples taste and how they harden and swell against my tongue."

Shocked, her mouth opened on a gasp, but no other sound came out. Under the bright, fluorescent lights in the kitchen, the look he gave her was hot and wicked. It seemed so out of place in the cheery room and yet...not. This man and his earthy sensuality fit into her life in surprisingly adept ways.

Because as startling as his unrefined words had been, they had also aroused her. She licked her lips, tasting tea and the honey she'd used to sweeten it. "That's not something a person usually discusses."

"But I like telling you how sweet you taste, how good you feel inside my mouth."

Her breath stilled somewhere between inhaling and exhaling. "You can be very...basic."

He leaned forward and brushed the back of his knuckles over one—yes, very erect—nipple.

She moaned.

He smiled, a man who clearly liked the impact he had on her. "I think despite your prim public image, primitive excites you. You like to hear these words from me."

He was right, but no other man she'd ever known would have considered saying such a thing, not to make the first comment, much less *tell her that she liked it*. For goodness' sake. Sandor was so different. Was that why she was drawn to him?

He defied the molds life would say he had to fit inside...just as she tried to. Or thought she did.

"You think I'm prim?" She looked down at the simple Albert Nipon suit in oyster shell silk she'd chosen to wear to dinner with his mother. Though its chic styling was form-fitting, it wasn't exactly sexy. The jacket buttoned up as a top showed nothing of her unimpressive cleavage and the skirt stopped modestly just shy of her knees. "Do you think I dress too conservatively?"

"The way you dress is perfect for you, Ellie. I like knowing that the rest of the world looks at you and sees what appears to be a coolly elegant woman, but I know that under the prim facade is a body made just for mine that responds with an uninhibited passion that delights me." His knuckles continued to brush up and down over her sensitized nub. "And sometimes you dress more provocatively than I think you intend to."

"You don't believe I *intend* to provoke you?" She could barely breathe, much less think with the way he touched her and the sensual timber of her voice saying such intensely erotic things just for her.

"I do not believe you have any idea how very sexy I find both the prim little suits or clothing like the dress you had on last night."

She'd wanted to be sexy the night before. It *had* been on purpose, but he didn't know that? "Why do you say that?"

"If you did, you would never have questioned the passion between us."

A man's brain was certainly a mysterious puzzle, especially Sandor's. "Was I supposed to read your mind?"

He shrugged. "I hope you now have a better basis to draw your conclusions from."

"I suppose I do." She grabbed his wrist, stopping that tantalizing touch that was melting her brain and other body parts. "I felt the passion in you before...leashed," she got out, "but I doubted my instincts when you did nothing to act on it."

"And now?"

She took a deep breath, but it didn't help get her senses under control. Her breasts felt full inside the lacy cups of her bra and the breath actually made them move against the silky fabric, arousing her further. She bit back a moan and closed her eyes, trying to find her control in blackness behind her lids. "Now I concede that we are very good together that way."

If only she knew whether, or not, he was that good with every other woman he'd been with. She knew how special it was for her, but what about him?

For her, last night...even right now...was a totally unique experience, but maybe he always found that much satisfaction in the act of lovemaking. She wanted to believe otherwise, but deceiving herself as to the meaning of sex with a man had broken her heart once before. She refused to do that to herself again.

He stood up from the table and came around to lift her to her feet. She was so close to his body, she could feel his heat, but they were not quite touching except where his big hands cupped her elbows. Her eyes opened of their own accord, taking in his heated brown gaze.

He caressed the sensitive area of her inner elbow with both thumbs. "Let us go be good together again, hmm?"

"So we are done talking about your father?"

"Yes." He cupped her face, tilting her chin with his thumbs. "We are done talking at all, I think."

"I suppose I can live with that," she husked. Her body was clamoring for his touch, but she fought the urge to press into him.

She wanted to play it cool, not to give too much of herself away. But that hope disintegrated with the first brush of his lips against hers. The brief contact zinged through her like an overload of electric current, making her body jolt and stiffen and her lips part and beg silently for more.

He gave it to her, covering her mouth with his completely, taking possession and yet inviting her to share in it...to make it mutual. And she wanted that, too. She needed to know that she was branding him as hers as effectively as he had marked her as his. He accepted the tentative slide of her tongue and invited her to go further. It was amazing.

Where had he learned to make love so completely with nothing more than lips against lips? Or had he been born with the ability? Sandor was a special man, part of her insisted it had to be inherent to him. The other part of her tried very hard not to be jealous of the women who had come before.

He kissed down along her neck and she shivered. "Sandor?"

"Hmmm?" He nibbled at a particularly sensitive spot, making her whole body shake with reaction.

"You know the whole don't have sex with virgins unless you're married to them or very close to it thing you've got going in your brain?" She wasn't sure where the words came from or the ability to speak coherently enough to voice them, but they came from that part of her brain that was not properly protected when he touched her.

The vulnerable part.

He laughed against her collarbone. "Ellie *mou,* how do you have the wherewithal to ask me questions? I must be doing something wrong."

"No." She panted a little as his tongue darted out to taste the hollow of her neck. "That's the point. You do this so well. I just wondered?"

"What?"

"How did you learn all this stuff? You're so good at it."

He groaned and buried his mouth against her. "You taste so good. I cannot believe you asked me that."

"It's just...I couldn't decide if your grandfather and you thought it was okay for you to have sex with women who are experienced. That seems like such a double standard, and then of course, there's *your* virginity to consider."

"I assure you, I am not a virgin."

"But didn't it bother you having sex when you were? You know the first time. Or did the woman plan to marry you and something go wrong?" The thought of him engaged to another woman was not a comfortable one.

His body shook with laughter even as his mouth kept doing truly decadent and delicious things to her. "You are right. I am guilty of a double standard."

"Explain it to me."

"There are women who are open to sex without commitment."

"Yes." That was true.

"You are not one of them."

"But I'm not a virgin."

"Yet, you are still very innocent."

That wasn't something she wanted to dwell on, but compared to him...maybe. "So, you've had sex with lots of women?"

He sighed and straightened so their eyes met. "Not lots. I am no playboy."

"But you know so much...you like it a lot." He'd been really attentive the night before. Hungry even. "I can't see you celibate."

"Then your imagination has let you down, though mine could not conceive of this conversation. So, perhaps we are even. Only consider that for years I worked twenty-hour workdays and took only the breaks my mother demanded I give her. Neither instance is conducive to ongoing sexual liaisons."

"But you have had lovers?"

"I have had sex partners. Even when the same woman met that need for more than a few nights, the relationship would never be something I would describe as lovers. Or even a relationship really. We scratched a mutual itch."

"That sounds so cold." And crude, but she was getting used to his earthy way of discussing certain things.

He had not been raised in the refined and often stifling atmosphere she had been subjected to.

"It was. I did not realize how cold until I warmed at the fire of your honest passion the first time we kissed."

CHAPTER SIX

WETNESS BURNED BEHIND her eyes, her emotions choking her. He might not believe in love, but that sounded like she was special to him. She said so.

"Of course you are special. I want to marry you. You are my lover and you will one day be my wife."

She didn't have the strength to deny him right then—wasn't even sure she wanted to, so she avoided answering altogether by kissing him. He growled and yanked her body into his, pressing his hardness against her in a blatant demand and claim at the same time. She had no intention of refusing that demand, no hope to do so even if she'd wanted to.

He swept her into his arms and carried her into the bedroom, laying her down on the bed carefully as if she were both fragile and precious. She looked up at him, her heart in her eyes, her teeth clamped together to bite back the words of love that wanted to tremble from her lips.

He stood and began to undress. "Tonight, I want to take it very slow."

Her body was already suffused with heat and longing and they'd barely done anything. "I don't think I'll survive slow."

"You will more than survive it, you will enjoy it." His husky laugh warmed her. "I guarantee it."

"You're very confident."

"According to you, I have reason to be. You like my lovemaking. You think I am so good at it, you wonder how I learned such skill." Oh, he sounded arrogant, but pleased, too, and she couldn't help smiling.

"Yes, well…"

He smiled, taking those two words as wholehearted agreement. "There you see?"

But she was beyond answering. He was peeling off his shirt and revealing bronze skin covered with silky black hair over sculpted muscles that tapered to a narrow waist and an intriguing arrow of hair that hinted at more. He was so incredibly gorgeous and overwhelmingly masculine.

He undid the button on his trousers and she sucked in air. It didn't help her feeling of light-headedness, though.

The man was simply too delicious for words.

He started pushing his trousers down his hips and she thought maybe she should be doing something, too. Though it was hard to move when her body was trembling so hard. She reached for the buttons on the front of her silk jacket.

"Don't," he said with a shake of his head. "I want to undress you."

"You're going to torture me, aren't you?"

"With pleasure….perhaps."

She quaked inside where he could not see. "I'm not going to survive."

"I had not pegged you for such a pessimist."

She laughed, but the sound choked off as he divested himself of his briefs. His erection sprang out from a nest of curly black hair. Even though they'd made love twice the night before and once again that morning, she still felt a frisson of trepidation skitter up her spine at the prospect of taking the big shaft inside her.

"You are looking at me as if I am a snake ready to bite."

She bit her lip. "More like a tree trunk ready to impale."

He laughed out loud, his head going back as amusement shook his tall frame. "You are priceless, Ellie."

Her heart squeezed. To see him like this was so rare and *she* had made it happen. It increased her sense of being special to him.

He was still grinning, looking at her. "You know we fit. Perfectly."

"Yes."

"But you still look nervous."

"I am, a little."

"Let me see what I can do about that." He moved toward the bed and the closer he got the faster her heart sped.

He stopped when his knees pressed against the end of the mattress and reached down to take one of her feet in his hand. He slid the sandal off. "Did you know that there are numerous pleasure points in your feet?"

She shook her head, her throat suddenly too dry to speak.

He cupped her heel in his big palm and used his other hand to massage her arch, sending pleasure arcing through her.

She gasped and moaned, her head falling back against the bed. "I do now."

He chuckled. "You like it?"

Her only answer was a moan as he found one of the pleasure points he'd mentioned. He massaged both feet thoroughly, pressing between her toes and making her squirm with feelings that did not resemble ticklishness in the least. It was both strange and wonderful to have a gorgeous naked Greek caressing her feet while the rest of her body was still fully covered. It was also highly erotic.

Slowly his touch moved up her legs, finding sensitive dips and hollows on her ankles and behind her knees. One spot had her keening his name and arching off the bed.

"You are so beautiful in your passion, Ellie."

"I've never felt like this before," she gasped.

"I am glad."

She was, too. Once again the word special came to her mind, but she still had no idea if what they felt was out of the ordinary for him.

But his fingers had just the slightest tremor as they made their way under her skirt. "Your skin is like satin, so smooth and soft. So perfect, Ellie *mou*."

He massaged her, working his way to her inner thighs and touching flesh that felt as private as her feminine center. In a way it was. No other person touched her thighs like this. She'd never thought about it before, but many parts of her body were actually pretty private and Sandor would touch them all.

He caressed her there, not even slipping a fingertip under the elastic band of her panties and her pleasure grew until she was making little mewling sounds and had spread her legs in silent, begging invitation for more. But he slid his hands back down her legs.

She made a sound of distress and he smiled. "It is time to remove your skirt, I think."

She was more than willing and cooperated by arching off the bed so he could undo the zip and slide it down her hips inch by excruciating inch. It wasn't tight and the lining was smooth so it slid easily, but he was drawing out the un-veiling. That's what it felt like. An unveiling.

"You make me feel like you're unwrapping a present, but it's the only one you've got on Christmas morning, so you're taking a long time with it." She could barely speak above a whisper...she could barely speak at all.

"You are a precious gift to me."

The words warmed something deep inside her that had always been cold. That place that needed to be treasured by someone, to know that she held a unique place in someone's heart and life. She'd always thought that if she disappeared from her father's life, he wouldn't even notice. Not really.

But while she might not have a special place in Sandor's heart, he was showing her that he intended her to have a special place in his life. That was better than what she'd had for so long, she almost blurted out her agreement to marry him right there. But some tiny lingering sense of self-preservation stopped her.

Making a decision like this during lovemaking would be stupid. She'd done that once before and she wasn't making that mistake again.

She was panting and ready to rip the rest of her clothes off herself by the time he was done with her skirt, though.

He stayed her hands when she tried. "Not yet. You promised, *pethi mou*."

Had she promised, or simply acquiesced? It didn't matter. She would let him continue because the pleasure was so intense and so was he.

He ran one fingertip along the top edge of her lacy bikini briefs that matched her cream lace bra. "Very nice."

"I don't wear thongs," she said almost apologetically. But she'd worn this particular set with the thought in the back of her mind that as much as she'd known it might not be smart to invite him to her bed a second night in a row, he might end up there anyway.

And here he was.

"These are quite sexy enough." He dipped one fingertip under the elastic of the waistband. "But I am eager to see you naked."

"Then take them off."

"Not yet."

She pouted for the second time in remembrance.

He pounced, blanketing her body and taking her mouth with a storm of passion that had her arching under him and rubbing the silk clad apex of her thighs against his heated manhood.

He broke the kiss, panting. "You are dangerous, you know that?"

"I like that."

"You are so far from prim, my little Boston princess."

"My wild side only comes out with you."

"As it should be."

It was her turn to laugh. "Your arrogance is showing again."

He shrugged and moved to straddle her thighs so he could start unbuttoning her top. He watched intently as her torso was revealed. She warmed under his gaze, but her own was snagged by the body straddling her. She reached out to touch him, wrapping her fingers around his erection.

The feel of his heated flesh against her hand was so incredible. "It's like satin over steel."

"It feels like steel," he growled.

She smiled and caressed him from top to bottom.

He moaned and she echoed the sound. There was something ferociously arousing about having the freedom to touch him like this. His velvet length jumped in her hand, throbbing against her fingers. But he didn't stop what he was doing.

He made her sit up to remove her suit top and undo the catch on her bra before pulling it off, too. She couldn't help noticing this unveiling had gone much faster than her skirt. Touching him was having its effect.

Naked skin pressed against naked skin and their heat mingled while frissons of sensation sparkled along every point of contact. She squeezed his hardness in reflexive action.

He groaned low and long. "You are dangerous."

"You said that."

"It is true."

"I think we are dangerous together."

He pushed her back onto the bed.

She met his gaze, her own determined. "I want you now, Sandor. No more games."

"This is no game, *pethi mou*."

And it felt all too serious when one hand cupped her breast, the thumb brushing over her nipple while his other hand clasped her shoulder, holding her body in place as she tried to arch off the bed at the contact.

She moaned, unbearably aroused by his refusal to let her move. She didn't understand why it should be so, or why he felt the need to keep her still. But it didn't matter. Because it was the way it was and it was so intense she could barely stand it.

Her eyelashes fluttered shut and all she could do was feel. Feel his hard thighs straddling her hips. Feel his hands both cupping her breasts now, teasing the rigid tips with his thumbs. She didn't try to move as if they had made a silent agreement for her not to do so. Gently he pinched, then pulled the hard nubs until she wanted to scream.

"Please don't stop," she whispered into the dark void behind her eyelids.

She continued to feel. Feel the pleasure-tension spiraling inside her. Feel her body suffuse with heat and need that grew so big she felt like it would explode out of her before he ever made her his. The scent of their arousal surrounded her as did his personal fragrance.

She could hear her own panting exhalations and his harsh breathing, both sounds like an internal caress that added to the desire coiling tighter and tighter within her. He shifted and the darkness behind her eyelids grew more acute as if she was in his shadow. Then his mouth was on hers—first devouring, then tenderly teasing and then devouring again.

He played on all of her senses, building her to a fever pitch and then drawing her back again. Repeating the process over and over again, but he was right. It was all much too intense to be called a game.

This man was determined to show her that they fit. That their bodies were perfect complements for each other, or maybe simply that his body could give her more pleasure than any other man would ever be able to.

She had no doubts as she writhed under him.

"Sandor! Please..." But she didn't know what she was pleading for. Completion? Or more of this maddening pleasure?

Sandor's heart contracted at the sound of his name whispered so desperately on Ellie's lips. She was so passionate. So responsive. In every way she fit him. Soon she would understand that truth as well.

He laved the sweet hollow in her throat. "You are so perfect for me, *pethi mou*," he said gutturally.

Her head was twisting on the pillow, but he knew she was not denying him. She was simply beyond the ability to respond verbally. And he had brought her to this state.

Pride surged through him. She had not been a virgin, as she had said she wasn't, but her responses were too overwhelming for her to have ever known what she felt with him with another man. She had said it was different for her, that she had not known this and he believed her.

In this way, he knew he was her first and for no reason he could logically explain, that was very important to him. He had never considered himself a possessive man when it came to his female companions, but then he had never made love to a woman with the intention of claiming her for a lifetime, either.

He moved back off her thighs and removed the last scrap of cloth standing between her and total nudity. No time to draw it out. No will to do so. It was time to claim her. He made quick work of donning protection.

He was pushing her thighs apart, preparing to enter her when he realized he wished to be claimed as well. He did not want mere compliance about this marriage thing. He wanted Ellie to be sure of him. To want more than his body.

For a moment in that bed, the small boy who had withstood the taunts of other children in his small Greek village because he had no father broke through Sandor's adult armor. He needed to know he belonged.

He looked down at Ellie. "Do you want me inside you?" He stopped moving…stopped touching…and waited.

Her eyes fluttered open. The deep-blue green of the Mediterranean stared at him, shiny and damp with emotion. "Yes, Sandor, only you...inside me."

How did she know those were the words he needed? How had she known to clarify...to use that *only?* That small child inside him, the one who had determined at an age so young he could no longer remember it to be everything others thought he was not—important, powerful, strong—that child knew that Sandor needed that word *only.* His being important to this woman was key to healing wounds he had refused to acknowledge were even there since before they ever left Greece for America.

"You belong to me, Ellie."

"Yes." Her gazed locked with his. "Only you."

He surged inside her, feeling as if for the first time, he had come home. Her body jolted, clenched around him and then she climaxed with a scream as primal as any mating cry. He let her body soak all the joy from that moment it could before he began to move, building the momentum again with thrusts that sealed her as his own.

"Sandor...I can't...it's too much."

He didn't stop, but rotated his pelvis with each thrust. "You can, Ellie. Give me the gift of your pleasure. Come for me, my own."

Her head went back, her heels dug into the mattress and she exploded as he found his own release. His arms barely had the strength to hold his weight off of her and when she tugged him down, he had no reserves to protect her.

She did not seem to mind, but mumbled sweet nothings against his neck, telling him how amazing he was, what an incredible lover, how strong, how perfect. She even told him he was beautiful and while he would never admit it out loud, he liked hearing all the praise from her sweet mouth. Even those words.

"I have to take care of the condom," he muttered at some point.

She smiled, letting her arms slip to the bed and nodded. "Thank you."

"For what?"

"You know."

"No, I do not."

"For not trying to trap me."

Did she really think him so weak he would resort to trickery to win his case? He had no need for tricks like that and with his background, even if he feared she would not come around otherwise, he would never use them.

Besides, she'd admitted she belonged to him.

When he came back into the bedroom after washing up, she was snuggled under the covers, barely conscious. She made no demur when he climbed into bed beside her.

He pulled her into his arms. "You belong to me, Ellie."

"Sandor…"

"Do not deny it." He rolled her onto her back and looked down at her. "You acknowledged my place in your life when we made love."

Her blue-green gaze slid away from him, then she sighed and met his eyes. "I don't deny that my body belongs to you, but that doesn't mean I'm going to wear your ring, Sandor."

So much for being barely conscious. She looked ready to fall asleep any second, but she was thinking clearly enough to argue.

Frustration roared through him at her words. "What does it mean then?"

"That I doubt I'll ever let another man into my bed, but I don't know if I can spend the rest of my life with you."

What the hell was that supposed to mean? He sat up and glared down at her, the small light given off by the bedside lamp illuminating an unfathomable feminine expression. "If you will not give yourself to another man, how can you deny my place beside you?"

"I'm not *denying* anything. Please believe me. I'm just not…just not confirming it."

"Semantics."

"No…Sandor…truth. I told you I needed time."

"But after what we have just done—"

Her finger pressed against his lips to silence him. "It was wonderful, Sandor. The most special experience of my life. Please don't ruin it by starting an argument." Her eyes shone with a vulnerability he could not fight.

He nipped her finger gently in retaliation and she pulled it away, but not before he'd laved it with a healing tongue kiss. Still, he growled, "I am not the one arguing here."

Were all women this confusing, or just her? He'd never spent much time trying to understand the workings of the female mind. The only one who had ever mattered enough to him was his mother and that relationship was in no way similar.

Her aqua-blue eyes were filled with feelings he could not identify. "I'm not arguing. I'm scared, Sandor. I don't want to be hurt."

"I will not hurt you."

"But you will. You can't help it." Her eyes drooped as exhaustion overtook her, but the words kept coming as if the thought behind them was so ingrained she did not need to be fully alert to express it. "You don't love me. That is going to cause me pain. I have to decide if it's going to be worse than the pain of letting you go."

He could not believe what he was hearing. "Damn it, I will not hurt you."

"You won't be able to help it." She sounded so sad.

And it made him furious. There was no need. "You tell me what you need and I will make sure you have it." To him, it was that simple. Why could she not see it?

"You can't."

"I can do anything."

Her lips curled in a small, melancholy smile. "I know you believe that, but it's not true. You can't give me the most important thing of all."

"What is so important?"

"Your love."

He felt like he'd been kicked in the chest, but didn't know why. "I can give you everything you need." He knew it was true. "If you want affection, I will give it to you. If you want gifts, I will buy them for you. If you want companionship, it will be yours. There is nothing I will withhold from you."

Her eyes closed, but moisture leaked from the corners and it made him feel helpless, not a sensation he was used to. And certainly not one he liked.

"Except the emotion I've spent my whole life living without." She turned on her side, away from him. "All the things you offer should come from love, but you will give them to me *if I ask*. There's a difference, even if you can't see it. I know that difference intimately."

He put his hand on her shoulder, needing to comfort the raw pain he heard in her voice. "Explain."

Her shoulder rose and fell beneath his hand. "My father

feels responsibility for me, but he doesn't love me. I figured that out when I was little. He's never loved me. Everything he has ever done for me has been out of duty. Now, you are telling me you want to do the same...you will give me what I say I need out of duty as my husband." She turned back to face him and the deeply embedded pain he heard in her voice was in her moisture filled eyes. "There's never been anyone like that for me. No one to love me. No other family after my grandparents died. No long-term friendships to fall back on. Life without love is so lonely, Sandor. I don't want that kind of loneliness in my marriage."

He did not know what to say. He'd always had his mother's love and before his grandfather had died, the old man had loved him, too. In his way. Even so, Sandor had never valued love because he considered it responsible for too much pain.

Ellie was saying the lack of it was just as painful, but she was wrong that it had to be lonely.

"Do you feel lonely now, Ellie?"

She didn't answer, but something in her eyes said she was lonely...deep inside. Even after they had made love so beautifully. He did not understand it. He felt more connected to her than he had to any other person. How could she not feel the connection?

"I don't want to spend the rest of my life waiting for the people I love to love me back," she said into the silence between them.

"Are you saying you love me, Ellie?"

The moisture in her eyes overflowed, tracking down her cheeks in a stream of tears and she whispered, "Yes."

Had he considered it two days ago, he would have said that her falling in love with him would help him convince her to marry him, but now he knew it was far more likely to cause her to turn her back on what they could have. She was genuinely afraid of being hurt by him. Because he did not love her.

Something squeezed inside him, making it hard to breathe. He knew what it was to hurt. As impossible as it should be, he was hurting right now. For her. But also for himself.

Her uncertainty was tearing at old wounds. Memories best forgotten, but that haunted him all the same. He had spent his childhood rejected for what he was. The illegitimate son of a Greek woman and her American lover. The best in sports and academics, his schoolmates and even his teachers had still looked at him as if he did not measure up because he did not share his father's last name.

No amount of effort on his part could force their full acceptance, or his grandfather's unconditional approval. And he could not force Ellie to accept him, either. He did not want to even try. She deserved to come to terms with their relationship on her own, but he also needed to know that the choice had been completely hers.

Would her love be like his grandfather's, tempered by expectations and needs Sandor had little hope of fulfilling? Or would it be like his mother's love…unconditional and willing to accept him for who he was? He was self-aware enough to realize that while he did not need her love, if he had it, he wanted it to come with acceptance.

He said nothing in response to her declaration. He did not know what to say that would not hurt her further. He could not return the words in all honesty and it seemed wrong to thank her for something he was not sure would not end up hurting him as love so often did.

So, he kissed her instead. Gentle, coaxing kisses that lasted until she stopped crying and slipped into sleep, her arms wrapped tightly around him, her head resting on his shoulder.

CHAPTER SEVEN

ELLIE SAT ON THE BEACH, looking over the ocean as the sun slowly sunk in the sky behind her. She was tired from the long plane ride and two-hour drive from Barcelona to the small coastal town that boasted its own castle and a pebbly beach perfect for sunbathing.

It was empty of sun-worshippers now, the small town's night life in full swing. It felt strange to be truly alone and she could not remember the last time she'd gone anywhere without her security detail.

She'd woken that morning in the bittersweet comfort of Sandor's warm embrace, her own hold on him just as strong. While her eyes were closed and his arms held her so securely, she could pretend he loved her. Once he'd woken, he'd made love to her and then…he'd left. After telling her that she had the weekend to think.

It was so typical of him to put a time limit on her ruminations, but the fact that he was giving her that time without further argument shocked her. It really did. It was so out of character for him.

Or was it? How well did she know him? She loved him, but that didn't mean she had an automatic in to the way his mind worked. Her dad would never have given an opponent time to regroup. Sandor hadn't even tried to tell her she had no reason to be scared. He'd said he expected her to come to terms with that truth on her own.

He'd stood there in front of her door, his big hands cupping her face and said, "You will either accept me for who and what I am, what I am capable of giving you, or you will not. You will either realize you have nothing to fear from me, or you will allow your fears to derail our future. It is your choice."

Then he'd kissed her and walked out the door.

While she doubted she would come to the conclusion that she had nothing to fear, she was rapidly approaching the one that life without him seemed much bleaker than life with him and without his love. Her own love was the biggest weapon against her in this battle. A battle that no matter how much the wounded parts of her heart left bleeding by her dad's lifelong indifference told her she had to win, she was uncertain of. Because the stronger, more complete part of her heart—the part that loved Sandor and believed in life's possibilities no matter what pain her past held, said the battle was in living and she was better off fighting for love than against it.

Sandor was everything she could imagine in a lover, but so much more, too. He was loving...to his mother. He was caring...with her. He was fair. He was honorable. And he was just so darn good. She couldn't believe the way learning he could never lie to his mother had impacted her.

His grandfather's strictures on integrity had taken deep root inside Sandor Christofides. And that just impressed Ellie to death.

Her dad had no problem lying to Ellie when he thought it was for her own good, but then he didn't love her. Not really. She'd wondered before if he'd ever loved anyone. Her mother? She got the feeling that losing her mom right after Ellie's birth had destroyed his heart. But she could be wrong. She had no way of knowing.

Both sets of her grandparents had died by the time she was six years old. Her dad's father had died of a heart attack at work the year Ellie turned six and his mother had been gone before Ellie had ever been born. Her mom's parents had died in a car accident caused by a drunk driver going the wrong way on the freeway two years before that.

She hadn't told Sandor the complete truth last night. She had been loved once. She could remember the warm feel of her grandmother's arms around her when she was really little. The way her grandpa had smiled at her as if she was the sunshine in his sky, but it had been so long, sometimes she forgot what it was like to be loved.

She remembered that warmth when she was around Hera, though. The older Greek woman made Ellie wonder what it would be like to have a mother. And part of her craved marriage to Sandor because she knew that if she married him, his mother would become her mother and someone in the world would actually love her. Sandor, who refused to acknowledge the emotion had no idea how very lucky he was to have had not one, but two people love him in his life.

And now she loved him, but she didn't know if she loved him enough to give the emotion freely without expectation of its return. If she couldn't, would their marriage work? Could it work? Was she strong enough to love unrequited and not grow bitter? And if she wasn't, how *real* was her love?

The answer to many of her questions lay in her response

to her dad. She looked inside herself and felt a measure of peace steal over her. Because while she got frustrated with her dad and sometimes the pain of not being loved like she needed hurt more than she wanted to admit, she'd never, ever hated him. She didn't hate him now. She never would.

And for all their similarities, Sandor was not a carbon copy of her dad. He paid her more attention than her dad ever had. He also showed tolerance for family priorities with his mom. That was something. Because Ellie wasn't going to raise her children alone, a work-widow. She got the feeling that Sandor would think it was doubly important for him to be there as a dad for his children. Because his own father had not been there for him.

She couldn't help wondering how he was going to react to learning she'd guaranteed herself more than a weekend to make her decision. She'd taken the week off from work, managed to fool her security detail into thinking she was still in her apartment and flown to Barcelona. She hadn't had any real destination in mind when she arrived at the airport; she'd simply taken the first international flight available.

That had landed her in Barcelona, where again she'd made her travel plans based on availability and hopped the first outbound bus with an empty seat. That had brought her to this small coastal town. She'd never ridden a bus before and it had been kind of neat.

She'd checked into an older hotel, the kind that still used high ceiling fans instead of air-conditioning to control the heat. Her room was small, but clean and the decor was old world with a charm often missing in the upscale hotels she stayed at when traveling under her father's aegis. She liked it, too.

Just as she enjoyed sitting on the beach for this short

moment in time as if she was just anyone, not the daughter of a super wealthy businessman. But it couldn't last. She had to go back to her life eventually.

When she left Boston, she'd been running, she freely admitted. From Sandor. From her own feelings. From the decision she fatalistically realized was a foregone conclusion. Especially since allowing Sandor into her body. He'd been right. She'd been arguing semantics. Once she'd given herself to him, there had been no hope.

Not for a future without him if he wanted to share hers.

Remembering back to just before they first made love, she'd had that moment of lucidity...the point at which she'd realized the outcome if she gave in. Stupidly...or courageously? Or simply unavoidably...she'd given in anyway.

She knew that sex didn't mean the same to women that it did to men. She didn't need her own painful past to learn that, the media screamed the message in every medium. But that sure knowledge had not saved her. Simply *because* sex meant something so different to her, she'd had no chance. If it was only her body she was holding back, she could have done it, but once her heart was involved, she was lost.

She was going to marry Sandor. The alternative...life without him and life without the mother's love she would be gifted with in Hera, was an untenable choice.

Her heart beat a rhythm of hope as she accepted the decision. Sandor wasn't her father. He loved his mother, which meant he was capable of the emotion. And he cared about Ellie. He was afraid of love as surely as she feared the emptiness of a life without it. She would teach him that love did not always hurt, that it could be the biggest blessing in a person's life. She'd seen it in the lives of others and she had known in that place all certain knowledge is born, not learned, that it would be the same for her if she had it.

He had reasons for his fear, just as she had reasons for hers, but that didn't mean he couldn't learn something new. She was taking a chance.

She refused to believe he had any less courage than she.

Ellie stayed in Spain for the rest of the week, missing Sandor, but reveling in the freedom. The security team didn't catch up with her until Thursday. After a very different return trip to Barcelona, this one in a chauffeured car, she flew home, this time first-class, Friday afternoon.

Sandor flipped open his cell while he clicked the send button on an e-mail to a subordinate in Taiwan. "Christofides here."

"Sandor, it's Hawk."

"Have you found her?"

"Yes."

Something in the other man's voice alerted him. "Where?"

"She's in Spain."

"She said she wanted time to think. Apparently she decided she needed distance, too."

"And other things."

"What is that supposed to mean?"

"Check your fax machine."

Sandor lithely jumped to his feet and crossed the room to where his personal fax whirred. Two sheets were in the printer tray. He picked up the top one, it had Hawk's company's logo and said, "For your review."

The sheet underneath was a newspaper clipping in one of the smaller European tabloids. It was obviously not a cover shot, but an interior article. It showed Ellie dressed much more provocatively and trendily than her usual attire. She was with an attractive dark-haired man standing beside a casino table. The man had his arm around Ellie's shoulder and his expression was nothing short of possessive.

For some strange reason, Sandor felt like he couldn't breathe.

"Go back to your computer. I sent additional photos in an encrypted file."

Sandor didn't know how the other man knew he'd gotten to the fax machine and had looked at the tabloid picture proclaiming a well-known playboy had a new plaything, who had been labeled as nothing more than his "woman of mystery."

Evidently Ellie's identity was unknown. Considering the fact that she did not court publicity, he was not surprised. And if the playboy was as wealthy as he looked, he could keep her name from even determined reporters.

Sandor checked his e-mail and there was the one from Hawk. He opened it, typed in the password Hawk fed him over the phone and a picture materialized on the screen. It was of Ellie and the man kissing on the beach. He scrolled down and the pictures got more condemning. Ending with one obviously taken through a window of the couple together in bed...naked.

"Destroy the pictures at your end," he barked.

"Done."

"Thank you, Hawk."

"I'm sorry, Sandor."

Sandor nodded and hung up the phone, realizing as he did so that Hawk would not have seen his head's movement.

The pain of betrayal tore through Sandor as he tried to

wrap his mind around the evidence presented to his eyes. Ellie had slept with another man.

He muttered a very ugly Greek word.

It did not help.

He'd believed she was a woman of integrity. He had believed her when she said she loved him. So, what had this been? A last fling before marriage? He could not accept that. He wanted nothing of marriage to a faithless woman.

The pain coalescing inside him was from disappointed hopes he told himself. It had nothing to do with a lacerated heart. His heart had stopped bleeding a long time ago.

George Wentworth called an hour later. "The security team have located her."

"In Spain?" Why he asked when he had the evidence of the pictures right in front of him, Sandor did not know.

"Yes. She's flying home today."

"Thank you."

"So, are we on target for the merger?"

"We will discuss it after I have spoken to Ellie." Why he felt compelled to tell her that the relationship was over before he told her father, he did not know.

She'd shown that their relationship meant nothing to her.

"Fine, fine. I'll talk to you Monday then."

Sandor allowed George to think all was well and hung up the phone. They would talk on Monday, but it would not be about the full merger that would be based on marriage between Ellie and Sandor.

Ellie called Sandor when she arrived at her apartment Friday night. It was late and she was tired, but at peace about her decision.

Silence greeted her at the other end of the line when he picked up. It was his cell, maybe the connection was bad. Though she'd noticed that his cell phone had problems much less frequently than hers. Sandor just seemed to control whatever was around him better than the average person.

"Sandor?" she asked, trying to see if the call was still connected.

"I am here."

"I'd like to see you."

"Tomorrow."

"Okay. Do you want to come by here?"

"I will."

"When?"

"I will be there after breakfast."

"Great." Maybe they could spend the day together. She'd missed him.

The line went dead and she realized the call must have dropped. She didn't bother calling him back. She was too sleepy and she would be seeing him in the morning.

The next day, Ellie was up early. She didn't know what time Sandor considered after breakfast, but she was ready at seven-thirty. He didn't arrive until nine.

When she opened the door to him, he did not kiss her, or even smile.

She wasn't so reticent. Begin as you mean to go on. And she meant for her relationship with him to be affectionate. Not that she had a lot of experience with that, but they could both learn. She leaned up and kissed his chin.

He didn't tilt toward her so she couldn't reach his lips, but she didn't let that bother her. "I missed you."

"Did you?"

She stepped back, biting her lip. "You're upset I was gone for a week."

"You could say that." She'd never seen him look so cold and remote.

If she wasn't sure she was mistaken, she would think his brown eyes were filled with disgust. But that would be much too strong a reaction for her little burst of independence.

"Are you angry I took longer than the weekend to make my decision?" she asked, trying to gauge his mood exactly as she turned and led him into her living room.

She sat down on the yellow sofa.

He took a chair as physically far from her as it was possible to get in the room. "So, you have made your decision?"

She tried a smile. "Yes and you might as well get used to the fact that I don't take orders well. It will make our life together less bumpy if you accept it. I'm also not fond of the cold shoulder treatment."

"So, you desire to marry me?"

"Yes."

"That is interesting. I must wonder why."

Her buoyant confidence that had carried her home began to falter. This conversation wasn't making any sense to her. "You haven't changed your mind just because I was gone for a week."

"No, I did not change my mind because you chose to take longer for your decision than I told you to."

"Good."

"However, other considerations have come to light." That was definitely disgust in his eyes.

"What do you mean?" What other considerations?

"You were no virgin when we made love the first time."

"I told you I wasn't."

"But what I did not appreciate was that lack indicated a deeper flaw in your character."

"You consider my status as a nonvirgin a lack?" she asked carefully.

He simply looked at her.

"Should I then consider your similar status the same way?"

"I, at least, understand the meaning of fidelity to one partner."

"And you're saying I don't?" she asked incredulously. No way were they having this conversation. "Because I had one lover before you, you've decided I couldn't be faithful? I don't believe this."

"No."

"What are you saying then?"

"That you have done a very good job of hiding your true character, both from your father and from myself as well as my investigator. At least at first. Clearly you are very clever at leading a double life. I should salute your ingenuity. It takes much to fool my investigator and your father's security team, but you have managed it."

"Sandor, I don't know what you are talking about. I haven't hidden anything from you." Well, she hadn't told him the details of her single past liaison, but that would hardly fall under the misnomer of hiding her true character.

"On the contrary, you did a very good job of deceiving me. Looking back, I can see the signs I was too blinded to take heed of before."

"What signs?"

"The condoms. If you were so innocent, why did you have condoms the first time we made love?"

"Because I assumed you'd want to make love eventually and I didn't want to risk pregnancy."

His lip curled. "That is a convenient excuse, but not a realistic one. Until last week, I made no moves to take our relationship to the bedroom."

"I know, but—"

He sliced his hand through the air, cutting her off. "I do not wish to sit here arguing with you."

"What do you want?" Inside, everything was freezing, but she didn't feel numb. It hurt, like being outside in below zero weather without her gloves. Cold so biting, it cut to the bone. That's what her insides felt like…painfully frozen.

"To say what needs saying and go."

"Then say it," she demanded from between lips that could barely move.

He looked hesitant for a second, but then the cold mask descended again and he said, "Your father wants an heir for his business. You refuse to be that heir, so he went looking. He found me."

More shards of ice pierced her heart and somehow she knew this wasn't done. "What?"

"He offered an impossible to resist dowry. Half of his company upon marriage to you and a will stating the other half would go to our children upon his death."

She shook her head, denying her father's culpability and Sandor's as well. To accept that they could treat her like a piece of barter hurt too much to deal with. She was nothing to either of them. She never had been.

"Yes. However, even half of your father's shipping business is not enough to entice me to marry a woman who would sleep with another man when the sheets had not even cooled from sleeping with me. A woman who was supposed to be considering my proposal of marriage."

As she forced the words to penetrate her mind, they

began to take horrible shape and two facts became clear. The first was that Sandor thought she'd had sex with another man while she'd been away from him. The second was that she would never have known about the business deal he had with her dad if Sandor had not become convinced of the first fact.

"You believe simply because I went out of country sans my security detail for a few days that it naturally follows I was having sex with someone else?" she asked, finding that as difficult to accept as the knowledge that she'd been played like a pawn between the two men in her life she loved.

She was used to indifference from her father, not this all out brutality toward her feelings. And from Sandor she had expected so much more. What a fool.

"I do not make such sweeping judgments on that flimsy a pretext."

"Are you saying someone told you I was cheating on you?"

"In a way."

"Explain," she demanded, the cold inside her growing until she felt like she was filled with ice that would shatter with the next blow.

He dropped a manila folder on the coffee table.

She picked it up, refusing to hesitate or fear what she would find inside. She pulled out several sheets of paper. The top one listed a prominent worldwide detective agency. It looked like a fax cover sheet. Underneath it was a copy of a sleazy tabloid article. A woman was standing at a roulette table with a man. The woman could have been Ellie's sister, she looked so much like her.

She was thinner, though, by at least ten pounds. Her eyebrows were waxed to a popular thinness, whereas Ellie left hers untouched because they were tapered naturally. The other woman dressed in the latest sexy fashions and held herself with the confidence of a cover model, or an actress.

Ellie always looked so stiff in photos like this. It was as if she had a sixth sense the press was zeroing in on her and would tense up just before any shot. She really disliked having her photo taken. The fax was black-and-white, so Ellie couldn't tell what color of eyes the woman had or if her companion's hair was black or brown.

She flipped to the next page and one of her questions was answered. The man's hair was brown. The full color sheet photo was of the same woman and man, this time kissing on the beach. The woman wore a bikini and hip sarong. She was so thin, her bottom rib was outlined. She didn't look sick like some Hollywood starlets, but she was definitely ultrathin.

As Ellie flipped through the pictures, she realized the woman's eyes were the same color as hers. She looked even more like Ellie than a sister would. Except for the weight thing and a few other cosmetic differences, the woman could have been Ellie's double.

The last picture was of the two people in bed together. She felt like a voyeur looking at it, but she could not tear her eyes away because it spoke so deeply to her. As Ellie recognized the same vulnerable look on the woman's face as she herself wore after making love to Sandor, she knew this woman *was* her sister. She did not know how it was possible. She tried to tell herself the doppelganger was just that…some stranger who shared enough genetic makeup from a distant past that they looked like twins though were probably not even considered really related.

But her instincts screamed it was more. She knew somewhere deep in her soul, somewhere so primitive she could not deny it…that this woman was her twin.

Her father had told her that her mother had died after giving birth to her. He'd never said anything about another baby being born. But it had to be. And her father had lied to her. How she and her twin had gotten separated, she didn't know. And she didn't care.

All she knew was that out there was a human being who would have loved her because sisters loved each other. A woman she would have loved and been there for, too.

She turned to Sandor. "Get out."

"That is all you have to say to me?"

"No."

He looked like he was almost hoping she could explain the pictures, but that had to be a trick of the lighting. He didn't care. He'd wanted to marry her in order to make his business bigger. Even his mom had gotten it right, while Ellie had lived in dumb ignorance. Enough was never enough for Sandor and his company would always come first. Just like her father.

"I think you are contemptible."

That seemed to rock him back on his proverbial heels. "What the hell did you just say to me?"

"You lied to me. You said you wanted me, but all you wanted was my dad's company."

"You think to use this to justify your behavior?"

"No. I don't have to justify my behavior and yours is irredeemable. Get out of my apartment, Sandor, and don't come back. Ever."

He didn't move. "Ellie…"

"Stop talking and leave." Too much was going through her mind. Too much pain. Too many surprises. Terror that all she had believed about life and herself was one big deception.

"At least tell me why you went to him. Was he an old lover…was it a last fling?"

"I don't owe you any explanations."

"You came home prepared to marry me."

"Yes, more the fool me."

"Ellie, make me understand."

She stared at him. The words felt like a plea from the heart, but he didn't have a heart. He only really cared about his company, about proving he was bigger and better than his father. He didn't care about her. His deal with her dad and the fact he had not told her about it proved that.

"You said you couldn't hide truth from your mother."

"It is not the same."

"Patently. You love her and I am nothing more than a pawn my father and you have played between you. I could hate you, Sandor. I really think I could hate you."

He laughed harshly. "One of the things I found so intriguing about you is how much we had in common. Even to this. I could hate you, too, Ellie."

"Go away, Sandor." Hot tears burned her eyes. She blinked furiously, determined not to let them fall while he was still in her apartment. "I don't want you here. Not ever again."

He stood, a flash of weary pain sparking in his eyes before it disappeared to be replaced by that glacial cool he'd worn upon entering her home. "And I do not want to be here. It seems we both made a mistake believing we could trust the other."

"Yes." Her voice cracked on the single word.

Sandor stopped on his path across the hardwood floor, but then he straightened his shoulders and kept going.

CHAPTER EIGHT

ELLIE WANTED TO scream out in pain.

She'd felt this way once before and promised herself she'd never let herself be used again. She'd failed and it hurt. It hurt so much, she didn't know if she could keep the pain inside like she had the last time. It was too big. Too deep.

But then her love for Sandor was so much more intense than what she'd felt at nineteen, the two feelings did not even compare. She felt like there was a steel band around her chest and it was contracting.

She couldn't deal with it. It was too much. But there was nothing there...no one to help her through the pain. Nothing to blunt its shattering intensity.

Then her gaze slid to the pictures spread out on her coffee table. The truth. She had to learn the truth.

She grabbed the fax cover sheet and stumbled to the phone. Blinking away tears, she read the number listed for the agency's landline. There were offices all over the world according to the stationery, but the one that had generated this fax was in New York. Her fingers were clumsy and she had to redial twice before she got the number right.

The sender, a person named Hawk, no last name given,

was not in the office. She left her name and both cell and home numbers with the answering service, requesting he call her immediately. She told the service it was an emergency.

In her mind, it was.

She couldn't let herself dwell on Sandor's betrayal. She heard you could not die from a broken heart, but you could not tell that by the way she felt. She couldn't afford to let the wound inside her grow. She had to contain it, lock it away with all the other pain of past rejection.

Desperation clawed through her as the agony threatened to shred her. She picked up the pictures and rushed to the computer, determined to research what she could. Anything to keep her brain occupied with something besides her bleeding heart.

She started with the article in the tabloid. Hawk had efficiently supplied the name of the weekly along with the page the article had been found on. She found the paper online. It was a Spanish tabloid, but since she was fluent in the language, that wasn't a problem for her.

Only there was no additional information. The name of the man with the woman who looked like Ellie's twin was given in the original article. Ellie did a site search on his name and discovered several more articles on him. But all that did was depress her.

Apparently she and her sister both had lousy taste in men because this guy had dated a half dozen women in the last year that he'd been photographed with. Who knew how many others he'd been with? There was no follow-up article to the one with his mystery woman.

Then Ellie decided it was time to go to the source. Her work with the unemployed had taught her how to research a person's background for the purpose of supplying sufficient documentation to get into continuing education programs. She started searching for her own birth records and from there, record of any sibling's birth.

She'd been at it about forty-five minutes when she stopped, so shocked, her eyes could barely focus enough to read the words on the computer screen. She *had* been born a twin and according to the records she was looking at, there was no record of her sister's death.

Following a hunch, she called a friend at the library. The other woman was a former client Ellie had helped to get into night school and eventually into a position as a reference librarian for a small town west of Boston. She asked the librarian to do a microfilm search on newspaper articles with her family's name in them around the time of her birth.

Two hours later, her friend called back with news that rocked Ellie's world right off its axis.

Ellie wasn't surprised to find her father in his office on a Saturday afternoon, but he was surprised to see her.

He stood up from his desk, a smile of welcome curving his lips. "Eleanor, what are you doing here?"

"I came to ask why you lied to me."

"Lied to you?" His pale blue eyes narrowed warily. "About what?"

"What's the matter? Are there so many lies between us that you can't guess which one I'm angry about?" she asked scathingly.

"I told Sandor not to mention the business deal. I knew it would only upset you."

"I don't care about the business deal between you two sharks."

"You don't?"

"No."

"So, you're going to marry him anyway?"

"Never!"

George Wentworth seemed to shrink, looking older than his fifty-four years. "I thought…"

"Whatever you thought, you were wrong. But I'm not here to discuss Sandor, or the almost disaster I narrowly avoided in marrying him."

"You aren't?"

"I'm here to discuss her." Ellie threw a picture on the desk.

It was one in which her sister's lover was difficult to recognize. Ellie had no doubt that her father would start looking for her sister, but the fact that he'd stopped looking at all and filed his lost daughter away with other bad business made her determined not to make it easy for him. She was perfectly capable of finding the other woman, or at least as capable of hiring a good detective agency as he was.

Her dad stared down at the picture and turned gray. "Where did this come from?"

"Ask Sandor."

His head snapped up. "What does Sandor have to do with it?"

"He thinks I cheated on him."

"But I told him you were in Spain."

"Did you?"

"Yes."

"There are stalking laws in this state. Call off your security detail, or I will invoke them."

"Damn it, Eleanor, you know I can't do that. It's not safe."

"You mean like she was safe?"

If anything, his complexion turned more pasty. "There was nothing I could do once she was gone. No leads to follow."

"You gave up."

"It was the only way to maintain my sanity." He made a visible effort to swallow. "How did you find out about her?"

"Certainly not from you."

He flinched, but said nothing.

"I played a hunch and had a newspaper search done of the time near my birth. The kidnapping made the papers."

"By the time it did, there was no hope left."

"Why didn't you tell me about her? I had a right to know."

"What would have been the use? By the time you were old enough to understand, I knew we would never see her again. Knowing about her would only have hurt you."

"Since when did you ever care whether or not I was hurt? You didn't tell me about my sister because you didn't want me to keep after you to find her. You knew I would. I'm stubborn that way about the people I love."

"I couldn't stand it. It hurt too much," the admission came out in a low, tortured voice.

"What hurt exactly? Writing your daughter off like bad business?"

"I didn't write her off. There was nothing to go on," he practically shouted, surging to his feet behind the desk.

"Who said I was talking about her?" Ellie asked, then turned and left his office.

He called her name, but she ignored the plea in his voice, just as he had ignored her pleas for affection for twenty-four years.

When she got home, there was a message on her answering machine. It was Hawk.

She called him back, irritated all over again by men whose priorities didn't match hers.

"I told your answering service it was an emergency," she said after he picked up and without even identifying herself.

"Miss Wentworth?"

"Yes."

"It has only been five hours since you called."

"An emergency implies immediate reaction is necessary, Mr. Hawk. I'm surprised your clients are tolerant of your definition."

"You are not one of my clients."

"Nevertheless…"

He sighed. "I will admit that I would prefer not to have this conversation, but to clarify, the demise of a relationship due to information I provide is not a five-alarm fire in my book."

"It should be when you got your facts wrong."

"Please, Miss Wentworth. I've heard it all before. Tearful begging and bribery are going to meet with the same non-results. Nothing is going to convince me to call my client and tell him there was a mistake. There was no mistake."

"You're so sure of that?"

"Absolutely positive."

She shook her head at his arrogance, but only said, "I have no interest in you calling the deceiving rat who employed you."

"Then what do you want?" the man asked, sounding skeptical.

"I want to know where you, or your operative was, when these pictures were taken."

"I cannot answer that question. My operatives are all very good at being discreet. Do not feel badly that you did not realize one was following you."

"I don't mean where the operative was in relation to the people in the pictures, I mean where he was geographically."

"He was in Spain," Hawk replied in a tone that said he was humoring her.

"Spain?" she choked out in disbelief.

The article had been in a Spanish tabloid, but the playboy with her sister was something of a Spanish celebrity, being a member of the family that ran one of the country's largest privately held business conglomerates. The article did not give any information regarding location of where the picture was taken with the man's mystery lady however.

"You know he was."

"No, Mr. Hawk. I don't know." She felt sick. She'd been in the same country, even on the same coast from the look of things, with her sister. "What city was he in?"

"Is this game necessary?"

"Just answer my questions and then I'll hang up and leave you in peace."

"The pictures were taken in and near Barcelona."

"If I'd stayed in the city, I might have seen her," she breathed incredulously. Why had she taken the bus out of the city to the smaller town further down the coast? Because she'd been running from Sandor. Pain sliced through her and she cut those thoughts off midspate. "Did you follow this couple anywhere else?"

"No. My client told me to stop surveillance so I called my operative in from the field."

At least she had a place to start. And a name. The playboy her sister had been seen with.

"Mr. Hawk, can you recommend an agency to help me find someone?"

"You're asking me for a recommendation?"

She almost laughed at his incredulity. "Yes. Sandor used you, which means you're the best there is. It follows you would know who I should call if I can't use you."

"Who do you want to find, Miss Wentworth, if you don't mind me asking?"

"The couple in the pictures you took. Specifically the woman."

"No agency I recommend is going to fabricate evidence of a second woman to get you off the hook."

"I'm not on the hook. In fact, because of you…I'm off of it permanently. Which gives me two things to thank you for, Mr. Hawk."

"Just Hawk," he growled. "What two things?"

"If you hadn't screwed up, Sandor never would have told me about the business deal he and my father intended to use me as the contract guarantee for. I might have married him. That's the first thing. And because you took those pictures, I now know I have a sister and even where to start looking for her. If you weren't in New York and I hadn't come to the conclusion that all men were a waste of good DNA, I might be tempted to kiss you."

Sandor stared down at the pictures of Ellie and the other man. When he'd first gotten the photos, he'd looked at them only long enough to assimilate what he was seeing and then he'd refused to look at them again. He'd meant to delete the images off his computer after he printed them off, but he hadn't.

Then he'd gone to Ellie's and told her it was over. And now he sat like a moonstruck calf, looking at the pictures in obsessive, meticulous detail. Ellie looked thinner in the pictures, but that wasn't right. Wasn't the camera supposed to add ten pounds? And there was something different about her eyebrows.

He tried to think back to when he'd met with her earlier. Had she looked any different? He couldn't remember. He'd been upset, damn it.

He didn't like admitting that any more than he liked the fact that he couldn't seem to look away from the pictures of his woman with another man. She *was* his woman. Ellie belonged to him. But if she'd gone to bed with another man, she wasn't his. According to the way they'd left things when he'd walked out of her apartment, she wasn't his. He'd even agreed to it.

His pride had. It had demanded he leave rather than push for explanations she was unwilling to give. Not that any explanation could make it okay. He was disgusted with himself for even wanting to know what she'd been thinking. For wanting to *understand*.

Only he couldn't get past one salient fact. She'd come home prepared to marry *him*. Why? Why, if she wanted to have sex with another man had she been willing to marry him? He knew it wasn't the money. It wasn't his position, either. Those things did not hold sway for Ellie. Or so he had believed.

But he had also believed her incapable of infidelity.

They were not married yet, but once she had taken him into her body, she had belonged to him. He crumpled one of the pictures in his hand as thoughts of her with another man tormented emotions he refused to acknowledge. He should not feel like this. If she wanted someone else, he should be able to deal with that the same way he did a business deal that fell through.

But he'd told her their relationship was not a business deal. And it wasn't. It was more, damn it.

He stared down at the picture again. Why did his instincts keep telling him something wasn't right about the photos? Obviously he didn't want to see his woman with another man. That was what was wrong.

He stared at the one of the woman on the beach. Was it a trick of the camera, or did Ellie's body look as different as he thought it did?

His phone rang and he picked it up. "Christofides."

"Sandor, it's Hawk."

"Yes?"

"I just had a strange phone call from your fiancée."

"We aren't engaged." Saying the words out loud made him feel hollow and he had to concentrate on ignoring the reaction.

"That's what she said."

"Was she angry with you?"

"No. Actually she thanked me."

"You find that strange?" Actually he did, too. He wouldn't have anticipated Ellie thanking Hawk for exposing her activities with the Spanish playboy.

"Not after she explained. She seems to think you and her father have messed her over royally."

Sandor made a noncommittal male sound he knew Hawk would understand.

"She asked for a recommendation for a firm to help her find someone."

"Who?"

"The woman in the picture."

Everything inside Sandor froze. "She's claiming it's not her?"

"Yes."

"And she wants you to find this other woman?"

"Not at first, no. She wanted me to recommend another agency. But if the woman in the photos is not your fiancée, then my operative made a mistake. That puts my agency at fault. I don't like mistakes, Sandor."

"I am aware of it. That is why I use your agency exclusively." He paused. "Are you going to find the woman?"

"Yes, but I wanted to give you the courtesy of knowing I was looking."

"I appreciate that."

"Sandor?"

"Yes?"

"I'm sorry."

Sandor knew the words were hard for the other man to say. He and Hawk shared that trait. They both hated making mistakes and admitting them equally as much. But the words meant something more. Hawk would not be apologizing if he wasn't convinced of Ellie's claim. If he believed her, then the evidence she had against the photos being her had to be pretty significant.

A sensation like heady relief washed over Sandor and he had to fight to keep his voice level. "Who does Ellie say the woman is?"

"Her twin sister, kidnapped from the hospital almost immediately after their birth. There were no leads and the baby just disappeared. No request for a ransom was ever made."

It took several seconds for Sandor to assimilate Hawk's words because they were so different than anything he would have expected the other man to answer. "I did not know Ellie had a sister."

"Neither did she."

"Her father did not tell her?"

"No and I get the feeling he's on her black list at the moment."

"Along with me."

"Afraid so."

Sandor swore, but he still felt lighter than he had in a long time. Ellie had not gone to another man's bed. She *was* his. "How did she find out?"

"She knew the pictures were not of her."

"So, she immediately thought she had a twin?"

"No. She told me she tried to believe the woman was just a doppelgänger, but her instincts were telling her otherwise, so she searched her birth records."

"And discovered another baby had been born?"

"Yes. I verified the birth records and newspaper accounts of the kidnapping as well as the fact that Miss Wentworth was staying in a small hotel in a town further along the coast than Barcelona during the time my agent was following her twin and Menendez around the city."

Trust Hawk to have double-checked the facts to be sure.

"I see. What are the chances they would have been in Spain at the same time?"

"Slim, but in my line of work, you learn to accept that kind of thing does happen. A lot more often than people want to believe."

"I believe."

"It upset her."

"You mean Ellie? What upset her?"

"That she was so close to her unknown sister and that they did not meet."

"She is no doubt upset about a lot of things right now."

Hawk's silence was agreement enough.

"Have you spoken to Wentworth yet?" Sandor asked.

"He's the next call I'm making."

"Let me know what you find out."

"No can do. Telling you I am looking is a courtesy, but in this case, Eleanor Wentworth is my client."

"Understood."

Sandor picked up the phone and dialed Ellie's number. She didn't answer and he wasn't surprised. She had caller ID. He tried three more times before deciding his best alternative would be to do what they had both said they did not want for him to do ever…return to her apartment.

He'd changed his mind, but he was under no illusions that she was in a similar place. Getting through the door was going to be no easy task. She'd said she never wanted to see him again. And she'd meant it. But he had not gotten to where he was by giving up.

He was on his way to her apartment when his cell phone rang.

It was Hawk again.

"What is it?" he asked without preamble.

"When I called to try to talk to George Wentworth, I discovered he had been rushed to a nearby private hospital. He was found collapsed on his office floor two hours ago."

"Did someone call Ellie?"

"She's not answering her phone."

"I am on my way to her apartment right now."

"Good. When you see her, tell her I'm working on finding her sister."

"Will do."

He tried calling Ellie's apartment again, but there was still no answer.

His next call was to his mother. That conversation was

almost as difficult as the one he anticipated with the woman he fully intended to claim once again.

Sandor knocked on Ellie's door, having gained access to the building without her assistance. She hadn't been answering her apartment buzzer, either.

There was no answer to his knock. That did not surprise him, either, but he did not give up, knocking again. No sound came from the other side of the steel door.

The next time he knocked, he called her name. Then called out, "Ellie, it is Sandor. I have news of your father."

Still nothing.

He strode quickly to the apartment that housed her security detail and banged on the door.

A tall man in his fifties, but obviously fit, opened the door almost immediately. "Yes?"

"You know who I am."

"Yes, sir."

"Has Miss Wentworth left her apartment this evening?"

"No, sir."

"Are you certain?"

"We have taken additional precautions since the slip she gave us last week, sir. There is no way she has left the building without us being aware."

Sandor nodded and turned, going back to Ellie's door and pounding on it until he heard a voice from the other side.

"For goodness' sake, Sandor, one of my neighbors is going to protest the disturbance." Her words were muffled by the door, but the scolding tone was clear. "Go away."

He stared straight at the peephole, hoping she was looking through it. "No."

"I'm not letting you in!"

"Your father is in trouble, Ellie."

"Yes, he is." She sounded both angry and hurt.

Sandor grimaced, hating having to impart this news. She had been through enough today, but there was no help for it. "He is in the hospital as we speak."

Silence reigned on the other side of the door. Then his cell phone rang.

It was her. He flipped it open. "I am sorry, *pethi mou*."

"What do you mean he's in the hospital?"

"Hawk informed me that he was discovered collapsed on the floor of his office over two hours ago. He was rushed to a private hospital."

The phone went dead. Then the bolts *snicked* signaling she was unlocking the door and then it opened. She stood with her hand on the knob, her eyes a chilly blue, the green almost completely absent. They were also red and puffy. "This had better not be a trick."

"I would not make something like this up."

"So you say."

Sandor did not take umbrage. He was well aware he could not afford to in their current circumstance. He was firmly in the wrong and they both knew it. What he did not know was how to undo the damage of their earlier conversation. He thought she could forgive him for believing her unfaithful; the evidence had been overwhelming. But he did not think she would forgive the business agreement he had with her father where she played a key role.

Sandor sighed. "As I said, George was discovered collapsed on his office floor this afternoon. His staff has been trying to reach you, but you are not answering your phone."

"I don't want to talk to him or you."

So, she had ignored caller identification that had indicated him, his company or her father's company. "I understand."

"No, you don't." Her chin trembled. "You don't love me. You can't understand at all."

CHAPTER NINE

HE DID NOT KNOW what to say to that. "I will take you to the hospital."

She shook her head, but he could see that her slim body trembled. "I can drive myself."

"You should not drive in your current state."

"What state is that, Sandor?" Anger leaked into her gaze. "Bleeding inside after finding out how thoroughly you and my father deceived me?"

"I knew nothing of your sister's existence."

"But you knew about the business merger. You knew that you saw me as nothing more than a contract guarantee. You were set to use me until you got what you considered evidence that proved me unworthy of being your pawn."

"That is not the way it was." But he'd known she would see it that way. Women and men did not think the same. He and Ellie seemed even further apart in the way they processed certain information than most. "I did not plan to use you. I wanted to share my life with you."

She shook her head. Denying his words? Denying herself? He did not know.

She swallowed convulsively, clenching her jaw to stop

her chin trembling. Yet he sensed the stoicism was only a step away from emotional breakdown. Something in the fragile way she held herself.

"I'm not going to discuss this right now." She sounded firm enough, but then she just seemed to crumble. "Is he really in the hospital?"

He pulled her into his arms rather than let her drop to the floor. "Yes, *pethi mou*. I called to check his condition on the way over here. He is stabilized, but they do not know yet what caused it."

He was grateful, but surprised when she did not pull away.

"*I* know," she mumbled against his shirtfront and then her lithe body shook with a sob. "It's my fault."

"No. That is not true."

"I told him about her. About my sister. Without any warning. Then I accused him of giving up on her and me. Then I left. I wouldn't listen to anything he said."

If he had realized the woman in the photos was not Ellie, he would have been with her when she confronted her dad. He could have made it better for both the woman he wanted to marry and her father. But he'd been deceived by his own eyes and now they would all pay the price.

"Shh…" He smoothed his hand down her back. "You were hurt. I should have been there with you. If we had not argued, I would have been. I am sorry."

She pulled away, somehow managing to stifle the emotions emanating off of her like an electric storm. She wiped at her eyes with the back of her hands and sniffed. "We need to go. I have to see him."

Sandor breathed a silent sigh of relief that she had decided to let him take her. She needed him even if she did not realize it.

They were in the car when Ellie asked, "How did you know about my sister?"

"Hawk called."

"Oh." She sighed. "That's right. You said something about talking to him. He told you about my dad?"

"Yes, in a later phone call."

"It was so shocking to find out I had a sister."

"No doubt horrifically so for you. But I had begun to suspect something was not right with the photos before I spoke to Hawk."

"What…why?"

"The woman in the pictures looks like you, but there are subtle differences."

"Why didn't you notice those before you accused me of sleeping around?" He could feel her intent stare as he negotiated city traffic.

"I was too angry to look at the pictures closely at first."

"But you weren't too upset after?" She sounded very confused.

"After you threw me out of your apartment, I went to my office. The pictures were there…" He let his voice trail off, unwilling to admit to the compulsion to be connected to her even if it was through looking at pictures of her with another man.

"And you looked at them?"

"Yes."

"Closely enough to notice the differences in the way my twin and I look?"

"Yes," he ground out.

"I would have thought you'd burn them and say good riddance."

"They were on my computer hard drive."

"Delete them then."

If doing so could have erased the feelings that came with looking at them, he would have. Nevertheless, he said, "I am glad I did not."

"Why?"

"I saw the truth."

"But I bet you didn't accept it until after Hawk's phone call."

"You are right."

"But you found it comforting?"

"Yes."

"I'm not sure I understand why. Since your watchdog was so obviously observing the wrong person, there's nothing to prove that I wasn't having a hot affair with some Spanish stud at the same time. Maybe I discovered the joys of fulfilling sex with you and decided to experiment a little."

He tried not to let her flippancy get to him. In some ways he definitely deserved her derision, but a primitive part of him wanted to growl at her to shut up. He did not like those words coming out of her mouth. "You came home prepared to marry me, you would not have done so if you were interested in experimenting sexually with others."

"Maybe I decided you were better in bed than my other experiments."

He couldn't help it. A growl escaped. "You would not do that," he said as evenly as he could, his grip on the steering wheel white-knuckled.

"That's not what you said this morning."

"I believed the evidence of my eyes." Maybe he had been premature in believing she would understand and forgive that aspect of their argument more easily than the other.

She turned to look out her side window, creating a mental distance that was intolerable. "It doesn't matter."

"I do not agree," he ground out. "I owe you an apology."

"For what?"

"For not trusting you. For accusing you of infidelity."

"We aren't married, I can't be unfaithful to you. Even if I had sex with ten other men—and you can't be sure that I didn't—it wouldn't mean I was unfaithful."

"You did not have sex with someone else. Stop implying you might have."

"Why?"

"You are goading my temper."

"So?"

"So, I do not want to have another argument with you."

"Maybe I do."

"Later…when you are not so fragile, pick a fight. For now, please…I am pleading with you, Ellie. Stop provoking me."

She gasped as if in shock.

Did she think he did not care enough about her to put his pride aside to protect her? He was not so weak.

After a couple of tension-filled minutes of silence, she sighed. "It really doesn't matter, but I didn't have sex with anyone else," she grudgingly admitted.

"I know."

"That doesn't make any difference. I'm not going to marry you, Sandor. You may have decided you can trust me, but I *know* I can't trust you now. That's not going to change."

He did not agree. "Because of the business merger?"

"Yes."

"We will overcome that."

"No, we won't."

They arrived at the hospital and he accepted now was

not the time for this conversation. He had lost ground with Ellie, but she had come home willing to marry him. He would bring her to that place again. "We will discuss this later."

"There's no point."

Instead of arguing, he parked the car and went around to help her out of her seat. Her face was pale, her eyes were still red and once again filled with moisture.

He leaned down and kissed her temple. "He will be all right, *pethi mou*. He is a tough man."

"I know." But, once again, she had to blink away tears.

He clasped her elbow and took it as a good sign that she did not pull away. It also disturbed him. George was not the only tough Wentworth. For Ellie to be willing to lean on Sandor feeling toward him the way that she did, she had to be feeling incredibly vulnerable.

He slid his arm around her waist and kept her close as they entered the private hospital.

Ellie walked into the hospital room, a cauldron of emotions swirling through her. She was still angry with her father, but she felt guilt, too. There was pain there as well, both at his and Sandor's betrayals. And fear. Horrible, mind-numbing fear. She didn't want her father to die. He was all she had, even if they weren't as close as she would like.

He was awake, his light blue eyes fixed on her as she approached the bed. He didn't smile. He didn't speak.

She stopped about three feet from the bed, not knowing what to do. Wishing he, or Sandor, would say something. Her throat was too clogged.

Then George Wentworth did something he hadn't since she was very little and then so infrequently, her memories of it often felt like dreams. He put his arms out. "Come here, sweetheart. Please."

And she ran to him.

He pulled her into his embrace and held her tight against his chest and she started to cry. "I'm s-sorry, D-daddy. I d-didn't mean f-for this to h-happen."

"I know, baby, I know." He rubbed her back, his hold warm and strong. "You didn't do anything wrong. I'm here because of my own mistakes, not yours."

She lifted her head, trying to hard to control her tears, but they just would not stop. "But I s-said…"

"The truth." He cupped her cheek. "Listen to me, Eleanor. I've made a lot of mistakes with you. I've made a lot of mistakes period, but I'll never regret the words you said this afternoon. They woke me up. You gave me hope for the first time in over twenty years that I would see my other little girl again. And as angry as you were, you made me realize that I had a daughter who needed me now, if I never find your sister."

"How could you not know I needed you?"

Agony darkened his eyes. "For more than two decades, I've practiced at ignoring your needs because I could not deal with feelings at all. Not yours. Not mine. I was a lousy father and I wish I could go back and change the past, but I can't. When your mother died, I shut myself off. It happened so fast, by the time your sister's disappearance came to light, I was already closed off from my babies. I didn't try hard enough to find her. I accepted without question…" His voice broke and it was a second before he could continue. "When the investigators told me there were no more leads to follow, I didn't argue. A year after her disappearance from the hospital, the police put her case on indefinite hold due to lack of new information. I closed the case with the investigative agency I'd hired as well."

Unbelievably he started to cry, turning his head away from her. "I have no excuse. When I look at your childhood, I feel as if I shut you out as completely as I did her. I failed you both on so many levels."

The monitor beside his bed began to beep and a nurse came rushing in, followed closely by a doctor. Ellie tried to get up and out of their way, but her dad wouldn't let her go.

"No. It's just my heart. It will get better. It's not used to feeling and it's having a hard time with the new experience." His attempt at a laugh ended in a pain-filled wheeze, but he wouldn't let her go.

"Please, Daddy, let them take care of you. Please. I don't want to lose you again."

"You won't leave?" His tone was pleading, his normally strong voice choked with tears she'd never, ever seen him shed before.

"I won't go further than the hall, I promise."

"I love you, Eleanor. Please believe me. I know I've done a lousy job of showing it, but I love you more than my own life."

She didn't know if she believed him. She wanted to. So much. And she felt badly, but twenty-four years of neglect didn't get wiped out with even heart-rending tears and confessions of affection. For all she knew, his illness was making him maudlin and he'd go back to his distant self once he was feeling better. She didn't say any of that, though.

She gave him a watery smile. "I love you, too. I always have."

He let her go and she moved back so the doctor could get to him. Then she stumbled toward the door and Sandor was there, his arm around her, guiding her out of the room and into the hall. Once outside the door, he pulled her into his chest, sheltering her from the noise coming from the room and the sense of desolation trying to wash over her.

Suddenly another pair of arms was there, hugging her. And a warm, comforting scent. "Is she all right, Sandor?"

"She is strong, Mama."

Ellie lifted her head. "Hera?"

"Yes, my child. I am here." The older woman's eyes were filled with compassion. "Come, let us go to the waiting room."

"I told him I wouldn't leave the hall."

"The room, it is right here, off the hallway. Not more than ten steps. You will know instantly if he has need of you. Sandor will make sure of it, but child you need to sit down."

Sandor agreed and between the two of them, he and his mother managed to convince Ellie to go to the waiting room and sit. They took a place on either side of her on the small sofa against one wall. There was no one else there and Ellie was glad. She never fell apart like this. She'd hate to have strangers witness her weakened state.

Sandor had his arm around her shoulder and she leaned against him, drawing on his strength.

Hera held Ellie's hand with one of hers and patted it with her other one. "You have had a difficult day, no?"

Ellie gave a shaky sigh. "Yes."

"Sandor told me all about it."

Ellie's head came up at that and she looked from mother to son. "All of it?"

Hera's dark eyes so like her son's, were filled with compassion. "Yes. All. My son, he was very stupid, but you must give him some credit. He did not know of your sister any more than you did."

"Did he tell you about the business merger?"

Hera's expression turned infinitely sad. "Yes. He and your father, they do not understand a woman's heart, do they?"

"No. I don't think they do."

"I am sitting right here," Sandor complained.

"And you are lucky to be so. Do not push it, my son."

Ellie choked out a laugh. "He's been watching out for me. He came to get me. I wasn't answering my phone."

"I know. He called me from his car on the way to your apartment."

"I might not have known." Tears threatened again. "What if Dad had died and I didn't know it?"

"Do not think this way. All will be well."

Ellie nodded, choking back tears.

The doctor came into the room. "Miss Wentworth?"

Ellie looked up at him. "Yes?"

"We've sedated your father. He needs rest right now."

"What happened?"

"You've heard the phrase, 'His heart couldn't take it'?"

"Yes."

"That's exactly what happened. It's actually very rare, but the shock of learning your sister was alive and apparently combined with some painful personal inner revelations, it was all simply too much for him. The good news is that tests show minimal damage to his heart and he should enjoy a full recovery, but he needs rest and relief from stress."

"He runs a multinational company…I think he lives on the stress."

"He'll have to learn to live on something else for a while."

Ellie looked up at Sandor. "How?" That's all she asked, but she knew he knew what she meant.

"I will work with his executive officers and keep the company running smoothly. Hawk will find your sister and all will be well. Believe me, *pethi mou*."

"I want to, but I'm scared."

"You have to have faith," Hera said, squeezing her hand. "Sandor will help you."

"But…"

"Despite his ignorant handling of his courtship with you, he is a smart and capable man. He will protect your father from further business stress until he is well again."

"That is good to hear," the doctor said. "You can go home, Miss Wentworth. Your father will not wake for several hours."

"I promised I wouldn't leave."

"So, you will stay." Hera patted her hand again. "And I will stay with you. Sandor, you must go home and rest. You have much to take care of tomorrow caring for two big companies."

Sandor tried arguing, but it did him no good. Hera Christofides was more than a match for her son when it came to being stubborn. Sandor arranged with the doctor for the two women to share a room near her father. Wealth brought with it certain privileges, especially in a private hospital.

Ellie slept fitfully and was beside her father's bed before breakfast the next morning.

His eyes opened and he searched the room with his gaze, stopping when he saw her on the far side of his bed away from the door. He smiled, his expression filled with gratitude. "You're here."

"Where else would I be?"

"I wouldn't have blamed you if you'd gone home and refused to come back to see me."

"Ellie would never do such a thing," Hera said from the doorway.

"Mrs. Christofides, I did not realize you were here."

"Ellie needs me right now."

Those words were so sweet to Ellie's ears. No one had ever "been there" for her like Hera was insisting on doing, or even Sandor had done the day before, or with his phone call just after 6:00 a.m. that morning. He'd somehow known she wasn't sleeping and had called to make sure she was okay.

He had offered to come to the hospital, but she'd known he had enough to keep him busy with his company and her father's so she'd told him not to come.

"Thank you for being such a good friend to my daughter."

Hera waved her hand dismissively. "It is my pleasure. She would be my daughter-by-marriage soon if you and my son had not messed up so spectacularly."

George winced. "Point taken."

"*Ne*…yes, I can see that it is."

Ellie reached out to take her dad's hand. "We don't have to think about that right now."

He squeezed her hand convulsively, as if he was afraid she'd pull away. "I would like to talk about it, though…if you don't mind."

Ellie chewed her lip nervously. "I don't want you upset again."

Hera pulled a chair near his bedside and sat down. "I've spoken with the nurse in charge. Breakfast will be delivered in twenty minutes."

It was such a mundane sentence, but it broke the tension starting to permeate the room.

Ellie's dad nodded. "Honey?"

"Promise you won't get overwrought again."

He smiled at her use of the old-fashioned term. "I promise."

"What do you want to say?"

He sighed and smoothed his blanket before he began to speak. The uncharacteristic hesitancy caught at Ellie's heart. "I approached Sandor with the merger idea after the way I saw he looked at you."

"What are you talking about?" Sandor had looked at her?

Her dad met her gaze, his own unflinching. She could tell he was determined to be fully honest. "I won't pretend it was all altruism on my part. I'd realized long ago you had no interest in running the company. Taking on a partner who could give me grandchildren to inherit the company made sense."

"He could hardly make those grandchildren without my cooperation."

"Exactly."

"So you offered him half your company if he would marry me?"

"Yes, but Ellie, I knew he wanted you, too. Personally."

That was something she was still very much uncertain of, but she didn't deny her dad's take on it. She saw no point in doing so. Apparently he had believed Sandor wanted her and that's really all the was relevant to this conversation.

The thing was, he'd overlooked something pretty major in her estimation. "Is that supposed to make it all better? What about what *I* wanted?"

"You looked at Sandor Christofides the way your mother looked at me when we first met."

"Like what?" Ellie asked, more because she was hungry to hear about her parents and what it had been like between them than because she wanted to know how her dad thought she saw Sandor.

"Your mother looked at me like a hungry hunter. She was an adventurous woman, your mother. So, her sweet eyes, the same color as yours, they were filled with both wariness and attraction. She wanted to tame the lion, but wasn't sure I could be tamed."

"You were a playboy?"

"No. Like Sandor, I was a businessman. A shark. I'd inherited wealth, unlike your young man, but it wasn't enough for me. I was only twenty-eight, when I met your mother, but though we worked side by side for years, I'd already almost doubled my father's business holdings."

"Did you love her?"

"Very much."

Something inside Ellie cracked at that assurance. He had loved once.

"How did she die?" She'd always known her mother died after giving birth, but there'd been an accident, too. She'd never asked for details because, well…that wasn't the kind of thing she asked her dad and there'd been no one else.

"She was in a car accident. It was bad. She went into premature labor…she delivered you girls and then slipped into a coma. She never came out and died less than a week after giving birth."

"I'm sorry."

"I am, too. She was a wonderful woman and she would have been so good for you. I didn't raise you the way she would have wanted me to. I failed her and you both…just like I failed your sister. I fight for every business concession I want, but I was too weak to fight past the pain of her loss."

"Failure is not a terminal disease unless you allow it to

be," Hera said from her chair beside the bed, sounding comfortingly practical.

George's head snapped up and he met her gaze. "I'm not going to let myself die. I'm going to make it up to my girls. Somehow. Someway."

Hera nodded. "That is an admirable sentiment, but it will not be easy."

"I know."

"If it becomes too difficult and you retreat to your work again, you will not get another chance. Your daughter is very self-sufficient."

"Too independent."

"You would rather she was weak?"

"No."

"Good."

Ellie didn't mind the conversation that did not require her participation. She had a lot to assimilate and as much as she wanted to trust her dad again, she just didn't know if she could. He'd hurt her so many times both as a child and then as a woman. And she'd been hurt by others, too…she was discovering that past pain could be a huge barrier to present acceptance of things like love and affection.

CHAPTER TEN

BREAKFAST ARRIVED AND they ate together, setting the pattern for days to come. Ellie came to the hospital each morning and ate breakfast with her father before going on to work. She knew that Hera spent a couple of hours every afternoon with him and Ellie returned in the evenings to spend time with him before bed. Sandor spoke to him daily.

Sandor called Ellie two or three times a day, too, but they didn't see each other. He was working twenty hour days covering for her dad and taking care of his own business.

In a way, Ellie was grateful for the respite from his company. She knew that since he'd decided she was trustworthy, he still wanted to marry her. She just was not up to arguing with him about it right now.

Hawk was still looking for her sister, but the man she'd been seen with had disappeared from sight and Hawk's agents were having difficulty locating the tycoon. The investigator had learned what the tabloid reporters had…no one else seemed to know who Menendez's mystery woman was.

In the meantime, Ellie was getting to know her dad like she never had. He told her things about her mom, her grandparents…*himself* that she'd never known. And each day, she got a little closer to believing the change in him was a permanent one. That maybe he really did love her.

But part of her acknowledged that until he was back to work and in his old world and *still* interested in her life and spending time with her, she wasn't going to trust that change completely.

He went home from the hospital the following Friday afternoon. It was the longest break from work Ellie had ever known him to take. Even though the following day was Saturday, he went into the office for a few hours. Sandor made sure those hours were short, escorting him back home before lunchtime.

He'd arranged with Ellie to be there to share the meal with her father. She waited for them, butterflies playing volleyball in her stomach. She hadn't seen Sandor since the Saturday before.

When she did see him, she had to fight the urge to take him into her arms. He looked exhausted, but then running two multinational companies would be enough to drive most men into the ground. Not Sandor. He looked tired yes, but still so strong and masculine that Ellie's knees had weakened at the sight of him ushering her father into the room.

She'd set up fruit juice spritzers on a tray before their arrival and served both men as soon as they seated themselves.

Her dad had taken an armchair kitty-corner to where she sat. He reached for the drink. "Thank you, sweetheart."

"You're welcome. How did it go at work?"

"Sandor did an excellent job keeping everything running smooth. There wasn't much for me to do."

"There was enough to keep you there four hours," she said with a wry smile as she offered Sandor his drink.

He'd folded his six-foot-four-inch frame onto the

cushion beside her. He took the drink and winked. "He had to check everything I had done to make sure I had not messed anything up too badly."

"Baloney. I knew you'd handled everything fine, Sandor, but there are always things that simply cannot be delegated. No matter how savvy the delegate."

Ellie sat back down, keeping as much distance as she could between her and Sandor. "How are you feeling," she couldn't help asking him.

"Surely that is a question for your father."

"Dad looks healthier than I've seen him in a long time, you on the other hand are almost gray with fatigue."

"It has been a long week, but I survived it."

"You need more rest, Sandor."

He merely shrugged.

She frowned. "You aren't going back to the office after lunch, are you?"

"There are things I could take care of."

"Let them wait."

His dark eyes widened.

Her dad laughed. "She's getting bossy. That's got to be a good sign. With her mother it indicated she felt possessive of me."

Heat climbed into Ellie's cheeks. "Even if we are no longer dating, I still consider Sandor a friend. I don't feel possessive of him, but I care about him. As a friend."

It was a huge understatement, not to mention a lie. She did feel possessive toward him, but to admit it would imply he had rights over her and that she would not do. She loved him and one thing she'd realized over the last week was that love, no matter how battered took a lot to die. Hers was bruised and maybe even bleeding, but still very much alive inside her.

For both of the men now looking at her so speculatively.

"I would be happy to stay out of my office if you would agree to spend the afternoon and evening with me," Sandor said.

"I have things to do this afternoon."

"Like what?" her dad asked.

"I'm expecting a call from Hawk on the search for my sister. And I need to do some laundry and clean my apartment. I haven't been home much lately."

"I would be happy to help you do your laundry."

That made her laugh out loud. "I can just see that."

Sandor shrugged. "My mother and I had very little disposable income when we arrived in America. I can sort and fold clothing with professional efficiency, I assure you."

The thought of having him in her small apartment with her for several hours was nothing short of terrifying. "I don't think that's a good idea."

Sandor laid his hand on her thigh. "We need to talk, Ellie."

"I don't want to talk," she admitted in a low voice, wishing her dad was not there with them, overhearing their conversation.

"Please, Ellie…"

She closed her eyes against the appeal in his but nothing could stop the warm, rich tone repeating in her head. "I don't want to be hurt anymore, Sandor. Please don't push me."

She hated saying the words in front of her dad, but both men knew they'd hurt her. She wondered if they realized how much. She was working toward a relationship with her dad again, but she didn't know if she could ever give Sandor another chance. Not after learning she was nothing more than a business pawn for him.

Sandor sighed. "I won't push you *now, pethi mou.*"

He wondered if she noticed the emphasis he put on the word, now. He knew she couldn't be aware of how damned fragile she looked. She needed rest as much as she claimed he did. So, he would not push her today, but soon, he and his Ellie were going to talk out their relationship. And she was going to give him another chance. She was too damned gentle and kind not to.

Besides, she'd said she loved him. He knew she'd meant it. If she was capable of turning off her emotions, she would have stopped loving her father a long time ago. She never had and it gave Sandor hope.

Hawk called the next morning with the news that he'd found Ellie's sister. She went by the name Amber Taylor and she was staying on Miguel Menendez's yacht with him. They'd just come into port after spending more than a week at sea.

Once Hawk knew her sister's name, he'd learned quite a bit more about her. She was a model, successful, but not with supermodel status. Which was why Ellie had never seen her on the cover of any major magazines. Amber did mostly fashion shoots and trunk shows with a few commercials. Ellie's lack of public profile had contributed to the fact that no one had ever latched onto her resemblance to a fairly successful model.

In addition, Amber had grown up in a small town in Southern California with her mother, Helen Taylor. Father deceased. Or supposed father. She'd only recently moved into international modeling circles and at twenty-four, her career was only a few years from peaking.

She didn't date much and her current relationship with Miguel Menendez was the first evidence Hawk could find of her living with a lover. There was no evidence of a formal adoption, but that had been expected. What had not been expected was that she was living under the identity of the baby daughter Helen Taylor had given birth to.

A baby who had been born premature and died soon after birth despite the best efforts of the doctors at the time.

"I don't want the authorities brought in on this right now, Hawk."

"I didn't think you would, Miss Wentworth."

"You aren't going to tell my father you've found her, are you?" She wasn't sure how she wanted to deal with the information, but she didn't want to risk another shock that could lead to a heart attack.

"You are my client, Miss Wentworth. Not your father."

"Right. Okay. Give me the information you have on her current location."

She scribbled down what Hawk told her. Then she hung up the phone. Considering how she was living, Ellie doubted very sincerely that Amber knew anything about her real family or that she even had another family.

Hawk was investigating the circumstances of her kidnapping further and trying to figure out how Amber had ended up with Helen Taylor, who did not fit the profile of a kidnapper in any shape or form. From all accounts, she was a dedicated mother who had sacrificed a great deal for her daughter to succeed in her chosen profession.

Not really sure why she did so, Ellie picked up the phone to call Sandor after hanging up with Hawk.

He picked up on the first ring. "Ellie?"

"I just got off the phone with Hawk."

"Has he found your sister?"

"Yes."

"Where?"

"In Spain. She's been at sea on her lover's yacht, but they put to shore yesterday."

He said nothing.

"I don't know what to do, Sandor. Do I just show up out of the blue with no warning? Do I call her first and tell her I want to meet her? Her mom might very well be her kidnapper. How is she going to feel about that?"

"Tell me everything Hawk said."

Ellie did, leaving nothing out.

"Her mother does not sound like a criminal. In fact, she sounds very much like a woman who cares deeply for her daughter."

"I thought so, too."

"There must be extenuating circumstances."

"I don't want to hurt Amber."

"But the circumstances of her birth cannot be ignored."

"I know."

"Perhaps it would be best to wait until Hawk has discovered more about how Amber entered Helen Taylor's life."

And that's what she did, but as each day went by Ellie's stress levels increased. She missed Sandor, though he called her several times a day. At night, she craved the comfort of his arms around her. And no matter how many times she reminded herself that comfort was a false one, the feeling would not go away. She did not realize how much an integral part of her life he had become until he was gone.

She was the one the pushed him away. He invited her to dinner, to lunches, to the theater, and she turned down every invitation. He never got angry with her. Just reminded her that when the time was right, he was going to corner her and there was nothing she would be able to do to get out of it. The most frightening realization of all was that she wasn't sure she wanted to. In fact, a big part of her wanted him to take the choice out of her hands and simply show up at her apartment.

But he didn't and she didn't sleep, spending both the dark hours of night and the spare moments of her days worrying.

She wanted to tell her dad that Amber had been found, but was afraid of what it would do to him to hear the news.

Hawk called and said he couldn't find any indication of how Amber had come to live with Helen Taylor as her daughter.

"If she's not the kidnapper, Miss Wentworth, then I have no idea how she came to be your sister's mother."

Hawk had learned more about Helen and Amber Taylor during his investigation and it all pointed to Helen being as good a mother as Hera. It hurt to think it had all started with a kidnapping. She couldn't imagine how her sister would feel to find that out. Choking out a goodbye to Hawk, Ellie was already mentally dialing Sandor's number when she disconnected her call with the world renowned investigator.

Sandor swore in Greek when Ellie told him what she had learned. "I'm so sorry, *agape mou*. But we will not let this situation tear lives apart."

He said it with such confidence that she believed him.

"What am I going to do?"

"We begin by telling your father."

"We?"

"Naturally. You do not think I would leave you to do this thing alone, do you?"

She had no right to call on his support since their breakup, but she wasn't about to turn him down. "Thank you."

* * *

Sitting in his favorite armchair close to Ellie's place on the couch in his oversize living room, her father paled as Ellie told him all that Hawk had learned so far.

"So, this woman…Helen Taylor…most likely kidnapped my daughter and brought her up to believe she was the baby she had lost two months before?"

"Yes, that's what we think." Sandor held Ellie close to him with one strong arm and she wasn't about to protest.

Nor did she protest him answering for her. She was shaking inside from the stress and worried that talking about her sister was once again going to prove too much for her dad.

Ellie added, "Her husband had died in the tragic car accident that sent her into early labor. Hawk thinks the similar circumstance surrounding mine and Amber's births may have triggered the kidnapping."

"But the woman was a good mother?" her dad asked in a hoarse voice.

"From all that Hawk could discover, she was exemplary in every way. She really loves her daughter. She lives for her." Ellie kept the wistfulness from her voice.

It was wrong to envy her sister a lifetime with a loving parent, especially knowing that she would face the pain of difficult revelations soon enough. But part of Ellie couldn't help wondering what it would have been like to be raised by someone who considered her more than an adjunct in his life.

"I think we should approach Helen Taylor first," Sandor said.

"I agree." Her dad ran his hand over his face and sighed. "She's no doubt been living in abject terror of being caught out for more than two decades. We need to deal with her first."

Ellie had reached the same conclusion. "It's going to be

awful for everyone. I've never met the woman, but I can't help but pity her. Whatever led to her taking Amber, she really seems like a decent person who loves her daughter." She took a deep breath and said what needed saying. "I don't want the authorities brought in. This is going to be hard enough on everyone without that."

Her dad nodded. "We will find out what happened... why she took my daughter and kept her...and we'll go from there."

Relief that he was taking the news so well and that her father was being so tolerant flowed through Ellie. "You're a lot more understanding about this than I expected you to be."

He grimaced, his light blue eyes shadowed with guilt and pain. "I can't get past the fact that she gave Amber the love I withheld from you. Maybe you would have been better off if she'd taken you both."

Ellie didn't know what to say. She was a poor liar, so she could not claim she'd hadn't had the same thought. Until her dad had "gotten human" she would have questioned whether losing her would have impacted his emotions at all. She felt guilty for thinking that way and knew it was wrong, but she'd spent most of her life believing that if she were to disappear—for whatever reason—the only thing her father would feel is a sense of failure in living up to his responsibilities.

She was beginning to believe she meant more than that to him now, but twenty-four years of thinking a certain way did not disappear overnight.

Letting her heart lead, she dropped to her knees beside his chair and hugged him. "I don't regret the fact that you raised me."

That, at least, wasn't a lie. No matter what strange

thought had flitted through her head upon discovering each new aspect of this situation, she loved her dad. She always had. The more he told her about her mom, the more Ellie realized in that way, she took after the woman who had died before she'd had a chance to hold her babies.

His laugh was hollow, but his return embrace was tight. "You're a gentle soul, Eleanor Wentworth. Very much like your mother," he said, echoing her thoughts. "I didn't deserve her and I don't deserve you."

"Maybe," she allowed with a small smile as she returned to her seat beside Sandor, leaning against him slightly and drawing on his strength. "But you're stuck with me regardless."

"We'll fly to California to see Helen Taylor tomorrow," her dad decided.

Sandor's arm returned to her shoulder and squeezed. "I am going with you."

Ellie didn't even consider arguing. She craved his support. She turned to meet his dark gaze. "I would appreciate that."

He kissed her, his lips tender, his expression unfathomable. "Then it is settled."

They flew in Sandor's private jet to a small airport near the town that Helen Taylor called home. She wasn't sure why they'd taken Sandor's plane instead of her father's. But when Ellie asked, her father said only that Sandor preferred to do so. He and her dad worked while Ellie fretted, but hid it behind a facade of relaxed boredom while flipping through one of the fashion magazines that featured shots of her sister.

Hawk had provided a wealth of information on Amber's

career. Ellie had spent countless sleeping hours looking at pictures of her sister in "model mode" and wondering what went on behind her beautiful aqua gaze. Funny how the same color of eyes on Ellie felt like nothing special, but on her model sister, they looked exotic and mysterious.

She rubbed at her own eyes, wishing she could take a nap, but knowing sleep would be ever elusive. She simply could not turn her brain off. She'd done a good job of keeping up the stoic front she'd spent a lifetime cultivating, but underneath, she wanted to crumple.

But a Wentworth did not crumple and even if they did, she couldn't. Her father and her sister needed her right now.

They were less than an hour into the flight and Ellie was yawning for the fifth time when, without the slightest warning, she felt herself bodily lifted from her seat.

Gasping, she clutched at Sandor, the magazine fluttering to the floor of the cabin. "What are you doing?"

"You need rest." She wasn't having any trouble reading his expression now. He looked angry. "Have you slept a full night since the day you returned from Spain?"

"No," she admitted and let her head drop to lie in the curve of his neck. "But I'm not going to sleep now, either."

"We shall see."

She found herself smiling against his chest at his arrogance. "I can't. Honestly, Sandor. Too many things are whirling inside my head."

He ignored her words and carried her to the tiny bedroom in the back of the plane, kicking the door shut behind him once they were inside.

"This is pretty nice. My father's jet doesn't have a bedroom," Ellie remarked.

"I know. That is why we took mine."

"For the bedroom?"

"Yes. You are not sleeping. That is obvious to anyone with eyes. I was determined you would rest comfortably during the flight."

Unused to being cosseted, Ellie found herself swallowing a suspicious lump in her throat. Even if she couldn't sleep, she appreciated the gesture. A lot.

"Thank you," she whispered.

"You are welcome." He laid her down on the bed, arranging her so that her head rested on a nice fluffy pillow. "Comfortable?"

"Mmm…hmmm."

"Good." He sat on the end of the bed and took her shoes and thin socks off.

She wiggled her toes. "Um…thanks."

"Again…you are welcome."

But he did not stop there. Before she knew what he was doing, he'd unbuttoned her dark silk slacks and had them halfway down her hips.

She grabbed his wrists. "What are you doing? You can't undress me," she hissed in a fierce whisper, not wanting her father to hear.

Though it was highly unlikely, even in the well insulated cabin, flying created a lot of white noise that masked conversations even between people seated near one another.

"You cannot sleep with your clothes on. Relax, *pethi mou*. I will take care of you."

"I'm not going to sleep anyway," she protested. "There's no reason for me to get undressed."

"You will be more comfortable." With a deft move of his hands, he broke her hold on his wrists and had her slacks down her legs and off before she could do more than gasp. He folded them on a neat crease and hung them in the miniscule closet before turning back to face her. "Is that not better?"

Ellie could only gape. Whether it was from sheer shock or that combined with her exhaustion, but her mind wasn't working properly. She should have scrambled under the covers, but she lay there in her blouse and panties and wondered what he would do next.

She found out when he sat beside her and began to unbutton her blouse.

Finally getting some semblance of wits about her, she twisted away and jumped off the bed. "I think I'll leave my blouse on. In fact, I should probably put my slacks back on and rejoin Dad."

The look in his eyes said she was going to get undressed and in that bed, like it or not. Too bad he was on the side by the closet and coincidentally, the door through which she wanted to escape. Though not half-dressed as she was.

She crossed her arms over her chest. "I don't like being bossed around, Sandor."

He leaned back against the door, crossing his arms as well and giving her a look she was fairly certain outdid hers in the intimidation stakes. "I do not like seeing my woman ready to collapse from exhaustion."

"I'm not your woman."

He crossed that small room with the speed of a Jaguar and then stood towering over her. "We are at odds. I accept this. But you *are* mine."

"No," she whispered the denial that felt like a lie.

"Just as I am yours."

The words touched her deep inside where she did not want

him to go again. And she shook her head, unable to give voice again to the denial her heart said she should not make.

His hands curved around her shoulders and he stepped closer so their bodies were mere inches apart. "So, you do not care if I bed another woman?"

Her heart screamed a denial, but she merely said, "Don't be crude," in her best approximation at a distant tone.

"Do not lie to me," he countered, his tone pure male censure.

She swallowed, wishing he wasn't so close...or that his nearness did not impact her so much. "I have no right to stop you from going to bed with another woman."

"I give you the right."

She opened her mouth, but she could not force a rejection to his offer from her throat.

He kissed her, briefly but firmly. "I give you the right," he repeated.

She couldn't say a word. To refuse the right was beyond her, but to accept it carried far too many connotations she was not prepared to deal with. She tilted her head back and kissed him, just as briefly and much more softly.

His eyes closed and he inhaled a deep breath before opening them again. "We will get there," he promised her. "Now, come. Let me care for you."

He lifted her again and put her back on the bed, his movements careful as if he did not want to startle her, but the implacable expression in his eyes said he expected her to rest.

Then, his eyes filling with a tenderness she could not fight, he finished unbuttoning her top and pulled it from her body. He hung it up and while he was beside the closet, he hung up his jacket, too. Their gazes locked. She sat up and curled her arms around her knees, but did not protest when he started taking off the rest of his clothes. He did not break the eye contact while he stripped to his silk shorts, neatly hanging everything up in the closet to be donned again later.

He came back to the bed.

She licked her lips. "Sandor?"

"I, too, could use a nap, Ellie. I have slept poorly since the night you disappeared from Boston. We will rest together. And for now, that is all we will do."

She should argue, but deep inside, she didn't want to. She trusted him not to push for anything sexual if he said he wouldn't. And she wanted to be held. So much. Her world was a maelstrom of frightening events and even though he had betrayed her trust, Sandor looked like an island of comfort for her storm-tossed heart.

Silently she uncurled from her protective position and climbed under the covers, leaving room for him to lie beside her. She wasn't sure, but she thought he sighed with relief. He joined her, pressed the button above the bed to cut the lights in the tiny cabin and then pulled her into his arms.

She didn't fight, but she didn't relax, either. She couldn't. With loving came wanting and since her love for him continued to beat inside her heart, her desire for him was there, too. But she didn't want to act on it. She didn't think she could handle it right now if she did.

She was barely holding it together and the way he made her feel when he touched her would rip away the barriers she'd manage to erect to protect herself since discovering both his and her father's duplicity. Besides, he was right…she both needed and wanted the healing rest of sleep. She was hungry to be held and to feel safe, if for just a little while.

He seemed to understand and did not try to cajole her into relaxing. He curled his big, warm body around her stiff one, wrapping his arms around her and spoke soft, soothing things into her ear until she grew drowsy. Bit by bit, her body gentled into his until she fell into a more restful sleep than she'd had since the last time he shared her bed.

She awoke sometime later to the sensation of someone gently brushing her cheek. Her senses told her it was Sandor before mind even became fully aware.

CHAPTER ELEVEN

"WAKE UP, *agape mou*. We will be there soon."

Her eyes fluttered open to a vision of him dressed and sitting beside her on the bed.

"I slept the whole flight?" she asked disbelievingly.

"You needed your rest."

She'd needed her rest the night before, too, but she'd tossed and turned until giving up on sleep and had gotten up before dawn to work on client files. "So you said."

"I was right."

"You don't have to sound so happy about it."

"What man does not like to be right?"

She wrinkled her nose. "I don't know one." It was all she could do not to snuggle into his hand. "I can't believe I slept so well."

"It was being held in my arms. I confess I, too, slept better than I have in weeks."

She scooted into a sitting position, holding the sheet against her chest. "Yes, well…we'll have to get matching teddy bears or something."

"Or something."

She wasn't touching that. "How long until we land?"

"Thirty minutes."

"Oh." She looked around the well lit, utilitarian cabin. Thank goodness there was a door to the small bathroom from the sleeping area. "I need to freshen up."

"You look very good to me, but I can understand you might think the just-been-loved look is better saved for our times of privacy together."

"I haven't been loved."

"Are you sure about that?"

What was he saying? That he loved her? No. He didn't believe in the emotion, but could he have changed his mind? Her dad had changed and she thought that was impossible. Had Sandor had some kind of emotional breakthrough? But if he had, surely he would have said something. Not made some oblique reference and expect her to get it.

She swallowed questions she wasn't sure she wanted answers to in her current emotional state and stared at him. "I mean we didn't have sex."

"That I concede. It comes later, I think."

"No," she breathed, more for form than vehemence.

He leaned forward until his mouth was a bare centimeter from hers. "Are you sure that is the word you will be saying?"

She opened her mouth to answer, but whatever she would have said remained locked in her throat because he kissed her. His mouth totally claimed hers, his lips molding to hers and his tongue sweeping her interior. Any protest she would have made died before she even breathed it and she kissed him back until she was panting and his hands were clenched in fists on either side of her hips.

"We will revisit this discussion later," he said and then stood up just as if he hadn't kissed her to within an inch of her life and made implications that were soul-shattering.

He tapped the end of her nose. "Get ready, Ellie *mou*. I will see how your father is holding up." Then he was gone.

Dazed, she climbed out of the bed and made a quick trip to the bathroom to brush her hair and other things before getting dressed again. Sandor had been right. She'd slept much better without her clothes and they were certainly fresher looking than they would have been if she'd worn them to bed.

The drive from the small municipal airport to Helen Taylor's home was less than an hour, but the tension inside the limousine was palpable by the time it pulled up in front of her modest ranch style home.

Ellie put her hand on her father's arm. "Are you going to be all right?"

His smile was reassuringly warm, so different than the way he used to look at her. "Yes, but what about you?"

"I'm scared," she admitted, surprising herself.

But then, maybe she was changing, too. Knowing you were loved changed the way you reacted to another person, she found.

He laid his hand over hers. "It is all going to be fine. Trust me, sweetheart."

"I don't want Amber hurt." Or her dad. Or herself. Or Helen Taylor, for that matter. Yet, she didn't see how at least some emotional bloodshed could be avoided.

"Neither do I. We're going to handle this the best we can and trust for the outcome."

She swallowed and nodded. He left the limousine first, then Sandor, who turned to help her out. He pulled her into his side with an arm around her waist as they walked up to the front door and she was grateful for the contact. Despite the warmth of Southern California's weather, she felt chilled. She cuddled against him in a public display of affection that she would not have shown a month ago.

Something inside her had definitely shifted.

Her father rang the bell. Less than a minute passed before it swung inward. A woman stood there, her wavy blond chin-length hair, cut in a bob and petite frame with trim figure proclaimed her Helen Taylor. She looked exactly like the photos taken of her recently as well as those Hawk had procured from years past. There was an almost fey quality about her that enhanced Ellie's already signaled protective instincts.

Helen's hazel eyes widened and darkened with distress as she seemed to recognize George Wentworth. Her gaze skimmed to Ellie, jolted up to Sandor's impassive features and back to Ellie again. "You look just like her. You look just like my baby."

Her mouth moved, but no other words came out as her eyes filled with tears and her knees gave. Ellie's father grabbed her before she could fall to the floor. Swinging her up into his arms as if she weighed no more than a child, he carried her inside. Sandor ushered Ellie in after them and closed the door behind them with his foot.

His arm was still locked securely around her waist and she leaned even more heavily into him.

Helen's quiet sobs were the only sound any of them made as Ellie's dad led them unerringly into the living room. He carried Helen to the couch and gently lowered her onto it. Helen stared at him through rain drenched eyes as if she could not believe what she was seeing.

He dropped to his haunches beside the sofa and took her hand. "It is going to be okay."

But the blond woman shook her head, unending rivulets of tears rolling down her cheeks. "It can't be. I knew this day would come, but I kept hoping it wouldn't. That wasn't fair of me. I know. I've been so selfish."

"Tell me why you took my daughter." He said it so gently that Ellie wanted to hug him.

She hadn't known he had this kind of patience and gentleness in him. Not even with his behavioral changes since his collapse.

Helen made an obvious bid for composure. "I…"

"Mom, what's going on?"

Ellie felt everything inside her freeze. She spun out of Sandor's grasp to face the newcomer whose voice was so like her own. She'd already been fighting tears and now her eyes burned with them as she furiously blinked, trying to keep some semblance of control. "Amber…"

Amber was staring at her as if she was seeing a ghost. "Who are you?"

"I'm…"

"She's your sister," Helen said, her voice wobbling only a little.

"My sister?" Amber shook her head, frowning at all of them. "No. That's not possible." Her gaze shifted to her mom. "You didn't give birth to twins. I checked. I always felt like something was missing, you know? So, I checked and there wasn't another birth record. I was the only baby born to Helen and Leonard Taylor."

Ellie knew her sister was shaking inside, even though her chatter and uncracked composure gave nothing away. She was a master at hiding her emotions herself.

Sandor seemed to sense the hurricane of emotion under the surface because he took a step toward Amber, his hand out as if to help her. "Miss Taylor, perhaps you should sit down."

"Who are you?" Amber demanded, taking a step back.

"I am your sister's fiancé, Sandor Christofides."

"The shipping tycoon?"

"You read the financial pages?"

"Sometimes. When I'm bored on a shoot. And you're George Wentworth," she said to Ellie's dad, still sounding very much in command of herself.

But Ellie saw another story in the eyes that could have been her mirror. Her sister's worry for Helen Taylor was there, as well as confusion and anger that these strangers had brought obvious upset into her home.

Gently placing Helen's hand down, their father stood. "I'm…" He cleared his throat. "Yes, I'm George Wentworth."

Helen sat up, wiped at her tears and then dried her hands on her jeans and put her arms out. "Come here, baby. I have to tell you something."

Amber walked slowly toward her mother, her eyes fixed on George Wentworth as if he was a snake prepared to strike. He stepped back, moving to sit in a chair close to the sofa. It was so like how he always sat with Ellie that she felt a twinge in her heart. They were a family even if they didn't all know it yet.

Amber let her mother pull her down to sit beside her. Her gaze jumped from Ellie to her dad, back to Sandor and then finally came back to rest on Ellie. "You look just like me."

"Almost."

"Your hair is darker. You don't highlight it at all."

"No."

"It's shorter, too."

"Yes. And my eyebrows have their natural shape and I weigh at least ten pounds more than you. I don't dress as trendily and I'm not fond of running," she said, naming a pastime Hawk said that Amber spent a lot of time engaged in. "But I love old movies, we wear the same size shoe and I prefer silver over gold jewelry as well."

Helen Taylor made a sound of distress.

Amber took her hand and held it. "What's the matter, Mom?"

"Please don't hate me, Amber. I deserve it, I know I do, but I can handle anything except that."

"No one is going to hate you, Mrs. Taylor. We're going to work through this," George Wentworth said in a firm but kind tone.

Ellie was so proud of him.

"I could never hate you," Amber vowed.

Helen shook her head, her expression turning both resigned and determined. "Before you came into the room, Mr. Wentworth asked a question. He wanted…" She stopped, seemed to collect herself and went on. "He wanted to know why I'd stolen his daughter."

"What?"

The shock of the traumatic words reverberated through Amber to the room around her. Ellie could feel the shock wave hit her with physical force as her sister's whole body went stiff. Then Sandor was there, wrapping both arms around Ellie, pulling her with him to a love seat, where he tugged her down right next to him. He kept her locked tight in his protective embrace while Helen blinked back tears and took several deep breaths.

CHAPTER TWELVE

"WHEN I DID IT, I didn't think I was stealing anyone. Please believe me. I-I thought you were mine." Helen brushed the hair from Amber's temple. "I love you so much." She swallowed and then went on. "I'd lost my baby after the horrific accident that took Leonard's life and caused me to go into premature labor."

She looked at George Wentworth then, as if trying to explain what she herself found inexplicable. "Some teenagers high on pot ran a red light and plowed right into our car. I barely survived the accident. We were living near Boston at the time. They life-flighted me to the hospital from our smaller town. When my daughter died, I started haunting the baby nurseries at all the hospitals. I was there the night your wife was brought in. Everyone was running around talking about the accident. It was so much like mine. If it hadn't been so identical, I don't think it would have happened, but it was as if I was reliving it all over again.

"Everywhere around me, doctors and nurses were saying the exact same things they'd said the night of my accident. It's hard to explain, but something snapped inside me. It was as if I was living out what had happened all over again, but with a different result. I created a whole new set of memories that I could deal with better than reality. Your wife went into coma, but her babies lived. I lived, but my baby died. In my mind that night, my baby lived and she was Amber."

Ellie's dad nodded, as if he understood such a thing. Again, she felt a spurt of pride for him.

Helen turned back to Amber. "Don't ask me how I managed to get you out of the hospital because I don't remember. When I got you home, all the baby stuff was still there, I thought you were my little Amber." Her voice cracked. "I loved you so much and you were all I had left."

Amber put her arm around her mom's shoulder. "It's okay, Mom."

"It's not okay. I lived the fantasy and *believed it completely for five years*. Except for recurring nightmares of losing my baby, everything was so good. I had this overwhelming urge to move across the country, though. I thought I wanted to get away from the painful memories of your fath...I mean my husband. Later, I realized my subconscious knew that I was running from something much worse than painful memories. We moved here when you were less than a year old."

"But something made you remember," Amber said gently, her tone so like George's had been minutes before that Ellie found herself blinking back more tears.

Helen nodded. "I saw an article on George Wentworth in a business weekly." She looked around at the rest of the people in the room. "I'm a financial analyst."

"We know," George said quietly.

She swallowed convulsively and nodded. "Of course." She took another deep breath and clenched her trembling hands together. "The article mentioned the disappearance of your daughter and suddenly *I knew*. I couldn't remember taking her, but I remembered my baby dying and knew that the little girl who I loved more than my own life belonged to someone else."

"I don't understand…you would have taken me back. Mom, I know you…"

"Yes. I tried." She was looking at Amber again, her hazel eyes filled with appeal. "But when I arrived in Boston with you, I had to research George Wentworth. I couldn't give my baby over to just anyone even if he was your biological father. I was frightened of what would happen to me, but even more terrified of losing you. I was going to plead for mercy…I hoped…" She swallowed a sob. "I hoped that he would let me visit you. But when I researched him, I discovered he was a merciless shark. The article had said something about how even personal tragedy had not slowed him down businesswise. He acted as if he'd never lost a daughter and didn't notice the one he still had.

"I knew the man described in the articles I read about him and by the employees I managed to talk to would press charges and I would end up in prison. I would have faced that…but learning how he treated the daughter he still had was something else altogether. He ignored her. She was raised by nannies and servants and hardly ever saw him."

She looked at George as if she couldn't quite believe he was the man she was describing and then back to her daughter. "You were such a loving little girl and affectionate. You would have shriveled up and died under that kind of care. I couldn't do it. I couldn't give you back. And he never changed. I kept tabs and watched his daughter Eleanor be sent to boarding school when she was barely eight years old."

Helen's eyes filled with tears as she met Ellie's gaze. "It hurt so much to see you treated like that. I loved your sister with all my heart and you by proxy. I couldn't change your life, but I couldn't let your father do the same thing to Amber."

"I understand," Ellie said. And she did. Someone looking from the outside might not, but she'd lived that emotional wasteland. "I'm glad my sister escaped having a childhood like mine. I'm glad you were there to love her."

"But she needed me. If you'd given me back, we would have had each other," Amber said in a low whisper.

"I thought of that and I just couldn't sacrifice your happiness for hers." Helen buried her face in her hands and started to sob. "I'm sorry."

Ellie's dad moved to sit on the other side of Helen. He pulled her into his arms and just held her as if he alone in that room could understand her mother's pain and guilt. And perhaps it was true. If everything he'd said over the past week plus was true, he carried a load of guilt for his treatment of Ellie easily as heavy as Helen's.

"If my biological father was such a horrible man why isn't he threatening prison and yelling at her?" Amber asked Ellie, her eyes filled with a confusion Ellie understood only too well.

"He almost died a couple of weeks ago and it changed him. I think he really loves me finally and I know he's going to love you."

"But, Mom?"

"Nothing is going to happen to your mom. Dad doesn't want to hurt her and neither do I. I only want to know you. I'd like to know her, too, if she'll let me. She was a good mom to you. She took care of you and after hearing her story, I'm convinced she didn't do anything with malice."

"Are you for real?" Amber asked. "Nobody reacts like that to something like this."

Sandor laughed, hugging her. "Ellie is a special woman."

"I'm glad." The controlled facade cracked for just a second as Amber's chin wobbled. "I don't want my mom hurt."

"She won't be," George said with conviction as he continued to hold the crying woman. "She did better by my daughter than I did. I stopped looking for you after only a year. I have no excuse for that. I was a rotten father to your sister, but she loved me in spite of it."

"There are worse fathers than you were, much worse," Ellie said.

"Thank you, sweetheart, but when I remember the times your eyes so like your mother's begged me to show a spark of affection and then I didn't...I'll never forgive myself."

"You hugged me sometimes."

"I bet you remember every single time because those times were so rare."

"You really were a bastard," Amber breathed.

George flinched. "Yes. I was and I thank God, Ellie never gave up on me. I've seen the error of my ways. I want to make up for them. I think we can build a family now. All of us, if you're willing."

"I won't leave my mom out."

"Like Ellie, I would appreciate the chance to get to know her, too."

At that Helen pulled out of his arms, wiping her face. She looked ravaged, but at peace and just a little bemused. "I've been so terrified for years. I can't believe things are happening this way."

Ellie's dad grimaced. "They wouldn't have...a few weeks ago."

"It's a good thing you didn't find me then," Amber quipped.

Ellie agreed, but said nothing. The visit continued on a more positive note from there. Strangely, though, Ellie felt herself pulling into the background, listening to her dad talk with Amber and Helen. She soaked up everything they all said and enjoyed hearing it, but she couldn't participate.

If Amber felt stunned and traumatized by events, so did Ellie. She still wasn't used to having a dad that wanted to be a dad and now she had a sister and that just blew her away. She'd been alone so long, she wasn't sure how to be part of a family and she wondered in a distant part of her mind if that was one of the reasons she'd put off talking about her relationship with Sandor.

She was scared of giving in and becoming part of a family and having it all taken away again. It was the kind of fear only someone who'd lived so long on the fringes of other people's happiness could understand. Her mind worked out the disturbing thoughts as she listened to the others talk.

She learned that Amber was in town for a shoot and planned to meet back up with Miguel afterward. She was very animated when she talked about him and that made both Ellie and her dad smile. At some point, Sandor ordered dinner to be delivered. They all ate, still talking.

It was late when Sandor stood and said, "Ellie needs rest. It has been a very traumatic few weeks for her. Perhaps this visit can continue tomorrow?"

Amber looked at Ellie and bit her lip in a gesture Ellie recognized. "You haven't been talking much."

"I'm soaking it all in. I'm um...not used to being part of a family," she said, exposing one of her inner revelations.

"Our dad seems so wonderful now, it's hard to believe he raised you the way he did."

Ellie smiled. "He's not as bad as everyone is painting him."

"Yes, I was."

She shrugged. "Then it doesn't matter. You're my dad and I love you. I always have and I always will, but this family thing…it's going to take some getting used to. I like it a lot, though." She smiled again, hoping they could all read her sincerity.

Amber nodded. "I have a feeling I'm going to like you a lot, too."

"You are going to love her, just as she will love you," Sandor corrected with a warm smile. "She is infinitely lovable and it is clear you are a very special woman, too."

Ellie felt faint. Okay, that was the second oblique reference and that meant she wasn't imagining them.

Her dad cleared his throat. "I would like to stay here a while longer…to talk out what I learned from my legal counsel with Helen in regard to the kidnapping and the statute of limitations and such."

"Is everything going to be okay?" Ellie asked. "She won't go to jail?"

"She will not. I have already put efforts into motion to assure that Helen suffers no more from the tragedy of her past."

"You did that before you even met us?" Amber asked with awe in her voice.

"Yes."

"Thank you." She jumped up and hugged him.

Ellie felt a twinge…not of envy, but of sadness. She did love her dad, but she wondered if she would ever have the easy relationship with him that her sister was already developing. Even if she didn't, what they had was so much better than what she'd known growing up, she wouldn't ever moan for things to be different. She felt truly blessed. Overwhelmed, but blessed.

"Then you all don't mind if I go to the hotel?"

"No, of course not. I am very glad you have someone to take care of you like Sandor," Helen said, just as if she was Ellie's mom, too.

It was nice.

Ellie discovered that Sandor had booked them into the same room at the hotel when he followed her into it and closed the door behind them. She noticed his suitcase as well as hers had been delivered from the plane and stood against one wall side by side.

"We share a room?" she asked.

"Always."

She nodded and Sandor went very still. "What did that little nod mean?"

"What did the oblique references you've made to love today mean?" she countered.

"That I love you," he replied without hesitation.

"No. You can't."

"I assure you, I do."

"But you don't believe in love."

"Belief is not always necessary for a state of being. I learned quickly enough how much I love you when you refused to come back to me, or talk to me about our future."

"Not before then."

"I was slow, but what I lack in speed to the mark I make up for in longitude." He pulled her into his arms. "I will love you forever."

She buried her nose in his chest, breathing in the beautiful scent she associated only with him. "I thought a man loved me once, but I was wrong," she whispered against him.

"Your other lover?"

She tilted her head back to see his face. "You're so sure there has only been one?"

"Yes. Your heart is connected to sexual intimacy for you. You would not allow a man you did not love into your body and if you had loved another after him, you would have married."

"You're sure?"

"Positive. Only a fool would let you go if you loved him."

"You are so sure another man would have loved me back?"

"I am positive it is a foregone conclusion." He kissed the tip of her nose. "You are irresistibly lovable."

"He didn't think so."

"The first lover?"

"Yes."

"He was an idiot."

She nodded, having come to the same conclusion but for different reasons. "I was nineteen. He was my bodyguard. I mistook sexual pleasure for the love of a lifetime until I overheard him talking about what a score he was going to make marrying me. He wanted a piece of my dad's empire and wasn't above using me to get it. He had it all planned. He wasn't even normally a bodyguard. He was trained in business, but took the job to get close to me. Apparently everyone knew how my dad ignored me and he thought I'd be lonely and easy to seduce. He was right. He even had sex with me without protection in hopes of getting me pregnant. Thankfully it didn't happen."

Sandor's arms tightened and anger radiated off of him with palpable force. "That bastard."

"Yes, he was. He taught me a valuable lesson, though, sex is not love." Would he understand what she was asking without her actually asking anything?

"No, it is not." This time he kissed her temple and then her lips, oh so softly. "Sex is something a person can live without, but if you take your love from me, I will wither and die."

"You did not just say that," she choked.

"I did."

She shook her head.

He nodded. "Oh, yes. What happened to the bodyguard?"

"I told my dad I thought he was sexually attracted to me. That he'd made advances. He fired him. He never knew it had already gone way beyond mere attraction to final follow-through."

Sandor pulled her to bed and tumbled them both down onto it without letting her go. They remained facing each other, lying on their sides. "I am sexually attracted to you, Ellie. More than is comfortable in any sort of clothing." He illustrated by pressing an unmistakable hardness against her. "But I love you, too, *agape mou*."

"What does that mean?"

"My love."

"Oh." He'd called her that before.

"Is it my crazy man behavior before you realized you had a sister? You forgave your father far worse, can you not forgive me for accusing you of being with another man?" He really seemed agitated about it.

She cupped his cheek. "I know the pictures were damaging. If I'd argued with you, I would have convinced you it wasn't me and to help me find out who she was. I knew that. I was much angrier about your deal with my dad."

"You use the past tense. You are no longer angry?"

She shook her head with a sigh. "What would be the point? Holding onto anger just leads to bitterness and that twists a person's soul."

He didn't look appreciably comforted by that statement. "But you still do not wish to marry me?"

"I can forgive, but I don't know if I can trust and I need to trust you to marry you."

"I did not tell you about the deal because I knew it would upset you."

"You were right."

"But I would have wanted you even if your father had not made his offer. From the first moment I saw you, I wanted you. Your father noticed my interest. It was only after doing so that he made his offer."

"He told me that. He said he thought I was interested, too."

"You were."

"I was," she agreed.

"Ellie, I need you to be mine for a lifetime. You can trust me. I will never hide anything from you again."

"Because you love me?"

"Yes."

"Like with your mom?"

"Exactly."

"I'm scared, Sandor. I realized tonight that I don't know how to be part of a family. I don't know how to believe in the goodness going on around me…how to believe that you can love me." The admission hurt.

But he shook his head decisively. "You are fooling yourself to think that. Belief is something you are very good at. You had faith in your father for years when anyone else would have given up on him. You had faith in me, or you never would have come back from Spain prepared to marry me. You're a woman full of faith and I'm the man prepared to prove to you that it's grounded in something real."

"You think you can do that?"

"Give me a try."

She stared at him. It couldn't be that easy. "Is this the happily ever after from the fairy tales?"

"I am no knight, but I think, Ellie *mou*, that this is the happy beginning of two people so much in love they cannot live apart."

"You won't leave me?"

"Never."

"I won't have to be alone ever again."

"I will be your anchor and you will be my sea, surrounding me, washing over me, keeping me always with you."

"And you will stay steadily always with me."

"Yes."

"I do love you, Sandor."

"Mama said you did."

"She did?"

"Uh-huh."

"When?"

"When I cried in my coffee over losing you."

"You did not."

"I most certainly did. You can call and ask her, but later…right now I have something else in mind to do with your mouth."

She'd opened it to ask him what when he kissed her.

She'd been isolated for so long, and now she had a

family. A whole family. Warmth and gratitude filled her as her brain lost contact with reality under Sandor's loving and provoking kiss.

Ellie went back to visit her sister the next day as promised and this time, found that she could not keep quiet. They talked and talked until once again Sandor was declaring it time to return to the hotel. They stayed in Southern California for three days, returning to Boston with Helen and Amber's promise to come to visit very soon.

When Ellie and Sandor were married a month later, Amber stood up for Ellie while George Wentworth, Helen Taylor and Hera Christofides looked on in teary-eyed bliss. There was another man there. He looked familiar, but Ellie was sure she'd never met him. When he put his arm around Hera Christofides and smiled down at her, Ellie almost fainted.

She turned to Sandor right in the middle of their wedding vows and blurted, "You found your father."

"More precisely, Hawk did."

"He wasn't married."

"Never had been. Apparently when a man in our family loves, it is for a lifetime."

Joyous tears washed into Ellie's eyes as she turned back to the minister to finish repeating her vows.

But Sandor squeezed her hand before she spoke. "I also destroyed the merger contract your father and I signed."

Her knees did buckle this time and Sandor swept her up against his chest, her voluminous skirts cascading over his arms.

"You did what?" she demanded.

"Took away your last reason for doubt."

He had and she felt light-headed because of it. "But what about Dad's company?"

"I've got a lot of good years in me yet. Helen is coming to work for me as a close advisor. She's a savvy business-woman. And one day I'll have grandchildren."

Ellie looked around her from the grinning minister who didn't seem to mind the odd ceremony to the small group of people all of whom were now her family. Finally she met Sandor's possessive and adoring gaze.

She was loved and she loved in return.

She was finally part of the family she'd longed for her entire life. And it felt so very good.

She finished speaking her vows without ever looking away from the man who had in his way made all of this possible.

He was her knight in shining armor, no matter what he said and their future looked so bright she would need a new pair of sunglasses to handle it.

* * * * *

Bought for Marriage

MARGARET MAYO

Margaret Mayo was reading Mills & Boon® romances long before she began to write them. In fact she never had any plans to become a writer. After an idea for a short story popped into her head she was thrilled when it turned into a full-scale novel. Now, over twenty-five years later, she is still happily writing and says she has no intention of stopping. She lives with her husband Ken in a rural part of Staffordshire, England. She has two children – Adrian, who now lives in America, and Tina. Margaret's hobbies are reading, photography and, more recently, watercolour painting, which she says has honed her observational skills and is a definite advantage when it comes to writing.

CHAPTER ONE

'THEO TSARDIKOS? You expect me to go and beg him for money?' Dione stared at her father in disbelief. 'I can't do it.'

Theodossus Tsardikos was a man to be reckoned with. His name was revered throughout the whole of Greece, and maybe the world for all she knew. He was her father's sworn enemy. He ran a very successful and very luxurious worldwide hotel chain; only the rich and famous could afford to stay there.

Yannis had once tried to persuade Theo to let him franchise his restaurants inside the hotels—the suggestion had been received with raw contempt. Theo made no secret of his dislike of Yannis Keristari. And Dione couldn't blame him.

Yannis slumped back against his pillow. 'Then this will be the end of me.'

'I think,' said Phrosini, with a worried glance at her husband before looking pleadingly at her stepdaughter, 'that your father meant you to think about it. Let's go home. We'll come back later and talk about this.'

As they left his hospital room Dione glanced over her shoulder at the man who had been such a big controlling influence on her life and found it hard to believe that he was asking her to do this. She'd done most things; she'd been the best daughter she could under the circumstances, but begging for money? From his arch-enemy? How insulting could he be?

Her mind flew back twenty-four hours to when she'd received the phone call from a distraught Phrosini saying he was ill and was asking for her.

'Of course I'll come. I'll be on the next available flight.'

Dione turned to her mother, an anxious expression on her lovely face. 'I need to return home. Father's in hospital; he's had a heart attack.'

Jeannie's hand flew to her mouth. 'Oh, dear! Naturally you must go. I'll tell Chris for you. I do hope Yannis will be OK.'

A magnanimous thought after the way he had treated her, decided Dione. But that was her mother; she rarely thought ill of anyone. She was quiet and undemanding and Dione privately thought that she let people walk all over her. Not that she would ever tell her parent that; she loved her too dearly.

To her dismay there were no available seats on flights to Athens until the next day, but at least it gave her the opportunity to tell Chris herself.

'I'll come with you,' he said at once when he saw her that evening. 'I can't let my fiancée go through this alone.'

He'd said it so proudly that Dione felt guilty. She had been planning to take Chris to Greece to meet her father, to get his approval for their wedding, but not under these circumstances. The shock of discovering that she was going to marry an Englishman would probably kill her father altogether.

Yannis was Greek through and through. Very proud, very traditional, and it was his ambition that Dione should marry one of his own kind. Dione, though, had other ideas. She wanted to escape her father's domineering nature and the only way she could do it, as far as she could see, was to marry and settle in England.

She had met Christopher Donovan on one of her frequent visits to the UK and when he proposed she had thought about it long and hard before finally accepting. It wasn't that she didn't love Chris, she did, but it was his love for her that she wasn't so sure about.

He had gone out with her on the rebound from a previous relationship and assured her that it was all over. But she had heard from a third party only the other day that the girl still hankered after him and that he had been seen with her. She had tackled Chris and he had looked startled at first, and then said that there was no truth in it.

'I think it would be best if I went alone,' she said to him now. 'My father's too ill to meet strangers.'

'You're probably right,' he agreed. 'You will phone me?'

'Naturally.'

The plane landed at Athens Airport and Dione strode through the arrivals lounge, a stunningly attractive woman in a cream trouser suit teamed with a chocolate-coloured top. Her long blue-black hair brushed her shoulders sensuously with each step that she took in her high-heeled sandals, causing many a male head to turn.

Dione was oblivious. She headed for the taxi rank, not expecting anyone to meet her, but surprised and pleased to see her stepmother.

'Phrosini, how nice of you! I didn't anticipate this.' She hugged the woman warmly, easily falling into her second language. 'Shouldn't you be with Father? How is he? Is he any better?'

Phrosini was short and plump but extremely beautiful, and it was easy to see why her father had fallen in love with her. She was as different from Dione's mother as it was possible for two people to be. His first marriage had been a definite mistake. They had probably loved each other to begin with, surmised Dione, but her mother had been too weak to stand up to his bossy nature. Phrosini could handle him beautifully without him even realising it.

'There's no change,' answered Phrosini. 'Except that he's excited you're coming. He really is ill, Dione. I'm worried to death.'

'Why didn't you let me know sooner?'

Phrosini grimaced apologetically. 'I didn't want to spoil your holiday. I know how much you enjoy being in England with your mother. At first I thought he'd recover quickly, but he didn't and he started asking for you. I couldn't reason with him.'

They drove straight to the hospital. 'I'm sorry, I know you'll want to freshen up, but your father's anxious to see you,' explained Phrosini.

And when Dione walked into Yannis' room she was shocked by his appearance. He wasn't a tall man, had always been slim and dapper, but he'd lost so much weight that he looked gaunt to the point of danger, his skin grey and drawn, and he was hooked up to a host of machines that monitored his every function.

'Dione!' he croaked. 'You're here!'

She crossed the room and hugged him. 'Yes, Father. How are you feeling? It's so naughty of you not to let me know you were ill.'

He stroked her hand. 'Didn't want to worry you, child.'

'So what brought on your heart attack?' she wanted to know. 'I thought you had the constitution of an ox.'

'Not any more.' Yannis glanced at Phrosini. 'You tell her,' he said in a hoarse whisper.

'Tell me what?'

Phrosini closed her eyes, and when she opened them again Dione saw a wealth of worry. 'Your father's business is failing—badly.'

'What?' Dione frowned. How could that be? Yannis had inherited a restaurant from his father and turned it into a successful chain. There had been no talk of it losing money.

'Trade's been dropping off considerably,' Phrosini informed her, her voice quiet and desperate. 'It needs a big injection of money for a facelift and your father hasn't got it. He's paying out more than he gets in. We're almost bankrupt, Dione.'

Dione was shocked but not truly surprised. She had trained in England as an interior designer, hoping to move there permanently and get a job, but Yannis had insisted she work for him. She spent her time travelling between the different restaurants, renovating where necessary—but always under Yannis' eagle eye.

He was a pure traditionalist, so old-fashioned that he would never let her impose any of her modern ideas. He

said traditional values gave the restaurants atmosphere
and would not be shifted. Dione had privately had her
doubts. People wanted modern and lively these days.
They didn't want to live in the past.

'This is awful,' she said. 'I had no idea.'

'Nor did I,' confessed Phrosini. 'Your father kept it
from me—and as a result he's in here.' She put her hand
over her husband's and squeezed gently. 'You're a very
stubborn man, you know that.'

Yannis grimaced. 'It's all up to you now, daughter,'
he said quietly, looking at Dione. 'You're my only hope.'

'Me?' Dione touched her fingers to her chest. 'How
can I help? I don't have that sort of money.' She really
didn't have a lot of savings. Her father paid her the
minimum wage he would have paid anyone else and it
all went on her flights to England.

'I want you to go and ask Theo Tsardikos for a loan,'
he explained in a hoarse, breathless whisper. It clearly
cost him to even talk. 'He'll drive a hard bargain, I know
that, but if anyone can do it you can.'

'I know it's a lot to ask of you,' said Phrosini now as they
sat and drank coffee back at home in their beautiful villa
and talked about Yannis. 'But you're our only hope,
your father's only hope. If he doesn't get this money his
life will be over. He won't have the will to live. He's
dying now. The doctors are doing all they can but...' She
let her voice fade away and even she looked pale and ill.

'Surely there must be some other way?' pondered
Dione. She wasn't afraid of Theo Tsardikos, even
though he was a powerful man; it would be more embarrassing than anything else. 'What about the banks?'

'They're closing in on him.'

And Dione knew that he didn't have any friends who would help. There were not many people who liked her father; he was a tyrant of the highest order, and she had more reason than most to hate him after the way he had treated her mother. But he was her blood after all and though she found it hard to forgive him she loved him. She kept the peace mainly for her emotionally vulnerable mother's sake, not knowing what he might say or do to her if she got on the wrong side of him.

Jeannie and Yannis had divorced sixteen years ago. When their marriage broke up he had moved back to his native Greece, taking Dione with him. Reluctantly he had let her visit her mother during school holidays. Now she spent as much time in England as she possibly could, and had been on the second week of a month's visit when she had got the call.

'It's a lot to ask of me.'

'I know,' said Phrosini.

Dione had grown close to her stepmother and loved her dearly but at this moment in time she wished that she wasn't asking the impossible of her. Phrosini had never had any children of her own, much to Yannis' disappointment because he'd always wanted sons, and so she looked upon Dione as her own daughter.

Now Dione faced the little Greek woman with compassion in her eyes. 'It looks as though I have no choice.'

And when they went back to the hospital to tell her father Dione was glad that she'd made the decision. He looked if possible even more sallow and ill than earlier. He lay in his bed, his breathing laboured, but as soon as he heard her news he smiled and a light appeared in his eyes.

'Thank you, Dione. Thank you from the bottom of my rotten heart.' And he took her hands and squeezed them.

Dione took a deep breath as she stood outside the door and prepared to face the legendary Theo Tsardikos.

Her father's life depended on her succeeding.

But how easy would it be, when they were total enemies?

CHAPTER TWO

THEO looked with interest at the woman standing in front of him. He was aware that Yannis Keristari had a daughter but he had never met her and was pleasantly surprised.

She was tall and slender and very fine looking, somewhere in her twenties, he imagined. She wore a grey jacket with a matching pencil-slim skirt and high-heeled shoes. The jacket was fastened to just above her breasts and a gold pendant dangled enticingly close to her cleavage. He couldn't help wondering why she had chosen to fasten it so demurely on such a warm day, and it amused him to assume that she wore nothing beneath.

Her eyes were dark and sloe-shaped with a fan of thick lashes, her nose straight and small, and her mouth—was delicious. He forced himself to look from it. She was nothing like her father, which came as something of a surprise. And totally unlike any other Greek woman he'd met. He was fascinated. Even more so than with the reason she was here.

Which had yet to be revealed.

Clearly Keristari had sent her. Theo had heard through the grapevine that Yannis Keristari's business was in trouble. Had his daughter's visit anything to do with it? Perhaps he was offering to sell him his restaurants?

He showed his visitor to a seat, not once taking his eyes off her, and waited for her to speak. She was graceful in her movements and smelled like a dream.

'Mr Tsardikos.'

'Please, call me Theo.'

'This isn't a social visit,' she declared with a delightful toss of her head that revealed a long, slender neck simply begging to be kissed. Theo sat down behind his desk to stop himself from advancing towards her. 'Maybe,' he growled. 'But there's no need for formalities, especially when you're the daughter of an old...acquaintance of mine.' He'd been about to say enemy, but realised that this could get her back up before she'd even given her reason for being here. 'Would you like coffee? I can get someone to—'

'No!'

It was an instant decision. She was clearly on a mission and wanted to get it over with. 'So how can I help you?' He folded his arms, allowing his eyes to half close as he studied her intently. He could feel a stirring in his groin that shocked him to the core. This was the daughter of a man he hadn't the faintest admiration for. He should be totally indifferent to her. So why wasn't he?

'My father needs money.'

He felt quite sure she hadn't intended to blurt it out like that because a tell-tale colouring to her skin belied her cool outer image. But he was glad that she had because he now knew where he stood. His mind had run to the fact that her father could be offering him first refusal on the business. But money! How much had it cost Keristari to send her here?

'Is that so?' he asked with cool indifference. He had no intention in the world of helping this man out.

Dione nodded. 'He believes that you might be able to help him.'

Theo wanted to tell her straight away that he wouldn't. Keristari was a bully of the highest order and most definitely not a man to do business with.

But he didn't want to let Dione go yet. He was fascinated. She was quite the sexiest woman he had met in a long time. There was something refreshingly different about her. It was as though she had no idea of her own sexuality. How he would like to introduce her to it.

'Why ask me?' he asked, leaning back in his chair, his hands linked behind his head. 'Why not his bank?'

'I think he's in too deep for that,' admitted Dione. 'He says you're his only hope. He's counting on it.'

Dione saw the disbelief on Theo Tsardikos' face, the hint of anger quickly suppressed, and knew that her mission was doomed to failure. But she still needed to try. The image of her father lying helpless in hospital flashed in front of her mind's eye. Much as she feared him, much as she sometimes despised him, she couldn't bear to see him so ill and worried.

'He's counting on it!' repeated Theo disbelievingly, dragging dark brows together over velvety brown eyes. 'Why would he ask me, the man he probably hates more than anyone else in the world, for money? Unless, of course, he's exhausted all his other options.'

'I don't know,' said Dione, her eyes steady on this

tall, undeniably handsome man with a shock of dark hair that looked as though he constantly ran his fingers through it. 'I didn't know anything about it until yesterday. I've been visiting my mother in England.'

'So Phrosini isn't your birth mother?' he enquired, sharp interest on his face.

Dione shook her head. She wished he wasn't quite so good-looking. She wished his eyes wouldn't rake over her as though he wanted to take her to bed.

'That explains why you look nothing like either of your parents.'

'Which has nothing to do with the reason I'm here,' declared Dione heatedly. She certainly wasn't here to discuss her parentage.

He allowed himself to smile and his very even white teeth looked predatory in her heightened state. Like a wolf about to pounce, she thought. This was a man she had to watch closely. He looked relaxed leaning back in his chair, his shirt collar undone, but his mind was as sharp as a razor.

'Your father's using you, you do know that?' he pointed out. 'Like he uses everyone he comes into contact with. The best thing you can do, Dione—do you mind if I call you Dione?—is to go right back and tell him the answer's no.'

Dione drew in a pained breath. What a heartless brute the man was. 'You haven't even asked how much he wants,' she retorted, her back stiff, her eyes sparking resentment.

'It's immaterial,' he said. 'I wouldn't lend your father one euro, let alone thousands of them, which I presume is the kind of amount he'd want. What's happened?'

Dione shrugged. 'All I know is that he's nearly bankrupt.'

'Bad management,' drawled Theo uncaringly.

'So that's your final answer?' she snapped, her heart dipping so low it almost touched her shoes.

Theo leaned back in his chair, a smile playing on well-shaped lips, and an unfathomable gleam in his eyes. 'There could be another solution.'

Dione's heart leapt with hope.

'I could save your father's business—on one condition.'

'And that is?' asked Dione eagerly.

There was a long pause before he answered, a space of time when his eyes raked insolently over her body, sending a shiver of unease through her limbs. But she didn't let him see it; she sat still, her hands folded primly in her lap, and waited to hear what he had to say.

'That you become my wife.'

The shock of his suggestion couldn't have been greater. This man was a stranger to her, as she was to him, and yet he was talking about marriage! Was he out of his mind? Would he lend her father money just to get his hands on her? What sort of a monster was he? Dione shivered as rivers of ice raced down her spine.

She jumped to her feet and glared. 'That is the most outrageous suggestion I've ever heard. What makes you think I'd marry a total stranger?'

A faint, insolent smile curved his mouth. 'I thought you had your father's best interests at heart. Otherwise why would you be here?'

'I do,' she admitted, 'but that doesn't include giving myself away to you.' The man had no idea what he was asking. He was probably a fantastic lover with years of experience, but it meant nothing to her. She didn't know the first thing about him. And nor did she want to if these were his tactics.

'It's your choice,' he said, as simply as if they were discussing a normal business proposition. 'If your answer's no then we have nothing else to discuss.'

'Of course my answer's no,' she spat at him. 'What do you take me for?' And with that she whirled on her heel and stormed out of the room.

His mocking voice called after her. 'I'll be waiting should you change your mind.'

'Then you'll wait a lifetime,' she hissed beneath her breath.

Dione didn't go straight to the hospital; she was far too wound up for that. She had taken a taxi to Theo's office but now decided to walk. Even then she took a circuitous route and by the time she did reach the hospital she was almost able to laugh at Theo Tsardikos' suggestion.

But her father didn't laugh. 'You could do worse,' he said. 'I've always wanted you to marry a proud Greek male and Tsardikos is as good as they come.'

Praise indeed coming from her father, thought Dione.

'I've been so afraid that on one of your trips to England you'll fall in love. It would break my heart.'

It was on the tip of Dione's tongue to tell him about Chris, but at the last moment she decided against it. Yannis' health was so bad that such an admission might finish him off altogether. In fact he looked even worse today that he had yesterday. His breathing was laboured and his skin a ghostly yellow and Phrosini hovered, not knowing what to do to help her beloved husband.

'I can't marry a complete stranger,' Dione said miserably.

'Not even for me?' demanded Yannis in a rough, angry voice. 'Not even though my life and my livelihood depend on it? What sort of a daughter are you?'

He made Dione feel guilty, but even so she stuck to her guns. 'I'd be prostituting myself.'

'With Tsardikos? He's an exciting male. Half the female population of Greece are after him. You'll be the envy of thousands.' And then he slumped in his chair and hardly seemed to be breathing.

Phrosini beckoned her out of the room. 'We must leave him for a while,' she said.

'Don't you know he's asking the impossible?' asked Dione, as they made their way to the hospital restaurant. 'I haven't said anything to my father, and I don't want you to either, but there's a man in England I've promised to marry.'

'Oh, Dione, why didn't you say?' Her stepmother was full of concern.

'How could I when my father's so ill, and more especially after what he's just said?'

'And this boy, you love him?'

'Of course.' But Dione's face gave away the fact that it wasn't exactly going to be a marriage made in heaven.

'You're doing it because you don't want your father to arrange a marriage for you?' she asked intuitively.

Dione nodded faintly, her lips clamped together. When it was put to her like that she realised it was probably true. The love she felt for Chris wasn't like the stuff you read about, but she had been happy enough—until she heard that he'd been seen with his ex-girlfriend!

'Oh, Dione, is that really the answer? I don't want you to be unhappy like I was with my first husband, like your mother was.'

'I'd be happier with Chris than Theo Tsardikos,' said Dione quietly.

'Theo's a good man. His offer is a lifeline to your father. In fact it might save his life. The doctors are very fearful today.' There were tears in Phrosini's eyes. 'And if he doesn't recover…well, your father's always wanted me to carry on the business if anything should happen to him.'

Meaning she would be letting them both down. Put like that, how could she refuse? Dione breathed in deeply, closed her eyes, then took the plunge, hating herself for it but knowing it was something she had to do.

'OK—I'll—marry him.' Her words floated in the air like a storm cloud threatening to bear down and drown her in a black deluge of unhappiness.

Phrosini hugged her tightly, tears streaming down her cheeks. 'My precious child.'

There was nothing precious about it, thought Dione, but she made up her mind there and then that Theo Tsardikos would not get it all his own way. This marriage would be on her terms.

He was savagely handsome, quite the best-looking man she'd ever seen—tall, with a perfectly honed body and long-fingered, well-manicured hands. It was one of the first things she'd noticed about him. But it didn't mean that she would eagerly jump into his bed. Quite the opposite! She would be a good and dutiful wife in every other respect. She would cook for him, entertain for him, accompany him whenever necessary, but nothing more.

Maybe this was what he wanted her to be—a good hostess? A man in his position would need someone at his side on special occasions.

And who was she trying to kid?

She had seen the way he looked at her, the way his eyes had raked insolently over her body, and she had known what he was thinking, even though she'd done her very best to ignore it.

Already she was beginning to lament her decision but her father was overjoyed when they went back to tell him, his eyes brightening and becoming alert and interested. 'My darling daughter! You won't regret this, I promise you.'

Dione wasn't so sure.

She spent a sleepless night worrying about it, telling herself there was still time to back out, but then recalling her father's pleasure. How could she deny him his dying wish?

As Dione sat outside Theo Tsardikos' office for the second time in the same number of days her heart leapt with alarming violence. This was going to be the hardest thing she had ever done. Giving herself to a man she didn't know was crazy. She had to be insane to do it.

And the man in question was taking great delight in keeping her waiting!

And the longer Dione waited the more irritated she became, until at last she jumped to her feet and prepared to leave. She couldn't do this, not even for her father's sake. No one knew the courage it had taken her to come here this morning; courage that was fast deserting her.

'Leaving, are we?'

Dione spun round at the sound of a deep, gravelly voice and looked into a pair of amused dark eyes. 'I'd begun to think you didn't want to see me. I've sat here for twenty minutes.'

'I'm a busy man, Dione. And you did arrive without an appointment. But now I'm all yours. Do come in.' And he touched a hand to her arm as he led her into his office.

It was a large, airy room with a wooden floor and pale grey walls hung with photographs of his various hotels. His desk was in front of the massive window with its views over Athens, and in one corner was a trio of armchairs. Against another wall was a series of bookcases. It was clean and clinical and efficient. Like the man himself.

She headed towards the desk, prepared to sit in the seat opposite him, as she had before, but instead he steered her towards the armchairs. 'We'll be more comfortable here.'

Dione did not want to be comfortable; she wanted to say what she had to say and get out quickly. Not the right sort of thought when Theo was her prospective husband—though actually she was hoping that he'd had a change of heart. A hope that was quickly dashed when he flashed his wolfish teeth.

'Can I presume that the reason you're here is to declare that you'll marry me after all?'

Two pairs of brown eyes met and warred, and Dione was the first to look away. 'I'd like to be able to say no,' she snapped, ignoring the stammer of her heart. This man was lethal. Deadly attractive but a danger all the same.

'You're a free agent.' The words were tossed lightly and dismissively into the air and Dione gained the impression that he couldn't care less. That this was all some sort of game to him.

'Meaning *you've* changed *your* mind?' she enquired sharply, mentally crossing her fingers that this was so.

'Not at all.' It was a simple, matter-of-fact answer; he was giving her no help whatsoever. In fact he was enjoying her discomfort.

'In that case,' she said in a voice not much above a whisper, 'I'll do as you ask.'

'I'm sorry, I can't hear you.'

Damn the man! A satisfied smile played about his sculpted lips and his eyes were filled with amusement. She felt pretty sure that he had heard. He just wanted to hear her say it again. He liked seeing her squirm.

'I said, I'll do as you ask.' There, was that loud enough for him? She'd projected the words as though she was throwing a missile, hoping they'd smash into his face and wipe some of the pleasure off it.

No such luck! His smile widened and deepened and he leaned forward and took her hands into his. 'There, that wasn't so bad, was it?'

Dione huffed and said nothing.

'You're not happy?'

'No, I'm not.'

'But I'm guessing your father's delirious?'

'He was pleased, yes.'

'He must really have hit rock-bottom.'

Dione flashed furious dark eyes at him. 'He has, and he's in hospital fighting for his life because of it.'

Theo frowned. 'I didn't know that.'

'There's a lot about my father you don't know.'

'And a lot I do,' he growled. 'He's unscrupulous. I bet he had no hesitation in saying you should marry me. How he could have produced a daughter like you I don't know.'

'How do you know I'm not unscrupulous too?' she riposted, wishing she could jump up and run. This was the most humiliating experience of her life.

'I'm good at reading people.'

'How do you know that if I marry you I won't take you for every penny you've got?' she slammed at him.

'Because I've already had a contract drawn up. I—'

'You've what?' interjected Dione in horror. 'You were that sure I'd say yes?'

'Absolutely,' he agreed, stretching out his long legs and linking his hands behind his head.

He looked so relaxed she wanted to take a swipe at him, knock some of that pleasure off his damnably handsome face. 'You bastard!'

Theo's well-shaped brows rose. 'Tut, tut, Dione! Here was I, thinking you were a lady.'

'You bring out the worst in me,' she savaged.

'It's not all I plan to bring out in you,' he said with a cruel smile. 'Let's get down to business. You *are* here to say that you will marry me in return for me bailing your father out of trouble?'

Dione swallowed hard, ignored the little voice inside her head that told her to get up and run, ignored the thought of a nice, safe English marriage to Chris Donovan, and nodded.

His lips curved in satisfaction. 'I never thought I'd say this, but your father's a very lucky man, do you know that? Not many girls would do this for their father. Pray tell me, why do you love him so much? Or is it perhaps because you fear him?' He saw the flicker in her eyes and nodded. 'He has you in the same stranglehold as everyone else. I pity you, Dione, having a father like that, though I applaud what you are doing.'

'Only because it's in your favour,' she snorted, deeply annoyed that he had summed up the situation so correctly. Did everyone know that her father was a control freak?

'As I said, I've had a contract drawn up; all you have to do is sign it.' He rose from the chair and strode across to his desk.

Dione watched, her heart aching with a pain she had never felt before. Sorrow, anger, despair. Not that she let Theo see any of this. When he returned to his seat she lifted her chin and sat that little bit straighter. 'I have a few stipulations of my own before I sign anything.'

Dark brows rose. 'Are you in any position?'

'I think I am.'

He lifted broad shoulders. 'I beg to differ on that point, but go ahead. Unless, of course, you'd like to read my contract first? You might be pleasantly surprised.'

Dione privately doubted it, but maybe she ought to take a look before she jumped in with her own criteria.

It wasn't a long document, but in essence it gave him full power to treat her as he liked in return for helping her father out of his financial troubles. *'To become my wife in every sense for as long as I desire,'* were the words that sprang out from the page.

Not on his life!

She thrust it back at him. 'No! Absolutely no!'

'To what exactly?' he enquired insouciantly. He had clearly expected her denial and was now going to take great pleasure in having her spell it out to him.

'I will not go to bed with you.' When all her friends had been sleeping around Dione had kept her virginity,

saving it for the man she would eventually marry—
someone she loved and respected. She had thought
Chris that man until very recently. But she was definitely not giving herself to Theo Tsardikos. Not ever!
'Nor will I remain married to you for longer than one
year,' she added stormily. 'In all other respects I will be
your wife.'

'There are no other respects,' he growled. 'A wife is
a wife. A wife spends time in her husband's bed. A wife
pleasures her man.'

'A wife also cooks and cleans and entertains.'

'I have people to do that sort of thing,' he answered
dismissively. 'It's a bed companion I want and I think
you'll fit the bill admirably. You're beautiful, you're
spirited, you're caring. What more could a man ask for?
But—maybe I can agree to your condition.'

Theo smiled to himself. It had never been his intention
for them to sleep in separate beds. On the other hand it
would be interesting trying to change her mind. In fact,
the chase could be as enjoyable as the kill.

He had wanted her from the first second he saw her.
She was quite the most striking and intriguing woman
he'd ever met. He had dreamed about her last night, and
what an exciting lover she had been! If dream became
actuality, however... His gut twisted at the very thought.

In one respect he felt sorry for Dione, and the
pressure Keristari had put on her. He wanted to make
their sham of a marriage reality; he wanted her to learn
to love him as a woman should love a man, not to marry
him under duress and out of loyalty to her father.
Keristari was a man whom no one liked except for his

very loyal wife. Phrosini deserved a medal for putting up with his bullying ways.

What had happened, he wondered, between him and Dione's mother? Clearly she hadn't tolerated his dictatorial manner; she had got out while she could. And good for her! Maybe Dione would tell him the story one day.

'So do you intend drawing up another contract?' she asked him now, her chin determinedly high, her lovely, liquid brown eyes revealing her distaste of what was about to happen.

Lord, he wanted to take her into his arms and assure her that everything would be all right. That he wasn't an ogre, that he wouldn't hurt her. And that he admired what she was doing. But that wasn't part of the game.

He was frankly appalled that she would marry him simply to please her father and drag him out of the mire he'd got himself into. It was misplaced loyalty as far as he was concerned.

Naturally he was sympathetic towards Keristari's illness, but that didn't change him from the bullying tyrant he'd always been. And even in his illness he was controlling all those around him. It was no way to behave towards your loved ones. He did not deserve their devotion.

He was so angry with the man that his tone was sharply aggressive when he answered her question. 'Naturally. I will have it ready for your signature this afternoon.'

Dione's head jerked as she stared at him wild-eyed. 'So soon?'

'Why wait?' he asked smoothly. 'I don't imagine your father will want to drag this thing out. If he's in

as much trouble as you say he'll want the money now.
But no marriage, no funding! Shall we set the wedding
for Sunday? Is two days enough for you to get your
head round it?'

CHAPTER THREE

THEO almost laughed when he saw the consternation on Dione's face.

'Two days?' she choked. 'You can't wait to get your hands on me, is that it? Damn you, Theo Tsardikos! Damn you to hell.'

Lord, wasn't she gorgeous when she was angry? He felt his testosterone levels rising and it was all he could do not to drag her into his arms and kiss her senseless. 'I was thinking of your father's money,' he answered, amazing himself at his coolness when inside he was on fire.

'I bet you were,' she snapped. 'I've seen the way you look at me. But don't forget, we shall have a piece of paper forbidding you to touch. And heaven help you if you renege.'

What a spirited person she was. What an exciting woman. His male hormones danced all over the place. 'I wouldn't dream of it,' he said slowly, levelly. 'Anything in that direction will have to come from you.'

'Then you'll wait till hell freezes over,' she tossed cruelly.

He folded his arms across his chest, dropped his head

to one side and studied her. 'You're amazing, do you know that?'

'Amazing?' she scoffed. 'I'm simply telling you how it is. This is a business contract. Nothing more, nothing less, and you'd best remember it.'

'I will remember,' he told her. Whatever happened between him and this intriguing young lady, whether they made a success of the marriage—wishful thinking—or it failed abysmally—more like it—it would stay in his memory for the rest of his life.

'Good,' she snapped, standing up, and with another flash of her lovely dark eyes she headed for the door.

He did not want to let her go yet—he wanted her to stay, to talk some more; he wanted to get to know this gorgeous creature better. But sanity told him to take things easy. In any case, she had to come back to sign the new contract. His lips quirked at the pleasure of seeing her again so soon. Perhaps at his home rather than here, where they could talk longer, get to know each other better.

And then on Sunday—she would be his!

He had a lot to organise, a lot of arrangements to make. No time to detain her. He walked to the door and bade her goodbye. 'Till later, Dione. I'll ring you when the contract's ready. Will you be home?'

Dione glared into his face. 'I have no idea.'

'Then give me your mobile number.' He half expected her to refuse; was surprised when she wrote it down without argument. He tucked the slip of paper into his pocket and held out his hand. She ignored it, spinning on her heel and rushing out of the office as though all the hounds in hell were chasing her.

Theo smiled to himself. He was rarely short of female company but no woman had appealed to him as Dione Keristari did now. She had turned up under the most distressing of situations; she'd been forced to approach him by her demanding father, but beneath her hostility, beneath the fear she had felt when confronting him, was a beautiful woman simply waiting to be loved.

Dione marched out of the office building with her mind in torment. Theo wanted from her exactly what she'd feared. A wife in every sense of the word! Thank goodness she'd been able to talk him around; though in actual fact she wasn't totally convinced that he would keep his word. He was the sort of guy who if you gave him an inch would take a mile.

Not wanting to go back to the hospital yet, she took herself into the village where they lived near Athens, sat outside a café and ordered coffee.

It was hard to believe that Theo Tsardikos had expected her to become his wife in every sense of the word right from the moment the ring was put on her finger. Had he no idea what it would be like to let a complete stranger make love to her? She couldn't even visualise letting it happen.

No, if he didn't stick to his side of the bargain, she would walk away from the marriage regardless. And if Tsardikos demanded his money back then her father would have to find someone else to dig him out of the mire he'd got himself into. It was as simple as that.

Or so she told herself. In fact it wasn't. She couldn't let her father down. She had let herself down by agreeing to this marriage, but if Theo drew up the contract in accordance with her request then she couldn't see anything going wrong. He was a man of his word, she felt sure, and, although he might enjoy goading her, he wouldn't force her to do anything she didn't want to do.

How long she sat there drinking coffee Dione wasn't sure. A few people she knew paused to pass the time of day but by and large she sat there alone and tried to digest the very big step that she was going to take.

She had to phone her mother, of course. And Chris. But it wasn't something she was looking forward to. Procrastination would be the name of the game here. Maybe after the marriage? When it was a *fait accompli* and they could do nothing about it. Was that too awful of her? But how could she tell them right at this very minute, when she had never felt so vulnerable in her life?

She had been driven into a corner by two scheming men, both of them as bad as the other. Twelve months was a lifetime when you weren't happy. It was a prison sentence. Her head spun and she sat there for hours until Spiros, the owner, came to ask whether she was all right.

'Dione, you sit here so long. You look very troubled.'

She had known him virtually all her life and smiled wanly. 'My father's ill,' she declared. 'I'm worried about him.' If only it were that simple.

'I am sorry. Please—give him my best wishes. I hope he is better soon.'

'Me too, Spiros. Me too.'

The phone call came sooner than she expected and her heart jerked into overdrive at the sound of Theo's deep, warm voice.

'Dione, it is time. I will pick you up. Where are you?'

'No!' She almost spat the word. 'There's no need. I will come to your office.'

'I'm at home,' he told her, and Dione's heart sank.

'You—you want me to come to your house?' How awful would that be!

'I thought you would be more relaxed.'

'If you think I'll ever be relaxed marrying an arrogant beast like you then you're very much mistaken,' she told him boldly.

Theo laughed. 'What a charming vocabulary you have.' And then his voice hardened. 'I repeat, where are you?'

Best not get on the wrong side of him, at least not until the money was safely in her father's bank account, thought Dione. 'I'm at Spiros' Café. Do you know it?'

'No.'

She hadn't thought he would. It was not the sort of place he would use. 'Give me your address and I'll find my way there,' she suggested coolly.

Theo made some sort of disagreeable grunting noise. 'Take a taxi. I'll see you soon.'

His villa was as large and impressive as she had imagined it would be, with the usual white stucco walls and red roofs but approached by a long drive and guarded like a fortress. She let the taxi drop her off at the gates and didn't buzz to announce her arrival until the vehicle had gone. Then she walked up the drive, lined on each side by olive trees, and saw Theo waiting for her.

He had changed from his business suit into a pair of casual trousers and a white shirt that stretched across a broad, powerful chest previously hidden to her enquiring eyes. His arms were muscular and tanned and he looked like a man who wasn't afraid of hard work. He also looked younger and less formidable but Dione knew that she must still be wary of him. This wasn't a social visit; this was business with a capital B.

Never had Dione felt more like turning and running. In two days' time this would be her home. She would live here with Theo; she would be his wife in the eyes of the law and every one of his acquaintances. But not in her eyes; never in her eyes! The marriage would never be consummated.

It was too embarrassing by far to ever tell anyone the real reason she was marrying Theo. For twelve months she would act as she'd never acted before, she would carry out her father's wishes, but she would walk away at the end of it with her head held high, confident in the knowledge that Theo Tsardikos had not had his evil way with her.

The villa was spacious and airy and expensive—and beautifully furnished. She fell in love with it straight away. Although it was large it was not pretentious. Theo, she hated to admit, had excellent taste. 'Why, this is lovely,' she said, unable to help herself.

'Wait until you see outside,' he answered, leading her through the villa and looking pleased by her enthusiasm.

And there in front of them was the ocean. Tiered down to it was a series of swimming pools and sun decks, some sheltered by palms and other plants, others bearing the full brunt of the hot summer sun. It was paradise.

'You have a perfect home,' she told him reluctantly.

'And it's going to be your home as well,' he said, turning to face her. 'Do you still think you're getting a bad deal?'

'As far as my emotions go, yes,' she told him truthfully. 'But as far as my senses are concerned, this is sheer heaven.' Her own home with her father was very beautiful but it would never match up to this. They had a pool, yes, but quite a small one in comparison, and they certainly didn't have a sea view. Her father would be as jealous as hell if he only knew.

And she must remember that it was for her father that she was doing this. He was the one forcing her to live in this idyllic spot. Maybe it was wise if she didn't tell him.

'I'm glad you approve; it's half the battle. Let's get down to business, shall we?'

They returned indoors and in his study, a cool, air-conditioned room with very little in the way of furniture apart from a hugely functional desk and a couple of chairs, he handed her a sheet of paper.

Dione sat and read it and she was satisfied. He was demanding nothing from her that she was not prepared to give, apart from her time. The contract was to run for twelve months from the day they married, and after that she was free to leave. He would divorce her without question and he would deposit into her father's bank account, the day after their marriage, whatever sum of money Yannis needed to build up his business again.

It was a very generous agreement under the circumstances, thought Dione. Theo was getting nothing out of it and it was costing him dear. There had to be a catch in it somewhere. But she read it through three times and it was all very straightforward. She took the pen he offered and signed. Theo countersigned.

And it was all done.

On Sunday she would become his wife.

All she hoped was that her father appreciated exactly what she was doing for him.

* * *

The day dawned with a cloudless blue sky and a hot sun powering down on them. Dione had still not telephoned her mother. She wanted to protect her parent, not let her worry and fear that in some incalculable way Yannis still had a hold over her. Jeannie never said much about him but Dione knew that she sometimes feared that her past would come back to haunt her.

And Dione had not seen Theo again either. A special delivery had revealed a stunning wedding dress in ivory silk and every accessory she would need to go with it. Dione guessed there had been some collusion with Phrosini because how could he have possibly known her size?

But she did not question her stepmother; she saw no point in it. The deed was done. She was to become Theo's wife and that was that. Personally she would have worn an oyster-coloured suit that was her favourite; now she was being forced to dress up as though it were a real wedding and she and Theo were very much in love.

Through the grapevine she'd heard that a whole host of guests had been invited. They were getting married in the hospital chapel so that Yannis could be present. No doubt, thought Dione bitterly, he wanted to make doubly sure that she wouldn't run away at the last minute.

Which was extremely tempting.

It was all very emotional and when finally, at a few minutes past three, she became Theo's wife, Dione burst into tears. Everyone cheered and clapped and no one knew, except for Phrosini and Yannis, that it was not a real wedding.

'You're very beautiful, Mrs Tsardikos,' said Theo softly as they walked out of the chapel that had been decked with a myriad of flowers tied with soft satin ribbons and looked charming.

'I don't feel it,' she said, so quietly that no one else heard. 'I feel a fraud.'

'I won't allow you to say that,' he announced curtly, taking her hand and squeezing it. 'To the outside world you are the beautiful girl who has captured Theo Tsardikos' heart. You will become quite famous, *agapi mou.*'

Dione groaned inwardly. She hadn't realised how much of a stir Theo's marriage would cause. She had hoped—she had prayed, in fact—that it would be a quiet affair, but the guests had poured into the hospital, overflowing into corridors, and congratulations had fallen thick and fast.

The reception was being held at Theo's villa and they made their way now in streams of cars that ferried people across the city. The gardens and terraces were decked with flowers and garlands, a band played and exquisite food was served.

Theo made a speech saying what a lucky man he was and Dione blushed her way through it. Theo's parents told her that she had made their son a very happy man, and his sister, Alexandra, couldn't quite believe it either.

'I never thought that Theo would marry again after what happened,' she said to Dione. 'In fact, he swore he wouldn't. You must be someone very special to get him to change his mind.'

CHAPTER FOUR

THEO had been married before! Dione stared at Alexandra in disbelief.

'He hasn't told you, has he?' enquired his sister. 'I'm actually not too surprised because he never talks about it. Not ever. It's as though he's shut what happened completely out of his life.'

'So—what did happen?' questioned Dione. For some reason her heart was thumping wildly.

'Maybe I ought to let Theo himself tell you,' said Alexandra, looking suddenly uncomfortable.

She was almost as tall as Theo and willow-thin. Her dark hair was cut stylishly short and she looked striking in a pale green designer dress. But her appearance meant nothing; it was the information she had imparted. 'You can't stop now,' protested Dione.

'You two haven't known each other very long, have you?' enquired Theo's sister cautiously.

Dione shook her head, unwilling to tell her exactly how quickly this marriage had been arranged. She had gone through the ceremony as if in a dream and if anyone had asked her about it she wouldn't have been able to remember one thing. Not even declaring that she would be Theo's wife. All she had been aware of was him standing tall and strong at her side, and once, when she had faltered, he had caught her hand and squeezed it encouragingly.

Alexandra grinned now. 'Love at first sight? And they say it never happens. It's easy to see that you two are made for each other. He's been living in a world of his own since his divorce. It was never a happy marriage, kept together only for their son's sake. You're the best thing that's ever happened to him.'

Dione frowned and if possible her heartbeat quickened even more. 'Theo has a son?' she questioned breathlessly.

Alexandra shook her head. 'He died when he was only eleven months old. I don't think Theo's ever got over it. And Katina walked out on him afterwards. A swift divorce followed.'

'How awful for him,' said Dione reverently, seeing Theo in a new light. 'It's no wonder he can't bear to talk about it.' And she made up her mind there and then that she would never let on that she knew. Not unless he brought the subject up himself. And that was extremely unlikely under their surreal circumstances.

The day seemed endless. Theo dutifully stood at her side as a constant stream of his friends and relatives came to congratulate them and no one would have guessed that theirs was a marriage in name only. The way he looked at her, the way he touched her elbow, the way he smiled, made it all look very real. And Dione, too, smiled until her face ached, pretending a happiness she was far from feeling.

'You should have been an actor,' said Theo softly at

one point when she had just agreed that they were made for each other.

'You too,' she tossed back.

Phrosini dragged herself away from the hospital and came to add her further congratulations. 'Your father is very grateful for what you're doing,' she reassured Dione.

As well he should be Dione almost said, but she did not want to upset her stepmother so she smiled instead.

'Theo made a good choice with the dress.' It was slender and elegant and made Dione look even taller than she was.

'She is very beautiful,' agreed Theo, looking for all the world as though he was the proud groom. 'I think our marriage will be most agreeable. And definitely exciting.'

Dione wanted to ask him in what way, but not in front of Phrosini. All the arguments they would have perhaps? Definitely not exciting in a sexual sense. Of that she was very sure. And when Phrosini drifted away and for a few moments they were alone she asked him what he had meant.

'How will our marriage be exciting?'

'That's easy,' he said with a shrug of his wide shoulders. 'There will never be a dull moment with you, my sweet Dione. Sparks will fly, I'm very much aware of that, as I am aware of the fact that all day long you've wished yourself anywhere but at my side. You've stood the test admirably. Maybe it's time I added my congratulations?' And with that he bowed his head to kiss her.

Dione stiffened and moved so that his lips brushed her cheek, and she would have pushed him away had he not gripped her arm in warning. 'Careful, *agapi mou*, we're being watched.'

So Dione fixed the smile back on her face, hiding gritted teeth and a dislike so intense that it burnt into her soul. Thank goodness, she thought, that she hadn't agreed to his initial contract or she would have found herself in his bed tonight. In bed with a stranger! She shivered.

Immediately attentive, Theo asked, 'Are you cold?' And his liquid dark eyes were filled with concern.

Dione shook her head. 'Someone walking over my grave.' And, although it was a common expression, she felt that in this instance it was the truth. She might as well be dead as married to this obnoxious man.

No, that wasn't true. He wasn't obnoxious. He was virile and handsome and astonishingly wealthy, which made him attractive in most female eyes. It would have all been so much easier had she felt the same way. But being bought put a different perspective on things. She meant nothing more to Theo than a possession, nothing more than anything else he could have bought with his millions.

In fact she felt unclean and she would have liked nothing more than to run into the house and take a shower, and stay there for however long it took to make her feel whole and pure again. She had committed a sin in marrying Theo. She had made promises in the chapel that she knew she would not keep.

It was a relief when the day was over, when everyone had gone and she could relax her aching face.

'Well, Mrs Tsardikos,' said Theo with a satisfied smile, 'I've made many purchases in my life, but none as satisfactory as this.'

Dione frowned and her heart stammered fearfully. 'Satisfactory?' She didn't like the look on his face; it was as though he was contemplating pleasures to come.

If he thought he could ignore their contract he was wrong, very wrong. She wouldn't be averse to walking out of here right this very minute.

'I mean that you're the most beautiful wife any man could wish for. Congratulations have flown thick and fast.'

'And exactly what do you mean by wife?' asked Dione, appalled to hear how shrill her voice sounded.

'Just that. A beautiful, gracious lady. Someone I shall be pleased to show off.'

'And that's all?'

'What else could there be?' A well-shaped brow lifted enquiringly. 'Unless of course you're having second thoughts and are willing to share my bed?' Dark eyes captured hers so that it was difficult to look away.

Dione's heart drummed even faster. 'Not in a million years.'

Theo smiled in a way that told her he was confident that one day she would change her mind.

'I mean it!'

'Then why do you look so scared?' he asked. 'You can lock your door if you like. I'm a man of my word, Dione, in case you didn't know. As I said once before, the first move will come from you.'

Dione felt her body relax and she managed her first genuine smile of the day. 'You're a very honourable man, Theo, and I thank you for helping my father.'

'He doesn't have the money yet,' he pointed out.

Dione drew in a swift breath. 'I hope you're not going back on your word. I've completed my side of the bargain.'

'And it will be in his bank account first thing tomorrow morning.'

His steady eyes met hers but a faint feeling of unease returned. What if he was lying? What if he wanted to take her into his bed before paying her father? The sooner she went to her room and locked the door the better. She faked a yawn. 'I'm tired, Theo. I'd like to go to bed.'

'Running away?' he mocked.

Dione stood her ground, lifting her chin and looking right into those dark, dangerous eyes. 'Not at all. It's been a long day.' And she cursed herself when she felt something approaching a flutter in the pit of her stomach. She put it down to nerves. It couldn't possibly be anything else—could it?

'I'll walk you up. Maybe I'll retire myself. As you say, it's been a tiring day. But a satisfying one all the same, don't you agree?'

'Where my father's concerned, yes,' she snapped. 'For myself, no. The next twelve months are going to be sheer hell.'

A harsh shadow darkened his face as they mounted the stairs together. 'And you'd do that for your father— put yourself through hell?'

Dione nodded, not trusting herself to speak. Put like that, it seemed like an enormous unselfish gesture on her part. If Yannis hadn't been at death's door she wouldn't have done it; that was a fact. If Phrosini hadn't per-suaded her... Tears began to sting the back of her eyes and she turned away. 'Goodnight, Theo.'

'Goodnight, my beautiful bride,' he answered as they reached her door. 'May I be permitted one kiss? To seal the deal perhaps?'

Dione wanted to say no, she wanted no contact between them, but she knew it would be churlish to refuse. It was going to be a brief kiss, though; nothing prolonged or sexual. Just a touching of lips.

She put her hand on his chest, prepared to push him away should he attempt to get too close, and felt passionate heat beneath her palm and the thud of his heart and knew immediately that she was in danger.

But it was too late to back away.

As his head swooped down narrowed lids hid the expression in his eyes, but his finger beneath her chin felt like a branding iron. This wasn't going the way she wanted.

Surprisingly, though, the kiss itself was restrained. His lips touched hers and then pulled swiftly away.

He was a man of honour after all.

Swift relief flooded through Dione's body and she felt herself go limp and would have fallen to the floor had Theo not caught her. His arms were strong and safe as he kicked open her door and carried her into the room, laying her gently on the bed.

'Thank you,' she whispered. 'I don't know what came over me.'

'The events of the day,' he tossed curtly. 'Will you be all right? Shall I send someone to help—'

'No!' cut in Dione swiftly. 'I'm fine now. I'd really like to be left alone.'

He nodded, his lips grim, and spun on his heel. Dione's relief knew no bounds when he finally shut the door behind him. She didn't even stop to question his sudden abruptness. This had been the worst possible day of her life and all she wanted to do was go to sleep and forget it.

Theo stalked into his room and tore off his clothes, leaving them untidily on the floor, before climbing beneath a fierce cold shower. Damn Dione! Damn the whole Keristari family! They were putting him through hell.

The money didn't count; it was a drop in the ocean to him, but Dione—she was a different proposition altogether. He had signed the wretched contract, he had promised to keep his hands off her. How the hell could he do that?

One touch was all it had taken to make him realise that he wanted her so badly that it would kill him to leave her alone. She was temptation incarnate. He could not imagine the days ahead without touching her, without kissing her, without making love to her. It would be sheer hell.

Maybe he should get out of here and leave her to her own devices? Maybe he should go on a world tour and forget her? Maybe he should just storm into her room and take her! This last thought fired the heat in his belly until it was at boiling point.

Damn! And damn again! What had he done?

It was a long time before Theo stepped out of the shower, feeling no better than he had before. This was a nightmare, a nightmare from which there was no escape—at least not for twelve long months. And maybe not even then. She would have got under his skin even more deeply.

With a towel wrapped around his loins he paced his room. Up and down he went like a caged lion. Up and down, round the bed and back again, until finally he went out onto the balcony and sat and watched the ocean. The restless ocean, a bit like himself with its endless to-ing and fro-ing.

He closed his eyes but all he could see was Dione's

beautiful face, and the thought that she would never be his pierced his heart like an arrow. He had intended to play the game slowly, to make her fall for him gradually without her knowing it—but how the hell could he do that when his body was on fire at the very thought of her lying in bed in the room next to him? When all he wanted to do was go in there and make love to her all night long?

It was what newly married couples usually did.

What a mistake it had been to believe that he could play these sorts of games. With other women, yes, perhaps. But not with Dione Keristari. He had fallen for her hook, line and sinker the first instant he saw her, despite how desperate she had looked. He admired her courage and her loyalty; she was a stronger person than he would ever be.

He got up and paced the balcony. It ran right around the house and all the upstairs rooms opened onto it. He came to a halt when he rounded the corner and saw Dione leaning against the rail, watching the ocean as he had done only seconds earlier. As soon as she saw him she turned to go back into her room but he held out his hand. 'Please, don't go.' And when she reluctantly halted he moved slowly towards her.

She had changed out of the wedding dress he had chosen with such care—how beautiful she had looked in it—and now wore a cream satin nightdress that barely covered either her breasts or her bottom. It had clearly been designed to tempt even the hardiest of men, and he wondered why she had chosen to wear it tonight of all nights.

Then suddenly she picked up a wrap and held it

tightly and defensively around her, as though she'd just realised that she was almost nude. It was a hot night, though, and he couldn't blame her for not wanting to wear much. He never wore anything in bed himself, and he was conscious now that all he had on was the towel. Perhaps she was thinking that his intentions were completely dishonourable.

'I couldn't sleep,' he said, by way of an apology.

'Me neither,' she admitted.

'I thought the sound of the ocean might lull you to sleep.'

'Well, it didn't. There's too much on my mind.'

'The same here.'

Lord, what a banal conversation to have with one's wife of a few hours, but what else could he say? He had promised to keep at arm's length but she was driving him crazy. That tempting glimpse of her body had sent his testosterone levels rising higher than they had ever been in his life. What was a man to do?

'Let's sit and watch the ocean together,' he said, in as normal a voice as he could muster. 'Would you like a drink, perhaps?'

'No, thanks, but yes, I will sit with you.'

Was that pain he heard in her voice? Was she doing it simply because she hadn't the strength to fight him? He sincerely hoped not. He didn't want her to hate him, even though he had more or less forced her into marriage.

It had been the only thing he could think of at the time so as not to let her slip away. The thought of never seeing her again had been abhorrent to him. It had been a foolish suggestion, he realised that now, and he could only hope that time would temper her resentment of him.

The moon was almost full and it lit the water like a fluorescent light, so that even without any lamps on in the house Theo could see Dione's face clearly. She looked sad and ethereal and it was the hardest thing in the world to keep his hands off her.

'How is Yannis?' he asked.

'I don't know.'

'He looked very frail at the wedding.'

'He is. Phrosini's very worried.'

'And you, are you worried?'

'Naturally,' she answered after a slight pause. 'I love my father. Why else would I have got myself into this situation?'

He wanted to say that Keristari didn't deserve her love, but he also wanted these few minutes together to be a time of peace not dissension and so he held his tongue. 'Do you think the money will help his health?' Privately, after having seen him today, Theo wasn't sure. He had looked at death's door.

'It's a lack of it that caused it,' she told him ruefully, 'so maybe it will. All we can do is pray and hope.'

'You're a good daughter to him.'

Dione didn't answer. She appeared deep in her own thoughts and they sat side-by-side in basket chairs and reflected over the turn of events that had brought them together.

Very soon he noticed that she had fallen asleep and gently he gathered her into his arms and carried her to her bed, where he laid her down and covered her with a single sheet. She did not wake and he stood there for a long time looking at this beautiful, untouchable lady.

So heavy was his heart when he finally went back to

his own room that he did not sleep. He spent the whole night thinking about Dione and wondering if it really would be possible to make her change her mind.

When Dione awoke her first thoughts were that she didn't remember getting into bed. She could remember sitting out on the balcony and Theo joining her, but nothing after that. Her body ran first hot and then cold at the thought that he might have put her to bed. And if he had, what else had he done? Had he looked at her? Touched her? Her robe had gone; she wore nothing but her ridiculous, minuscule nightdress. What had possessed her to wear it last night of all nights? What impression had she given?

Bouncing up, she took a cooling shower before dressing in a loose-fitting cotton top and a pair of cut-off jeans. She wanted nothing to give Theo the wrong impression.

But she had wasted her time. When she went downstairs he was nowhere in sight, and his housekeeper told her that he had gone to the office. 'He said to tell you that he is deeply sorry, this being the first day of your marriage, but something important came up. He says he will make it up to you tonight.' There was a twinkle in the buxom woman's eyes as she spoke, but to Dione it was a death sentence. Besides, Anna surely knew that they were sleeping in separate rooms?

'Thank you,' she said quietly.

Dione spent her day swimming and sunbathing and visiting her father. He didn't look any better and worried when the money was going to reach his account.

'I've kept my side of the bargain,' she assured him.

'Theo's gone to the office today; I expect he's arranging it.'

'He'd better be,' grumbled Yannis.

He didn't seem interested in the fact that she'd virtually sold her soul; all he wanted was the money. Dione hated him for it and didn't stay very long. And when she got home Theo was there.

'Where have you been?' he asked with a scowl dark enough to turn day into night.

'To see my father,' she answered haughtily. 'Is it any business of yours what I do with my time?'

'I thought you'd left.'

'Why would I do that?' she asked.

'You weren't happy last night.'

'I'm not happy today either, but that doesn't mean I won't keep my side of the bargain,' she retorted heatedly. 'Have you finalised things?'

Theo inclined his head. 'So now we can go away on honeymoon. I thought England. I thought you'd like to introduce me to your mother. Have you told her yet that she has a son-in-law?'

CHAPTER FIVE

AS THEO'S plane touched down in England Dione felt her heart sinking even lower. The thought of telling her mother that she had secretly got married was bad enough. But there was Chris as well. How was she going to explain it to him?

Theo had done his best to engage her in conversation during the flight, but all Dione had wanted to do was shut herself away in her own miserable world and pretend he didn't exist. In the end he had lost his temper with her.

'If you don't make some sort of effort, Dione, everyone will know that our marriage is a sham. And I'm warning you, if it ever leaks out, your father will find himself in more trouble than ever before. A contract is a contract. You'd best remember that.'

His dark eyes, almost jet-black, had bored into her skull like surgeons' drills, and Dione's whole body had frozen. There was no disputing that this man meant what he said.

'I shall do nothing to back out of it,' she riposted, her head held high, her eyes as dark and threatening as his. 'You need have no fear of that.'

'Then why the distance?' he demanded, shoving his

face up close to hers. 'Why a journey as silent as the grave? Don't you think this is as bad for me as it is for you?'

Her eyes shot wide. And although he smelled gorgeous, although his sexuality was undisputed, she glared fiercely. 'Go to hell, Theo. You're enjoying this. Power is your life-stream. It's your succour; it's your everything.'

'Power in a business sense, yes,' he agreed, 'but in my private life it's very different. I don't want you to feel that you have to put a face on to the world; I want you to enjoy being married to me. I want you to relax and have fun, and I want to enjoy it too. We could do that, Dione, if you'd not look on me as some sort of monster.'

Dione almost laughed, for that was exactly how she did see him. A great big predatory monster, taking but never giving. He'd taken her in payment for helping out Yannis, and she didn't think she'd be far wrong in thinking that at some stage in their relationship he'd demand his pound of flesh. Promises were made to be broken and Theo Tsardikos wouldn't lose a second's sleep over it.

'In front of anyone who matters I'll be the perfect wife,' she assured him coolly, 'but when we're on our own…' She let her voice tail off, telling him without words that he'd best not expect anything that wasn't in their contract.

Theo's nostrils had flared as he turned to look out of the window, and now that they had touched down, his hand on her arm as he helped her alight was like a grip of iron.

A car met them and whisked them to a penthouse apartment on London's South Bank and all the time neither of them spoke. The views across the city from the floor-to-ceiling windows were amazing but Dione was in no mood to admire. Nor did she comment about the tasteful décor, or the fact that her room and Theo's had an adjoining door. She silently noted that there was a key in the lock, which she intended keeping firmly turned.

'So when am I going to meet your mother?' he asked, when they had showered and changed. 'Maybe we should invite her out for dinner if you think that would be easier. She won't be able to have hysterics in a crowded place.'

He had changed into black chinos and polo shirt open at the neck to reveal dark whorls of hair on his broad chest. Dione didn't particularly like men with hairy chests, but she had to admit that seeing Theo like this made her want to touch, to find out whether the hairs were softly smooth, or strong and springy. And he was wearing a different aftershave too, something less exotic but fresh and exciting, and which sent a surprising tingle through her nerve-ends.

'My mother will never have hysterics,' she informed him tersely, hating herself for feeling anything other than dislike. 'She'll be surprised, shocked even, but she'll accept the news quietly, like she does everything else in her life.'

Theo settled deeper into his chair, legs outstretched, ankles crossed. 'It doesn't sound as though she was much of a match for Yannis Keristari.'

Dione shrugged. 'I guess not.'

'So tell me about her. Tell me why their marriage didn't work out.'

But Dione shook her head. 'I'd rather not talk about it.' She wasn't ready to discuss such matters with Theo.

In reality he was her mother's son-in-law and should be told, but in her mind he was still an outsider, an outsider who had no time for her father, and he didn't merit such intimate details. She doubted she ever would tell him.

'It sometimes helps,' he said, with an understanding that surprised her. She hadn't realised that she was giving away her inner torment, though why it should still hurt after all these years she didn't know. Perhaps it always would. It was a popular belief that time healed but this particular wound seemed as though it would never go away.

Dione pushed herself up from the chair and walked across to the window, her back to Theo. 'Not on this occasion! In any case, considering our marriage isn't a normal one, I don't see that it's any of your business.'

'I'd like to make it mine.' He had risen silently and moved with surprising quietness for such a big man, and his gruff voice in her ear made her jump.

She swiftly turned and found herself chest-to-chest with him, only a hair's breadth separating them. The heat of his body reached out to her like an unseen hand and although she wanted to move she didn't want to give him the satisfaction of knowing that he disturbed her.

So she stood stock-still and looked into the amazing darkness of his eyes. Reflected in them was the blueness of the sky and the greyness of the buildings, making them a mixture of all three colours. They were shiny like glass and held her in their thrall for several long seconds.

Unaware that she had been holding her breath, Dione let it out on a sigh. 'Not now, Theo,' she said quietly, unsure whether she was saying not now to something more than his request. Something much more danger-

ous. For that was how it felt. Every one of her nerve-
ends was vibrating as he continued to look at her with
such deep meaning in his eyes that she knew she ought
to move, and move quickly. Why was it, then, that her
feet felt as though they were glued to the floor?

In the end it was Theo who turned away, but not
before a satisfied smile curved his generous lips. 'If you
can't make a decision then I'll make it for you,' he said.
'We'll go and see your mother, tell her our news, and
then if she hasn't eaten we'll take her out for a meal.'

'What if she's not in?' she asked, wanting to put off the
moment for as long as she could, but thankful that Theo
had moved because she could now draw in a deep breath
without feeling that she was being consumed by him.

'We'll cross that bridge when we come to it. Something tells me that you're not looking forward to telling
her that we're married. It will be a shock, I know, and
she'll be disappointed that she wasn't invited, but leave
it to me—I'll win her over.'

And Dione didn't doubt that he would.

Theo Tsardikos was a charmer of the highest order.
Already, after only one day of a marriage she hadn't
wanted, she was beginning to feel a faint physical attraction. It could never be anything else. She hated him
for trapping her the way he had, but she had to admit he
was the sexiest male she had met in a very long time.
Chris was nothing compared to Theo.

Perhaps she ought to tell Theo about Chris now,
before her mother dropped it out? But he was already
ushering her towards the door and the moment passed.

Dione had a key to her mother's house but today she
did not let herself in. She rang the bell and waited, con-

scious of Theo standing, tall and authoritative, behind her shoulder. She had to ring a second time before the door was opened and she'd been hoping that she had a reprieve.

'Darling,' said Jeannie, her pale blue eyes lighting up as she gave her daughter a hug. 'What a wonderful surprise! I thought you were still in Greece.' And then she saw Theo and there was an unspoken question in her frown. 'Do come in.'

They followed her mother into her small, cluttered, but comfortable sitting room and Dione was conscious of Theo filling it with his presence. He was such a big man and her mother was small and quite frail, with brown hair already beginning to go grey.

'How's Yannis?' asked Jeannie, though it was clear that she was still wondering who her daughter's companion was.

'Not good,' answered Dione, glad of a reprise from the moment of introduction. She had no idea how her mother would take it. At this moment Jeannie couldn't take her eyes off Theo. And who could blame her? He was terribly handsome and simply oozed charm. Even though so far he hadn't spoken a word his smile had said everything.

'I'm sorry to hear that,' answered her mother. 'And is this—a friend of your father's?'

'Mmm, actually, no. Well, yes, I suppose in a way; he's a business acquaintance,' muttered Dione, feeling her face flood with colour.

'I see.'

Dione knew that she didn't, and the more she fought for the right words the hotter she became. This was going to be far worse than she had imagined. And unconsciously she began fiddling with the rings on her finger, the huge solitaire diamond and the exquisite gold band.

Jeannie let out a scream. 'Dione, you're married!'

Theo came to her rescue. 'And I'm the lucky man. How nice it is meet you, Mrs Keristari.'

Silence filled the room, the sonorous ticking of an old grandfather clock the only sound.

How much time passed Dione didn't know, but it felt like hours. Her mother's face was filled with both surprise and dismay. Not a woman to give vent to her feelings, she let her eyes do the talking. And she didn't look happy.

Theo was the first to speak. 'I'm Theodossus Tsardikos, usually called Theo.' And he held out his hand.

Jeannie was a long time in taking it, and even then she didn't speak; her blue eyes were clouded and distrusting.

'I'm sorry our marriage has come as such a shock to you, Mrs Keristari,' he said, smiling warmly and reassuringly. 'It did happen rather suddenly, I admit. But when love strikes, why wait?' And he put his arm about Dione's shoulders and kissed her full on the lips.

A shiver ran through her, trickling down her spine like melting ice. Although the kiss had meant nothing it set off a chain reaction that was completely unexpected. Something she would have to analyse later. She didn't know whether to curse Theo or thank him. She hadn't completely made up her mind whether to tell her mother the truth, or stick to the lie that she and Theo were happily married. He had taken that option away from her.

Jeannie certainly wouldn't approve of her marrying Theo to help out her father. Not after the way he had treated them both. So perhaps it was as well that her mother didn't know the truth. Not at this stage anyway. Maybe some time in the future when it was all over. When she and Theo were divorced and she could get on with her life.

Jeannie's eyes were on Dione now, asking her how it had happened.

'I'm sorry, Mum,' she said quietly, her lovely dark eyes sad and caring. 'I know it's come as a shock, but it really did happen like Theo says. Lightning struck us. We knew we had to be together.'

'You could have told me,' whispered the older woman.

'I know, but there wasn't even time to fly you over to Greece for the wedding. I didn't think you'd come anyway because of—'

'Yes, I understand,' said Jeannie, though it was clear that she didn't see the reason for such urgency. Then she added politely, 'Welcome into the family, Theo.'

'I apologise for keeping you in ignorance,' he said, taking her hand and kissing the back of it in an exaggerated gesture. 'We only married the day before yesterday—it was a complete whirlwind affair—and we made it our first priority to come over here and tell you. Your daughter is wonderful and I know that we're going to be very happy.'

Goodness, don't lay it on with a trowel, thought Dione, though she dutifully smiled into Theo's face. 'We are,' she agreed.

And after a few more consoling sentences from Theo Jeannie finally relaxed and smiled and wished them all the best.

Hurdle number one over, thought Dione as they sat drinking tea a few minutes later. Theo already had her mother eating out of the palm of his hand, even blushing when he complimented her on looking too young to have a daughter of marriageable age.

'Does Theo know about Chris?' asked her mother, when Theo excused himself with a business call some time later.

Dione shook her head and looked guilty.

'Why not?'

'I saw no point.'

'And Chris himself, I know he isn't aware of your marriage because I saw him only yesterday. What are you going to say to him? Really, Dione, this is very unlike you. You always swore you would never get married to a Greek because of what happened with your father.'

Dione could understand her mother's concern where Chris was concerned. She was worried herself about how she was going to tell him. Maybe she could persuade her mother to do it for her? No, that wouldn't be fair; it was the coward's way out. She would have to go and see him and hope he wouldn't be too angry.

'Theo's different from my father,' she said defensively. 'He'll never hurt me the way Father hurt you.'

Jeannie pursed her lips. 'I hope you're right.'

'Mrs Keristari.' Theo came back into the room. 'I'd very much like to spend more time getting to know you. Let us take you out to dinner. We'll have your favourite wine and your favourite food and—'

'Please, call me Jeannie,' she said, interrupting him. 'And thank you for the offer but I've eaten. I was about to settle down and watch my favourite TV programme.'

'Then we are interrupting you. I'm so sorry. How about tomorrow night?'

'Tomorrow I'm…'

When her mother hesitated Dione knew that she was trying to make excuses. She didn't want to dine with Theo. Her mother wasn't used to such flattery, such attention—she found it embarrassing. And when the doorbell rang Jeannie fled to answer it.

'Don't push my mother,' warned Dione quietly. 'You're overwhelming her. She leads a very simple life.'

'So I'm beginning to realise. You're really nothing like her, are you? You're the feistiest woman I've ever met. I guess you take after your father in that respect.'

'I just know how to stick up for myself,' answered Dione. 'My mother doesn't. But nevertheless she's the sweetest woman alive. I've hated lying to her about us.'

'I thought she took it remarkably well, after her initial shock. And I—'

'Dione! You're home!'

Her words were cut off by an all too familiar voice, and a pair of strong arms lifted her off the floor and swung her around. Dione caught sight of her mother shaking her head, informing her that she hadn't told Chris about Theo. She looked terrified. Jeannie hated altercations, would do anything to avoid them, and now she was going to be stuck in the middle of one.

And of course Theo didn't know about Chris either.

CHAPTER SIX

WHEN Chris put her down and tried to kiss her Dione pushed her hands against his chest. Goodness, this was a worst-case scenario. She had no idea that Chris visited her mother. She had been hoping to go and see him alone, break the news without Theo breathing over her shoulder.

Chris was much shorter than Theo with sandy-coloured hair and a pale complexion. For several months she had thought she was in love with him , and had been truly upset when she'd heard that he was seeing his ex-girlfriend again. In fact when she went to Greece she had taken her ring off. For one reason she hadn't wanted her father to know, and for another she'd begun to have second thoughts about marrying him. If he could go out with a former girlfriend before they were married, what would he do afterwards?

Perhaps it was one of the reasons she'd agreed to marry Theo? Surely she wouldn't have done so if she'd been really, truly and deeply in love with Chris? If she'd trusted him with her heart and soul?

Finally Chris noticed that there was someone else in

the room. A tall, dark, Hellenic-looking man with a harsh frown on his handsome face.

Dione hesitated for only a fraction of a second, knowing the disclosure was going to hurt him, but she had to get it over with and the sooner the better. 'Chris, this is Theo, my—my husband.'

'Husband? You're married?' Chris' voice rose to ear-splitting proportions and his faced flushed an ugly red. 'What the hell's going on? You're supposed to be engaged to me.'

Dione heard Theo draw in a harsh breath and knew that she dared not look at him. 'I—I was going to tell you, Chris, but it all happened so quickly. Theo swept me off my feet. He proposed, I accepted, and two days later we were married. I'm so sorry.'

'I bet you're sorry,' Chris sneered. 'Some jerk with loads of money turned your head.' He flashed a disparaging look in Theo's direction. 'And don't bother to deny it, big guy, because I've met your sort before. I saw the limo outside, wondered whose it was. Quite a catch, aren't you?'

'I don't think you entirely understand,' said Theo, his voice very even, though Dione could see fire in his eyes.

'Then make me,' tossed Chris, his blue eyes hard and belligerent.

Dione had never seen this side of Chris. Initially she had felt sorry for him but now he was behaving like a maniac and she was afraid.

'The way I see it,' retorted Theo, his voice crackling with tightly controlled anger, 'Dione couldn't have been truly in love with you or she wouldn't have given me a second glance.'

'Oh, you think that, do you?' scoffed Chris. 'It proves how little you know. It's easy to see that you turned her head by flashing your wallet.'

'And you think money is important, do you?' demanded Theo. 'You think Dione would throw away the love of her life, if that's what you believe you are, for the security of knowing that she need never work again? I think, my friend, that you do not know Dione very well at all.'

Dione glared at them both and put her hand on Chris' arm. 'Please stop it!'

'Why should I,' raged Chris, 'when you drop me for some scheming bastard?' He shook her away and stood in front of Theo. 'I ought to knock the living daylights out of you.'

'Feel free,' answered the handsome Greek, arms folded across his magnificent chest.

Chris was the first to back down, though his eyes were still murderous.

'I think we should go,' whispered Dione to Theo.

'Not until he's left,' he answered calmly. 'I don't want him upsetting your mother any further.'

Chris looked at Jeannie, as though imploring her to let him stay, but Dione's mother nodded. 'I think it might be best.' She looked tortured at the scene that had just taken place.

When Chris had left, banging the door loudly behind him, Dione took her mother's hand. 'I'm truly sorry. I never expected Chris to behave like that. He's not the man I thought he was. Does he visit you often?'

Jeannie shrugged. 'A couple of times a week; sometimes more. He comes for his dinner and we sit and chat and—'

'He's taking advantage of you, Mother,' insisted Dione. 'You know he hates cooking for himself. You must stop it.'

'I don't expect he'll come again now that he knows you're—married.' She said the word with difficulty and Dione hugged her.

'I'm sorry, Mother.'

'It's all right. Didn't you say something about going for a meal? Isn't it time you went?'

'You mean you want to be alone?'

Jeannie nodded.

'Then we'll go,' said Dione.

It was Theo's turn to voice his concern. 'Are you sure you'll be all right, Jeannie?'

Again Jeannie nodded. 'I'm sorry Chris spoke to you the way he did.'

'No need to apologise,' he said at once. 'I guess I wouldn't have been happy if the positions were reversed.'

Indeed, thought Dione. He would have been spitting mad; the other guy might not have got off quite so lightly.

Outside in the car there was a terrible silence and she realised that Theo hadn't started the engine. Instead he sat there looking at her, anger on his face, and his voice was dangerously cool when he spoke. 'Why didn't you tell me about your fiancé?'

'Would it have made a difference?' she demanded to know. 'Would you have given my father the money without any conditions? I don't think so.'

'So you selflessly gave up your boyfriend?' His dark eyes were savage on hers. 'Or perhaps it wasn't so selfless. How the hell could you have got yourself engaged to an unscrupulous swine like him? He's treating your mother abominably. He's using her, he's sponging off her.'

'I know,' said Dione quietly. 'And I'm appalled. He used to come round for his dinner quite often when I was there, but I never imagined that he'd carry on doing it.'

'Your mother's too kind.'

Dione nodded. How very true that was.

'It looks to me as though I've saved you from a fate worse than death. How the worm turns, isn't that what they say?'

Dione said nothing. She was too busy wondering about the change in Chris.

Theo's lips tightened and he turned the key. The car roared into life and sped down the road. But they didn't go out to dinner; they went back to his apartment instead.

Once inside, a glass of whisky in his hand, he resumed the conversation. 'How much does this man mean to you?' Dark eyes were hard and questioning and his whole body was taut with suppressed anger.

Dione shrugged, trying to appear uninterested, whereas deep inside she was a mass of unhappy nerves. 'Does it really matter?' Actually Chris meant nothing now. He had well and truly blotted his copybook as far as she was concerned. Never for one minute had she expected him to behave so bullishly. And to take advantage of her mother—that was the last straw.

Theo snorted. 'I can't see you giving up a man you truly love to help your father. No girl would do that. Especially for a bully like Keristari! Or is that it? He bullied you into it. Threatened to make your life hell if you didn't help him out?'

'Nothing of the sort,' declared Dione with a toss of

her head, eyes flashing pure resentment. 'The choice was purely mine.'

Dark brows rose. 'And I'm expected to believe that? I did do, until I found out about your fiancé. He had every right to be angry. I'd have killed if the positions were reversed.'

'Just before I left England I found out that he'd been seeing his ex-girlfriend,' said Dione quietly.

'Ah!' Enlightenment filled Theo's eyes. 'So you'd have ended the engagement anyway?'

'I guess so,' she acknowledged, not wanting to keep up the tension any longer. She felt drained of all energy. It had been a long day. All she wanted to do was go to bed; she wasn't even hungry.

'Perhaps I did you a favour?' His lips curled in amusement and his body relaxed. 'Care to join me in a drink before dinner?'

Dione shook her head. 'I want neither. I'm tired.' But she was glad that the topic was over, that he'd accepted her engagement would have ended anyway. Not that she could see him caring even if she'd been truly and deeply in love with Chris. He was playing a game with her and her father, and enjoying it. It wouldn't matter to him one jot if he hurt anyone's feelings.

She turned and headed for the door but Theo was quicker. A heavy hand dropped on her shoulder and spun her round to face him. 'You're not turning in yet. You're my wife, Dione, and I want your company. Indeed, I demand it.'

After the last few days when she'd gone around in a trance, not really believing all that was happening to her, this was the last straw as far as Dione was concerned. 'You demand it?' she flashed. 'Well, tough luck, because I'm going! There's nothing in our contract to say that I have to play the part of a loving wife when there's no one else around. Or had you forgotten that?'

Theo didn't seem in the least perturbed by her outburst. In fact, he smiled and shook his head. 'Have you any idea how tempting you look when your eyes are flashing fire and your whole body is alive?' His normally faint accent had deepened, as had his voice, and his meaning was very clear.

Theo was disappointed when Dione backed away. He didn't want her to be afraid of him; it wasn't in his plan of things at all. She was totally, gorgeously sexy, and every part of him strained to touch and to kiss and finally to take her into his bed.

Although he had agreed to her ridiculous contract he had no intention of biding by it. He was a red-blooded male not used to keeping his hands off his women friends.

And this was not just a friend, she was his wife!

This was their honeymoon!

Her place was in his bed!

He would allow her some freedom but his patience wouldn't last long. Even now his male hormones were running riot. And when Dione moved away he had to bite back a savage response.

'Don't be afraid, my beautiful wife. I have no intention of going back on my word, but there's nothing to stop me complimenting you! You're every man's dream, do you know that?'

'No, I don't,' she snapped. 'And compliments like that will get you nowhere.'

'I don't expect they will,' he answered evenly. She was an amazing girl, nothing at all like her mother, who was gentle and quietly spoken. What Jeannie had ever seen in Yannis Keristari he didn't know. They were poles apart. Maybe Keristari had thought he could mould her into his way of thinking. Obviously the woman had a backbone of steel; otherwise she would never have been able to back out of their marriage. Good for her, he thought.

He liked Jeannie; he liked her very much. But he had taken an instant dislike to Chris Donovan. What a swine the man was. What a manipulative swine. He couldn't understand what Dione had ever seen in him. She could certainly have done better. If at the end of these twelve months they went their separate ways then he hoped she would find someone who truly loved her and whom she loved in return.

She deserved that at least.

'I'd like you to have dinner with me,' he said, not wanting her to go to her room yet. Not at all, if he could help it. He wanted her to share his bed, tonight and every night. It was going to be sheer hell keeping his hands off her. 'My housekeeper's an angel; she'll be able to rustle something up in no time at all.'

'I'm not hungry,' she insisted.

With difficulty he held back his anger. 'You've had nothing since breakfast, Dione. You won't be able to sleep on an empty stomach.'

'That will be my problem, not yours,' she retorted.

Harshness crept into his voice. 'You're my wife; I want to look after you. I insist that you eat.'

Dione glared at him, her eyes brilliant with anger, and he wanted to take her into his arms and tell her that everything would be all right. But would it? She had married him for one reason only. A ridiculous reason, as far as he was concerned. Keristari didn't deserve her loyalty, and he wouldn't be averse to telling him so if the opportunity ever presented itself.

'It looks like you're giving me no choice,' she said, her head tilted high, her eyes bright with indignation and anger.

Lord, she looked beautiful. His hormones surged once again and he had to move away or he would have taken her into his arms and kissed her.

When he gave his ultimatum he hadn't realised quite how irresistible she would be and he took a few deep breaths as he went to find his housekeeper.

Left alone, Dione breathed in deeply as well. She was fully aware that Theo found her attractive and she wished that she had been strong enough to stick to her guns and go to her room. On the other hand, it could be fun taunting him but remaining cool and unobtainable at the same time. It was no less than he deserved.

When he returned she was sitting in one of the easy chairs, her legs crossed, revealing a tantalising amount of thigh. If he saw he ignored it, crossing to the corner bar and pouring himself another Scotch. 'What can I get you?' he asked after he'd taken a long swallow. 'A gin and tonic? Martini? Wine?'

He knew so little about her that he had no idea she never drank. 'Just a tonic water, thank you, with ice and lemon.'

'Nothing stronger?'

'I don't touch alcohol.'

Brows rose. 'Any particular reason?'

'I saw my father drink enough,' she answered tersely.

'Ah! I wondered why you didn't touch your champagne at the wedding.'

Dione hadn't realised that he'd noticed. She'd made a pretence of drinking, raising her glass to her lips whenever the occasion demanded it.

'Would you rather I didn't drink?' he asked.

'Of course not,' she said at once.

He handed her the crystal glass and sat down opposite, studiously ignoring her legs, letting his glittering eyes rest on her face instead.

So he could be a gentleman!

And yet Dione didn't think that his thoughts were quite so gentlemanly. She wasn't an idiot; she knew that he wanted her, and that this whole marriage agreement was going to be harder than she thought. It would be up to her to be the strong one.

They sat talking about not very much until his housekeeper told them that dinner was ready. The table was set in a formal dining room and they had chicken consommé followed by cheese omelette and salad and then raspberry parfait. All very light and delicious and Dione surprised herself by eating every bit.

Afterwards they took their coffee back into the living area and moved out onto a wide, glass-enclosed balcony with sliding doors that could be opened or closed at will. It was enhanced with exotic palms and colourful plants, and they sat and watched the lights coming on over London. The sky turned dramatically pink and grey and finally into midnight blue, and for the first time Dione felt relaxed in Theo's company.

'I love your apartment,' she said impulsively.

'It does have its finer points,' he agreed.

'Do you spend much time here?'

'A couple of months a year, maybe, split up into the odd week or even a day, depending on my workload.'

'It seems a waste,' said Dione pensively. 'It's so lovely.'

'But not as lovely as you.'

Dione suddenly realised that he was watching her and not the beautiful vista in front of them, and heat filled her body. 'You don't have to flatter me,' she said smoothly, 'this isn't a proper marriage, you know.'

'If it were we wouldn't be sitting here now,' Theo returned. 'We'd be in bed, Dione. This is to all intents and purposes our honeymoon.' There was a moment's silence before he muttered, 'I never dreamt that I'd be spending it in this way.'

His face was in shadow, almost as dark as the night because there were no lights on in the room behind them, but both his words and his harsh voice told her that he wasn't happy at the prospect of sleeping alone.

'You knew what you were letting yourself in for,' she pointed out, even though her heart was drumming against her chest wall. There was no denying that Theo was an exciting male animal and remaining immune to him didn't look like a very good possibility.

Without any warning Theo pushed himself to his feet. 'I'm going to bed. Stay here if you like.' His voice was cold and abrupt and Dione guessed it was because she had reminded him of the terms of their contract.

'I think I will,' she said softly. At least until she felt sure that Theo was safely in his bed. Their rooms were far too close for comfort and she had no idea whether the adjoining door was locked or not. She ought to have

checked it in front of him, when he was showing her
around, made sure that he knew what the rules were.

'Goodnight, then,' he said tersely.

'Goodnight, Theo.'

He brushed past her and her skin tingled, and even
when he had gone she could not relax. Exactly what had
she let herself in for?

It must have been a good half-hour later before she
finally went to bed, and by then Dione was so tired that
she forgot to check the key in the lock.

CHAPTER SEVEN

'DON'T fight, you're coming with me!'

'No, Daddy, no! You're hurting!'

'Then do as I say, child!'

'I don't want to go with you; I want to stay with Mummy.' And she screamed as loud as she could.

Dione felt strong arms around her and struggled violently. 'Get away, *get away*!'

'Dione,' came the insistent voice, a different voice this time, 'wake up! Do you hear me? Wake up.'

Dione struggled to open her eyes, and instead of her father she saw Theo. A strong, protective, concerned Theo. And realised that it had all been a dream, the recurring nightmare that had haunted her over the years.

Tears rolled down her cheeks unchecked as she let Theo hold and comfort her. He found a handkerchief from somewhere and dabbed her cheeks, and she took it from him and held it to her eyes.

Several long minutes passed before her sobs subsided and her shoulders stopped heaving. 'I—I'm sorry,' she stammered.

'Don't be, *agapi mou*. Are you all right now?'

Dione nodded.

'Would you like anything? A glass of water perhaps? Or would you like me to keep holding you?'

'Yes, please,' she whispered, snuggling into his chest. Surprisingly she felt safe in Theo's arms; safe and cared for. And although she knew it was dangerous, although he wore nothing but a pair of black boxers, she wanted him to stay with her for the rest of the night.

He stroked her sweat-streaked hair back from her face and murmured words of comfort, and not until she had completely calmed down did he say, 'Do you want to tell me about it?'

Dione had never thought she would disclose to Theo what had happened to her as a child, but suddenly she wanted him to know. There could be other nights when she screamed and thrashed in her bed and woke him. She owed him the truth at least.

'It's about my father,' she said unevenly.

Theo drew in a swift breath and held her even more tightly. 'Go on,' he said, and she could hear a thread of anger in his voice.

'I was only six years old,' she confessed, 'and he thought my mother was having an affair with another man—not that I knew that at the time—and he turned out to be wrong anyway. But because of that he decided she wasn't fit to bring up his child and he dragged me from my bed in the middle of the night and bundled me in his car and flew me to Greece.'

She faltered a moment. This was the first time she had told anyone what had happened and it was a momentous occasion for her. 'He never returned here,' she finished with a break in her voice. 'He hasn't seen my mother since.'

Against her body Dione felt all of Theo's muscles tighten and a hiss of anger escape his lips. 'The swine! You must have been terrified.'

'I was,' she agreed huskily. 'I didn't stop crying for days and days, and when I could cry no more I was terribly naughty, the most evil child imaginable. I think there were times when he wished he'd left me with my mother. But then he had a letter from my mother's solicitor about her rights, and he used to let me go to see her, not without a bodyguard of course. He needed to make sure I'd return,' she added disparagingly.

Dione's heart had used to break every time she had to leave her mother, and Jeannie would hug her through their tears and tell her that it wouldn't be long before she saw her again. In later years Dione had grown to understand that her mother had been too scared to go against Yannis' wishes in case he stopped her from seeing her daughter altogether.

'And yet you stayed with him, even when you were old enough to do your own thing?' questioned Theo in a quiet, puzzled voice. 'I don't understand that.'

Dione drew in a deep breath and let it go slowly. 'Because I was afraid he might still do something to hurt my mother. She's always felt deeply vulnerable where my father's concerned. He hurt her so much that she's never really got over it.'

Theo's arms tightened around her, and his mouth dropped tiny, comforting kisses on her brow. 'Poor lady! For what it's worth, I like her. She's sweet and gentle and she hated to see me and Chris fighting over you. It's what held me back. What did you ever see in him?'

Dione shrugged, glad for a moment of a change of topic. She had felt as if she was baring her soul, and it was painful, even though Theo seemed to understand. 'Maybe I was looking for love. He seemed like the right guy at the time.'

'And now?'

'I think you know the answer to that.' Dione could feel herself growing more and more comfortable in Theo's arms. Perhaps a little too comfortable, because somewhere deep inside her stirred dangerous feelings.

'My parents eventually got divorced,' she said, trying to ignore what was happening to her, 'and Yannis married Phrosini. I grew to love her. She's very dear to me. And she's good for my father too.'

'He doesn't bully her like he does everyone else?' asked Theo tersely.

'Phrosini gives as good as she gets. She's a very strong woman.'

'She'd need to be,' muttered Theo. 'And it's made you strong too, though not strong enough to tell your father to go to hell when he asked you to come and see me. Not that I'm objecting to it,' he added, tapping her nose with a gentle finger. 'You're the best thing that's happened to me in a long time.'

'Even when I scream like a baby and wake you from your sleep?' she asked with a rueful smile.

'Even then,' he agreed and, gathering her even more closely against him, he added, 'You don't deserve any of this, Dione.'

'It happened a long time ago,' she said. 'I should be over it.'

'Childhood memories are difficult to erase, especially of something as traumatic as that. Maybe you need to see someone.'

'A therapist, you mean?'

'Perhaps.'

Dione shook her head. 'It's only under times of stress that my nightmare returns.'

'So being here with me is a strain for you?' His lips firmed, and she felt a slight shift in his body. But he didn't move away because he was enjoying holding her, enjoying the warmth of her body against his, and she was very well aware that his hormones had kicked in and were ready to bounce into action.

As were her own! But she ignored them. 'Of course it's a strain. Being driven into a loveless marriage would be a strain for anyone.' As if he didn't know! But to him it was a pleasant game, maybe even an exciting one. He had no current girlfriend—at least she didn't think so— so he could afford to take a year out of his life and play games with her.

'I don't want it to be a strain for you,' he said, his voice a low rumble of sexuality. 'I want you to relax and enjoy our time together. Twelve months will be an age if you fight me.'

'So long as you keep your side of the bargain, I won't fight,' she reminded him, trying to ignore the swiftness of her heartbeats when his fingertips brushed the soft skin of her cheek. They traced her high cheekbone and the contours of her eyes and then trailed down the length of her nose. And finally he cupped her chin and turned her face up to his.

His eyes were as dark as the night, with just a tiny highlight in the pupil from the lamp he had switched on. Ninety-nine per cent of her told her to move away swiftly. The other one per cent was held in his thrall.

The male scent of him assaulted her nostrils, filtering through her senses until she felt drugged. And when his mouth came down over hers Dione had neither the strength nor the will-power to turn away.

Theo also seemed to forget that kissing or even any form of contact was taboo—unless, of course, he'd taken her lack of resistance as acceptance. Dione didn't even begin to think about that possibility, not when his mouth began a fiery assault that wrestled a powerful response from her. It was the most drugging kiss she had ever experienced and a murmur of satisfaction escaped unchecked from her lips.

'*Theos!*' groaned Theo, and, taking the sound as a form of surrender, he deepened the kiss, his tongue now entering her mouth, exploring, entwining, tasting and taking.

Dione felt herself spiralling up to an hitherto unexplored plane, sensation following sensation, touching nerve-ends, racing through veins, until it reached the most private part of her body, where it tightened and throbbed and made her very much aware of her vulnerability.

Theo was a highly dangerous man; he would be an even more dangerous lover. If he could arouse her like this by one simple kiss, what could he do if he really tried?

And why wasn't she fighting him off?

She had no wish to participate in sex with Theo Tsardikos for the next twelve months—for sex was all it would be—and then dissolve their marriage as though it had never happened. If it was what *he* wanted, it certainly wasn't on her agenda.

And yet she was allowing the kiss, not wanting it to stop; wanting Theo to stay with her for the rest of the night in case she had her nightmare again. But expecting him to lie with her and not touch her would be asking the impossible, she knew that, and it would be best to banish him now.

How could she, though, when she was enjoying his kisses so much? So much that they frightened her! Even so, she found herself kissing him back, so desperately that shame should have hung over her. Instead she felt a strange exhilaration, something that had never happened before.

Maybe because she'd never kissed anyone like Theo before!

He was a man of stature, of means, of immense sex appeal, and he was surely irresistible to any girl he met. And shame on her, she had joined the list, the only difference being that she had a gold band on her finger.

A band that meant nothing, she reminded herself, even as she trailed her fingers through the dark, springy hair on his muscular chest. Soft they were, the hairs, soft and silky, and she had an urge to nuzzle her face into them and inhale his manly fragrance. Of course, she didn't. Instead she splayed her fingers and pushed him away.

A faint smile curved his beautifully sculpted lips. He didn't look disappointed, but neither did he look triumphant that he had achieved something that she had vowed would never happen.

'Feeling better?' he asked.

Dione nodded, not trusting herself to speak. She was so filled with emotion that her throat had closed up.

'A kiss soothes most wounds,' he said with a faint smile, his eyes dark and unreadable. 'At least, that's what my mother used to tell me.'

'Not quite the sort of kiss you just gave me,' she countered.

Theo shrugged. 'If it did the trick, who cares?'

I care, she thought, because you've opened my defences. 'I think I'll be all right now,' she told him, her voice low and faintly shaky. Not surprising considering that her insides still sizzled. Kissing Theo was the most alarming thing that had ever happened to her. An experience she did not wish to repeat.

A little voice inside her head told her that she was lying, that she would dearly love Theo to kiss her again, that in fact she would like him to spend the rest of the night with her. But she ignored it.

'Are you sure?'

Dione nodded, not trusting herself to speak again.

Theo eased himself reluctantly from the bed and stood looking down at her, his arms folded over his hard, wide chest. His skin gleamed gold in the lamp light; even his ebony hair had a sheen. He was a perfect specimen of manhood and yet Dione knew the danger of getting too deeply involved.

As if marrying him wasn't deep enough!

'I'll leave the door open,' he said now, 'and then if you should need me you only have to call.'

Dione smiled faintly. She wouldn't be calling out again. In fact, it was doubtful whether she'd sleep. His kisses had completely obliterated all other thoughts and emotions.

He bent low over her. 'Goodnight, then, Dione.' And he kissed her again, but this time it was the sort of gentle kiss one would give a child. Nevertheless it had an alarming effect on her and she closed her eyes tightly and held her breath, listening as he moved softly out of the room, only then releasing it on a low, deep sigh.

At first she lay awake thinking about what had happened, wondering what the repercussions would be; whether Theo would now expect more from her. If so he was going to be deeply disappointed. He had caught her at her most vulnerable but she would make sure that it never happened again.

And as she lay thinking sleep overtook her, a dreamless sleep this time, and she woke to feel the warm rays of the morning sun streaming over her through the half-open curtains.

'How are you feeling? No more bad dreams?'

Shock made her eyes shoot open and she sat bolt upright in bed. 'What the devil are you doing here?'

Dark brows rose. 'Now, there's a friendly greeting after what happened last night.'

'I appreciate you comforting me,' she answered, feeling uncomfortable with Theo in the room, 'but as for anything else, it's totally out of order.'

'It didn't seem like that a few hours ago,' he snorted.

'I didn't know what I was doing.' She doubted he'd believe the lie because even to her own ears it sounded feeble.

'So that's how you usually get comforted, is it?' he sneered.

Dione shook her head in disbelief. 'You have a sick mind. I wasn't thinking straight last night; I didn't know what I was doing. But now I do, and rest assured it will never happen again.'

A tight smile twisted his lips. 'Is that a promise?'

He looked as though he didn't believe her and that made her even angrier. She slid out of bed and stood facing him with her arms akimbo, heedless of the fact that she wore only a short cotton nightdress, made even shorter where her hands bunched it up on her hips.

'I thought you were a man of your word, Theo Tsardikos. Clearly I was wrong. You took advantage of me in my hour of need and for that I hate you.'

'I took advantage?' snorted Theo, raising disbelieving brows. 'I didn't notice you attempting to fight me. I remember very clearly saying that you'd have to make the first move, and in my eyes you did just that. Rubbing your body against me as you did was nothing short of an invitation. Hell, Dione, I'm not made out of stone.'

'I hate you!' she flared. 'Now, get out of here and let me get showered and dressed.' Thankfully Theo was already dressed so his magnificent body was covered. Not that she couldn't remember what he looked like almost naked! The sight of all that bare flesh would remain with her for a very long time to come.

There was a distinct atmosphere over breakfast and when he asked her what she would like to do afterwards she glared at him. 'I'd like to go and see my mother—alone.'

'I'm afraid not,' he announced grimly. 'This is our honeymoon.'

'Honeymoons are for lovers, not enemies,' she retorted, her voice edged with anger.

'Then we'll have to see about turning me from an enemy to a lover, won't we?' he growled.

And Dione could see that he meant it. There was grim determination on his face, and cold, hard sincerity in his eyes. 'You'll have your work cut out,' she tossed back. 'Every time I look at you I think of my father. I'm doing it for him, not for your personal gratification.'

'But imagine the fun you could have while your father's counting my money.'

'My father's very ill,' she spat. 'How dare you talk about him like that?'

Theo shrugged. 'Not so ill that he didn't think twice about using you! And since I've parted with a very large sum I intend getting my money's worth. Remember that, Dione, the next time you think about hitting back at me. We can do this the easy way or the hard way; the choice is yours.'

CHAPTER EIGHT

THEO knew that he shouldn't have got annoyed with Dione, but it was hard trying to keep his hands off her. He had seen his opportunity last night and taken it and he didn't have any regrets.

Kissing her had been even better than he'd imagined. In his mind he'd not only kissed her but also made love to her; long, passionate sessions when the world had spun on its axis and he had gloried in the deal that he'd made.

And last night, after he'd gone back to his room, his body in torment, he'd hoped that it was the beginning of something special and exciting. Dione was a league apart from other girls. Usually they were out for what they could get; you could almost see the pound signs dancing in their eyes. Even his ex-wife had been interested in his bank balance and his divorce settlement had cost him far more than he cared to think about.

Dione, on the other hand, didn't even seem to like him. Admittedly she had responded to his kiss, which he had thought a good sign. How wrong could a man be? It was nothing more than gratitude for helping her overcome her nightmare problem.

His lips thinned at the thought of Keristari wrenching her away from her mother at such a tender age. What a brute the man was; even worse than he'd always thought. He had ruined two lives with his selfishness. He was a totally uncaring swine of a man and Theo wished now that he'd never given him the money.

Except that he would never have got to know Dione if he hadn't! And he wouldn't be feeling her harsh rejection! Her outburst this morning had surprised him because he'd begun to think that he was getting somewhere. Now it looked as though he was back to square one.

He'd given her an ultimatum but he would never force himself on her. On the other hand, he knew that he couldn't live with her day in and day out and not even touch her. He would have to use all of his charm and wiles.

He smiled in satisfaction; he was going to enjoy it.

'I'm glad you find it amusing,' said Dione testily.

'Come on, Dione, don't be so uptight. We have a further twelve months to get through; you can't spend all of our time together hating me.'

'But I don't have to let you make love to me,' she retorted hastily. 'A deal's a deal as far as I'm concerned and you crossed the line last night.'

'You didn't stop me.' In fact, he felt sure she had enjoyed it as much as he had.

'I needed comfort.'

'But not the sort I offered?' he asked, his turn to speak sharply. 'You needn't answer that; you've made yourself very clear. Feel free to go to your mother's today if you want to.' And with that he walked out of the room.

Dione didn't stop to wonder why Theo had had a change of heart; it was sufficient that he had, and within the next twenty minutes she was hailing a taxi. But before he could even pull up Theo had driven into the space in front of her. 'Jump in.'

He was giving her no option and Dione slid into the seat beside him. 'Thank you,' she said quietly.

'You're welcome.'

It was a tight-lipped reply and Dione guessed he was angry with her for wanting to go off on her own. But she didn't care; she needed space, she needed time to sort out her muddled thoughts. Since the kiss she'd had mixed feelings about Theo, not least of which was the fact that she'd enjoyed it.

He dropped her off at her mother's, declaring that he'd pick her up again at twelve and take her to lunch. His words were brusque and Dione knew that she dared not argue.

Jeannie was surprised to see her again so soon and Dione hugged her warmly. 'I'm sorry you had to find out about Theo like that,' she apologised. 'It really did happen like I said. The instant we met we both knew we were meant for each other.'

'You could at least have phoned me,' said Jeannie, her hurt showing in her pained blue eyes.

'I could have,' admitted Dione, 'but I knew there wasn't time to fly you over—and I doubt you'd have come because of Yannis. It was Theo's idea that we tell you face to face. Do you like him?' she asked, trying to sound eager when in fact she was hurting inside at having to deceive her mother.

'He—seems very nice,' answered Jeannie, 'from what I've seen of him. He's very good-looking and has perfect manners. I hope he'll make you happy. I was happy with your father once, but he changed when we were married. I trust Theo won't do the same.'

Dione shook her head. 'He won't; he's a different person altogether from my father. He doesn't even like Yannis.'

'Not many people do,' Jeannie admitted. 'I'm surprised you've left him, considering he's still in hospital. What did he have to say about you marrying Theo?'

'He's happy for me.' Which wasn't a lie. Yannis was ecstatic, though she wasn't sure that he'd be entirely happy when he found out that they'd gone to England on their honeymoon. She had left Phrosini to tell him.

'Why am I not surprised?' asked Jeannie drily. 'He's always wanted you to marry one of his own. And now his wish has come true. Are you going to settle in Greece?'

'Theo's business is based there.'

'What does he do?'

'He owns a worldwide chain of hotels. I believe there's one in London.'

'So he's very rich?' Jeannie's tone was unusually disparaging.

Dione nodded. 'That's not why I married him, Mother, if that's what you're thinking.'

'Yannis' ambition was to be rich,' pointed out Jeannie. 'In my opinion it sours men. They have a very narrow view on the rest of the world. Don't let yourself get sucked into a trap.'

'Theo isn't like my father.'

'Are you sure?'

Dione nodded.

'Then I'm happy for you, my darling.'

Jeannie made some tea and they sat and talked some more until finally the subject of Chris was brought up.

'I never knew he could be like that,' said Dione.

'Me neither,' admitted her mother. 'It certainly opened my eyes. If he dares show his face here again I shall tell him exactly what I think of him.'

Dione smiled. Somehow she couldn't see her mother doing that, although there did seem to be a much stronger backbone in her today.

'Do you know what?' asked Jeannie. 'He actually asked if he could move in with me. Be my lodger. Apparently he's being thrown out of his flat.'

'You've not said yes?' asked Dione, appalled. It seemed to her that all Chris would be after was free food and lodgings.

Jeannie shook her head. 'In fact I always thought there was something odd about him, although for your sake I did try to like him. But I like Theo better,' she added with a smile. 'I'm glad to see that you're following your heart. I have my reservations, obviously, as it's all happened so quickly—but the same happened with your father and me. I fell in love with him at first sight.'

It was the first time her mother had told her this and Dione touched her hand. 'You think Theo will treat me badly?'

'I wouldn't be a caring parent if I didn't feel a little concerned, but on the surface he seems very nice.'

'He's much nicer than Chris,' said Dione forcefully. 'Do you know that just before I left for Greece I found out that Chris had been seeing his old girlfriend again?'

Jeannie shook her head. 'No, I didn't know that.'

'He denied it when I asked him. But my source was

very reliable. He had no right to say those things to me about marrying Theo when he'd already two-timed me behind my back.'

'How right you are,' said Jeannie. 'I wonder if he'll turn up for his lunch today?'

Dione's eyes shot wide. 'He wouldn't dare. Maybe I should wait and see, though. I don't want you tackling him on your own.'

'I can deal with Chris,' said her mother in a much more confident voice than usual. 'I've seen him now for what he is. You don't have to wait.'

Dione was shocked. Yannis had knocked her mother's self-confidence to such an extent that she rarely stood up for herself. This was an amazing turn-around. But still she hesitated about leaving her.

When Theo came to pick her up she opened the door to him. 'Would you mind coming back later?' she asked. 'I need to see Chris; he'll be here shortly.'

Theo's face darkened, and his eyes became bullets of steel. 'What for? What else is there to talk about?' he asked harshly.

About to tell him that it had nothing to do with their relationship, Dione changed her mind. 'There are things that need to be said,' she told him coolly.

'Perhaps I should stay and hear them?'

'And perhaps it's none of your business,' she snapped.

He met and held her eyes for several long seconds. It was a battle of wills and Dione had no intention of backing down. In the end he snarled, 'Very well.' And spun on his heel. Car tyres squealed as he sped away, and almost immediately Chris came around the other corner.

'Dione!' he exclaimed, alighting from his car. 'I

didn't expect to find you here. Was that your—er—husband just leaving?'

She nodded briefly.

'What's happened? Fallen out already?' Chris' eyes gleamed with delight.

'Nothing of the sort,' she told him shortly, leading the way back into the house. 'My mother has something to say to you and we thought it best done in private.'

Chris lifted his untidy brows.

Jeannie kept it short. 'I'm sorry to say this, Chris, but you are no longer welcome in my house.'

He frowned and then glared at Dione. 'This is your doing, isn't it? Now you're married to that man you think you can dictate to your mother, tell her what to do.'

'It has nothing to do with my daughter's marriage,' said Jeannie sharply. 'I've let you take me for a fool, but not any longer. I want you to go, Chris, and I don't want you to come back.'

Chris frowned, as astonished as Dione at the change in her mother. And then he turned to Dione. 'What's this, a conspiracy?'

'If you like to see it that way,' said Dione. 'My mother and I both agree that it's no longer acceptable.'

'And guess who put the idea into your mother's head,' he scorned. 'Well, thanks very much, Dione! First you run off and marry the first rich man you meet, and now you're banning me from this house. You're not the girl I thought you were, Dione. Theo's welcome. He'll soon find out what an unpleasant little witch you are.'

And with that he spun on his heel and left.

Dione and Jeannie looked at each other and smiled in disbelief. When Theo turned up they were sitting sipping tea. In contrast he looked far from happy. Dione promised her mother that she'd come to see her again before they left, and then followed her husband out to his car.

He drove silently and grimly but thankfully not at high speed. Dione felt his presence almost as much as when he had comforted her last night. Even though he was still angry it was overridden by his high sexuality. She could almost breathe in the passion inside him.

As they pulled up outside a private club the car was taken from him to be driven to some secret parking area, and Theo ushered her inside, where the atmosphere was hushed and opulent and everyone seemed to know everyone else.

Theo shrugged off their greetings and took Dione into a quiet corner of the dining room where their conversation would not be overheard. He came straight to the point.

'What was so important that you had to talk to that idiot of a boyfriend of yours without me being present?'

Dione glared. 'Chris is no longer my boyfriend.'

'Naturally,' snarled Theo. 'It was a mere figure of speech. But I hope you weren't telling him about our marriage, promising that once it's over you'll go back to him.'

If the fierce light in his eyes was supposed to frighten her, it didn't. Dione was used to men like him. 'No one has any idea about our arrangement, you can be sure of that. I wouldn't humiliate myself.'

'So you find being married to me humiliating?' he jeered, not looking pleased by the inference.

'What do you think?' she riposted, her dark eyes flashing her displeasure. 'Being forced into marriage wouldn't be anyone's idea of delight.'

'No one held a gun to your head,' he pointed out, at the same time indicating to a hovering wine waiter that they weren't yet ready to order.

'True,' Dione admitted, 'but it's what it feels like. I know I did it for my father, but I can't say that I'm getting any pleasure out of it.'

'You could if you tried.' His voice had gone a degree lower. 'You proved that last night. Tell me, did you respond to Chris' kisses the way you did to mine? Maybe you're not aware of it, but you revealed a hidden passion that it will be my pleasure to explore.'

'Never!' she cried, ignoring his question about Chris because the truth would have scared her. No one had lit her inner fire better than Theo. It both frightened and excited her at the same time. 'You're forgetting the terms of our contract.'

'Oh, I haven't forgotten, believe me.' His smile was wickedly assured. 'I'm simply assuming that one day passion will overtake us.'

Dione felt like striking out at him; at the same time she knew that what he said was true. She only had to let her guard slip once and he wouldn't hesitate to take advantage. When that happened she would be lost. 'You assume too much,' she told him testily.

'You're saying that you're not passionate? That you and Chris never made love until you felt that you were floating on a different planet?'

'What Chris and I did is none of your business,' she retorted angrily, at the same time feeling her cheeks flush. What would Theo think if he knew she was a virgin? Would he think her too pious for her own good? Would he call her an ice maiden as Chris had sometimes done? Chris hadn't been at all happy when she wouldn't go to bed with him, declaring that she was saving herself for when she got married.

And now she was married!

And she still didn't want to be made love to!

She was relieved when Theo beckoned the waiter and ordered their drinks. They studied the menu but she didn't know what she wanted, so Theo ordered for her. He had an alarming effect on her that at times made her feel strong and in control, and at others as weak as a kitten.

Damn the man for doing this to her!

'Have you any plans to see Chris again?'

The question took her by surprise. 'For your information, my mother's told him not to darken her doorstep again. I'm playing this game the way you want it.'

'So you see our marriage as a game?'

'Isn't it?' she thrust back. 'A game of power between you and my father! I hate the fact that I have been put in this position.'

Theo's brows rose and he leaned back in his chair and studied her, his dark eyes extremely intense, as though they were trying to look into her very soul. 'If you hate your father, why would you tie yourself to me for him?'

Dione immediately regretted her outburst. She did hate her father sometimes, but she loved him as well. And she would always be loyal to him. Perhaps he'd bullied her into thinking that way, but whatever she would never let him down. 'I didn't say I hated him altogether—only for what he's made me do. And I did it for his health's sake. I don't wish to discuss it any more.' She wished their meal would arrive so that she could concentrate on that instead.

'He's a very lucky man. And I'm lucky too to have such a delightful bride.' His black mood seemed to have left him and with a smile he reached across the table and took her hand.

Dione felt a whizz of something electric shoot through her arm, continuing into her body until it felt on fire. And all this because he had touched her! Hell, what was happening?

His thumb stroked and tormented and she wanted to snatch away; on the other hand she didn't want to give him the satisfaction of knowing that he disturbed her. Last night had been such a big mistake. She had appreciated him comforting her but she ought never to have let him kiss her. It had opened a door an inch and now his foot was in he wanted to take advantage.

During their meal they talked about everything except themselves, for which Dione was grateful. And by the time they had finished she was feeling more comfortable in his presence.

They walked afterwards, seeing the sights of London as though they were tourists. They took a boat trip down the Thames and a ride on the London Eye, exclaiming over the terrific views on such a clear day. And when they finally went back to his apartment Dione was tired but happy.

Theo had asked her no more awkward questions, made no untoward approaches apart from holding her hand, and if this was going to be his attitude for the rest of their so-called honeymoon then she could deal with it. She didn't dare think any further than that.

His housekeeper had dinner ready for them and after all their walking Dione had a good appetite. It was not until afterwards, when she and Theo were watching the darkening sky from the comfort of the balcony, Beethoven's Ninth playing in the background, that uneasiness began to assail her.

This was intimate; this was different from how it had been during the day. She could sense Theo looking at her instead of the view and wondered whether she ought to escape before it was too late. Or was she reading something that wasn't there?

'Doesn't London look beautiful at night?' she asked him.

'Not as lovely as you.'

She turned then and met the blackness of his eyes. 'You're not supposed to pay me compliments,' she said, alarmed to feel a sudden awareness. It was not easy ignoring this man's glances, especially when they expressed desire.

'Why? All women deserve compliments.'

'But our relationship is different,' she protested.

'Which makes it all the more exciting,' he growled. 'You're a very sexy woman, Dione.'

'And you're a smooth talker,' she flashed back, trying to ignore the fluttering of her heart. 'It won't get you anywhere.'

'Such a pity! I really would like to get somewhere with you.' The growl had deepened to a rumble within his chest and it was filled with innuendo.

Dione shot to her feet. 'This is a ridiculous conversation. I'm going to my room.'

'Not so quickly.' Theo's hand caught her arm as she jumped up. 'I've already promised that nothing will happen without your permission, so why the need to rush away?' And then he smiled, a devilish smile that revealed his wolfish white teeth and crinkled the corners of his eyes. 'Unless it's your own feelings that are running wild? Is that it, perhaps?'

'You're out of your mind,' snapped Dione. And she was out of hers because what he'd said was true. Pleasant hours spent in Theo's company had triggered emotions she would rather not feel.

'Mmm, I wonder,' he said in amusement. 'Sit down, Dione; you're going nowhere yet. I think you're forgetting that you're mine, and I happen to want your company for the rest of the evening. I have no wish to sit here alone.'

Although he was smiling there was a hard edge to his voice and, much against her better judgement, Dione dropped back into her chair. Damn the man. He was clearly used to getting his own way, and, fool that she was, she was allowing it. Why had she always thought that she could stand up to him?

She could have done if her weak body hadn't decided to respond. It was nothing to do with her head or her mind, it was her treacherous limbs, and all the nerves and pulses that were too sensitive for their own good.

Theo hitched his chair round so that he sat facing her, and, leaning forward, he took her hands into his. 'You have nothing to be afraid of, Dione. I'm not a big bad wolf.'

She tried to tug free but his grip was strong and in the end she gave in. A fatal mistake, because within seconds her heart raced out of control.

'We're in this together, you and I,' he growled. 'And twelve months is a long time if you're not enjoying yourself. If I were you, Dione, I'd stop fighting and start having fun.'

'It's different for you,' she flared, 'you're enjoying this situation; I'm not. Have you any idea what it was like telling my mother about us? I wonder what sort of a fool she took me for, marrying a man I hardly know.'

Theo shrugged. 'It looked to me as though she accepted the fact that it was love at first sight. You lied very convincingly, *agapi mou*. So convincingly, in fact, that I began to believe the story myself! Perhaps you are attracted to me, even though you deny it? Perhaps we should experiment again?'

'Don't you dare,' cried Dione in panic as his head drew closer to hers. But then she found that she could do nothing to stop him. With pounding heart, and a red-hot heat searing every limb, she allowed him to claim her lips in a kiss that set her soul on fire.

If he hadn't kissed her last night, if she hadn't felt the full portent of his kisses, she might have found the energy to reject him. But, fool that she was, she drank in every blissful second of it, and when he deepened the kiss, when he pulled her forward onto his lap, she did nothing to resist.

Beneath her she could feel the thundering heat of him and a throbbing readiness, and she wriggled uncontrollably, kissing him back, allowing her fingers to feel the harsh contours of his face and the shape of his head beneath the glossy dark hair.

'Ah, Dione, how I want you,' he breathed between kisses.

And Dione, to her shame, silently acknowledged that she wanted him too.

CHAPTER NINE

OUT HERE on this sultry summer evening Theo seemed more harshly Greek than ever, and he stirred her senses in a way no Englishman ever could. Despite all her reservations about marrying a native of her father's country, Dione could feel herself being drawn towards this vital, arrogantly handsome man in a way she had never expected.

Her nipples hardened and tingled as they brushed against the explosive hardness of his chest, and, ignoring warnings echoing repeatedly in the back of her mind, Dione sucked in his kisses, her tongue meeting his eagerly and sensually. She was giving all the wrong signals, she was very aware of that, but the will-power to move was non-existent.

The kiss grew deeply intimate and their individual body heat moulded into one smouldering fire. His fingertips touched and stroked the bare flesh on her arms and throat, igniting flames, and Dione wriggled uncontrollably, conscious of the heat between her thighs and her desperate need for fulfilment.

Never before had she felt such an urge, never felt the need to break her self-imposed vows. It became crystal

clear in her mind that Theo was an expert in the art of seduction, far more passionate than any Englishman she'd
been out with—and yet she'd been certain that she would
marry one. Greeks had been entirely off her agenda.

On the other hand, it didn't mean that she was falling
in love with Theo. This was nothing more than chemical
attraction. But what an attraction! Desire meeting
desire—though where hers had come from Dione had
no idea. Fire meeting fire! Animal hunger meeting
animal hunger! Whichever way she worded it, it all
amounted to the same thing.

She wanted Theo!

It was a new and alien feeling, a stimulation of her
senses, anticipation of the unknown, of the sheer
enormity of aroused feelings. She'd been called an ice
maiden many times and now she knew why. No one had
ever managed to intoxicate her into feeling heady with
an aching bodily need.

When she gave a shiver of pleasure Theo stopped
kissing and looked at her with concern. 'Are you cold,
agapi mou?'

She replied with the merest shake of her head, her
throat so tight that she could not speak.

Nevertheless Theo swung her up into his arms.
'Somewhere more comfortable, I think.'

Dione knew that she ought to protest; there was still
a sane part of her mind that told her she would despise
herself tomorrow morning if she let Theo have his way.
But insanity ruled. She allowed him to carry her to his
bedroom and lay her down on the bed.

'This is OK for you?' he asked gruffly. 'I don't want
you to do anything that you'll regret.'

In response Dione linked her hands behind his neck and pulled his face down to hers. Nothing else mattered at this moment of madness except feeling Theo inside her! The ache in her groin, the desperate need, would not go away until it had been assuaged by this spectacularly sexy man—who also happened to be her husband!

Whether it was this thought that made it all right in her mind Dione could not be sure; all she knew was that she wanted him to make love to her. *Now!* Never in her life had she felt such an intense ache in the pit of her stomach, or the honeyed sweetness that moistened the sexual heart of her.

She felt Theo's groan vibrate through the length of his body, and with excruciating slowness he popped the buttons on her blouse. Dione's breasts burgeoned and ached as inch by inch her flesh was revealed, and they seemed to lift themselves of their own volition for his touch.

A further tiny groan escaped him as he stroked and explored, easing his fingers inside her bra to squeeze her nipples in an exquisite taste of what was to come, before rolling her on her side so that he could flick it undone and whisk it away. A smile settled on his lips, one of pure pleasure and anticipation, his eyes feasting themselves on her curves.

When finally her breasts were exposed his eyes grew even darker as he sucked each of them in turn urgently into his mouth. Dione's body arched involuntarily, her hands gripping his head, fingers tugging at his hair, her hips gyrating as wave after wave of desperate need flowed through her.

But Theo was in no hurry. It was a deliberate, slow

seduction of her senses, bringing her further and further into the realms of no return. She heard her voice saying his name over and over like a mantra.

'This is good?' he asked, raising his eyes to hers, his lips moist and soft as he hovered millimetres above her tingling breasts.

She nodded. 'I don't know what you're doing to me but I want more.'

'You and me both,' he rasped, and his actions became more urgent, his hands moving to her skirt now to slide it down over her hips, revealing white lacy panties that matched her bra.

They felt damp and she was embarrassed as he slithered them off. 'Now you're all mine.'

There was a hot intensity in his wicked dark eyes, and with the frenetic energy of a man possessed he whipped off his own clothes and leapt on the bed beside her. All of a sudden it wasn't a matter of persuasion and seduction, it was a feverish hunger that needed assuaging—right now!

Dione had no time to feel afraid; her fingers tightened over Theo's shoulders as he drove himself into her. He hesitated only briefly when he felt resistance, but there was no going back. He could not stop, nor did she want him to. They were both being carried away by their own heated desire.

Her climax, when it came, sent her spinning into outer space. She was unprepared for the waves of sensation that pounded through her body, that made her gasp time and time again, her heart beating so loudly she felt sure that it could be heard all over the building.

She wanted to cling on to Theo, who was experiencing the same mind-bending convulsions, but he turned abruptly away when she touched him and rolled off the bed. His body was slicked with sweat but he regained his composure before she did and his voice was full of anger when he finally spoke.

'Why the hell didn't you tell me that you were a virgin?'

Dione swallowed hard, taken aback by his harsh words. He was spoiling a beautiful moment, didn't he know that? She had always wanted her first time to be special, and up until this point it had been. Now he was defiling it. 'If it doesn't matter to me, why does it matter to you?' she demanded, pulling a sheet over her still aching body.

'Dammit, Dione, it does matter. I would never have taken you so roughly had I known.'

'I'm not complaining,' she returned, getting up also and hugging the sheet around her.

Theo didn't seem to notice that he was still nude, that he wore nothing except a scowl. 'But I don't like it. I've never done that to a woman in my life.'

'Didn't you enjoy it?' she challenged, suddenly beginning to feel degraded.

'Of course I damn well enjoyed it—that isn't the point.' His tone suddenly changed to one of concern. 'Are you all right?'

Dione nodded. 'I just need a shower.' And, feeling utterly humiliated now, she hurried over to the adjoining door and slammed it shut behind her.

Theo let out a harsh breath. Damn! The worst thing was that he hadn't been able to control himself. He had known what he was doing, he had recognised that Dione was a virgin, and yet he hadn't stopped. What sort of a swine must she take him for?

His body still raged with rampant hormones and yet he had never been so angry with himself. Dione had said it didn't matter, but he had taken her without thought for her feelings.

He could never make love to her again because this moment would come back to haunt him. She'd felt so fantastic in his arms—she had the body of an angel and he'd felt hidden fires within her; he'd even begun to look forward to long, sensual nights spent together in bed.

If only she'd told him she was a virgin things could have been so different. He would have treated her with the tenderness she deserved; he would have enjoyed initiating her into acts of love. Instead…

Theo's shoulders drooped as he headed for his own shower. A long, cold shower, but it did nothing to lessen his anger. And he wasn't looking forward to speaking to Dione again. Somehow he would have to bluff his way out of it, not let her see how much his mistake had affected him.

She had put on a brave face, pretended it didn't matter, but he knew how much a woman's virginity meant to her, especially a woman of Dione's age. Clearly she had been saving herself for Mr Right, maybe even Chris Donovan, had they married, and now he had taken it.

Never in his life had he hated himself as much as he did at that moment, and when he heard the key turn in the door between their two rooms his heart sank even further.

Dione couldn't sleep. She had gone to bed telling herself that she didn't care, but deep within her heart she struggled to come to terms with what had happened. It wasn't as though it was solely Theo's fault. She was as much to blame. They had fallen on each other like two sex-starved animals, something she had never imagined herself doing!

On the other hand, perhaps it was a good thing that Theo was disappointed in himself. It might keep him away from her in future; because if they continued to make love during the whole of their twelve-month contract then one of them, maybe both, might find it hard to part at the end of the term.

Finally Dione fell into a dreamless sleep and woke feeling more at ease with herself—until a horrific thought struck her. What if she was pregnant? Theo had been too impatient to use protection and she hadn't even thought about it. Could it happen the first time? She was ashamed to admit that she didn't know. She could only hope not and she had no intention of passing any of her fears on to Theo.

They met over breakfast and both of them studiously avoided mentioning what had happened last night. Theo wore a white polo shirt and black chinos and Dione had chosen a simple beige dress with an orange and brown pattern. Had she subconsciously dressed to suit their mood? she couldn't help wondering.

Her mood was definitely brown and she wondered what plans Theo had for the day. If they'd been an ordinary newly wed couple they would probably have spent all their time in bed, never leaving the apartment, but due to their extreme circumstances this was hardly likely to be the case.

Theo looked as though he'd had a sleepless night as

well, with shadows beneath his eyes and his hair all over the place. 'What are we doing today?' she asked, partly to break the silence, partly because it would be good to know what he had planned.

'I think a good, long walk in Hyde Park might be the answer,' he declared. 'Blow the cobwebs away. Do you horse-ride? We could do that if you like.'

Dione shook her head. 'No, I don't.' And if she did it would have been uncomfortable sitting astride a saddle. Not that he'd think of that. What man would?

But he amazed her by pulling a rueful face. 'Sorry, wrong question to ask. Are you terribly sore?'

'I'm OK,' she lied.

He shook his head in anger at himself. 'I was stupid. I got carried away. Do forgive me.'

'Let's forget the whole issue,' said Dione hastily, although she appreciated his apology. 'What's done is done. I've finished. Let's go.'

Amazingly they enjoyed themselves, both making a determined effort to put the events of last night behind them. 'I guess this isn't how you usually spend your day?' queried Dione as they rested on a park bench after walking for a good hour and a half. They had spent their time chatting, pointing out different things of interest…a grey squirrel, a robin, blackbirds, ducks; anything that caught their attention.

Anything other than themselves!

'Indeed not,' he agreed, smiling into her face for the first time that morning. 'I'm usually dashing here, there and everywhere; my feet hardly touch the ground. I can't remember the last time I took a break like this.'

When Theo smiled, when his face softened and his

eyes crinkled, Dione forgot the atmosphere between them and felt a fresh surge of awareness. It was foolishness, she knew, and she kept it well-hidden. 'You should be ashamed,' she admonished instead. 'Everyone needs to relax some time.'

Theo shrugged his magnificent shoulders. 'I'll be the first to admit it. But running a business like mine doesn't leave much time for relaxation.'

'Am I right in believing you have a hotel here in London?'

'I do. One of my finest,' he answered proudly.

'Can I see it?'

Theo looked at her with raised brows. 'If you're really interested.'

'Of course.'

He looked pleased. 'Then I'll take you there tomorrow.'

After that the atmosphere between them seemed to lighten, and by the end of the day they were chatting like the best of friends. Dione knew that she ought to be pleased, that this was what she had wanted from the very beginning, but after last night, after he had sent her soaring with the stars, how could she be happy with a platonic relationship? Her whole body felt different. More alive, more feminine, more everything, in fact. She even wanted to be made love to again.

But it was not to be. After another of his housekeeper's scrumptious meals—poached salmon with garden peas and tiny new potatoes—Theo took a phone call in his study and when he came back his face was grim.

'I have to return home. Some damn idiot's hacked

into our computer system and has downloaded personal information.'

Dione frowned. 'And you're expected to sort it?'

'Not me personally—the police have been called in—but I naturally want to be there. It affects the whole company; we could be in big trouble. We're leaving in an hour. I've asked Mary to pack our cases.'

'I could have done that,' she protested but he was hardly listening. She could see his brain working overtime; she was non-existent at this moment. 'Would it help if I stayed here?' she asked hesitantly. 'Then you can go straight to your office.'

Dark eyes pierced her. 'And leave you to the likes of Chris Donovan? Not on your life. You're coming whether you want to or not.'

It was a silent journey in Theo's private jet. His thoughts were on what was happening and he seemed hardly to notice her existence. It should have suited her just fine except that she would have liked to be involved. She would have liked him to talk to her about it, share his thoughts and fears.

Two cars were waiting at the airport, one to whisk Theo to his office and another to take her home and, although she'd missed a night's sleep and went straight to bed, all Dione could think about was Theo's problem. She might have been forced into this marriage but even in these few days he had become a big part of her life and she was truly concerned for him.

Later in the morning she went to see her father and found him sitting up in his hospital bed, much improved.

'I have you to thank for this, my loyal daughter,' he said. 'How is married life? Is Theo looking after you?'

'Of course; he's very much a gentleman,' she answered, marvelling that her father could speak about it as though it were a proper marriage.

'Not too much of a gentleman, I hope?' he asked with a knowing twinkle in his eye. 'You are—sharing a bed?'

'I think what we do is none of your business,' retorted Dione, speaking more sharply than she usually did to her father. 'You got your money—isn't that enough? Where's Phrosini?'

'You've just missed her. But she'll be back; you'll see her later.'

'I'm not staying that long, Father.' She thought of telling him about Theo's problem but then decided against it. Knowing Yannis, he would gloat. So long as his business was picking up he really cared little about anyone else.

'I expected you to be away longer than this,' he said.

'You know Theo,' she said; 'he's like you—he can't keep away from his work.'

'But you're not entirely unhappy?'

As if he cared! Nevertheless Dione shook her head. 'We get on well under the circumstances.'

'Will he mind you still working for me?'

'What?' Dione's eyes shot wide. 'You can't expect me to carry on after you've sold me to him?'

'*Dione!*' Yannis sounded scandalised by her suggestion, his face more animated than she had seen it in a long time.

'Isn't that what you did?' she tossed angrily. 'Sold me! I don't belong to you any more. I'm glad you're getting better but believe me, I shan't be visiting you on a daily basis. In fact, you deserve no visits at all.' It was

the first time she had ever spoken to her father like this
but something inside her had snapped and she actually
felt relief. Maybe he had done her a favour after all?

CHAPTER TEN

THEO didn't even phone. Dione waited all day to hear how things were going and was hurt when he didn't contact her. Maybe he thought it was none of her business.

When he did finally come home it was almost midnight and she was in bed. Though not asleep! She had lain there listening for him, feeling more lonely than at any other time in her life. In the four days since their marriage she had grown used to his presence, had even begun to feel comfortable with him, and she missed him as she had never expected.

Pulling on a white towelling robe over her skimpy nightie, Dione made her way downstairs. Theo sat stretched out in a chair in the massive living area, a glass of whisky in his hand, looking so strained and tired that her heart went out to him. She flew across the room. 'Theo, how are things?'

He looked at her with red-rimmed eyes. 'We're getting there. What are you doing up at this time of night?'

'I've been worried about you,' she declared honestly.

'Why?'

'Why?' she echoed. 'Because...' She had been about to say 'because you're my husband'. But that would infer that theirs was a proper marriage and she loved and cared about him, and that wasn't the way of things at all. 'Because it's a horrible thing to happen to anyone. Is it very bad?'

'It could be worse if it hadn't been spotted. But it's going to involve many hours of work and could set the company back months. The police are working on it, thank goodness.'

'Do you think I could be of any help?' asked Dione. 'I'm completely computer savvy.'

'You are?'

She nodded.

'Didn't you tell me that you were an interior designer and that you worked for your father?'

'I did, but not any more.'

Well-marked brows rose.

'I went to see him today and told him so.'

'Good for you!' he exclaimed. 'I bet he wasn't happy.'

Dione shrugged. 'I said that since he'd sold me to you I owed him nothing.'

A harsh frown slashed Theo's brow but he didn't deny that he owned her and, although it shouldn't have done, Dione found it deeply hurtful. Somehow, since the night he'd made love to her, she'd felt differently towards him, and she had thought that maybe he had too. Not love, nothing like that, but more a friendship than an arrangement written on a piece of paper.

His non-answer confirmed that he didn't see it that way. He had bought her to do with as he wished. And if he chose to ignore her for twenty-four hours at a time it was something she had to put up with.

'You look tired,' she said, changing the conversation. 'Why don't you go to bed?'

'And you think I'd sleep?' he scoffed. 'Go back yourself, Dione; there's nothing you can do.'

Hiding her hurt, Dione turned and made her way upstairs. If that was the way Theo chose to play it there was nothing she could do. She lay listening for him to turn in too, but in the end she was asleep before he did. And the next morning he was gone when she woke up.

Instead she had a visitor. 'Mrs Tsardikos, it's Mrs Tsardikos,' said Theo's housekeeper with what sounded like an apology. 'I've put her in the living room.'

Dione frowned, wondering why Theo's mother had chosen to pay her a visit.

But the glamorous woman who turned to face her as she entered the room was not her mother-in-law but a complete stranger, and for the first few seconds she stared at Dione without speaking.

'I'm Theo's first wife, Katina,' she announced finally. But she didn't extend a hand of greeting. 'And you're the next fool.'

Dione frowned. 'I beg your pardon?' The woman was handsome in a hard sort of way, with her hair beautifully coiffed and her make-up perfect. The harsh red colour of her lips was echoed in her fingernails, but the black suit she wore made her look very severe.

'I felt it my place to come and warn you in case you don't realise exactly what you've let yourself in for.'

'I think,' said Dione, hating her on sight, 'that that's my business and nothing at all to do with you.' The woman was overbearing. It was no wonder their marriage hadn't lasted.

'Theo can be the perfect gentleman on the outside,' continued his ex-wife, as though Dione hadn't spoken, 'but he's a complete swine otherwise. I wouldn't wish him on my worst enemy.'

'I've seen none of it so far,' countered Dione.

'That's why I'm here so early in your marriage,' came the glib response. 'If you take my advice you'll get out of it as quickly as you can.'

Dione stared hostilely at her visitor, scarcely able to believe what she was hearing. 'I don't need any advice, especially from you.'

'What's he been saying about me?' came the quick and almost fearful response.

'Nothing!' spat Dione. 'But exes are always hostile. It's natural. Thank you for coming but I'll wait and find out for myself what Theo's like.'

'You're making a big mistake,' purred Katina, perching on the edge of one of the chairs, clearly not yet prepared to leave. 'In twelve months' time you'll be wishing you'd listened and done something about it. Please ask Anna to make me a coffee.'

'I'm sorry!' exclaimed Dione with exaggerated politeness. 'I'm forgetting my manners. Please excuse me.' Outside the room she felt like spitting fire. She wasn't in the least sorry that she hadn't offered this insufferable woman a drink. What had Theo ever seen in her?

It took her several moments to regain her composure and return to the room, and as they sat drinking coffee she willed the other woman to leave.

'You had an amazingly short honeymoon,' said Katina complacently. 'What happened?

'Are you trying to tell me that you've been keeping

tabs on us?' asked Dione indignantly. She was shocked to hear that the woman knew so much.

'Tabs? What are tabs?' Her English was good but clearly there were words she was not familiar with.

'Checking up on us. To hear you talk you're thankful to be rid of Theo. Why the interest now?'

'It's you I'm thinking of.'

Dione tossed her head, her eyes flashing anger. 'I don't think so. Something tells me that you'd like Theo back. You're trying to get rid of me, that's what you're doing.'

'I wouldn't marry Theo again if he got down on his knees and begged,' scorned Katina.

But Dione didn't believe her. If she wasn't interested in him, why would she be here? The story about warning her what Theo was like didn't ring true. She was out to cause trouble.

'He's a womaniser. He might have married you but you're not the only one in his life. Have you ever wondered why he spends so much time at work? It's nothing more than a cover-up.'

'Really?' asked Dione. 'And you have proof of this, do you? Perhaps he did it when he was married to you but our marriage is different.' In a way that Katina would never know about. 'He won't cheat on me.'

'You sound so sure that I pity you,' scorned Theo's ex. 'But of course you've only been married a short time. I was confident of him once. And look what happened when we lost our child—you did know about that?'

Dione nodded.

'He saw it as an excuse and left. He blamed it on me, of course. Said I'd changed, but the truth is Theo doesn't want to be tied down. You're nothing more to him than a novelty. If I were you I'd get out of this marriage before he throws you out.'

'I'm sorry,' said Dione stiffly, unable to remain civil any longer, 'I don't remember asking for your advice.'

'It's freely given,' said Katina, putting down her empty cup and standing up. 'Do tell Theo I called. I'll see myself out.' And she sailed from the room.

Dione was so angry that she couldn't rest and when Theo came home later that evening the first thing she did was tell him about his ex-wife's visit.

'She had no right coming here,' he roared, his eyes flashing golden anger. 'You should have phoned me. I would have come right over and told her to leave. Did she upset you?'

As if he cared! Dione didn't even deign to answer.

'What did she want?'

Dione lifted her shoulders in a helpless little shrug. 'To warn me against you!'

Theo's face became suffused with colour and he let out a hiss of rage. 'I wonder who the hell told her we'd got married.'

'I guess it's common knowledge,' acknowledged Dione wryly. The wedding had been no secret. In fact, it had been a far bigger ceremony than she would have liked under the circumstances, though she had never told Theo that. 'But I am interested as to why she would tell me you weren't a fit husband. Is there anything I don't know? Do you fly into fits of rage? Is my life in danger?'

'You know damn well it's not,' he thundered. 'Did you tell her about us?'

'Am I a fool?' she riposted. 'I may as well let you

know now I didn't like Katina. I can't think what you ever saw in her.'

'I sometimes wonder that myself,' he acknowledged quietly.

'She was clearly here to make trouble.'

'But you didn't let her get to you?'

Dione shook her head.

'If she ever comes again I want you to tell me straight away. In fact, I might go and see her. She had no right talking to you like that.'

'It's not worth it,' insisted Dione. 'She didn't get the better of me.'

'I'm glad you stood up to her,' said Theo.

'I'm not like my mother,' acknowledged Dione.

'I guess you've had years of practice with your father?' There was a wry twist to his lips as he spoke. 'Yannis is the biggest bully I know.'

'I agree,' she answered, 'and if he wasn't my father I wouldn't give him the time of day. But blood's thicker than water, isn't that what they say? He's given me a good upbringing... I've never been short of anything; I couldn't turn my back on him.'

'You're an amazing woman, Dione. Come here.' And he beckoned her to him.

Warily she approached and when he pulled her down onto his lap she made no attempt to resist. She could feel the good, strong beat of his heart against her side, and even after a long, hard day at work he still smelled good. The male scent of him was like an aphrodisiac and awareness sizzled through her with the speed of lightning.

'I went to see him today,' she said, trying to pretend

that it was quite normal to be sitting on his lap. 'He looks much better.'

'As well he should be,' snarled Theo, his mood changing. 'He got what he wanted.'

And you didn't, she was tempted to ask, when you were the one who gave the ultimatum? I was piggy in the middle. But she kept her thoughts to herself. 'Do you have any regrets?' she asked instead.

'Ask me that in six months' time,' he growled. 'Our marriage so far has been anything but smooth.'

'Did you expect it to be?' she enquired, wondering how they could be having such a conversation when hot desire filled her body.

'I didn't expect to have to fight off a jealous boyfriend,' he told her accusingly.

'And I didn't expect to have to deal with an ex-wife.' she retaliated.

'*Touché!* But it can't have been jealousy on her side because she was the one who walked out.'

'You never told me about her, though,' insisted Dione, finding it easier to ignore the tight tension inside her while talking about his ex.

'Why should I have done?' he asked harshly. 'This is hardly a marriage made in heaven, where both sides confess their past so that no skeletons turn up. There was nothing in our contract that said we needed to bare all.'

And then his voice lowered almost to a growl. 'I didn't ask you over here to talk about our past loves. It's the present I'm interested in. I need you, Dione, and I need you now.'

His arms tightened around her and his frank confession sent a further thrill spiralling through Dione's overheated veins. She tightened muscles in a vain endeavour to stem the hot hunger that stung the very heart of her and was almost afraid to look into his eyes in case he saw her very real need.

What she saw, though, was a question, one she hadn't expected, not after the last time. She had thought he would now take it as his right to make love to her whenever he felt like it. Unless, of course, he was asking whether it was still too soon?

Well, damn the soreness; she wanted him—badly. And he must have seen the answer in her eyes because with a groan he nuzzled the side of her neck, biting gently, sucking, kissing, moving his lips inexorably closer to her mouth.

Dione clutched his head, moaning her acceptance, her pleasure, her hunger. And her lips were parted and ready when he began his invasion. 'This is what a man needs after a hard day,' he muttered into her mouth. 'The sweet taste of woman! Someone to make him forget his worries.' His breathing grew harder, his voice more hoarse and his demands of her deeper.

The pulse in Dione's throat beat so hard it threatened to choke her, and her heart struggled to keep up with the demands made on it. By now she was putty in Theo's arms and when he snapped the straps on her nightie in his urgency to suck her stinging nipples into his mouth she felt nothing but extreme exhilaration.

His long fingers cupped her breasts, moulding and firming, and his teeth nipped and grazed, and when he looked up to judge her reaction his eyes were glazed. All worries over work had vanished and he was lost in a world where only senses mattered.

Dione wasn't aware of the moment that her night-dress had fallen even lower, conscious only that his fingers had blazed a trail over the flatness of her stomach and were now playing with the moistness between her thighs. He was incredibly gentle, but in so doing he was arousing her more than if he had taken her with urgency as he had before.

When she could stand it no longer, when her whole body writhed and wriggled and demanded fulfilment, when she cried out in both pleasure and despair, he swung her to her feet.

'Don't move,' he warned as he ripped his shirt over his head and removed his trousers. When he was glori-ously, excitingly naked he pulled her to him again and she felt him against her, and this time it was she who hooked her arms around his neck and pulled his head down to hers, all the time moving her body sensually against him.

'God, woman, what are you doing to me?' he groaned hoarsely. 'I can't stand any more of this.'

With the slickness of experience he turned her back on him, at the same time sliding a condom into place. Dione was thankful, even though she wouldn't have found the strength to stop him making love to her even if he hadn't. Never before had she felt such a powerful need. Her whole body throbbed and ached so much that it almost hurt.

His hands captured her sensitive breasts, fingers teasing aching nipples as he edged her towards a leather sofa. There he bent her forwards over the back of it and the coolness of the leather felt like heaven to her hot skin. Slowly he entered her from behind, constantly asking whether he was hurting, but each time she shook her head, completely incapable of speaking.

Even when she had taken the full length of him he still didn't rush. He took it slowly and sensually, riding her like a fine thoroughbred mare, until in the end it was Dione who begged for more.

'Faster, Theo, faster,' she cried. 'I can't stand any more of this.'

He was quick to obey and Dione shot to a climax a couple of seconds before Theo. Her knees gave way and they both ended up on the floor, heaving and writhing, gasping and groaning, feeling as though they'd died and gone to heaven. Finally, their limbs still heavy, they lay still.

'That was good for you, *agapi mou*?'

It was more than good—it had been out of this world, but did she want to admit that? What would she be letting herself in for? 'I never knew that making love could be so enervating,' she confessed with a wry smile.

Theo's skin glistened in the light from one of the floor lamps, and even in repose he still looked imposing. Naked or dressed, aroused or relaxed, he was one hell of an exciting male. She had never thought that when she agreed to marry him, had never expected that within a few short days she would be begging him to make love to her.

She had thought that the next twelve months were going to be hell; instead it looked as though she was going to enjoy them!

CHAPTER ELEVEN

IN THE weeks that followed Dione and Theo grew closer than she had ever expected. Not that she didn't always keep uppermost in her mind the fact that this was a temporary arrangement. Theo was still worried over his company affairs, though the police had traced and apprehended the hacker, who, it turned out, was a disgruntled ex-employee, but other than that they spent all of their spare time together.

She slept in his bed; they made love so many times that to even think about it embarrassed Dione. He teased her by saying that she had become obsessed by sex, but he also declared that he was one hell of a satisfied man. 'Persuading you to marry me was one of the best moves I've made,' he said one evening after a particularly long and satisfying love session.

Dione wasn't so sure. 'I hope you're not thinking of extending the twelve months. A contract is a contract, don't ever forget that.' She didn't want him getting any wrong ideas.

When Theo made love he was being driven by lust rather than any real feelings; and if she was honest with herself it was the same for her. It was amazing sex, but

that was all it was; she could never see herself tied to
Theo for the rest of her life.

Theo frowned. 'I'm a man of my word, Dione.
'You'll be free to fly when the time comes.'

When one morning she woke up feeling ill Dione
thought it must have been the fish they'd had for supper
the previous evening. But when it happened again, and
she added up the dates, she knew that her worst nightmare had just become reality. She was pregnant!

And she was trapped! Trapped to a Greek man just
as her mother had been! The very thought made her feel
ill all over again.

Theo always left for the office before Dione got up
and as yet he had no idea of the fear consuming her. Nor
did she want to tell him because she wasn't feeling
strong enough to deal with it herself just yet.

'Are you all right, Dione? You look pale.' They were
sitting outside by the pool one evening, letting their
meal go down, and Dione had closed her eyes. She felt
guilty about not telling Theo; on the other hand she
feared his anger more and intended putting off the evil
moment for as long as she could.

'I'm fine,' she said, looking into surprisingly concerned brown eyes and hoping she was actress enough
to get away with it.

'Perhaps you're not getting out enough? What do
you do with yourself while I'm at work?'

Dione couldn't believe he was really interested. All
that seemed to matter to him was that she was ready and
waiting when he got home. There wasn't a single night
when he didn't want to make love. His virility continu-
ally amazed her. Though she was forced to accept that

her own needs were pretty much on a par with his. And this she found even more astounding.

'Not very much,' she acknowledged. 'I almost wish I hadn't given up my job with my father. I'm not cut out to be a stay-at-home wife.'

She swam sometimes but she didn't like sitting out in the sun. She had her father's dark hair but her mother's fair skin and burnt easily. She spent much of her time reading, or surfing the internet on a computer Theo had made available for her. She visited Phrosini and her father, but all her friends were at work during the day. It was very much a life of leisure but it wasn't for her.

'Maybe I should introduce you to some of my friends' wives. They seem to spend all their time shopping or at each other's houses.'

'No, thank you,' said Dione quickly. 'There are only ten months left; I'll get by.'

A harsh frown attacked Theo's brow. 'You're counting?'

'Wouldn't you in my position?' she snapped.

'Maybe I'm wrong, but I thought you were settled and happy. You always seem pleased to see me when I get home.'

Dione lifted narrow shoulders but said nothing. Her pleasure was purely sexual; even Theo should know that.

He snorted angrily and, jumping to his feet, he marched indoors. Dione spent that night in her own bed. She oughtn't to have spoken to him so rudely, she realised, because now life would be unbearable.

The following morning Theo had gone off to work and she was retching over the toilet as usual, when she heard a sound. Glancing over her shoulder, she saw her husband watching her. She slammed a tissue to her mouth and spun to face him, her eyes wide orbs of guilt.

'Does this mean what I think it means?' he asked harshly.

Dione nodded. No need for words; he was as angry as she had expected him to be.

'Why didn't you tell me?'

'Why are you spying on me?' she riposted furiously.

'I forgot something. And it looks as though it's lucky I did. You're pregnant?'

He made it sound like an accusation.

'And if I am, whose fault is it?' she demanded.

'Needless to say, I take precautions,' he shot back. 'And needless to say also, you've given no indication that you don't enjoy it. In fact, your appetite is as great as mine.'

'Maybe it is,' she agreed, 'so it must have happened on that first occasion. You didn't care then that you might get me pregnant. All you wanted to do was satisfy your own carnal urges.'

Theo closed his eyes and she could almost hear him counting to ten. And actually she had no right being angry because she was just as much to blame. 'Have you seen a doctor?'

Dione shook her head, and then wished she hadn't because the room spun round. Instantly Theo was at her side, a strong arm supporting her. With his other hand he filled a glass with water and bade her take a sip.

Her mouth felt putrid and she gladly took it off him.

'That's better,' he said eventually. 'You're looking more like your normal self now. Go back to bed. I'll send for my physician.'

'I'm not ill,' she protested vehemently.

'Then I'll take you to see him. I don't suppose you've had your pregnancy confirmed?'

Dione hated him fussing. 'I'll go in my own good time,' she retorted, 'to my own doctor.'

Theo nodded grimly. 'Will you be all right if I leave you now? I have something important to take care of.'

Tell me something different, thought Dione. But it was a relief to have him go. A relief also that he had found out about the baby.

Dione wasn't looking forward to Theo coming home that evening. Usually she bathed and made herself ready for him, but now she suspected there would be a change in their relationship.

'What's the matter with you, Theo? You haven't been yourself today. Not trouble with your wife already?'

Theo looked at his colleague and managed a wry smile. 'Not at all; she's everything a man could wish for.' Except that now, because of his own stupidity, she was having his baby. The very thought was sheer hell.

'There's obviously something on your mind,' insisted Dimitri. 'Can I help?'

'You can keep your nose out of it,' rasped Theo, and immediately regretted his outburst when he saw the man's dismay.

Theo always had a good relationship with his employees; he treated them fairly and kindly and they respected him for it. It was rare that he ever needed to tell anyone off. And Dimitri was his right-hand man; he knew as much about the business as Theo did. It was wrong to take his anger out on him.

He clapped a hand on Dimitri's shoulder. 'I shouldn't

have said that. It's true, I do have a problem, but it's personal and I don't wish to talk about it.'

His colleague shrugged. 'That's your prerogative, Theo. But if you do need an ear you know nothing will go any further.'

Theo nodded.

He couldn't even begin to describe his shock when he had seen Dione vomiting and he'd immediately known the reason for it. Hadn't Katina been exactly the same? And hadn't she tried to hide it from him as well?

Her excuse was that their marriage had been going through a bad patch and she had thought he'd be angry. As if! What man could be angry when he'd procreated a child, especially in wedlock? A child was born to be loved and cared for. To be guided through life, to be taught values.

A child did not die at a very young age!

Thoughts came tumbling back and Theo had to blink back tears and push them away. They did not bear thinking about.

But what was Dione's excuse for not telling him? Had she too been afraid that he'd be angry? Was he really that unapproachable? Their relationship had gone up several notches recently and he had begun to think that something more serious was developing.

And now she wanted to shut him out!

Which proved only one thing. That Dione's view of their relationship was entirely different from his. In her eyes their marriage was no more real now than it had been on the day they wed.

And by impregnating her with his seed he had ruined her life!

He couldn't bear the thought that he had hurt her a second time and knew that he had to go home and try to put matters right. Difficult, under the circumstances, but somehow he had to try. He needed to reassure her that he would never desert her, that he would see her through this, make sure she never suffered. Even if she didn't want to remain married to him he would give her every support possible.

When he got home he found her lying in the shade by the pool wearing nothing more than a skimpy black bikini. There was no evidence yet of her pregnancy; she was stunningly slender and beautiful, and his male hormones swung into appreciative action.

She lifted wide, surprised eyes to his face and she was clearly not happy to see him. 'What are you doing here at this time of day?'

'Have you seen the doctor?' he countered, ignoring her question.

'Not yet.'

'Have you phoned for an appointment?'

'No.'

'Why the hell not?' His voice rose in accordance with his frustration. He had so wanted to comfort Dione, to reassure her that he would take care of everything, but the vibes coming from her were not conducive to kind words.

'Because I didn't realise it was so important,' she defended. 'Is that why you're here, to make sure I carry out your wishes?' She stood up now and faced him, hands on her hips, her chin thrust out.

'I'm here because it's my fault you're in this condition.'

'At least you've got something right,' she countered furiously.

'And I want to take care of you.'

'Because it's the honourable thing to do?' she replied. 'Thanks, but no thanks; I don't need your help. It has never been my intention to stay with you a day longer than necessary and nothing has changed.'

And she meant it!

And she looked beautiful in her anger. So gorgeous, in fact, that he wanted to wrap his arms around her and kiss her senseless. 'For heaven's sake, go and make yourself decent,' he rasped. Damn the woman, she'd got beneath his skin in a way he'd never expected. What had started as a game was turning into something much more serious.

Dione needed no second bidding; she scuttled into the house as though an army of ants was chasing her. Theo slung his jacket over the back of a chair, took off his tie and undid his collar. He'd been cool in the car, but now the full heat of the midday sun bore down on him and he'd have liked nothing more than to strip off and take a swim.

But since he'd commanded Dione to get dressed he could hardly do that. He closed his eyes instead and called himself all kinds of a fool for allowing such a situation to develop.

Dione took her time getting dressed. What she really wanted to do was walk out of the house and never see Theo again. He was the one to blame. She hadn't invited him to make love to her.

Nor had she stopped him, warned an inner voice.

That was true, but she was damned if she would admit it to him. This was Theo's fault! If he hadn't insisted on this ridiculous marriage then none of it would have happened.

It was with reluctance that she finally made her way outside again. Theo sat with his head back and his eyes closed, but he flicked them open the instant she walked past him. She perched on the edge of the canvas lounger she had vacated earlier, hugged her knees and glared at him.

For a few long seconds neither spoke, resentment pulsing between them like a giant heart. Theo's face was stern, his eyes unwavering, and when she could stand it no longer Dione spoke. 'Where do we go from here?' She knew where she wanted to go; home to England to her mother. Jeannie would take care of her; she would understand why she had been attracted to Theo, and why she needed to get away from him now.

But she couldn't see that happening. There was still a huge chunk of her contract left; Theo wouldn't let her go, especially now she was pregnant with his child.

'First thing, you need to see a doctor; you need confirmation that you are actually pregnant.'

'As if my body hasn't already told me!' she answered quietly, her brown eyes warring with his.

'And, as you seem so reluctant to organise it yourself, while you've been dressing I've made an appointment for you at eleven in the morning with a highly recommended gynaecologist.'

'How dare you?' Dione was incensed that he was taking matters into his own hands. 'You have no right!'

'I have every right, considering that I'm the father,' thrust Theo harshly.

'And then what?' she questioned fiercely. 'Do we

pretend to the world that we're deliriously happy? And what do we do when the contract finishes? Because I sure as hell am not staying with you.'

'We'll cross that bridge when we come to it,' he said with barely concealed anger.

'The coward's way out,' muttered Dione, but he was right, of course. There was very little they could do until the baby arrived. Lord help her if she was going to be tied to Theo because of one simple mistake.

Simple? Not simple! Tortuous perhaps. Stupid! Mindless! Anything but simple! One foolish error was going to affect the rest of her life.

They sat in silence, each deep in their own thoughts, until one of his maids came to tell them that their lunch was ready. It was served indoors, where the air was cool and Dione could breathe more easily, and consisted of a very simple omelette and salad with yoghurt for dessert. Despite her unease in Theo's company, Dione cleaned her plate.

'Are you going back to work?' she asked him, sipping iced water and contemplating the darkness of his brow.

'I'm going to work from home for the rest of the day,' he informed her tersely.

'You don't have to stay with me,' she protested, unable to imagine anything worse under the circumstances. 'I'm not ill; I'll be all right.'

'I'm fully aware of that,' he growled. 'But I intend staying all the same. I think you should rest this afternoon.'

'And what do you think I've been doing all morning?' she asked crossly. 'It's all I ever seem to do.'

'Good.'

'No, it's not good,' she slammed. 'I'm bored witless.'

'I'm sorry you feel that way,' he retorted drily. 'Is there anything you'd rather do?'

Dione hissed her displeasure. She didn't need him to be polite. She would have preferred anger. It was a surreal situation and she hated him for getting her into it.

When she didn't answer he smiled. 'We could go to bed.'

'And do more of the same that got us into this situation in the first place?' she yelled. 'No, thank you! There will be no more sex between us.'

'You can't get pregnant twice.'

Dione eyed him furiously. 'You really have no idea, do you? The very thought of you touching me makes me sick.'

Theo frowned, a deep, harsh frown that dragged his brows together and slashed his forehead. 'You can't mean that.'

'Can't I?' she thrust back.

'It would be impossible. Your body needs mine as much as mine needs yours. Maybe we should put it to the test?' He smiled grimly and walked towards her.

Dione shot to her feet. 'Don't you dare touch me!'

Theo halted mere inches away and to Dione's chagrin her traitorous heart clamoured to break free from her chest, her pulses throbbing in unison to its beat—even her nipples leapt forward in response to his nearness. Every fibre of her being ached for fulfilment! She hated him and wanted him at the same time.

With a groan Theo held out his arms and like a fool she walked into them. He folded her against him and she felt comforting heat as well as scorching awareness.

'It's no use us fighting each other,' he murmured,

nuzzling her ear. 'What's done is done. We might not like it, each for our own reasons, but there's no escaping the fact.'

'You're right,' she agreed, and lifted her mouth for his kiss.

The instant their lips met every sane thought melted away. She was lost yet again in a world where the only things that mattered were their senses. Senses that spiralled away out of control! Touch—the feel of him beneath her fingertips, of a finely honed body, of well-developed muscles, of a barely reined hunger!

'Let's go somewhere we won't be disturbed,' he breathed against her mouth.

Dione nodded her agreement, reluctant to let go, and gave a little squeal of delight when he swung her up into his arms and carried her upstairs.

With his bedroom door kicked shut behind him Theo wasted no time in stripping off his clothes while Dione did the same. They were both consumed by a primeval craving that needed to be urgently assuaged, and as far as Dione was concerned it was a mind-blowing experience, over too quickly, but beautiful all the same.

Did she regret it? She asked herself this frequently in the hours that followed while Theo was working away quietly in his study, and always the answer was the same. No, she did not.

CHAPTER TWELVE

AT PRECISELY eleven o'clock Dione and Theo were ushered into the gynaecologist's consulting room, and at ten minutes past eleven her pregnancy was confirmed. 'Congratulations,' the doctor said to them both.

It wasn't a surprise but even so Dione gazed at Theo in dismay. He took her hand and smiled and tried not to show the doctor that they weren't truly delighted. 'Let's go and celebrate,' he said.

'Mother, I have something to tell you.' Dione's heart was thumping as though she were a guilty sixteen-year-old instead of a married woman in her twenties. And although she hadn't meant to blurt it out quite so immediately she added, 'I'm pregnant.'

She had made a conscious decision not to keep the news from her mother. Jeannie had been hurt enough when she got married without telling her. She didn't deserve to be kept in the dark about her first grandchild.

There was a pause at the other end of the phone, a long pause. 'Do say something,' urged Dione.

'I'm delighted—if you are,' answered Jeannie cautiously.

'I think I'm more shocked,' confessed Dione.

'It is...a little soon in your marriage. How does Theo feel?'

'He's in a state of shock too. But I'm sure that when we've both got used to the idea we'll be over the moon. He's very protective of me; keeps wanting me to rest. I'm sure he thinks I'm ill.'

'Your father was the same,' advised Jeannie. 'Men don't understand these things. When are you expecting it?'

'Next March! Oh, Mother, I wish you were here.'

'You know I can't come over, sweetheart.'

Of course Dione knew. Jeannie would never set foot anywhere near Yannis.

'But you could come home nearer the time and have your baby here,' suggested her mother hesitantly.

'I'd love that,' breathed Dione, 'but I don't think Theo would be too keen on the idea.'

'Of course not,' said Jeannie at once. 'He'll want to be with you. He'll book you into the best maternity hospital and he'll hover over you like a protective butterfly. He loves you very much, Dione.'

It helped that her mother did think Theo was good for her because how could she tell her that the very thought of being tied to him for the rest of her life terrified her? How could she explain her fears that he might snatch the baby from her if she went against his wishes? It would be like a re-run of her mother's torture and she wouldn't wish that on her child for anything. She knew only too well the pain and distress it caused, the nightmares that never completely went away.

She still didn't know whether Theo would expect her to remain married to him permanently. It was something they hadn't yet discussed, and her hormones were too irrational at this moment to even think about it.

They chatted for a while longer and after she'd hung up Dione wandered around the villa like a lost soul. She couldn't drum up any excitement for this new life inside her. Any normal mother would have been making plans and preparations and sharing her excitement with whoever cared to listen.

By the time Theo came home that evening she had worked herself up into such a state that he took one look at her and asked whether she was feeling ill.

'What do you think?' she snapped. 'How would you feel in my position?' She'd been pacing the room, not looking forward to him coming home, wishing herself anywhere but here.

'I think,' he said quietly, taking her shoulders and forcing her to sit down, 'that you should try to relax. I know neither of us is happy with what's happened, but it's done and there's no going back. If you want your baby to be happy and contented then that's what you need to be too.'

'And how would you know?' she demanded with a flash of her lovely dark eyes.

In answer he took the seat beside her, and a deep sadness came over his face. 'There's something I need to tell you.'

Immediately Dione knew what he was going to say and guilt flooded her because she had spoken without thinking.

'Katina and I had a son.'

He didn't look at her as he spoke, for which she was thankful because she didn't want to give away the fact that she already knew.

'Our marriage was a mistake from the start. We never stopped arguing; we each had different aims in life.

Katina's was to play the bored housewife but the perfect partygoer. And that didn't suit my lifestyle. I'm a workaholic, as you've probably gathered, and when I come home I need to relax. Not so Katina. She's a night person. We were totally unsuited and were on the verge of splitting up when she became pregnant.'

Theo's hands were locked between his knees and he rocked ever so slightly backwards and forwards as memories returned. Dione kept as quiet as the proverbial church mouse. This was a side of Theo she hadn't seen before—deeply disturbed and retrospective.

She was almost tempted to put her hand over his but then thought better of it. He was best left alone until he had told her the whole story.

'Katina wasn't too happy at the thought of becoming a mother; she felt it would destroy her hedonistic lifestyle. But I thought it might help save our marriage and was delighted. Nikos was born and for a few months Katina seemed to settle down and be happy. But gradually her desire to party overtook her again.

Theo sprang to his feet and crossed over to the window. The sky had turned purple with faint streaks of scarlet reflected from the sun that had gone down only moments earlier. It was one of the most beautiful and dramatic skies Dione had ever seen. But she knew that Theo was blind to it. In his mind's eye he was seeing only the destruction of his son and his marriage.

Again she wanted to comfort him, but again she knew it was too soon. She waited with bated breath for him to continue.

'One night I was called out to a work-related problem. It was unfortunate that it was Nikos' nanny's night off. Katina had been planning to go out to some friend's birthday bash, and was far from pleased when there was no one to look after Nikos. She didn't trust our housekeeper and so took him with her. All this was without my knowledge, you understand?'

He spun to face her, and Dione drew in a swift breath when she saw the sheer hell in his eyes. But still she remained silent.

'Katina ran her car off the road, braked for a dog or some night animal. She got away with a few scratches and a broken arm, but Nikos was killed.'

Dione drew in a deeply horrified breath, appalled at what she was hearing, and instinctively she jumped up and ran across to Theo. He was blinded by tears and she wrapped her arms around him. 'I'm so sorry, so very sorry,' she said, and there were tears in her eyes too.

For several minutes they stood locked in each other's arms, tears freely flowing, thoughts spinning, until Theo finally pulled away. 'That was seven years ago, and there hasn't been a day gone by when I haven't thought about him.'

'I can understand that,' said Dione softly.

'Katina and I divorced pretty quickly afterwards. She's still single and childless and a proper party animal. We would never have worked. You can see why I was angry that day she came to see you.'

Dione swallowed hard and nodded.

'There have been occasions when she's tried to get back with me, though lord knows why—probably because her money's running out. I settled a pretty hefty sum on her after the divorce and if she's spent it it's her bad luck. She doesn't have a job; she likes to think of herself as a lady of leisure.'

He shook his head as if to clear it of all bad thoughts. 'I'm sorry; I didn't mean to burden you with any of this.'

'I'm glad you've told me,' she said with a quiet smile.

'Nikos would have been seven and a half by now. His birthday's the day before Christmas.' He was speaking more or less to himself, a faint smile curving his lips.

Dione would like to bet that Theo had pictured his son over the years growing into an intelligent young boy, full of mischief and questions, and maybe the very image of his father. It was a dreadful thing to have happened and she couldn't even begin to imagine how she would feel under the same circumstances. Katina had mentioned her son briefly but hadn't shown any signs of grief like Theo, which Dione found truly remarkable.

A long silence followed during which they were both busy with their own thoughts. Then, seeming to throw off the mantle of melancholy that had enveloped him, Theo took Dione gently into his arms. 'How would you like to help me forget for a few hours?'

How could she refuse? With hands linked they went up to their bedroom and then began the sweetest, most tender assault on her senses that Dione had experienced since meeting Theo. She had expected him to be driven, to take her instantly and fiercely in order to fight his inner demons—and she'd been ready for him. Shattering excitement was what their marriage was all about.

Instead he took the utmost satisfaction in undressing her slowly, kissing each inch of bare flesh as it was exposed. Dione had never been treated to such exquisite pleasures before; had never dreamt that such light kisses could be such torture. She wanted more and she wanted it quickly, but when she reached out to hold him closer he tapped her on the nose.

'Patience, my love,' he said with a soft, mysterious smile.

And so she was forced to stand there until she was completely naked, having suffered the torment of breasts and nipples being sucked into his mouth, of her stomach being smothered with kisses, and as he inched lower and lower so grew her desire.

When finally he knelt before her and his tongue and lips explored and tasted her most private of places, she threw back her head and mewed like a kitten.

She wanted to lie down on the bed She wanted to spread herself wide for him. She wanted him to enter her and make love in such a way that only Theo knew how.

But he was not ready for that yet. He looked up and saw the drugged pleasure in her eyes and with a satisfied smile he pushed himself to his feet. For a second, when he moved away from her, Dione thought that he was going to leave her like that and her whole being screamed out for release.

Instead he said in a voice little more than a hoarse whisper, 'My turn now.'

Dione had never had the pleasure of undressing Theo before; always he'd been so impatient that he tore his clothes off himself. Now, with nervous fingers, she undid the buttons on his shirt, kissing, as he had done, each exposed area of tanned and warm and incredibly potent flesh.

Always, every day, she was aware of the fresh masculine smell of him but never more so than at this moment. As she tasted and touched and inhaled she felt every part of her being sing with excitement. It took an age for her to undo his shirt buttons because her fingers trembled so much.

It was a whole new experience and when finally she slipped it back off his shoulders and the whole of his naked chest was exposed to her greedy eyes she did what he had done to her. She sucked his hard male nipples into her mouth, exulting when she felt his rise of pleasure, when she heard him groan with undisguised anguish, when his fingers gripped her shoulders so hard that they hurt.

She attacked his trousers next, again a totally new experience, and when she had difficulty undoing the waistband he impatiently did it for her. She slid the zip down with deliberate slowness; suddenly beginning to enjoy this game, she enjoyed seeing Theo writhe.

He had tormented her until she'd felt that she was going out of her mind, and now it was her pleasure to do the same to him. She waited until he had stepped out of his trousers and underpants before she touched and kissed and reverently stroked the object of her desire.

Long minutes passed before she tentatively took him into her mouth and if her own desperate need was anything to go by Theo should be almost dying with painful hunger.

When he stopped her, when he groaned and pulled sharply away, Dione knew that he had been on the verge of no return. Neither of them spoke, each aware of the other's need, aware of their own need, and this beautiful, slow seduction of senses.

Their eyes met and by mutual silent consent they fell onto the bed, and here Theo became the master again, entering her slowly, making love slowly, his eyes never leaving hers. Somehow he managed to save himself until he saw the telling reflex in her eyes, when he felt the tensing in her body as she was about to explode, and then, and only then, did he let his own feelings ride free.

Each time they made love was better than the last, but this surpassed everything. Dione thought that she was going to faint as she lay there fighting for breath and crying out Theo's name.

Theo too fought long and hard for control and when finally he moved from her, when he lay on his back, one arm stretched across her, the other hanging over the edge of the bed, she knew what it meant for them both to be truly happy.

Of course, it was going to be an infinitesimal moment in the time span of life, but here, together, there was no future, there was no past, it was just the here and now, and the ultimate release of emotions.

It had been hard telling Dione about Nikos, and he'd hated the fact that he'd broken down in front of her. But now, lying here spent, aware of her gorgeous body next to his, Theo felt his unhappiness over Nikos' death had been put back into that special place in his heart and safely locked away.

How she'd managed to arouse him so erotically, and how he'd hung on so long, he had no idea. Considering Dione had been a virgin when he met her, she had considerable flair. She was like a witch, weaving her magic; knowing instinctively how to turn him on.

And she did it so beautifully. He was lying here spent now but he knew that in a very short space of time he would be ready to start again. He turned his head and smiled lazily at her. She looked radiant, her skin soft and flushed, her lovely dark eyes luminous. 'You're incredible, do you know that?'

Dione gave a Mona Lisa smile, contained and mysterious. 'I did what came naturally.'

He turned onto his side so that he could look at her more easily, smoothing his fingertips over her breasts, feeling the hot moistness of her skin; the rise and fall of breathing that had not yet steadied. 'A natural siren. Aren't I a lucky man?'

Dione remained silent and he guessed that she didn't feel herself so lucky. And who could blame her? He trailed his hand over her stomach, quite flat at this moment, but inside was his baby.

He met her eyes and knew that she was thinking the same and in an instant he had sprung from the bed, guilt settling over him like a devil's cloak. How could he enjoy himself in her body ever again with such a heavy weight to carry?

In the days that followed Theo did his best to keep a distance between himself and Dione, but it was difficult if not impossible. She affected his senses to such an extent that there were times when he could not keep away from her. And she never stopped him when he wanted to make love; in fact, her need was often as strong as his.

It was the only thing they had in common, this hunger for each other's bodies. A crazy situation when looked at in the cold light of day, but a heady one when experienced in the velvet darkness of the night.

He knew that he had a liability towards this child, and he had no intention of shirking it, but he'd been haunted over the years by Nikos' death and, try as he might, he could not shake the thought from his mind that it could happen again to this as yet unborn child. It was an irrational fear, perhaps, but not one he could ignore. He shared his thoughts with no one, not even his mother and father.

'Theo, we've had an invite from your parents.'

'You didn't accept?' He had just come in from an exhausting day at the office and a further meeting with the police. They had indisputable proof now that his ex-employee was the hacker, and he'd been charged and was due to appear in front of the magistrate for sentencing in a few days' time.

'I said you'd ring them. They want us to go for dinner on Saturday night.'

Relief showed on his face. 'I thought you meant for tonight, and I couldn't face going out again.' He was mentally weary and wanted nothing more than a peaceful evening at home, perhaps burying himself in Dione's body! It was a pleasure that always made him feel better.

'Dione, it's good to see you again.' Theo's mother, stately in black, her greying hair fixed in a bun at her nape, beamed her pleasure as she led them through to the sheltered garden at the back of their villa. 'I thought we'd sit outside for a while now that some of the heat's gone out of the day.'

It was a much smaller house than Theo's and furnished in a very homely style. Dione felt instantly at ease. A sprinkler kept the lawn green and flowers nodded their lazy heads whenever droplets caught them. It was serene and cool and even Theo stretched out his legs and looked relaxed.

There had been days recently when he looked anything but. Whether it was the court case that bothered him or their own difficult circumstances Dione couldn't be sure. Maybe both! She'd forgotten about the hacker but it had naturally affected Theo and the running of his business affairs. She felt a bit guilty for not asking him how things were.

Theo's father, an older version of Theo himself, poured them drinks and once they were settled his mother looked directly at Dione. 'Tell me how things are going. It's very naughty of Theo not to have brought you to see us before now, but I know how busy he is. It shouldn't stop you coming, though, Dione. You're welcome at any time.'

'Thank you,' she murmured. It was true; apart from a few brief words at the wedding she'd seen nothing of Theo's parents, and he had warned her on their drive over that he hadn't yet told them that she was pregnant. 'Plenty of time for that,' he had said.

In other words, he didn't want her to blurt it out. He needn't have worried; she was doing her very best to forget that she was pregnant. Not that it was easy with morning sickness, but other than that she had never felt better.

'Have you settled into your new home?'

Dione nodded. 'I have; it's very beautiful.'

'I expect your parents are missing you. You did live at home?'

Again Dione inclined her head.

'And I believe your father has been ill. How is he now, poor man? I've eaten at his restaurants. Very good food.'

'He's doing well, thank you. He's over the worst. He's left hospital now.'

'That is good. Give him my best wishes. Theo, he has

not told us very much about you at all. Do you have any brothers or sisters?'

Dione didn't like being given the third degree and she glanced at Theo to see whether he would rescue her. But he was deep in conversation with his father and seemed not to notice. 'I'm an only child,' she answered.

'Such a pity!' consoled the older woman. 'Theo and Alexandra were excellent company for each other. There is only thirteen months between them. Didn't your mother want any more?'

Dione sucked in a breath and answered as evenly as she could, 'Yannis divorced my mother. She lives in England and has never remarried. And my stepmother's never had any children.' And please, she prayed, don't ask me any more personal questions. But it was not to be.

'That is so sad.' Mrs Tsardikos leaned forward and took Dione's hands into hers. 'How old were you when your parents divorced?'

Finally Dione caught Theo's eye and he came to her rescue. 'You ask too many questions, Mother. Why don't you tell Dione about your poetry? I'm sure she'd love to read some.'

Her attention distracted, Mrs Tsardikos released Dione's hands. 'Would you really?' And her pale eyes lit up with pleasure.

Dione nodded. Anything to distract her temporary mother-in-law from this invasion of her privacy!

Smiling happily, the woman hurried indoors.

'You'll have to excuse my wife,' said Theo's father. 'She has a very inquisitive nature. Drink up and I'll pour you another—you'll need it before the night's out. Once Helena gets going there's no stopping her.'

'Dione doesn't drink alcohol,' Theo informed him. 'I'm sorry, I forgot to tell you.'

'Dear me,' muttered the older man. 'And here was I, thinking she did not like it. So what would you like? Fruit juice? Mineral water?'

'Just water, please,' answered Dione, and when Theo's father disappeared too she looked at Theo crossly. 'Why didn't you warn me about your mother? I think she wants to know my whole family history.'

Theo grinned. 'She's just curious, that's all. There's no harm in her. But poetry's her pet hobby so you'll be asked no more questions, except perhaps whether you like it or not. I have to admit it's not to my taste.'

'And what if it's not to mine? Do I tell her?'

Theo shrugged and spread his hands. 'That's up to you.'

In other words, on her head be it.

But Dione got through the next half-hour quite happily. Fortunately she liked Helena's poetry: it was rich and thought-provoking; all about life. And it was easier to see now why she asked such a lot of questions. She knew so much about people, what made them act the way they did, their sorrows and happiness, their beliefs and opinions.

'Have you ever thought about getting them published?' she asked. They were written in a hard-backed book in the most beautiful handwriting and Dione could just see them in print, with perhaps telling illustrations beside each one.

'Nonsense, child; they're not good enough for that. I think it's time we had dinner. Let's go indoors.' And her poetry was dismissed.

It was a long, leisurely meal with an assortment of both meat and fish dishes that left the tastebuds bursting. After dessert, an out-of-this-world strawberry flan, Theo's father suggested they take their coffee outside. He loved his garden and was never happier than when he was working in it or talking about it.

When Dione made to follow Helena placed a hand on her arm and held her back until the men were out of earshot. 'There's something I must ask you, child. Why have you not told me that you're pregnant?'

CHAPTER THIRTEEN

DIONE'S eyes snapped wide and her heart ran amok. How had Helena found out about the baby? Had Theo told her after all?

'It's all right, child, Theo hasn't said anything,' reassured her mother-in-law, reading her thoughts. 'But I'm a woman; I know these things. It should be a happy time for you, but Theo, he is not so happy?'

Dione's fine brows drew together. How had his mother guessed? Surely she didn't know the circumstances of their marriage? Her face suddenly went bright red. If Theo had told her she would…

'I'm right, aren't I?' interjected the older woman quickly. 'He's not happy. And I will tell you why. It is because of little Nikos. My son, he doesn't say much to me; in fact, he doesn't speak about it at all, much to my sadness. But it broke his heart when Nikos died.' And then she clapped a hand to her mouth, her pale eyes suddenly horrified. 'You do know about him?'

'Yes, Theo told me,' acknowledged Dione with a nod.

A look of relief crossed Helena's face. 'He would never forgive me if I said something out of place. You see, I truly thought my Theo would have no more children. He idolised that boy and no one can ever replace him.' She lifted her hands and shook them in the air in desperation. 'I think he is wrong; I think this child you are carrying will be good for him. But you must be patient, Dione, if he does not at first seem happy.'

If only she knew the real reason for Theo's displeasure, thought Dione, but she smiled wanly. 'I'm sure you're right.'

'I'm glad we have had this talk,' said Helena. 'It will be our little secret for a while, until Theo himself sees fit to tell me.'

When they joined the men Theo looked at Dione with a questioning lift of a brow, but she smiled and began chatting normally as though nothing out of the ordinary had happened. A few minutes later Alexandra turned up. Her mother berated her daughter for not saying she was coming. 'You could have joined us for dinner.'

But Theo's sister shrugged it off. 'I didn't know you were having a party.'

And not long afterwards Theo announced that it was time for them to leave.

'Come again, Dione, any time,' said his mother, hugging her warmly. 'Don't wait for Theo to bring you.'

On their way home Theo asked her what his mother had been talking about after dinner. 'I saw her detain you.'

'Nothing much,' insisted Dione, not wishing to break his mother's confidence.

'I want to know,' he declared fiercely. 'I want no secrets.'

Dione sighed and knew that she'd get no peace until she had told him. 'Ok, but you're not to tell her that you know. She guessed about the baby.'

'What?' Disbelief flooded his face. 'How?'

Dione lifted her shoulders. 'Female intuition, I guess.'

'Damn!'

'Does it really matter?' she questioned. 'As soon as I begin to show it will be common knowledge.'

'I wished to choose my own time,' he answered. 'And it certainly wasn't now.'

Dione wasn't sure why but one look at his thunderous face and she knew she dared not ask.

Depending on his mood of the day Dione sometimes slept in her own bed, sometimes in Theo's. Tonight, when they got home, she went straight to her own room. She had no idea why the fact that his mother knew about the baby should upset him so much. Admittedly he didn't want this child, but the deed was done, there was no going back, so why keep it a big secret?

She woke on Sunday morning and Theo's housekeeper told her that he was out, presumably gone to his office, and that he'd left even before she had arisen.

It was something he did occasionally—his mother had told her that it had been a regular thing after his divorce. And now he was unhappy again and wanted to immerse himself in work! Was that it? Not that it was her fault his mother had found out. If he was mad with anyone it should have been his parent.

By mid-morning Dione was feeling well enough to work up an anger against him, and on an impulse she asked his driver to take her to his office. Theo had made sure from the outset that there was always a car and driver at her disposal. The fact that she had her own car seemed not to matter to him, and it sat idly in the garage, probably dying a silent death, wondering why on earth she had abandoned it.

Maybe she was wrong, maybe he had a lot to do, but for once she didn't feel like sitting at home twiddling her thumbs. This marriage had been Theo's idea and he couldn't shirk his responsibilities when something happened that he didn't like.

The office block was in the centre of Athens' business quarter, a magnificent marble building that told the world that this was a truly successful company. Heavy plate-glass doors and a thickset man in uniform guarded its entrance.

'I've come to see my husband,' Dione told him when he looked at her with suspicion. 'Mr Theo Tsardikos.'

The man frowned. 'Mr Tsardikos isn't in today.'

'Yes, he is,' insisted Dione.

'I've not seen him. Just one moment.' And he spoke into an internal phone. 'No, he's not here. I'm sorry if you've had a wasted journey, Mrs Tsardikos.' And then he smiled for the first time. 'I'm pleased to meet you. I've heard talk about the new Mrs Tsardikos. You're even more beautiful than people say.'

'Thank you,' she acknowledged, but too annoyed with Theo to be really pleased. 'Is there anywhere else he's likely to be? I know it's business that called him away.'

'You could try the hotel. He's sometimes there on a Sunday.'

The Tsardikos was one of Athens' premium hotels; royalty and the insanely rich stayed there and Dione had never even put a foot inside the place before. Now, as her driver dropped her off, she craned her neck to look at the towering building. Impressive didn't even begin to describe it and she felt distinctly overwhelmed as she was ushered inside.

It was all marble and mirrors and silent-footed staff and before she'd even reached the reception desk Dione caught sight of Theo coming down a flight of stairs with a stunning redhead on his arm. They were laughing into each other's face and looked completely at ease with one another.

Her stomach bunched into a tight knot and she felt sick; not with her morning sickness but something entirely different. Jealousy! In that instant it hit her. She was beginning to fall in love with Theo!

The shocking discovery stuck in her throat like a fishbone. This was the last thing she had expected or even wanted. Considering their marriage was nothing more than a sham, Theo was free to see other women. Wasn't he? It was amazing how much the thought hurt.

She walked across to him and the shock on his face was something that would stay with her for a long time.

'Dione!' he exclaimed, hurrying forward. 'Is something wrong?'

'No,' she answered as pleasantly as she was able under the circumstances. 'I needed to get out, that's all.'

To her surprise he looked pleased. 'I'm glad you did. Let me introduce you to Belinda, my PA.'

Belinda stepped forward and held out her hand. 'You're Theo's wife? I'm pleased to meet you at last.'

Her handshake was warm and her eyes were friendly but Dione held back. 'I didn't realise that he got you working on a Sunday as well.'

'I work whenever Theo wants me,' answered the redhead, with a warm smile in Theo's direction.

'Belinda's been with me for many years,' Theo informed her. 'She's half-English, like yourself, and I don't know what I'd do without her.'

'Lucky you,' said Dione, managing a faint smile. 'How did you know where to find me?'

'Your office doorman,' she answered. 'He obviously knows your movements better than I do.'

'Well, my work here's finished,' Theo declared. 'Belinda and I were both about to head home. Come, let us go,' and he put a hand beneath her elbow. 'I'll see you in the morning, Belinda.'

Once she had gone his grip on Dione's arm tightened. 'What do you hope to achieve by chasing after me like this?'

'I wasn't chasing,' she answered evenly. 'I was just fed up of being on my own. I'm sorry if I intruded.'

His eyes went rock-hard. 'I don't know what you're talking about.'

'It doesn't matter,' Dione answered quietly.

Theo's lips compressed until they were no more than a thin straight line. 'Am I right in thinking that you suspect there's something going on between Belinda and me?'

'Of course not!' But even to her own ears her words didn't ring true.

'You're wrong, you know. It's your hormones all out of kilter.'

'There's nothing wrong with my hormones,' she said evenly, not wanting to argue with Theo. She knew what she had seen and now all she wanted to do was go home.

'Believe me, I know. It is your hormones,' he rasped.

And he should know because he'd gone through it all before. That was what she expected him to tell her but he didn't. He dismissed Dione's car and driver and jumped into his own, which had glided to a halt outside the doors the instant he set his foot out.

But Dione didn't marvel at the slick organisation, she was too upset, too hurt by her own startling discovery. How it could have happened she had no idea. Falling in love with a man like Theo was a fatal mistake.

When they arrived home the first thing Theo did was pour himself a drink, the second was to stand staring out of the window while he presumably got his thoughts into some sort of order, and the third was to tower over Dione where she had slumped into an easy chair.

'So you think I'm having an affair?' Harsh, condemning lines scored his face and hardened his eyes. 'You think that I'm carrying on with my PA?' The words slammed into her like bullets from a gun. 'Do you really believe that I'd do such a thing while I'm married to you?'

'Ours isn't a proper marriage,' she reminded him quietly. 'You're free to carry on as many affairs as you like.' It hurt to say that but it was the truth whether she liked it or not.

'Even so,' he answered, 'I have principles. And more especially since you're carrying my baby.'

'*Your* baby!' queried Dione. 'I hope you're not trying to say that I'll have no part to play in bringing the child up?' She had thought about this over and over again, but hadn't actually made a decision—until now! She couldn't afford to risk that at some time in their future he would take their child from her. She needed it to be sorted from the very beginning.

In answer Theo took her by the shoulders and would have shaken her, she felt sure, if he hadn't had second thoughts about her condition. 'I'll ignore that remark, Dione, put it down to your hormonal changes.'

'What is it with you and hormones?' she asked. 'It was your hormones that got us into this mess in the first place.'

Their eyes met and held and Dione refused to back down so it was Theo who eventually moved. His fingers curled into his palms, his huge body taut as he stood looking down at her, and his eyes were so hard and black that they looked like time bombs about to explode.

Impatiently he swung away and picked up his glass, tossing the contents down his throat before crossing the room and pouring another, which went exactly the same way.

'I have no wish to argue with you, Dione,' he announced tersely.

'Nor do I,' she answered. 'Does Belinda know about the circumstances of our marriage?'

Theo's top lip curled in a snarl. 'What the hell do you take me for?'

There was something dangerously exciting about Theo in this mood and Dione shifted uncomfortably. 'I've not known you long enough to know what you're really like.' Except that he was beginning to get beneath her skin far more devastatingly than she had expected or even wanted.

'I have not told Belinda, I have not told anyone,' he announced harshly, 'and I hope the same can be said for you.'

'Naturally.'

He swung away again, his rage ebbing and flowing like the ocean that lapped down below them. 'This conversation is getting us nowhere, Dione. I'm going for a swim before lunch.' And with that he marched out of the room.

Dione exhaled slowly and closed her eyes. The morning's ordeal had taken a lot out of her. She felt drained of all energy and emotions. It would be comforting to have Theo's arms around her but she knew that she dared not sleep with him any more, or even let him kiss her, otherwise she would be in great danger of giving herself away.

She picked at her lunch and then, declaring that she was tired, took herself to her room and lay down. Theo did not come after her. She had half expected him to but was not entirely surprised that he didn't. The atmosphere over lunch, which Anna had set out in the shade by the pool, had been thick enough to cut with a knife.

Later, after her scanty meal had gone down, Dione felt it was her turn to swim. She used the pool often when Theo was at work but not very often did they swim together. Now she swam long, lazy lengths alone, the water silken and cool against her skin, and gradually some of the tension eased out of her.

Until suddenly she became aware of someone swimming at her side! She tried to ignore him but Theo was a larger-than-life person and could not be easily dismissed. 'Are you feeling better?' he asked as they reached the end and paused a moment before embarking on another length.

'I'm OK,' she acknowledged softly.

And that was the full length of their conversation. They simply swam up and down the pool, never hurrying, Theo keeping pace with her. The sun blazed down out of a cloudless sky but the water remained mercifully cool and when she'd finally had enough and hauled herself out Theo continued to swim.

Dione watched until her eyes grew heavy and she fell asleep. The next thing she knew Theo was sitting on a chair next to her, watching her through narrowed lids, and she grew uncomfortably warm, wondering how long he had been there.

And suddenly, as she looked down at herself, Dione realised that her stomach was no longer as flat as it had been. It wasn't rounded, but usually when she lay on her back it was hollow—and now it wasn't.

And it was this part of her that Theo was looking at.

With her clothes on it was indiscernible and she hadn't really been aware of it herself—until she followed Theo's gaze. Even her breasts seemed bigger and she grew hot again at the thought of what was happening to her body.

When he realised she was awake Theo got abruptly to his feet. On a table was a jug of iced water and a plate of biscuits. 'You ate hardly anything at lunch time,' he said, filling a glass and handing it to her.

But although Dione drank the water she declined a biscuit. 'I'm not hungry.'

'Even after all that swimming?'

'Yes.'

'It's not good for you to miss your meals. You have two to think about now.'

As if she didn't know it. Unconsciously Dione put her hand on her stomach.

'And this little fellow,' said Theo, placing his hands over hers, 'needs all the nourishment he can get.'

Having him touch her like this was very personal and Dione shifted uneasily. Theo in a bad mood she could handle, but in the light of her new-found feelings it was a different matter altogether.

She moved his hand away. 'Please don't touch me like that.' And she ignored the fact that little quivers of pleasure had begun to run through her.

Dark brows rose. 'You're still annoyed with me?'

'I have no feelings one way or the other,' she told him with an insouciant lift of her shoulders.

Theo frowned. 'In that case it might be best if I left you alone. Do as you like, Dione. Think what you like. But bear in mind that our contract isn't over yet.' With that he spun on his heel and headed indoors.

And the next morning his anger hadn't abated. He came into her room before she had got up, dressed in his suit, ready to go out. And the heavy lines on his face told her that he wasn't here to ask how she was.

'I have to go to Canada on a business trip,' he announced abruptly. 'And I don't know when I'll be back.'

CHAPTER FOURTEEN

DIONE stared at Theo as though he had just told her that he was going to jump off the edge of the planet.

'Don't worry; you'll be well looked after. And probably a whole lot happier with me out of the way,' he added harshly.

Maybe, maybe not! She didn't fancy being cooped up here in this fancy house with no one to talk to. Without a doubt she was going to miss him.

'And don't even think about leaving,' he added shortly when he saw the mixed emotions on her face. 'You're mine—don't ever forget it.'

If they hadn't had their argument yesterday Dione wondered whether he would have asked her to accompany him. She would have liked that. Canada was a place she had often thought she'd like to visit. Vancouver. Ontario. The Niagara Falls. But clearly he didn't want her with him.

Was he taking Belinda? she wondered as he turned and left the room. Would he have someone to keep him warm in bed at night? The very thought sent a stream of jealousy through her stomach. She would be lying here alone and he would be…

Later that morning Dione phoned her mother. 'Theo's gone away for a few days,' she told her. She was missing him already. Not that he was ever around during the day, but she'd got used to him coming home at night and they would sit and talk about all and sundry, sometimes his work, sometimes world affairs, sometimes his parents. They were usually comfortable in each other's company.

And of course often they made love. They had been the best times of all. This was what she was going to miss. She had to accept the fact that she was not the only woman in his life.

His marriage to her was nothing more than a convenient arrangement and she ought to be used to the idea. If it hadn't been for the life growing inside her she might have been. One unfortunate mistake had ruined everything. Actually, two mistakes. The second was discovering she had feelings for him.

'And it's business and he couldn't take you with him,' said her mother, understanding the situation instantly. 'Why don't you come home? I'd love to see you again.'

'I'd like to do that, Mother, but I feel my place is here. I'm settled now; I'm quite happy.'

'Of course you are. Is everything all right with the baby?'

'Perfect.'

'How's Yannis?'

'He's good; he's out of hospital.'

They spoke a few minutes more, and then Dione let her mother go. She supposed she ought to visit her father. Speaking about him had made her feel guilty. She didn't go as often as she ought these days. Even so, she had no intention of telling him about the baby. Yannis would be delighted; he would see it as a way of cementing their relationship permanently.

You can't do better than to marry a nice Greek man! His words haunted her; it had been his mantra ever since she was of marriageable age. Dione shook her head in despair. She would leave it until another day to pay him a visit. In the mood she was in now she might say something she'd be sorry for.

But the next day she regretted that she hadn't been to see him.

'Dione!' It was Phrosini's urgent voice on the phone. 'Your father's in hospital again. He's had another heart attack.'

Dione drew in a swift breath, her heart dipping. 'I'll be right there.'

When she got to the hospital they wouldn't let her see her father. Phrosini was outside his room, wringing her hands, and when she saw Dione she burst into tears. Dione hugged her stepmother and tried to console her. 'He'll be all right, you'll see. My father's a fighter if nothing else.'

But two hours later Yannis died.

Phrosini was beside herself and Dione was upset as well. No matter what she had thought about Yannis, he was her father, her own flesh and blood; he had created her the same as Theo had created the life form inside her own body. There was a bond that nothing could break; not hatred, not anger, not resentment. Nothing!

They sat in an ante-room consoling each other, and it was a long time before either of them felt strong enough to go home. It was sad to think that Yannis would never again be a part of their lives.

'Come home with me,' urged Phrosini. 'I can't be on my own right now.'

From there Dione rang her mother and Jeannie was truly shocked when she heard the news. 'I thought he was getting better?'

'So did I. I guess he's been under more strain than any of us realised.' And at least her mother was free of him now. She might not have seen him for almost twenty years but she'd always remained afraid of him; had never wanted to do anything that might rock the boat and keep her from seeing her darling Dione ever again.

'And how are you, Dione? This isn't going to be too much for you, in your condition?'

'I'm pregnant, Mother, not ill,' she answered, trying to inject a touch of humour into her voice. Not easy at a time like this.

'You will let me know when the funeral is? I'd like to send some flowers.'

'Of course,' answered Dione. 'Will you be OK, Mother?' For the first time she wanted her mother to have company.

'I'll be fine, Dione, don't worry,' Jeannie informed her. 'If you're thinking I shouldn't be on my own then don't. I'll be all right.'

Next it was Theo's turn to be told the news and because she didn't know where he was staying Dione rang his office and was put through to Belinda. Which surprised her, as she'd half thought that his PA might have gone with him on his North American trip.

'Belinda,' she said without preamble, 'I need to get in touch with Theo and he forgot to leave me his hotel number.'

'Are you all right, Dione?' asked the redhead, concern in her voice. 'You sound upset.'

'I just want his number,' said Dione, not wishing to talk about her father's death.

'One moment.' Belinda's voice became efficient and as soon as she had the information she wanted Dione rang off.

It was several hours before she was able to get in touch with Theo. She could have rung his cellphone but she didn't have his number with her. But Dione knew that it wasn't that urgent. Theo didn't give a damn about her father. He would probably think it a good thing that he'd gone.

And then another thought struck her.

Unless Phrosini carried on Yannis' business it would be sold. Theo could have his money back. She would be free of him!

Amazingly the thought saddened her. In fact she felt quite tearful. She didn't want to be free of Theo, not any more. She wanted him to love her the way she was beginning to love him. Not that there was any chance of that.

'Dione, what's wrong? Belinda told me you'd be calling.'

Dione didn't appreciate the fact that the redhead had felt fit to inform him that his wife had been after his hotel number.

'She said you sounded upset. Are you ill? It's not the baby, is it?' he asked with sudden concern in his voice.

'As if you'd care,' she thrust with a sudden gush of anger. 'It would be a relief for you if I lost it, wouldn't it?' And then she wished she hadn't said that. It was cruel and unnecessary and she didn't really mean it.

There was a long silence at the other end and Dione knew that he was hanging on to his temper by a thin thread.

'I'm sorry,' she said. 'That was uncalled for.'

'So why did you want to speak to me?' His voice was hard and entirely devoid of emotion and Dione could see in her mind's eye the harsh planes of his face.

'It's my father,' she announced in a voice scarcely above a whisper now. 'He—he had another heart attack. He died this morning.' And telling Theo like this made it a stone-cold fact.

Up until now she had not really taken in the fact that Yannis was no longer with them. It would leave a great big hole in her life, in all the lives of those he had touched—especially Phrosini, who had loved him unconditionally. And who even now had shut herself in her room. She had cried until she could cry no more. Whereas Dione had not shed a single tear!

She didn't feel guilty. She was sorry her father had died, of course she was, but he had hurt her so much over the years that tears refused to come.

'Dione! I'm so sorry,' said Theo, his voice reverent and hushed now.

But she knew that he wasn't. He'd had no time for Yannis and hadn't been afraid to show it.

'Is there anything I can do?'

'No,' she said quickly and firmly. 'Phrosini and I will take care of things. I'm with her now. I'm staying here until after the funeral.'

'Of course! I'll come home as soon as I possibly can.' And after a slight pause, 'Dione—'

'Yes?'

'Are you all right? Really all right, I mean? In your condition it's—'

And that was all he cared about, her condition. 'I'm fine,' she said quietly. 'I don't need wrapping in cotton wool, Theo.' And she put down the phone.

Almost immediately she wished that she hadn't. She had heard the concern in his voice; he could be a great source of comfort to her—if she gave him the chance! She dropped her head in her hands. What was happening to her? Why was she behaving so badly?

Theo claimed it was her hormones. Perhaps he was right. Or perhaps it was because she was falling in love with him and dared not let him see it.

'Mother! What are you doing here?' It was the morning of the funeral and a taxi had just dropped Jeannie off at Dione's father's house. A surprisingly confident Jeannie with a different hairstyle and new clothes.

'I thought you might need me, my darling,' answered her mother. 'You don't think Phrosini will mind?'

'Of course not,' said Dione at once, but Phrosini had never met Jeannie and Dione couldn't be truly sure what her reaction would be. There had been no consoling her since her husband's death. Dione herself had had to make all the arrangements, and Phrosini was even at this very moment shut in a darkened room. Crying tears for her beloved Yannis when Dione had thought she could not possibly cry any more. 'I'll tell her you're here.'

Phrosini at once took Jeannie into her arms and both women cried.

'Where's Theo?' asked Jeannie finally.

'Still in Canada,' answered Dione quietly and sadly. 'He said he'd try to get away, but—'

'And he did,' said a deep voice over her shoulder.

Dione felt the hairs on the back of her neck prickle and she spun around. Theo, in a black suit and tie, stood sombrely in front of her. 'Theo—you didn't tell me you were coming today.'

It was a flat statement of fact, yet inside her, despite the ordeal that lay ahead, she felt her body react to Theo's innate sexuality in a way that it shouldn't on a day like this. Or on any other day for that matter!

'You didn't really think I would stay away?' asked Theo shortly once they were alone. 'Keristari might not have been my favourite person, but he was your father and I respect that. I'm here for you, Dione. It can't have been easy arranging the funeral; if I could have got away earlier I would have, but—'

'I don't need you,' Dione told him coolly. 'My mother's here for me.'

'Not for Yannis?'

'What do you think after the way he treated her? My mother's a different person these days. She made the journey alone and I really admire her for that.'

Theo couldn't even begin to describe the feelings that ate at his gut. At first, when Dione had appeared to be jealous of Belinda he'd felt surprisingly pleased, but now that she still showed no sign of even liking him he was at odds to know what his emotions were.

Yannis dying put a whole new complexion on things. Strictly speaking there was no reason now for Dione to remain tied to him. She had probably worked this out for herself! But in truth he didn't want to let her go. She was carrying his baby! And, although he was deeply fearful of bringing another child into the world, it didn't alter the way he felt about Dione.

Dione had grown on him in a way he hadn't expected. He got angry with her sometimes, deeply angry, but in many other ways she was a delight in his life. Spending time away had helped him get things into perspective, but to return home and find Dione still very much out of favour with him was like someone driving a stake into his heart.

After the funeral, with only Phrosini and Jeannie and Dione left, Theo took Dione to one side and asked her what she wanted to do. 'Are you coming home?' he asked gently.

Dione appeared to consider his suggestion, and then shook her head. 'Phrosini still needs me.'

He felt his temper begin to rise. 'Phrosini has your mother now.' He hoped it didn't show in his voice. This was no place for an argument. 'She's not leaving until tomorrow—I asked her. They've discovered a strange alliance. In fact I think Jeannie might stay even longer.'

'Do you know,' asked Dione, 'that this is the first time she's visited Greece?'

Theo inclined his head. 'She told me so. I imagine she's feeling relief. And I don't mean that in a nasty way, Dione,' he added when he saw her lips tighten. 'Yannis was her nemesis.'

'I know,' agreed Dione reluctantly. 'And I'm happy she's here.'

'So you will come home?'

'I'm not sure, Theo.'

Exasperated, Theo saw red. 'You will come, Dione. Your place is with me now.' He hadn't wanted to come down the high and mighty, but she was driving him insane. All the time he'd been in Canada he had wanted her in his bed. She had no idea how empty his hotel room had been.

He watched as Dione struggled with her emotions. She was so beautiful; he had almost forgotten how beautiful. He had never seen her in black before, except for her bikini, which didn't count. No, that was wrong. It did count. He adored seeing her long golden limbs and her amazingly slender body. Which was already changing shape!

Pregnancy suited her, gave her a glow that had been absent before—except perhaps when they made love! She looked stunning now, though. Elegant, almost regal as she stood in front of him with her chin held high and her gorgeous dark eyes blazing.

'Very well, I'll come,' she answered quietly, almost submissively. Which wasn't the usual Dione style, and he hated himself for pressurising her on today of all days. He knew he was being cruel but the truth was he needed her

But when they got home it didn't turn out as he'd hoped. Almost before they'd set foot through the door she turned on him. 'Don't think we can pick up where we left off, Theo. It's the last thing I want to do.'

'Of course,' he answered as evenly as he could. 'It's been a horrible day for you. All I want to do is hold and comfort you, to let you know that—' he had been about to say that he'd always be at her side. Where had that idea come from? Dione was showing him in no uncertain terms that he would never be a permanent fixture in her life '—that I care.'

'Care?' she echoed. 'I bet you didn't even think about me while you were in Canada. You probably even had female company. And then of course you have Belinda waiting for you when your wife turns you out of her bed.'

'In fact,' Dione went on before he could say anything, 'I can't think why I let you persuade me to come home. You and I no longer have anything in common. I'm not staying. I'm going back to my fa—to Phrosini's.' And so saying she spun on her heel and rushed out of the house.

For a few moments Theo didn't follow; he simply stood there in a state of shock. He hadn't expected her to flare up like this. Both the funeral and her pregnancy must be playing havoc with her nerves.

He must go after her, calm her down, make her see that he only had her best interests at heart. But before he could even do that he heard a cry and a crash—and the next moment silence!

CHAPTER FIFTEEN

THEO raced to the front door, his heartbeats quick and hard, coming to a shocked halt when he saw Dione lying motionless at the bottom of the steps that led on to the driveway. Instantly he was kneeling at her side, calling her name, not attempting to move her in case she had broken something.

When she didn't respond he yanked his cellphone out of his pocket and called for an ambulance. 'Quickly!' he barked. 'My wife's knocked herself out and she's pregnant.' And all the time his eyes were on her.

She was breathing, thank goodness, but there was a nasty cut on her forehead that was oozing blood. He stemmed it with his handkerchief and held it there until Dione stirred and lifted heavy lids to look at him. 'What—?'

'Shh!' He pressed a finger to her lips. 'Don't say anything; don't even try to move. There's an ambulance on its way.'

'I don't want—'

'Just a precaution,' he told her. 'Hopefully they'll send you home, but you need to be checked over. That was some fall you took.'

Dione closed her eyes and lay so still that he was fearful she'd passed out again.

'Theo!' It was no more than a husky whisper.

He bent forward and put his ear close to her lips. 'Yes?'

'Do you think I've harmed the baby?'

'Of course not,' he said reassuringly, though his thoughts had already run along similar lines. What if he lost this child the way he had lost Nikos? It didn't bear thinking about; it would be his biggest nightmare come true. He shivered, his body ice-cold, and it seemed an age before the ambulance arrived.

When it did he went with Dione and walked alongside the trolley as she was wheeled to the emergency room. But he was not permitted to stay while she was examined, and he paced the corridor like a caged animal.

It seemed an age before someone finally came to tell him that she would be all right. 'She's bruised her head badly and has a severe headache, and we're keeping her in for a few days just to make sure.'

'Is that necessary?' asked Theo with a sharp frown. 'If it's just her head then—'

'She *is* pregnant, Mr Tsardikos,' reminded the doctor. 'A fall like this could cause a miscarriage. She needs to rest. And I'm sure she wouldn't do that at home.'

'No, I expect you're right,' agreed Theo, but even so he wasn't happy. She'd just buried her father, for goodness' sake; she'd had enough of hospitals. 'I could look after her myself,' he said. 'Make sure she rests.'

'No, Mr Tsardikos.' The doctor held up her hand. 'She stays here. You can obviously visit whenever you like, even stay here if you prefer; there will be a room next to your wife's for family.'

'I'll stay,' agreed Theo at once. 'I'll go home and get some clothes and be back before you know it. Can I tell Dione?'

'I'm sorry, she really does need to rest.'

In the hours that followed Theo watched Dione as she slept, knowing that it was his fault she was here. If he hadn't insisted on her accompanying him home they would never have argued and this wouldn't have happened. Hell, why could he never control his temper? Dione had grown on him more than he'd ever expected and he knew that he was already halfway to falling in love with her. If anything should happen…

Finally, though, he fell into a fitful sleep and the next thing he knew she was calling his name.

'Dione!' he breathed thankfully. 'You're awake at last. How are you feeling?' She looked pale and lifeless and he was dreadfully worried.

'I want my mother.'

It was like a blow to his solar plexus. Nevertheless he didn't show that it hurt. He glanced at the clock on the wall instead. 'It's the middle of the night,' he said gently.

'I still want her.'

'Won't I do? Is there something you need?' he asked. 'I'm sure that—'

'Theo,' she insisted, 'I need my mother.' She said it very firmly and very loudly and her eyes were hard on his, telling him without words that she didn't want him sitting watching her.

'Very well,' he said on a sigh and with great reluctance. 'I'll go and fetch her.' He supposed it was natural that at a time like this she would want her mother. But it hurt that she was turning to someone else instead of him. He should be the one uppermost in her mind; he was her husband after all.

But in what way? asked an inner voice. Your marriage is nothing more than a sham. Dione doesn't love you; it was out of loyalty to her father that she married you. You'd best remember that.

He didn't want to remember, damn it. Dione meant a lot to him now and he wanted to look after her the same as any husband would.

When he arrived at her father's house it took a long while for him to make anyone hear, and when the door was finally opened it was Jeannie herself who stood there.

'Theo?' Her eyes widened with surprise. 'Is something wrong?'

He didn't waste time with apologies. 'Dione's had a fall…she's in hospital; she's asking for you. Get yourself dressed and I'll take you right now.'

Jeannie's face blanched. 'She is all right?'

He nodded.

'And the baby?'

'So far everything seems fine.'

'What do you mean?' she asked with a further frown.

'Apparently there's danger of a miscarriage, so she has to rest. They're keeping her in for a few days.'

'Thank goodness I'm here,' breathed Jeannie as she turned away. Belatedly she said, 'You'd better come in. I'll leave Phrosini a note. I don't want to wake her; she had trouble getting to sleep.'

But while Theo was waiting Phrosini herself came to see what was going on and Theo explained all over again what had happened. 'I'll keep you posted,' he said. 'I'm so sorry, Phrosini.'

But all was well and after three days Dione was allowed home and Jeannie reluctantly flew back to England. She had wanted to stay and help look after her daughter but Theo had persuaded her otherwise. He wanted to take care of Dione himself; he wanted to show her in every way possible how much he cared.

'You gave me a big scare,' said Theo once he'd settled Dione in a comfortable chair.

'I scared myself,' she admitted with a wry smile.

'But you are OK now?' She still looked pale and tired and he couldn't help worrying.

Dione nodded.

Theo sat down close to her and leaned forward. He wanted to take her hands and blurt out the fact that he had fallen in love with her, but he knew that he dared not. Not yet, at least. 'I have something to tell you,' he said, his heart thumping as painfully as if he were a teenager on his first date. He hadn't felt like this in a long time.

Dione looked at him expectantly.

'I never really wanted this baby of ours,' he began.

'I know that,' she retorted quickly.

'No, hear me out,' he insisted, 'I've not finished. I've always been afraid that I'd lose him the same as I did Nikos. Life is such a precarious thing. I couldn't have handled it. I'd rather have no children than fear losing another. At least that's what I thought.'

He had her full attention now and he swallowed hard before continuing. 'But when the nurse told me there could be a danger of you miscarrying I knew that if that happened I'd want to kill myself. I love that little life growing inside you. The same as I've grown to love you, Dione.' He twisted his lips wryly and looked at her with his heart in his eyes. 'Do you think you could ever learn to love me in return?'

He watched as Dione's eyes grew wide and round and then she turned her head away and he knew that he had lost her.

Theo's admittance didn't altogether surprise Dione. His vigil at her bedside had proved how much he cared. And even though she'd been afraid to let herself believe it she had felt his love radiating out to her.

Nevertheless she remained silent.

'You think I don't mean it?' he asked harshly. 'You're surely not still thinking that there's something going on between Belinda and me?'

'You looked so close,' she answered miserably.

Theo closed his eyes for a brief second and took a breath. 'Belinda has a boyfriend; they're getting engaged at Christmas. She's extremely happy. She's been with me for a long time and admittedly we have a strong rapport that is sometimes misread. But believe me she means nothing to me in the way you think.'

He turned her to face him, his hands hot on her shoulders, searing her skin, making her want to lean into him and feel his strong arms around her. 'And that's all there is to it.'

Dione gave a small sigh. 'I know there's nothing going on between you, really I do. I'm sorry for doubt-ing you.' But there was still something else troubling her. 'Would you love me if I wasn't pregnant, Theo?' she asked in low, hushed tones. She needed to be absolutely sure that his declaration of love wasn't simply for the baby's sake.

'Dione, I think I fell in love with you the day you

came to see me on your father's behalf,' answered Theo with a smile. 'You were unlike anyone else I'd ever met. You intrigued me and I knew I had to make you mine.'

'So you thought up that heinous plot?' she challenged, her eyes growing softer, but still she didn't let their bodies touch. She was teasing him now, wanting to see how long it was before he could contain himself no longer.

'You have to admit that it was a pretty good one.'

'So what happens now my father's died?' she challenged.

'The contract still stands,' he declared firmly. 'In fact, I'm thinking of increasing it to life. Could you bear that, Dione?'

In response she lifted her mouth to his, at the same time pressing the full length of her body against him. His arousal was swift and exciting, sending fresh waves of sensation through every inch of her being. The kiss, gentle at first, increased in passion with each second that passed, until finally Theo swung her into his arms and carried her up to bed.

'One thing, *agapi mou*, before I ravish you sense-less,' he growled, his fingers trailing sensual delights over her already naked body. 'I haven't heard you say yet that you love me.'

'Isn't it obvious?' she asked, her tone so husky that he had to bend his head to hear. Lying in her hospital bed, wondering whether she was going to lose her baby, had made her realise how precious life was, and how short. There wasn't time for arguments, for hiding feelings. It was the here and now that mattered.

'I love you, Theo.' And she rather liked the sound of it. 'I love you, I love you, I love you.'

Theo groaned and held her so tight that she thought she would break in two. And letting him make love to her after a period of hating him was more fulfilling than she could ever have imagined. He took her to the heavens and back and when finally he let her go, when they were both sated as only two lovers could be, she felt oddly bereft. She never, ever wanted Theo to move from her side. He was her life now.

She turned her head, looked at the man lying beside her and smiled. She hadn't realised that he was watching her through lazy lids.

'That was something, wasn't it?' he asked.

'Mmm!'

He kissed her long and hard and then looked into her eyes. 'I know I put pressure on you; I know you reluctantly married me and couldn't wait for our contract to end, but as I said before I knew from the moment I set eyes on you that you were destined to be my wife. One way or another I would have captured your heart.'

'It's an odd way of doing it,' she mused. 'Marrying first and falling in love second. What if we hadn't fallen in love, what if there had been no baby? Do you think we would have been able to walk away?'

'We'll never know,' said Theo.

But Dione did. She hadn't been aware of it at the time, it was only now that realisation dawned, but she too had fallen in love with Theo right from the word go. She'd used the pretext of marrying him for her father's sake, but deep down inside something must have told her that he was her destiny.

She smiled. 'No, Theo! We'll never know.'

EPILOGUE

'WHAT did you say, Mother?' Dione had phoned her mother every week since Yannis' death, but she'd had no inkling that anything had changed in Jeannie's life.

'I said I'm going to get married again.'

Dione held her hand over the receiver and turned to Theo where he sat cradling their baby. 'My mother's going to get married.'

He grinned and stuck his thumb up. And Dione had never seen him look more content. He adored their son and wasn't afraid to show it.

'You never said you had a boyfriend, Mother.'

'I was scared in case it didn't last. But I think I've finally shaken off your father's ghost and I'm ready to live my life again.'

'Good for you,' said Dione fervently. 'When am I going to meet this lucky man?'

'I thought we'd fly over for Easter. If that's OK with you?'

'It's more than OK,' cried Dione. 'Oh, Mother, I'm so happy for you.' There had been a time when her mother wouldn't set foot in Greece, but now she had become a regular visitor and Dione had never been happier.

And Phrosini too was getting on with her life. She had thrown herself with gusto into running Yannis' restaurant business and things were looking up at last.

'Isn't he the most beautiful baby you've ever seen?' Dione put down the phone and perched on the arm of Theo's chair, looking at her son adoringly. Leander looked just like his father and she was happier than ever.

'Naturally,' agreed Theo. 'Any baby of yours would be beautiful.'

He had become a doting father-to-be over the last few months, treating Dione like a princess, showing her in every way possible how much he loved her. And he seemed to have got over his paranoia about losing Nikos. He was already planning for their baby's future, and the future of those who were not yet even a twinkle in his eye. Dione could see that she'd have her time cut out looking after all of Theo's babies.

Not that it would be any real hardship. He'd already employed a nanny, much against Dione's wishes, and he was prepared to employ a whole army of helpers if it eased the load of his princess.

'You're wasting your money,' she protested time and time again, but he took no notice. He simply smiled and did whatever he wanted to do.

And when Leander was seven months old Dione found herself pregnant again.

'We really will have to stop doing this,' she said to Theo as they lay exhausted in each other's arms a few evenings later.

'Don't you enjoy making babies?' he asked with a wicked smile, stroking her hair back from her damp forehead.

Dione grinned. 'It's the best pastime I know.'

'Then I think we should carry on until we're too old to do it.'

Dione pretended to groan. 'I think that will be for ever, my darling.'

'Then so be it,' he said.

* * * * *

*A collection of three powerful,
intense romances featuring sexy,
wealthy Greek heroes*

The Greek Millionaires' Seduction
Available 16th April 2010

The Greek Tycoons' Takeover
Available 21st May 2010

The Greeks' Bought Brides
Available 18th June 2010

www.millsandboon.co.uk

Fill your summer with four volumes of red-hot Australians!

Convenient Possession
by Helen Bianchin

Available 4th June 2010

Billionaires' Marriages
by Emma Darcy

Available 2nd July 2010

Ruthless Seduction
by Miranda Lee

Available 6th August 2010

Outback Engagements
by Margaret Way

Available 3rd September 2010

www.millsandboon.co.uk

M&B

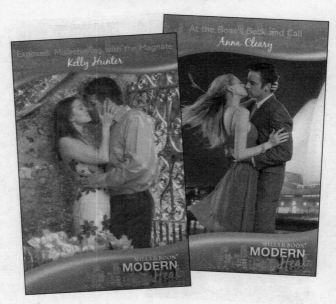

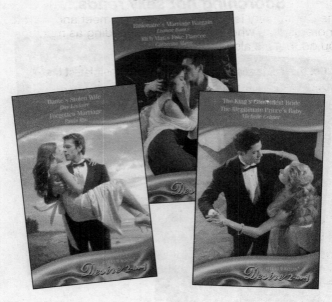

millsandboon.co.uk Community

Join Us!

The Community is the perfect place to meet and chat to kindred spirits who love books and reading as much as you do, but it's also the place to:

- **Get the inside scoop from authors about their latest books**
- **Learn how to write a romance book with advice from our editors**
- **Help us to continue publishing the best in women's fiction**
- **Share your thoughts on the books we publish**
- **Befriend other users**

Forums: Interact with each other as well as authors, editors and a whole host of other users worldwide.

Blogs: Every registered community member has their own blog to tell the world what they're up to and what's on their mind.

Book Challenge: We're aiming to read 5,000 books and have joined forces with The Reading Agency in our inaugural Book Challenge.

Profile Page: Showcase yourself and keep a record of your recent community activity.

Social Networking: We've added buttons at the end of every post to share via digg, Facebook, Google, Yahoo, technorati and de.licio.us.

www.millsandboon.co.uk